PERFECT CRIME

Helen Fields studied law at the University of East Anglia, then
we·   ·he Inns of Court School of Law in London. After
complet...g her pupillage, she joined chambers in Middle Temple
where she practised criminal and family law for thirteen years.
After her second child was born, Helen left the Bar. Together
with her husband David, she runs a film production company,
acting as scriptwriter and producer. The DI Callanach series is
set in Scotland, where Helen feels most at one with the world.
Helen and her husband now live in Los Angeles with their
three children.

Helen loves Twitter but finds it completely addictive. She can
be found at @Helen_Fields.

By the same author:

Perfect Remains
Perfect Prey
Perfect Death
Perfect Silence

Perfect Crime

HELEN FIELDS

MIX
Paper from
responsible sources
FSC® C007454

This book is produced from independently certified FSC™ paper
to ensure responsible forest management.

For more information visit: www.harpercollins.co.uk/green

avon.

Published by AVON
A division of HarperCollins*Publishers*
1 London Bridge Street,
London, SE1 9GF

www.harpercollins.co.uk

A Paperback Original 2019

1

Copyright © Helen Fields 2019

Helen Fields asserts the moral right to be identified as the author of this work

A catalogue record for this book is available from the British Library

ISBN-13: 978-0-00-827520-4

This novel is entirely a work of fiction.
The names, characters and incidents portrayed in it are
the work of the author's imagination. Any resemblance to
actual persons, living or dead, events or localities is
entirely coincidental.

Typeset in Bembo by Palimpsest Book Production Ltd, Falkirk, Stirlingshire

Printed and bound in Great Britain by CPI Group (UK) Ltd, Croydon CR0 4YY

Acknowledgments

My endless thanks for helping with this book – and keeping me writing in general – go, in no particular order, to . . .

Caroline Hardman (Agent Extraordinaire), Thérèse Coen on foreign rights, Joanna Swainson and Nicole Etherington from Hardman & Swainson (Best) Literary Agency (In The World). Phoebe Morgan for her pure good nature. Sabah Khan for her boundless energy. Helen Huthwaite for her outstanding instincts. Also to the superlative Avon and HarperCollins team who get these books from concept to production and out into the world – Molly Walker-Sharp, Elke Desanghere, Dom Rigby, Anna Derkacz, Rebecca Fortuin, Laura Daley, Katie Reeves, Hannah O'Brien, Jane Wisbey, Sarah Whittaker and Oli Malcolm. And a special shout out to Cressida McLaughlin for providing me with the name of one of the victims (and to the man himself).

To Tantallon Castle and the lovely people who work there and answer ridiculous questions from visiting authors (if you haven't been to Tantallon, you must!). To Whighams Wine Cellars in Edinburgh for great food, a wonderful place and a heavenly cocktail menu (I conducted thorough research). To Sandy Bell's, also in Edinburgh, the place to go. And to Ruth Chambers who tolerates endless location scouting, random archery and menu tasting in the name of authenticity (and possibly the odd hangover).

To my friends and family who listen to me drone on about plots and characters, deadlines and crazy new ideas – you know who you are – I love you all. Not a single word would have been written without you. And especially to David, who orders my favourite teabags from England in advance so that I never run out mid-book and hit a writing crisis.

Thank you x

For my mum, Christine May Fields.

Leading by example, inspiring through toil,
loving with gestures, even when the words were hard to say.

Chapter One

20 February

It seemed unlikely that there would be enough of his body intact to reuse after the fall, but in one final act of optimism, Stephen Berry left his organ donor card pinned beneath his mobile, keys and wallet at the side of the road. The impact of the fall, even onto water, would be devastating. He would suffer crushing injuries, probable brain damage, and if the force of his body hitting the water didn't kill him, the temperature would take care of it in a matter of seconds.

He'd done his research. After tumbling from the Queensferry Crossing into the River Forth, the breath would be knocked from his body, the sudden chill would make him gasp and he'd take in lungfuls of water before he had time to resurface. Death, if not instantaneous, would certainly be fast. Nothing to be scared of, he told himself. Fear was only anticipatory. In the moment, his brain would serve him a huge dose of mental opiate. Should he survive the drop, he'd have no memory of it.

The most dramatic of graves, millions of tons of water rushed beneath him, daring him to join it. He only had a matter of a few minutes to get it done and the truth was that he should have begun climbing already. Having purchased special gloves and boots to allow him to scale the inverted anti-suicide fencing, there was no excuse for his ambivalence.

When he'd called the taxi to his home address, he'd been ready to get on with it. The poor cabbie had already done an eight-hour shift and was on his way home. Stephen had hated pointing the carving knife towards his own jugular and threatening to cut, thereby forcing the driver to pull the car over on the bridge – a strictly no-pedestrians zone – but had been unable to think of a less abusive plan. At least he hadn't threatened the driver with it. He'd said sorry a dozen times before the driver had brought the vehicle to a halt, not that an apology would make up for the trauma of seeing a blade flashing in the rear-view mirror.

He climbed the easy vertical railings, then got a grip on the sharp layers of metal intended to ensure no one made it from one side to the other. It hurt a little, but he was in good shape. Better physically than mentally, that much was obvious. An hour a day at the gym meant he was well toned. A jog twice a week kept his cardio levels high. To look at him, you'd have no idea about the bipolar disorder he was suffering. It would all come out during the investigation into his death. His long flirtation with drugs designed to even out his moods. Periods when he'd gone off his medication against the advice of one doctor after another. Attempts at counselling that only made him feel weaker and more pathetic than his illness already did. Relationships that couldn't withstand the bluster of his stormy nature. Jobs that hadn't lasted as long as they should have when some days he simply couldn't face the concept of shifting from his bed.

The coroner would assume he was in the middle of one of his downward episodes. There would be some regret that there was no more effective treatment available, or that he hadn't felt able to reach out to a friend and ask for help. A small-type headline buried deep within a local newspaper would repeat that tired old truth that there wasn't enough care in the community. While he'd decided against leaving a note to explain his death, he wished briefly that he could have dealt with that ridiculous fallacy. No amount of care could have prevented him from getting to where he was today. He'd felt his premature death tugging at him, like a chain around his waist, since he was fifteen years old. He'd spent the next sixteen years fighting it, but today he'd become the postscript in his own story.

The girlfriend from whom he'd tried so carefully to hide his disorder had finally figured out that he was a worthless piece of shit who'd drag her down for the rest of her life if she stayed with him. There had been a lengthy session of me-not-you bullshit, which he could have done without, followed by an excruciatingly long packing period. It wasn't like in the films, where one of you simply monologued for a while then slammed a door and was mystically gone forever.

He and Rosa had been living together for a year and it was amazing how complex the structure of intertwined lives could get in twelve short months. Pots and pans, pictures, ornaments, books, extension cables, for fuck's sake. They'd argued over who'd bought the extension cable by their bed. Not – ridiculously – over who'd spent the money on it, but out of fairness, trying to remember the event because she didn't suddenly want to realise she'd taken something she had no right to. Bitch. Even at the fucking end she couldn't set him free by being selfish and unjust. She was a good person. How annoying was that? She was such a good person that the fault, as ever, lay with him. His moods, his needs, his fractured, ruptured psyche.

A passing car issued a long beep and someone shouted from a window. The wind swallowed the words, which pleased him.

There were times when the rest of the human race just had to butt out and the sixty seconds prior to committing suicide was one of them. He took another upwards step, jolting with the sudden clarity of the memory of buying the extension cable for Rosa when he'd bought her a new hairdryer. It had been obvious the cable would never reach the dressing table and around the back, so he'd added it to the Christmas list as a functional extra.

'Oh, for Christ's sake,' he muttered. It was still plugged into the wall. A stupid remnant of a good stretch when he'd been able to be thoughtful, living outside the trappings of his own mind for four months without interruption. Bliss. For a second he considered phoning Rosa to remind her of the extension cord's history. She could reclaim it when the flat was emptied out. Only then he'd have to explain where he was, and what he was doing, and she might talk him out of it. Rosa would be the only person who could. Too late, he thought. It was just an extension cable, after all. His snake of a brain had just chosen the moment to try to turn it into a lifeline instead.

Other cars beeped their horns as he took the final step up and over the railing. He stood, wobbling in the fierce breeze. Vehicles halted, forming an unofficial barrier. Doors slammed. Stephen turned around slowly. An arc of people had formed several metres away from him. He wasn't sure if the distance was because they thought he might grab one of them and take them with him, or for fear that approaching closer might make him jump all the sooner.

In the end, one man pushed between two onlookers, hands in his pockets, casual as you like, and wandered over to stand below his position on the fencing.

'Are you okay for me to stand here and talk to you?' he asked.

'Not much point,' Stephen muttered. 'You should probably back up a bit.'

'Why?' the man asked.

'I'm going to jump and I don't want you to feel responsible. No one else needs to be involved.'

'That's really thoughtful of you . . .' The man left the sentence hanging. 'That's the part where you fill in with your name,' he finished when there was no response.

'Oh, sorry,' Stephen muttered, feeling foolish and rude. 'Stephen.'

He had no idea why he felt the need to comply with social niceties at such a life-changing time. Years of conditioning, he guessed.

'Cool. Good to meet you, Stephen. I'm Rune Maclure.' Sirens echoed across the expanse of water. 'That'll be the police. Do you feel up to talking with them, or shall I ask them to stay back, too?'

'Keep them away,' Stephen said, taking deep breaths and focusing on the river. The pattern of the water was making him dizzy, or perhaps it was the adrenaline. Either way, he wasn't sure he could stay upright much longer.

'Feeling unstable?' Maclure asked.

He didn't answer.

'Relax one leg, get your balance back. Is this your stuff down here?'

'Yeah,' Stephen muttered.

Maclure reached down to pick it all up, pocketing the keys and mobile, holding the wallet and reading the organ donor card.

'Hey man, you want to be a donor? That's amazing. Too few people take that opportunity. I can't believe you're still thinking about other people when you're feeling so bad. That's pretty impressive.'

Stephen stared at him. The trick of relaxing one leg had worked. He was stable again.

'Probably no point. They might not even find my body.'

'That would be a shame. You look in good shape. Lots of people could benefit from those organs. It's amazing what they can transplant these days. It's always the part where it asks if you want to donate your eyes that blows my mind. How weird would that be, waking up after surgery, looking in the mirror to see yourself through someone else's eyes? Incredible, really.'

Through the growing crowd of bodies appeared four police officers, talking in whispers on their radios and moving people back, away from what Stephen assumed they'd already be referring to as 'the scene'. He hated that. Causing a scene. Being the scene. All he'd ever wanted was to blend into the crowd.

'Don't give it another thought. I can handle them,' Maclure said, raising his palms in the air in a gesture that said, effortlessly, calm down, I've got this. He moved away to speak to the closest of the police officers, greeting her with a handshake.

Stephen watched him go, wondering why Maclure seemed so relaxed. If someone had been seconds from suicide in front of him, he'd have been frantic. His shoulders weren't hunched, his voice was so low it was almost inaudible. There was no sense of crisis or hurry about him. He sure as hell wasn't bipolar, Stephen thought. He'd never been that relaxed or self-assured, not for one single second of his whole bloody existence.

'They're going to give us some space if you could just do me a huge favour and put your legs back this side of the fence. Not climb down, you have every right to do whatever you want. Stay up there by all means, but I was curious about what I should do with your belongings. Could you spare me one more minute?'

Stephen rubbed his eyes. One more minute? He'd come to the bridge to stop the pain, not prolong it.

'There must be someone who'd want to know what's happened to you. Did you leave a note so they can understand how you were feeling? If you did, that's great. You can give me your address and I'll make sure it gets to them. If not, give me a name and a number. I'll tell them you were at peace with your decision, rational, not scared. It'll make it easier for whoever you're leaving behind.'

'Why would you think I'm not scared?' Stephen blurted, the ludicrousness of that suggestion hitting him harder than he liked.

Suicide wasn't easy. It wasn't something you just did as a whim. Of course he was scared.

'I'm sorry, you just seem so . . . man, I hate to think of you up there feeling that way. Listen, I can't stop the police for more than another minute and I really want to know what's going on with you. Just take one step back over until we've finished talking. For me, if not for you? You seem like a great guy. Who else would have left a donor card when they're planning on killing themselves?'

Stephen considered the options. It was really just jump or take a step back to talk. And perhaps Rosa would want to hear some last words. Their break-up was so recent and raw that she was sure to blame herself. If he did nothing else, he could leave some reassurance that he'd have come to this whether or not the relationship had broken down. The thought of her spending a lifetime blaming herself was intolerable. He might be severely messed up in the head department, but he wasn't cruel.

Maclure was standing looking nonchalant, hands in his pockets once more, looking no more excited about life than if he were stood at a bus stop.

Stephen shifted one leg backwards over the upper railing, to the delight of the crowd, who gave a stadium-style whoop. Turned out that suicide was a spectator sport. Who knew?

'Good for you,' Maclure said, waving a hand vaguely at the police. 'Do you smoke?'

'No,' Stephen said.

'Me neither. I guess it's a standard play to offer someone in your situation, a cigarette, right?'

'I guess,' Stephen replied.

It was laughable really, having such an inane conversation while he stood on the suicide barrier of a bridge.

'So, can you give me a reason why you're doing this? That's bound to be what interested parties will ask. Not that there even has to be a reason, I get that. Sometimes it's just down to a feeling.'

Stephen thought about it. The truth was somewhere in between. He'd lost the will to live some time ago on a day-to-day basis but, longer-term, he had no faith in his bipolar disorder ever being effectively treated. He looked at the man with all the questions. Good-looking, athletic, black, slim, with a slight beard growth trimmed to maximise the squareness of his chin. The sort of person you both hated and wanted to be, wrapped into one.

'I'm bipolar,' was the answer Stephen settled for.

Maclure nodded. 'That's a tough one. And the treatment makes you feel like crap on the good days, so you stop taking it, then all the good days become bad days anyway. Is that about right?'

'Something like that,' Stephen said.

Only the truth was exactly like that and, annoyingly, he could never have put it that concisely, even though he was the one living it.

'But you're still alive. You're making it work. You have a mobile phone, which means you contact people. That's a great start. This wallet's pretty thick, which means you're living a normal life — credit cards, bills, driving licence, I would think, access to cash. You haven't been reduced to life on the streets. Pretty admirable, given what you're going through. A lot of people in your situation can't cope within normal social boundaries at all. You should be proud of yourself.'

That was certainly a new perspective on his life. Pride. Not something many people could have applied to him, however creative they were. Rune Maclure could talk the talk.

'I need you to tell Rosa that this isn't her fault,' Stephen said.

It was time to get down to business and he wasn't enjoying standing here in the cold.

'Rosa – girlfriend, I'm guessing. I'll need a surname if I'm going to be able to trace her.'

'Her contact details are in my mobile. The security code is 1066. And could you tell her the extension cable is hers. She'll know what I mean. I just remembered.'

'So you've split up?' Maclure asked.

'She couldn't take it any more,' Stephen muttered.

'I'm sorry, I really can't hear in this wind. Stepping closer, okay, but I'll keep my hands in my pockets.'

He moved to a position directly beneath Stephen, who turned his body more fully to the interior of the bridge to be heard.

'I said, she couldn't take it any more,' he shouted. 'She did her best. I'm not angry with her. It's important she knows that.'

'Okay, that sounds like an unresolved relationship, though. You should probably do her the favour of saying it to her yourself. What do you think?' He pulled Stephen's mobile from his pocket.

'Just jump already! I'm late for my shift!' someone yelled from the viewing sidelines.

'Ignore that,' Maclure said quickly, reaching a hand up towards Stephen, who frowned and shook his head.

'I'm annoying everyone,' he muttered, shifting his leg back over the barrier so his full body was on the water's side.

'Listen to me, there's always one, okay? One sick bastard

9

who wants to see carnage. Drown him out. Let's phone Rosa. She'll want to hear your voice. You know that in your heart, that's why you wanted me to talk to her for you. I'm coming up so I can hand you the mobile.'

'You're not wearing gloves,' Stephen said vaguely, the ache in his own body almost overwhelming him. It took so much energy to balance. 'Your hands will get torn to . . .'

Maclure was already climbing. Stephen contemplated stopping him by threatening to jump, but he really did want to hear Rosa's voice one last time. As Maclure climbed, Stephen studied the sea of faces behind the improvised crime-scene tape barrier the police had hastily erected. One man stood, eyes glittering, hands in pockets, grinning at him. Another woman was ranting at a police officer. An older lady was in tears, and although he hadn't thought it possible, Stephen hated himself just a little more for causing such distress.

The grinning man began to laugh, throwing the sound out so Stephen couldn't miss it. The noise was chalkboard awful. Jamming his hands over his ears, he lurched forwards, trapping the toe of one boot between two metal bars.

He went head first, grabbing for the railings, crashing a knee into metal followed by a hip, then rolling forwards onto his stomach, head down towards the water. The laughing man laughed louder. In spite of the wind, the roar of the water and the screams from the crowd, that cackling was all he could hear.

He gripped the fence with both hands, fighting his body's desire to pull himself back up and the voice in his head telling him to let go. It would all be over in seconds. He didn't need to speak to Rosa one last time. That would only cause more problems than it solved. There would be a rush of air as he fell, the chance to experience free-fall flight, then perhaps a fleeting sense of cold or of impact, but not for long enough to process it or to feel pain.

Stephen let go with one hand, closing his eyes.

'He's going to let go!' a woman shouted.

There were yells, the sound of boots hitting the concrete hard and an excited screech. It was the shiny-eyed man, Stephen thought. Here to see him die. Perhaps he was Death. He'd never been religious or superstitious, but maybe at the last he was seeing the world without blinkers. All those horror films, true-life experience programmes, children's stories, were real.

A hand clamped down hard on the ankle above his trapped foot.

'I've got you,' Maclure said. 'Talk to me, Stephen. This is no time to be making choices.'

'Death's here,' Stephen said, straining his neck to turn and look up into Maclure's calm brown eyes.

'If he is, then he's not here for you. Not today. Come on, grab that railing and use your stomach muscles to pull halfway up. I just need to get a grip on your belt.'

'I'm not sure,' Stephen said.

'Fair enough, but I'm your side of the barrier. You pull your foot out now and you're taking me with you.' Maclure smiled gently.

It wasn't a threat and it wasn't posturing. Stephen could see the truth of it.

As Maclure extended his grip to clasp more of the denim of Stephen's jeans, a mobile phone tumbled from his pocket and plunged towards the freezing flow beneath them, disappearing as if it had never existed at all.

'Shit, sorry about that. I wanted to give you the chance to speak to Rosa. I'll buy you a new one if it'll get you back up here. How about it?'

Stephen stared after his mobile phone. He didn't want to go like that. To simply cease to exist, wiped from the world without trace, his entire life made pointless. He tensed his core, suddenly grasping the real reason why sit-ups hadn't been a waste of time, and took a grip of the lowest railing, for the first time seeing what the climb up the inverted suicide fence had done to his rescuer's hands. Blood dripped in gashes from his palms and skin was flapping in the breeze as he reached out to take hold of Stephen's belt.

'I didn't mean for you to get hurt,' Stephen said. 'Thank you.'

He managed to get his knee into a gap between the metal struts and pushed his body up high enough for Maclure to get to him.

'Thank me later,' Maclure said. 'Let's just get you a cup of coffee and away from the spectators for now.'

There were shouts as police threw ropes over the barrier for them to tie around their waists, rolling the tyres of a police car over the ends to keep them safe.

'Why did you risk yourself?' Stephen asked as he finally got his face level with Maclure's and looked him straight in the eyes.

'We all have our demons,' Maclure said. 'Every one of us. Anyone who says differently just learned to lie better than you and me. My way of dealing with my own is to do my best to help other people. It's selfishness if you think about it.'

Stephen put an arm around Maclure's neck and pulled him into a quick, hard hug.

'I owe you my life,' he said.

And he meant it, but all he could think about were the demons Maclure had mentioned and the man still watching from the crowd. He wasn't laughing any more. Not so much as a glimmer of a smile.

Chapter Two

3 March

Detective Inspector Luc Callanach stood and stared at the man in the tatty armchair, wondering about the people who professed to forgive those who'd hurt them most. Terrorists who'd bombed indiscriminately and yet parents had forgiven them for taking their children so cruelly. Drunk drivers who'd caused crashes and still those who mourned the dead would not speak ill of the perpetrator. Never in his life would Luc be able to find so much space in his heart for such a gesture.

The man looked up at him, opened his mouth as if to speak, then blew a bubble instead, slapping at it before dropping his hand back into his lap. Bruce Jenson was suffering from Alzheimer's. It was too good for him, Luc thought, staring out of the window and across the rolling lawn of the care home as the day lost the last of the light. Any disease that let such an animal forget what he'd done was an injustice on a grand scale.

Luc took a step forwards to kneel down and stare into the watery blue eyes that saw but didn't see.

'Was it you who raped my mother?' he asked. 'Or did you just watch as your business partner violated her? Did you threaten to sack my father, if my mother told him what you did? Was it you or Gilroy Western who first came up with the idea?'

Jenson issued a strangulated groan, his shoulders juddering with the effort of making the noise.

Luc took a photo of his mother and long-dead father from his pocket and held it in front of Jenson's face. His head drooped. Luc took him by the chin and held the photo in front of him once more. He knew what he was doing was wrong. Bruce Jenson wasn't going to respond to anything he did. Sixty seconds after he left the room, his father's boss of thirty-five years ago wouldn't even remember that another human being had been in there with him.

Still, he couldn't stop. The rape his mother had suffered had echoed through the years, the trauma so bad that she'd deserted Luc when he'd been falsely accused of the same offence. Jenson and Western had never had to pay for what they'd done.

Luc had done his best not to pursue them, telling himself the past was best left, knowing he would lose his temper – perhaps fatally – if he ever did come into contact with either man. But he'd just spent a week in Paris with his mother, and being back in France had brought back all the horrors of his own arrest and the loss of his career with Interpol.

He'd had to walk away from everything he held dear when an obsessed colleague had told the worst lie you could tell about a man, and yet his mother's rapist was at liberty. Hard as he'd tried not to hunt down the two men who'd once run one of Edinburgh's most successful furniture companies, he'd realised the battle was already lost. So here he was – using his police credentials to get inside a nursing home, where Bruce Jenson would die sooner or later – still wanting answers. Still craving vengeance.

'Do you recognise them? Is there any part of you still in there? You wrecked her life, and then you wrecked mine. And the worst of it . . .' Luc spat the words out, a sob coming from deep inside his throat as he tried to keep going. 'The worst of it is that one of you bastards might just be my fucking father.'

Bruce Jenson's mouth lifted at the corners. It was a coincidence, Luc told himself. Nothing more than an involuntary twitch. But hadn't his eyes lifted a little higher at the same time, doing their best to meet Luc's even if they hadn't quite made it?

'My father worked for you for years. He looked up to you, trusted you. You sent him out to pick up a broken-down truck during the Christmas party and together you raped my mother. Her name was Véronique Callanach, and if you smile this time, I swear I'll choke the fucking life out of you.'

A string of saliva tipped over the edge of Jenson's bottom lip and made slow progress of lowering itself down his chin. Callanach's stomach clenched. He could see his mother, sack over her head, pushed to the floor of Jenson's office, wearing the party dress she'd been so proud of but thought too expensive for someone as lowly as herself. He could hear her cries, sense her anguish and revulsion. And then the shame, followed by the horror of finding herself pregnant with her first and only child, knowing she could never tell Luc's father what had happened.

Losing his job would have been the least of their problems. He'd have killed both Jenson and Western for what they'd done to her and she'd have spent the next twenty years visiting a good man, who'd never hurt a soul, in prison. The globule of drool ran into the wrinkled grooves of Jenson's neck. As if he'd been there, Luc imagined him drooling on his mother's flesh as Jenson or his partner had violated her, hands wherever they liked, bruising her, hurting her.

The cushion was in Luc's hands before he realised what he was doing. Propping one knee on the arm of the chair, he raised the cushion in his shaking, white-knuckled fist, teeth bared, every muscle in his body straining to let loose. Yelling, he aimed the cushion at the wall and lobbed it hard, knocking a vase to the floor as it fell, leaving a mess of smashed pottery and slimy green water.

He shoved himself backwards, away from Jenson, and staggered against the patio door that led into the garden. Forehead against the glass, hands in raised fists either side of his shoulders, he kicked the base of the door. The crack in the glass appeared remarkably slowly, with a creak rather than a crack, leaving a lightning-fork shape in the lower pane.

Callanach sighed. He was pathetic, taking out his anger on a man who had no fight left in him. Natural justice was in play. Jenson would never see his grandchildren grow up, or retire to a condo in Spain, which was where his former business partner was apparently now residing. He was seventy years old and to all intents and purposes, already dead. There was nothing more Callanach could do to him that he wasn't already suffering.

He took a few deep breaths and looked around the room. It was cheap and shabby. This wasn't luxury nursing. The bed had a rail to keep the patient from falling out, but the blankets looked thin. The paintings were the sorts of cheap prints you could buy in a pound shop. Other than a couple of ageing, dusty family photos, no personal touches adorned the surfaces. Jenson had effectively been ditched. It was as good a sentence as any court could have passed, if rather late in the day. Wandering over to the mess on the floor, Luc collected up the shards of vase and dumped them in the waste basket. He took a few paper towels from a dispenser on the wall and mopped up the water as best he could before some unsuspecting nurse walked in and slipped, then brushed off the cushion with his hand and tucked it into Jenson's side.

16

Satisfied that the room was back in order, he took a pair of gloves from his pocket and a sterile bag. Standing over Bruce Jenson, he plucked one of the few remaining hairs from the man's scalp, sealing it carefully into the bag to avoid contamination of DNA before stripping off the gloves and depositing them in the bin.

He accepted that it was beyond his power to punish this one of his mother's attackers, but he needed to know if the man had fathered him. He'd spent a long time weighing up that particular decision, but even now he wasn't prepared for how to face the outcome. If Jenson was his father, it would destroy everything he'd ever considered to be his identity. His mother was French and he'd grown up with her in France, never suspecting his time there would come to an end. His father, though, was a proud Scot. Born in Edinburgh, Luc could barely remember the first few years of his life. He recalled his dad as a warm, laughing man, who hugged often and hard, with huge hands and a quick smile. With his father gone too soon, his mother had struggled raising a young child alone and retreated to her family.

Luc checked the room once more to ensure he'd left it as tidy as possible, took a final look at the face of the man he would hate forever, and left. Passing by the nurses' station, he paused and leaned over the desk.

'I accidentally knocked a flower vase with my elbow,' he said quietly. 'I'm so sorry. Can I pay to replace it?' He let his French accent rumble along the words, making eye contact with the nurse.

'Oh no, don't worry at all. These things happen. We have loads of vases in the storeroom. I'll pop down and clean it up.' She smiled sweetly, running a self-conscious hand over her hair as it escaped from her ponytail.

'Don't worry, I made sure the floor was dry,' Callanach said.

'You have much more important things to do. Mr Jenson wasn't disturbed at all. As you said, he really wasn't aware that I'd visited. It's a tragedy.'

'I know. His son Andrew finds it difficult to visit him, too. Will you need to come back, do you think?' she asked.

Luc swallowed his guilt. He was flirting for his own purposes, well aware of the effect he had on women when he switched on the charm. His looks had got him modelling contracts and a stream of rich, good-looking girlfriends until he'd grown up and decided to do something with his life. Now living in Scotland, he supposed he was almost exotic with his deep-toned skin and still getting to grips with a second language. He might have been bilingual since childhood, but that didn't account for fighting with the Scottish accent and colloquialisms.

'I'm not sure. I may be back in a few days,' he said, showing perfect white teeth. 'Hopefully you'll be on duty again?'

'I might just be,' she giggled.

He'd pretended to be on official police business, thereby avoiding signing the visitor's book. No one had thought to take a note of his details. It was shocking how easily people let the rules slide when you flashed a badge. Giving the nurse a final wave, he took the corridor towards the car park.

If Jenson proved to be his father, it was more complex than just knowing he had the genetics of a monster. There was the issue of hereditary Alzheimer's to contemplate. Worse than that, he would either have to reveal to his mother that her rapist had indeed impregnated her, or spend the rest of his life lying to her about it. Neither prospect was a happy one. Then there was the complication of potentially having a half-sibling. Would he want to know more about Andrew Jenson, or was that a step too far?

If Jenson wasn't his biological father, that would mean tracking Gilroy Western down in Spain. Obtaining a reliable DNA sample from a man who would quite possibly remember Callanach's French mother, would prove much more difficult.

Callanach pushed through the double doors into the car park, sighing. He didn't want any of this. He longed for a simpler time, when he thought he'd known who his father was, even if losing him so young had pained him his whole life. If it was the living, breathing, golf-playing Gilroy Western, how was he going to make sure justice was done?

His mother had been adamant that she didn't want to make a historic rape report to the police. There was no corroborating evidence. Western might even plead that the sex had been consensual, and dealing with that would leave his mother doubly traumatised. That left either walking away, knowing his mother's rapist had gone unpunished, or ruining his own life and career by taking matters into his own hands.

There were few positive outcomes of continuing to investigate, yet he was headed for home, to put Jenson's hair into an envelope to send it off for forensic testing, alongside a hair from his own head. He despaired of himself. He was hoping the holiday in Paris would resolve matters between his mother and him. After a long period of separation, they'd made their peace with one another. The holiday had been as emotionally draining as it was pleasurable. Luc had felt unable to discuss the rape, and his mother had obviously picked up on his pity for her. The pain of a sexual assault didn't diminish over time.

He started his car, turning on the headlights in the fading light, and felt his mobile vibrating in his pocket, answering it as he pulled on his seatbelt.

'Luc, it's Ava,' a woman said before he could greet her. 'Listen, sorry, I know you're not due back from leave until tomorrow, only I'm at the city mortuary. A man was found dead, having fallen from a tower at Tantallon Castle. How quickly can you get here?'

His holiday, if you could call it that, was most definitely over.

Chapter Three

3 March

Detective Chief Inspector Ava Turner stood, arms folded, over-looking the corpse. She was only slightly saved from the trauma of the scene because the injuries were so horrific that it almost didn't look real. Dr Ailsa Lambert, Edinburgh's chief pathologist, a tiny, hawkish woman who might have blown away in a strong breeze, was moving around the postmortem suite with her customary speed and professionalism.

'Your first high-fall body?' the pathologist asked Ava.

'Yup,' Ava replied, lifting an arm with her gloved hand and looking underneath. 'Are all these injuries postmortem or are there signs of an assault before he fell? These gashes look like knife wounds.'

'Extraordinary, isn't it? I'm afraid with a high fall, in physics terms, the force applied to the body is ballistic. These huge splits to the fleshy parts occurred when the force radiated out and reached a critical point where this man's body could no longer contain the amount of energy within them.'

She lifted the sheet to reveal a split around the man's side that almost reached his navel and another down the back of his left leg. It was as if someone had taken a meat cleaver to his flesh. Ava took the corner of the sheet from Ailsa and laid it back down.

'Like blunt force trauma, then?' Ava asked.

'Sort of, only this works from the inside out. There are multiple fractures, as you'd expect. This gentleman landed flat on his back. His spine is severed in four different places, his liver burst and both lungs were punctured by broken ribs.'

'Did he suffer?'

'Not physically, I can say that with a high level of certainty. We know from high-fall victims who survive that their brain protects them immediately prior to impact. They pass out or go into a sort of impending trauma fugue. Very few have any memory of impact at all. In this man's case, I can tell you death was so instantaneous that he wouldn't have had time to have registered the pain. The back of his head hit the concrete hard enough to flatten a section of his skull. Shall I turn him over for you to see?'

'No need. I'll take your word for it,' Ava murmured.

'Very wise, but I'm afraid I have a caveat to your question about his having suffered, and it's linked to why you're here at all.' The door opened and a white-suited figure entered. 'Luc! Come and join us. We were just getting to the heart of the matter.'

'Hey.' Ava smiled at him. 'Sorry to deny you your final few hours of leave. Were you doing anything fun?'

Luc shook his head. 'I was at the gym. I ate too much in Paris. Got to get back in shape.'

It was a lie, but Ava let him get away with it. Callanach had the sort of slim build and washboard stomach that most men could only dream of.

'Didn't have gyms when I was your age,' Ailsa grumbled as she pulled over a mobile light with a magnifying glass on a flexible arm. 'We went for good long walks, didn't sit in front of screens for hours at a time and we certainly didn't spend all our spare cash on food that was more saturated fat than protein.'

Callanach grinned at Ava. Ailsa was an outstanding pathologist, but she didn't mince her words on any subject.

'Now, with any high-fall victim, we have accidental fall, suicide or criminal event. Look here.' She picked up the corpse's right hand, flattening his fingers out on her own palm. 'There's a substantial amount of debris under his fingernails – three out of five were broken off during the fall as there's fresh blood dried in with the debris. That debris is comprised of brick dust and dirt.'

'He clung on then,' Callanach said.

'He most certainly did,' Ailsa responded. 'Which is why I'm ruling out suicide.'

'You don't think he changed his mind? I mean, climbed to jump, started to fall and grabbed at the wall, or it just happened as a matter of instinct?' Callanach asked.

'Not a normal pattern. Suicides usually jump a distance when they've decided to go and he'd have had to jump backwards to have grabbed the wall. If that was the case, gravity would probably have tipped him onto his back very high up, making it impossible for him to have got a hold on the wall with his fingertips.'

'If I decided to commit suicide out at Tantallon, I'd jump off the cliffs into the sea, not from the castle walls to the ground. Too messy,' Ava added.

'So, not suicide. Accident, then?' Callanach asked.

'A much more likely prospect,' Ava said, 'and one I'm still seriously contemplating. It's possible he slipped, managed to get a hold for a while but couldn't pull himself back up, particularly given the ripping of the fingernails. Only, it's not that easy to fall off the walls at Tantallon. If it was, they wouldn't let anyone onto any part of the castle. He had to have climbed onto the outer aspect of the wall.'

'Misadventure?' Callanach queried. 'Being a bit brave, climbs up, slips, grabs hold and it all goes wrong. Any sign of drink or drugs?'

'No odour when I opened the stomach or brain to suggest serious alcohol intake, and I usually know pretty quickly if that's an issue. As far as drugs go, I've taken samples for a tox screen and put those on a high-priority request. What I wanted to show you is this . . .'

Ailsa put the man's hand back down on the metal pallet and positioned the magnifying glass over his middle finger, adjusting the light so it was flat over the top.

'Look here,' she said.

Ava and Callanach leaned in for a closer look, turning their heads to check from different angles.

'I give up,' Ava said eventually. 'The hand's badly bruised, with substantial grazing. I can see the three ripped nails. It's all what I'd expect.'

'All right, what you don't know is that only one of these fingers is fractured. Middle finger, right at the top, in the distal phalange near the base of the nail.'

Callanach slipped his gloved finger underneath the area and felt the bone.

'I can't feel anything,' he said.

'The break isn't displaced, so I wouldn't expect you to. It only showed up on the X-ray, but there's no healing at all, and fingers heal quickly, so it's a new break but not caused by the force of the fall. It's distinct from the other fractures.'

'Caused when he was gripping the rock?' Ava asked.

'I thought so, then I saw this . . .' Ailsa brought the magnifying glass even closer to the end of the middle finger and pointed at a tiny purple V-shape, just visible against the paler flesh of the hand. 'That mark wasn't caused by the rock. It's the wrong side of his hand for a start. When he hit the ground, his palm was facing the floor, I know that from the impact pattern. This bruise is deep and fresh. I've excised the skin and looked underneath. Recent trauma, hard. It's probably also what caused the fracture beneath.'

'Your best guess as to cause?' Ava asked.

Ailsa folded her arms and tipped her head to one side. 'I'm hesitant,' she said. 'This is a bit of a reach.'

'But it's the reason we're here, right?' Ava raised her eyebrows.

'Indeed. This definition and shape is unusual. Without the fracture, I'd have been less positive, but a substantial amount of force was applied, so weight was put onto the finger. It looks to me like the tip of a boot's tread mark. That would explain the fracture, too. As I say, that's not backed up by anything else. There are no other injuries that can't be explained by the fall. No other defensive wounds. In these circumstances, without witnesses or a clearer picture of what happened, I wouldn't be able to base a legal case on it.'

'Well, let's hope there's an innocent explanation. We haven't had a murder in Edinburgh since that gang retribution killing in Braidburn Valley Park at Christmas. I was hoping we'd manage to go more than a couple of months without another murder investigation.'

'I'm just telling you what I see,' Ailsa muttered. 'Maintaining law and order's your area of expertise.'

'Not really. My squad just gets to clean up after societal norms have been decimated. Anyway, standing here won't provide answers,' Ava said. 'Perhaps when we've identified him, we'll get a clearer picture. Send me your report. I'll open an enquiry but keep an open mind for other possibilities. Does that sound reasonable?'

'It does indeed,' Ailsa smiled. 'This man's only in his early thirties. I think we owe him this much at least. It's no age to die, under any circumstances.'

'It certainly isn't,' Ava agreed, walking to the postmortem suite door before removing her cap and gloves and depositing them in the bin. She reached out to hug Ailsa. 'How are you keeping?' she asked, stepping out of the sterile suit.

'You mean for an old person?' Ailsa grinned.

Ava tutted at her.

'I'm fine. Less stressed than either of you, I'm guessing. I'm glad to hear Luc's taken some time off. When did *you* last get a holiday, girl?'

Ava laughed. Ailsa, a friend of her parents from years back, would never cease to refer to her as a child no matter how old she got or what rank she was.

'I'll take a break soon, I promise. We've finally appointed a new detective inspector, so that should ease things a bit. We'll head out to Tantallon now. Anything in particular we should be searching for?'

'It's a needle in a haystack, but I'd like to get a look at the missing fingernails. They might just be harbouring a few cells that'll paint a fuller picture,' Ailsa said.

'Don't hold your breath,' Ava warned. 'It hasn't been treated as an active crime scene by forensics. What do you say, Luc? Are you up for a night-time stroll along the castle walls?'

'Perfect end to a perfect holiday,' Callanach smiled. 'I'll get my coat.'

Chapter Four

4 March

Stopping off at the police station, Ava and Callanach grabbed wet-weather gear, more substantial flashlights than were in the boots of their cars, and notified the control room of their plans. By the time they'd driven the thirty-odd miles east from the city centre towards North Berwick, taking the winding lanes from the main road to the tip of the coast with due respect for the rain and wind, it was just past midnight.

They sat quietly in Luc's car, having bypassed the car park at the end of the lane in preference for parking directly outside the entry booth-cum-gift shop. Looking across at the vast curtain wall that had once shielded the inner grounds of the castle from marauders, they listened to the increasingly thunderous rain.

'I came here for a weekend to do an archery course as a child,' Ava smiled. 'By the end of the first day, I thought I'd fallen in love with the instructor.'

'What happened?' Luc asked.

'Oh, you know, like most crushes you have when you're ten

and your instructor's twenty-five, it ended when he patted me on the head and said I'd tried really hard, then his bleach blonde girlfriend turned up in her miniskirt and my heart broke into a thousand pieces.'

'Are you over it yet?'

'Well, I still feel butterflies in my stomach when I see a man holding a longbow but other than that, I think I'm through the worst. Do you believe in ghosts?' she asked.

'No. It's simple statistics. How many people have inhabited this earth and died? Surely we'd be overrun with restless spirits if that was the case.'

'Cynic,' she replied. 'I thought Frenchmen were supposed to be romantic.'

'Is that what you brought me here for? Romance? I'm not sure looking for a recently deceased man's nails in a wall qualifies as a date.'

'Idiot. If this were a date, I'd be wearing my good socks,' she grinned, leaning forwards to look to the top of the castle walls. 'But for what it's worth, I agree with you. William Wordsworth wrote, "I look for ghosts; but none will force their way to me; 't is falsely said that there was ever intercourse between the living and the dead." Isn't that beautiful?'

'I'm sure it is, but I may be having trouble directly translating it. My English is still pretty literal and most words only have one meaning.'

Ava frowned in confusion momentarily, then closed her eyes and shook her head in mock disgust.

'Forget it, Romeo. If that's the best you can do when I'm providing a backdrop of poetry, you should probably just keep quiet.' She zipped up her waterproof and tried to open the door, the wind slamming it back hard against her shin as she went to exit. 'Ow! For fuck's sake!' she growled.

'Yup, you've got all the poetry tonight,' Callanach said. 'Let me get that door for you.' He exited and jogged round to offer her a hand up as she rubbed her bruised leg. 'Are you sure you want to do this now?'

'No, but the way this storm's rolling in, if there is anything to see it'll be gone before morning, so it's now or never. Come on.'

They went through the visitor centre, where some unlucky local uniformed officer had been stationed with an employee to allow them access, and walked towards the front entrance of the castle, still imposing even in its semi-ruined state. A gale was buffeting them from the north and the rain was only a degree short of freezing. Ava pulled up her hood and shook long dark brown curls of wet hair from her eyes.

They took the wooden footbridge over the old moat and entered through the arched doorway of a greenish brick structure. Below them and to the right, encompassing an area of loose fallen rocks and part of the moat, was a section of crime-scene taping. Beyond that, they were met with slippery cobblestones before the castle grounds opened up ahead of them. In front, a grassed area led to cliffs that crumbled into the sea. A fierce whistling echoed around the ancient structure and it was easy to see why visitors had imagined ghosts there, stepping back hundreds of years in time. It was clear that no attacker could have approached from the direction of the sea and also that Ava was right. Suicide in the direction of the cliffs would have been the much more obvious option.

Luc saw Ava pointing towards an internal doorway and they went inside to find a spiral stone staircase with little to assist their climb other than a rope attached to the central wall. He followed close behind her, watching her footing, fighting his desire to reach up and steady her. Ava wasn't the sort of woman who wanted or needed much help, but that didn't make it any easier for him to switch off how protective he felt of her. She'd become his closest friend in Scotland, which wasn't always simple given that she was also his boss.

Ducking under additional crime-scene tape, they moved to a level paved outcrop with a visitors' information board. The section was wide, easily three foot across, and level enough to have stood safely, if not advisedly on top of the wall, overlooking the bridge and the moat. Above them, higher walls blocked some of the wind but none of the rain.

'Apparently, this is the fore tower. When exactly did our man fall?'

'He was found at the bottom of the wall when staff got in this morning. The castle doesn't open until 10 a.m. at this time of year and the door we came through is locked at night. We won't know what time he fell until Ailsa completes her report and estimates time of death, but it was between about 7 p.m. and 8 a.m. They have cameras at the visitor centre, which we've checked, but they don't give a good enough night-time picture for us to see anything,' Ava shouted over the wind.

'He broke in?' Callanach asked.

'What?' Ava yelled, huddling into him to hear.

Callanach put an arm around her shoulders and cupped a hand over her ear to make himself heard.

'I said, did he break in or just stay after the centre closed?'

'I'm told there's no damage to the door or the lock, but there's no CCTV of the castle itself, so we can't be sure. Apparently, people have ended up locked in here at night before. Plenty of small corners to hide if you don't want to be spotted. Look . . .' She pointed over the edge, leaning perilously across the rough stone wall. 'He must have fallen from just here. Hold onto me.' She climbed the wall past the information board and lay on her stomach, head over the edge, indicating for Luc to hold the back of her coat.

'No,' he said, loudly enough for her to hear perfectly clearly over the gusts. 'I can't let you do that.'

'I think you mean, I can't let you do that, ma'am,' Ava corrected him. 'If you don't hold onto me tightly enough, I'm joining our as yet unidentified friend on Ailsa's table, so get a grip. Literally.'

'Come back. I'll climb it. Call me whatever names you like, I'm not okay with you taking that sort of risk.'

'Except there's no way I'm strong enough to pull you back when you slip. You'll just take me down with you and that's not how I want to go, so follow orders, Detective Inspector. I spent my childhood climbing walls like these and in worse weather.'

Dangling from the waist forwards, Ava leaned as far over the edge as Callanach would allow her. He guessed they were around fifteen metres up and even if his estimate was wrong, given the dark and precipitation, he was certain it was a sufficient distance to be lethal. Ava cursed every few seconds, shifting along the wall, moving the flashlight to and fro, up and down, until finally she shouted out.

'Camera!' Ava yelled, waving the flashlight towards Callanach's face.

'I need a free hand. You'll have to come back up a second.'

'No can do. I'll never find this again. My camera's in the left-hand pocket of my coat. Just grab it and pass it to me.'

'God, you stubborn, stupid . . .'

'I can hear you, you know. Take the torch.'

Callanach took it, keeping a grip of Ava with his right hand as he delved into her pocket and passed her digital camera to her.

'What is it?' he shouted.

'Flap of skin, I think. There's a thin line of it snagged on the rock.'

The flash went off several times and Luc braced himself to counterbalance Ava's increasingly outward-leaning weight.

'Take the camera and pass me an evidence bag.'

Callanach slipped the camera into his coat and reached into his trouser pocket for a plastic bag.

'Ava, we have to come back and do this in the morning.'

'It'll be gone by then. There must have been blood here given the amount of skin but I can't see any trace of it. If Ailsa's right about the boot mark, this might be our last chance to get the evidence.'

Callanach handed her the bag. 'Just give me a bit more room to manoeuvre, I think there's something else stuck in the rock.'

She shifted her weight in order to move her head downwards. The gust that took her came from the opposite direction than the predominant gale, rendering Callanach's balance useless and thrusting him forwards into Ava's body. She screamed, grabbed the rock face, rolling to one side and losing her grip, her right leg flying into the air then crashing back down into the jagged brickwork. Her jeans ripped from knee to ankle and her cheekbone smashed hard against the bricks.

Callanach threw himself forwards, wrapping an arm around her thigh, feeling her slipping away from him. Scrabbling at the rock face, the flailing of her body was making it harder to hold her. The wind whipped around her head, taking her screams down the sheer castle wall.

'Ava, I'm pulling you up on three. Tense your stomach, stop grabbing the walls and reach for my arm!' he yelled with no way of knowing if she'd heard.

Forcing his boot tips over the ninety degree angle of the wall he was lying on to gain some stability, Callanach tensed.

'One, two . . .'

She wrenched on his arm, moving too early, too jerkily. Her leg ripped away from him as she got a grasp of his hand.

'Hold me!' she screeched.

Blood was pouring down her face, and her grip was wet and weak on his hand. Both legs flew out behind her in the wind.

He scraped forwards across the flat of the wall, twisting his body to get better pulling power and dragging a knee up and under his core, roaring as he fought the wind for her, his right arm a vice around her back, launching himself backwards. They flew upwards and crashed against the rear of the visitor information sign, Ava like a rag doll in his arms once her weight shifted over the top of the wall. She landed on top of him, crying out and clutching him madly. Callanach cradled her head, whispering words of reassurance she would never hear over her cries and the storm.

It was minutes before she raised her head to look at him.

'Do you need an ambulance?' he asked.

Ava flexed both legs and ran her hand down her neck, tipping her head to one side then the other.

'I'm okay,' she decided.

'You're not okay. You've got a bloody death wish.'

Callanach took her by the shoulders and shook her. She looked at him, horrified, then her eyes filled with tears and she collapsed, shaking against his chest.

'I'm sorry,' he muttered into her hair. 'You scared me. Come on, let me look at that gash on your face.'

Ava turned so he could wipe the worst of the blood away to inspect the injury beneath.

'The cut on your cheek's not too bad, but you've got a hell of a bump on your forehead. We should get you checked out for concussion. Can you walk?'

Ava nodded, rolling to her knees to get upright.

'Slowly,' he said. 'Let me hold you.'

Standing, he pulled her up, sliding one arm around her waist and protecting her damaged face with his other hand. They took the spiral staircase at a snail's pace, with Ava gripping the wall on one side and Callanach's hand in front of her as if she were on a ship in a squall, pausing every few steps. He pulled her into one of the tiny but secure side rooms to rest before taking a look at her leg.

By the time they reached the ground, she was shaking so badly, Callanach was worried she might pass out.

'Let me carry you. It's flat from here.'

She looked up at him, her grey eyes huge in her ashen face, her hair bloody and flattened against her head.

'Like hell you will,' she managed with the smallest of smiles.

He laughed, loud and hard, the tension leaving his body in fierce waves that left him nauseous and breathless.

'We need to get you warmed up,' he said when he could finally speak again.

Finally, they staggered in through the visitor centre door, making the uniformed officer posted there jump up and grab for his ASP baton.

'It's all right,' Callanach reassured him. 'There was an accident, not an incident.'

'Shall I call an ambulance for you, ma'am?' the young man asked, keeping his distance from them as if they might be contagious.

'No, I'm fine. Nothing a couple of paracetamol won't fix,' Ava said. 'Lock up behind us then report back to your station, Constable. Would you mind being discreet about this? I don't want anyone thinking DI Callanach and I had a fist fight.' She did her best to smile, but her face was losing its numbness and redefining the definition of pain.

'Absolutely, ma'am, you can count on it,' he said stoically, opening the door for them to exit towards the car park.

'One thing,' Ava said, looking at the castle employee who was staring at her as if she'd just landed in an alien spacecraft.

'If you did get trapped inside the castle walls at night, is there any way at all you might get out? I mean, if it was something like a life-or-death situation.'

Kevin, his name badge proclaimed, snapped to remarkably quickly.

'Two options,' he mused, rubbing his greying bread and glancing back up towards the castle as if he could see the answers. 'If you were slim and wanted to badly enough, even an adult could maybe climb through one of the bomb holes then get out down the banks of the moat. Alternatively, if the tide was out, you could clamber down the rocks to the sea and walk along to the section of the beach from where it's possible to get back up. You'd have to be fit, though. Uninjured and strong. I wouldn't want to try it.'

'Thank you,' Ava said. 'I take it I can count on you not to say too much about the state I'm in . . .'

'I'm a Scot, madam,' Kevin said. 'We survived a tumultuous history by being loyal and having an uncanny ability to keep our lips sealed. Nothing's changed.'

Ava gave Kevin a smile that Callanach thought would have melted the heart of every Scottish warrior ever to have fought the English at Tantallon before taking hold of Callanach's hand and pulling him towards the exit.

Callanach opened the passenger door and helped Ava in.

'The Royal Infirmary's on our way back into the city. There won't be any traffic this late. Just relax. I'll have you there in fifteen minutes.'

'Stop, please, it's a few bumps and bruises. Nothing's broken except my pride. Just get me home.' Ava rested her head backwards and closed her eyes.

'Are you kidding? After what just happened? Can you feel the size of the lump on your head? Come on, Ava, that's more stupid than wilful.' He started the car and pulled away.

'Luc, please.' She extended a hand slowly to rest on his forearm. 'What I did was rash. It was unfair to you. If an officer in my command took a risk like that I'd suspend them. Even I'm not sure what came over me. If you take me to the hospital, this goes official. Give me a break, okay?'

He sighed, the admission that she was right unnecessary. 'What about going to see Ailsa at home? She'll look you over.'

'I'll scare her rigid. She'll be furious and I'll never hear the last of it. No. I just need a hot bath, a stiff drink and a first-aid kit.'

'Natasha?' he tried.

Ava's best friend would be just as angry, but she'd look after Ava overnight without a second thought.

'Spending most nights at her new girlfriend's house. Would you let it go? I'm not a child. The shock was worse than the injuries.'

'Do you even have ice in your freezer, because you're going to need some for your head?'

'Not sure, and the bump's come out so it's safe, right? You only have to panic when there's no lump.'

'Remind me never to let you make important medical decisions for me. You're staying at mine. There's still a chance you're concussed and you shouldn't be alone,' he said firmly. 'No arguments. And stay awake while we're driving. If you fall asleep now, you're waking up at the hospital whether you like it or not. Don't bother arguing.'

For once, Ava didn't, which told Callanach all he needed to know about her underlying state.

His apartment in Albany Street was the front first floor of a Victorian terraced house. He ordered her to sit on his sofa while he made up an ice pack and fetched her a blanket.

'I'm running you a bath,' he said. 'Can you get your jeans

off or do you need help? Your left leg's badly cut and I need to take a look at the damage.'

Ava stared down at her jeans, cut almost in two on the left where she'd snagged them on the wall.

'Hadn't noticed,' she said. 'I don't suppose you've got any whisky? Brandy or port would do at a push.'

'I'm making coffee,' he replied, running a flannel over the bump on her head before putting the ice pack on it. 'I'm afraid alcohol and head injuries don't mix, whatever you Scots might regard as being traditional in these circumstances.'

'Killjoy.' She unbuttoned her jeans and wriggled out of them, inspecting her left leg by kicking it out from under the blanket. 'I guess I'm not going to be wearing a skirt for a few weeks. That's nasty.'

The leg was blotched purple and black down her shin from the knee to the ankle and a four-inch cut, thankfully not too deep, was going to make an impressive addition to her collection of scars.

Callanach handed her a steaming mug and perched on the end of the sofa.

'Are we going to talk about what you did tonight?'

'Are you going to psychoanalyse me, because you know I find that boring?' She took a sip, screwing her nose up at the strength of the coffee. 'This stuff can't be good for you.'

'Don't change the subject,' Callanach said, kicking off his shoes and rolling up his sleeves. 'If you'd really wanted to scope the outer wall for forensics, we could have got a team in there. I know it would have taken longer, and it's still a fishing expedition until Ailsa's finished her report, but what you did broke all the rules. It's my fault too, I shouldn't have let you, but I didn't think you'd be so . . .'

'Foolish? Idiotic? Reckless? I'm not going to make up excuses. There were real reasons for going there tonight, to visit the scene and see if there was any evidence worth protecting or that might bolster Ailsa's theory. I hadn't intended to climb the wall. I just got that sudden burst of adrenaline. The dark, the wildness, the sense of adventure.' She put her coffee down and rearranged the ice on her head. 'I don't know, Luc. I spend so much time sitting at my desk, doing paperwork and giving orders, sending other people out to crime scenes, hearing about other officers' experiences. I feel as if I've lost touch with everything I joined the force to do. All police officers have a healthy dose of hero syndrome. It's why we throw ourselves into the middle of fights, and – yes – dangle off high walls to preserve that one piece of evidence that'll be gone by morning. I don't have a death wish. Quite the opposite. I need to feel alive again.'

'Damn, I forgot the bath,' he said, dashing off towards his bedroom.

She heard the water stop flowing and cupboard doors banging. He reappeared holding two huge crimson towels and offering her a hand up.

'Ava, I understand you're feeling stuck, but you could have died tonight. That's more than just desk boredom.'

'It's not just my desk,' she groaned as she hobbled towards his bathroom. 'There's nothing – and no one – to go home to. Work is my whole life, so when I'm not sure why I'm doing it any more . . . God, listen to me moaning. I love my job, you know that. But I'm in my mid-thirties. I haven't been in a relationship in forever, and the last one I did try was a disaster. My best friend calls me a work-in-progress and that might be funny if it weren't true. I don't go out. I don't do social media. I can't even bloody well cook! How sad is it to count down the hours until you're back behind the desk you're starting to hate?'

She dropped the blanket on the bathroom floor and pulled

her top over her head. Callanach turned away to give her some privacy. Ava winced audibly as she lowered herself into the hot water.

'I'll give you some space,' Callanach said, reaching for the door handle.

'Actually, could you stay?' she asked quietly. 'I mean, with your back turned, obviously. I may be sad and lonely but I'm not that desperate.'

'Charming,' he laughed, sitting in the bathroom doorway but staring out into his bedroom, his suitcase as yet unpacked on the floor and his passport thrown onto the bedcovers. 'Dizzy?'

'A little,' Ava admitted, dunking her hair backwards in the water and screwing up her face at the cloudy swirls of red that came out of it. 'Hey, thanks for looking after me. And I'm sorry for what I put you through up there. I haven't even asked if you're hurt.'

'Couple of bruises from when you landed on top of me. For someone who can't cook, you can certainly eat.'

Ava laughed. 'Bastard,' she said, throwing a wet flannel at the back of his head.

They both knew it wasn't true. Ava was thinner than ever. Callanach had only been away a couple of weeks, but he'd noticed it as soon as he'd seen her at the city mortuary.

'So, I hope you don't mind me asking, but of all the medical suggestions you had, you didn't mention Selina. Is everything okay, only it seemed logical to me that you might have offered to let your accident and emergency doctor girlfriend take a look at me?'

Callanach stretched his arms above his head and breathed deeply. 'Ex-girlfriend. Very amicable and I'm sure if I'd have asked, she'd have been only too happy to have helped out. It just felt like I'd be taking advantage, given how badly I've let her down.'

'Your decision then, not hers? Stop me if I'm prying.'

'Good. I'm stopping you. You're prying,' he replied gently.

'Did she not go to Paris with you?' Ava continued.

Callanach tutted. 'Really?' he asked.

'Well, I am naked in your bath, so I feel somewhat entitled to be questioning you about your private life, especially given that I've just poured my heart out to you about what a pathetic loser I am.'

'You recognise that I just saved your life, right? Was that not enough, or do you still feel as if I owe you the extra pound of flesh?'

He turned to stare at her, forgetting his promise to remain facing the other direction, not that her modesty was compromised from his angle. All he could see was the top of her head and her eyes, beneath which he knew she was grinning wildly.

'We talked about her joining me in Paris, but I had too much to sort out with my mother. Selina suggested we book a holiday together later in the year – something to look forward to in the summer. I knew it wasn't right. She's an amazing woman.'

'Way too good for you,' Ava said gently.

'Agreed. Anyway, I told her just before I left. She wanted me to think about it while I was away and maybe give it another try, but I'm wasting her time. She needs to be free to find someone who can be everything she deserves. I'd planned to call her tonight and make that clear, but then you decided to pull this little stunt.'

'Oh God, I'm sorry, Luc. Why is life never simple?'

'At least you took my mind off it. Are you ready to get out yet?'

'Yeah. Tired now,' she said. 'Would you mind helping me up? My muscles are starting to seize.'

'Sure,' he said. 'Eyes closed, I promise.'

'You'd better. I couldn't stand to see the look of disappointment on your face after being used to Selina's five feet ten inches of pure legs and all-round Spanish gorgeousness.' She reached a hand out to put on Callanach's shoulder as she climbed gingerly from the tub and picked up a towel. 'Okay, I'm decent.'

'Why do you always do that?' he asked.

'Ask for help getting out of the bath? I'm not sure I make a habit of . . .'

'Put yourself down and make a joke of everything. Is that really how you see yourself, or are you just pushing men away?' Callanach asked, letting her lean on his arm as she left the bathroom.

'It's too late for serious conversations,' she said. 'You take the bed. I'm already invading your space. I'll be fine on the sofa.'

'No, you won't. You'll sleep on the bed and I'm staying next to you. I don't like the look of that bump and you shouldn't be left alone. Now lie down. I need to put some Steri-Strips on those wounds.'

'How come I never noticed you were this bossy before?' she smiled, lying back against the pillows.

'You never nearly fell from a castle wall when I was responsible for your safety before,' he said, peeling the stitches from a pack and applying them every inch along the gash to her leg.

'It was awful,' Ava said, suddenly serious and biting her nails. 'I really thought I was going to fall. It seemed to take hours and I was aware of everything. Every part of my body, the weight going through my hands, the pain in my shoulders, you yelling. I could taste the blood running from my head. And I really, really didn't want to fall. I hope that's not how our dead man felt. I've been scared before, Luc, but never like that, so out of control. I felt utter hopelessness.'

Callanach finished what he was doing and looked up. Ava was tearful and pale in spite of the hot bath. The eye beneath the bump on her head was beginning to blacken. He could count on one hand the number of times he'd seen her cry since he'd first met her and she'd been through hell on more than one occasion. Drawing the covers up to get her warm, he went to dim the lights and draw the curtains before climbing onto the bed next to her and sliding an arm beneath her neck.

'It's all right now,' he said. 'You're safe. Go to sleep. I'll be right here if you feel ill or have a nightmare, or . . . anything.'

She was silent for a couple of minutes, crying against his shoulder.

'I'm not going to thank you for saving my life,' she said. 'It's not enough to say it. I'm not even sure how to start. I've never in my life been able to trust anyone the way I can trust you. Natasha maybe, but it's not the same. I owe you everything, Luc. I hate what brought you to Scotland, but I'm glad you're here. Don't ever leave.' She shut her eyes, relaxing into sleep with her arm across his chest.

'I won't ever leave you,' he whispered. 'You don't need to worry about that.'

Chapter Five

4 March

The Major Investigation Team was buzzing. Detective Superintendent Overbeck had even graced the briefing room for once and was standing in front of the crowd looking at her watch when Ava walked in. The right-hand side of her face was remarkably unscathed, but her left eye was black. The gash along her cheekbone was being held together with butterfly stitches and the bump on her forehead was such a perfect half-egg that it looked almost unreal. Overbeck stared openly at her, arms folded, mouth gaping. Ava went straight to her to apologise.

'Don't even bother,' Overbeck said before Ava could get a word out. 'Is Police Scotland pay really so bad you're having to audition as an extra in a fucking zombie movie? Just tell me you weren't on duty at the time, because you're not suing the department for whatever screw-up you got yourself into.'

'You don't have to worry about that, ma'am,' Ava reassured her.

Overbeck was nothing if not direct, which – being grateful

for small mercies — meant most conversations were cuttingly brief.

'Good, let's get on then.' Overbeck turned to face the crowd, banging a deserted mug on a table to get quiet. 'Right, now that the detective chief inspector has joined us, even though you might not particularly enjoy looking at her today . . .'

That got Overbeck a laugh. Credit to her, Ava thought. Her boss never missed an opportunity to work a room.

'I want to introduce you to MIT's new additions and to congratulate' — Overbeck paused to check her notes — 'Max Tripp on his promotion to detective sergeant. Most of you have worked with DS Tripp for some time now, and I'm sure you'll be relieved that there's now a younger, fitter and less offensive sergeant on your team than just DS Lively.'

That one was met with an absolute roar of laughter and Lively seemed to be enjoying the attention in spite of the fact that it came wrapped in a bow of insults. Ava looked from Overbeck to Lively. It was only a few months since she'd caught her heel-toting, self-declared queen bitch of a superior in flagrante delicto with the dour, die-hard sergeant and she still hadn't been able to wipe the memory from her mind. They were about as unlikely a couple as you could imagine and yet Overbeck had still managed to make Ava feel as if she was the sad case.

'Ach, you love me really, ma'am,' Lively aimed, bravely, at Overbeck.

Ava waited for the superintendent's explosion. Their affair wasn't public knowledge and Lively was asking for trouble by sparring with her in front of the squad.

'That's right, Sergeant,' Overbeck said with a smile. 'Like I love my shoes. I get to tread on them every day, they go where I decide and if there's any crap, the shoes get it on them rather than me personally. Then, when they get old and scruffy, I throw them in a bin and it's as if they never existed.'

That one got not just a laugh, but also a round of applause. Overbeck looked genuinely pleased with herself rather than merely supercilious. Ava couldn't believe it. Sergeant Lively got away with so much bullshit and now Overbeck wasn't even rebuking him, just adding to his kudos points with the lads.

'All right,' Overbeck said when her ego had sucked in enough of the jollity. 'Our newest team member worked with us before on a temporary placement before going off on maternity leave. I'm delighted to say she'll now be joining you full time, so please don't any of you reveal your true natures until she's settled in a while. Stand up, if you would, DC Janet Monroe.'

The short, neat Hispanic officer stood up, her dark hair shining in a perfect bun, looking completely at ease in the predominantly male room. Ava was keen to recruit more females into MIT, but it was slow-going and not helped by the locker-room atmosphere. Janet Monroe was tough, smart and more than a match for her new colleagues.

'And, finally, your new detective inspector. Not shipped in from Interpol, I'm afraid, but perhaps you'll actually be able to understand this one's accent . . .'

There it was, the dig at Callanach. Ava had been waiting for it. She looked across the room to Callanach, who gave a simple shrug. He was used to the abuse.

'Transferring to us with promotion after a long and distinguished period working with undercover teams across Scotland, Detective Inspector Pax Graham.'

Graham stood. He'd been sitting at the very back, but he couldn't hide in the most crowded of rooms. Ava wondered how he'd ever been selected for undercover work at his size, and it wasn't just his height. The man was a mountain – 100 per cent rugby-playing Highlander.

Overbeck had been almost girlish while they'd been interviewing him. She hadn't sworn once. Ava wasn't impressed by muscles, but Graham had proved himself invaluable in the department's last major operation. He pushed the rules when it was necessary to get results, and had shown himself to be both trustworthy and decent.

Ava was pretty sure he wasn't just playing the promotion game. She had no time for police who wanted to climb the ladder as quickly as possible. That wasn't the point of service. Pax Graham had seen his share of danger and discomfort. He was popular with his superiors, as his references had proved, but equally well liked by his peers, which was a much more significant compliment. You could be the best manager in the world, but if the men and women under your command didn't like you, they wouldn't respect you, either.

Graham moved to the front of the room to many slaps on the back and congratulations. Overbeck shook his hand and ceded the floor.

'Thank you,' he grinned. 'Some of you have worked with me in previous operations, but if not you'll find out I like to keep my head down and get on with the job. I'm looking forward to working alongside DI Callanach.'

As he continued to introduce himself, DS Lively stood up and made his way between bodies to stand at Ava's side.

'Were there no other options for the post?' he whispered. 'It's like someone drew a cartoon character of an eighteenth-century Scot and brought him to life.'

'You're not serious,' Ava muttered in response. 'Are you never bloody satisfied? Do you remember what you put DI Callanach through for being French when he started? Now you've got the archetypal Celt and you're still not happy.'

'You're right there. Do you see the look on the boss's face? That's more than just professional courtesy.' Lively crossed his arms and frowned.

Ava smiled at him. 'Sergeant, are you actually jealous? Please

45

say you are. That would make me happy in a way I thought I was too cynical ever to feel again.'

'Due respect, ma'am, sod off,' Lively said. 'So who did you get in a fight with?'

'A wall,' Ava said. 'Misjudged it.'

'Shame I missed that,' Lively said, back on his usual form.

'You'd have enjoyed it. I was wondering who to pair you with for the next investigation. Let me know if you'd prefer to be on DI Graham's team or back with Callanach.'

DS Lively groaned. 'Can I stay in the incident room and eat doughnuts?'

'I think you've spent enough time doing that already,' Ava said, directing a pointed look at Lively's midsection. 'Hey, maybe that's why Overbeck's so happy about recruiting Graham. Bit of eye candy. Perhaps you're not flavour of the month any more.'

'That's a bit personal, ma'am. I'm not sure you're supposed to speak to an officer in your command like that. I should have a chat with human resources.'

'You could' – Ava dropped her voice even lower – 'but then I'd have to explain that my comments were made in relation to seeing you naked with the evil Overlord up there. You might find that a less amusing conversation to have with HR, don't you think?'

'Low shot,' he growled. 'Hang on. You're up. Try not to drool over all six foot four of him at once, won't you?'

All eyes were turned in Ava's direction. She climbed between the rows of chairs and wished her squad were looking her in the eyes, but everyone was focused on the lump on her head. Her own fault. She'd woken up feeling utterly foolish, not to mention confused, in the bed of her detective inspector. That was a first, and she had no idea how she'd let it happen, even if they were close friends. Why she'd decided to climb over Tantallon Castle wall was equally puzzling. Ava had a dim recollection of feeling cool and heroic, almost as if she'd been showing off to Callanach, only that was ridiculous. They'd been in enough tricky situations that she didn't have anything to prove. But it had felt good initially to be leaning out in the wind, searching for clues and battling adversity like some ridiculous movie heroine. Now, there was only one question on everyone's mind, and MIT would be obsessed with gossip and speculation until she dealt with it.

'Welcome to both DC Monroe and DI Graham,' she said. 'They're both starting today, so everyone make sure you're showing them how we operate and our normal procedures. We have two cases pending trial, so please make sure all the court papers are in order for those.' There was silence. Fine. 'I went to take a look at a crime scene last night based on information received from the pathologist. I slipped and fell – they were difficult conditions – hitting my head against a wall. Looks worse than it is and I'm fully fit for duty.

'Now, as I recall, the newly promoted are duty bound to buy the rest of the squad drinks, so DI Graham and DS Tripp will no doubt make themselves available at a suitable pub after shift tonight.'

That took everyone's mind off her injuries and caused another round of raucous comments, allowing Ava to slip towards the corridor. She took the corner quietly and headed for her office.

'Ma'am,' a voice rumbled from behind. She turned back to see DI Graham approaching. 'You'll come for a beer tonight, then?'

'I'll have to see,' she said. 'The squad likes to let its hair down when they're out together and having your DCI there isn't very conducive to that.'

'My celebration, my rules,' he replied.

He was nearly a foot taller than Ava and close up, she had

to tilt her neck back to look into his clear blue eyes. It was easy to see why Lively was feeling intimidated by the new boy.

'Let me know where you're going. My mobile number's on the squad contact sheet. The first thing you should do is put all those numbers into your phone. I might pop in for a quick one.'

'I'd be offended if you didn't,' he smiled. 'Is there anything in particular you need me on at the moment?'

'Just settle in while you can. In MIT, the work finds us. You won't need to go looking for it,' she said, waving goodbye and trying not to limp as she continued walking.

By the time she reached her office, her leg was sore, and Callanach was waiting for her with coffee and paracetamol.

'Given that you saved my life, I'm pretty sure I should be fetching you coffee,' she said, dropping into a chair and putting a hand to her forehead.

'If you really felt indebted to me, you'd have called in sick as I suggested.' Callanach shook two tablets from the pot into her hand.

'Yeah, Overbeck really likes people not turning up to her briefings. I find her particularly sympathetic on that subject.'

Ava tossed back the pills and swallowed. The phone on her desk rang as she was still trying to wash a tablet down with coffee. She waved a distracted hand at Callanach, who answered for her.

'Is Ava there?' Dr Ailsa Lambert's reedy voice twittered down the line.

Callanach loved the way she never deferred to Ava by rank. 'She's not. This is Callanach. Can I help?'

'Indeed you can. We've made a positive identification of our fall victim. His fingerprints were on the national database, after an incident in which he'd had an offensive weapon in the back of a taxi. Looks like the procurator fiscal was still making a decision on whether or not to pursue the case.'

48

Callanach grabbed a pen and paper.

'Name?' he asked.

'Stephen Berry. Lived in the city. No other convictions. I've finished my report save for the tox screen findings and I'm hoping to be able to give you everything tomorrow.'

'I'll follow up now. Thanks, Ailsa.'

He sat down at Ava's computer and identified the case file on Stephen Berry that had been referred to the prosecutor's office.

'What have we got?' Ava asked.

'The man with the missing fingernails is Stephen Berry, thirty-two years old. Address is a flat on Comely Bank Row. He was on bail for possessing a large knife, which he revealed to a taxi driver during a journey. Hadn't proceeded to charge yet, but it's not clear why. I'll take Tripp and check it out. You stay in that chair and get some rest.'

'Uh huh, and send someone to massage my feet too, would you?'

'Still funny, even after you nearly fell off the top of a castle. I'll call in as soon as I have any information.'

An hour later, Callanach and Tripp were heading into the city, to what appeared to be a private house. The windows were blacked out and the door had a video security system. A minute after they buzzed, a young woman allowed them entry and sat them in a comfy lounge where soft music was being piped gently though speakers. All the artwork featured either calm seas, woodland mists or desert sunrises. Max Tripp picked up a leaflet from the table and read aloud.

'"The Reach You charity was founded in 2002. They have six drop-in centres, do outreach work at a variety of clinics and addiction groups, are accessible through your general practitioner, hospital or hospice, and run a 24–7 suicide helpline." These guys are really well set up. Says here they got a lottery funding boost in 2006 that allowed them to take on a number of new full-time staff who work with a large team of volunteers.'

'It did,' a man said as he walked in, holding his hand out to shake Tripp's. 'I'm Rune Maclure. How can I help you?'

'I'm DC . . . DS Tripp,' Max stumbled, 'and this is DI Callanach. I'm afraid we have sad news. You were instrumental in talking down a man who was ready to jump from the Queensferry Crossing last month. We got your name from the police statement.'

'Stephen Berry,' Maclure said quietly, his face falling. He sat down, taking a moment. 'Can you tell me what happened?'

'He died following a fall from the walls of Tantallon Castle. It was instantaneous. The pathologist was clear that he wouldn't have suffered,' Callanach said.

'Thank you. I'm afraid the problem with suicide is the amount of suffering it takes to get to the point of ending it all. A second of agony at the end doesn't even come close to being a concern for most of the people I see.'

'Of course,' Callanach agreed. 'Can you tell us what you knew about him?'

'Not very much, to be honest. Reach You is on the emergency services list to provide experts who assist in suicide attempts – either about to happen, or failures – for people who need help afterwards. I assume the taxi driver called it in as soon as he'd let Stephen out of the cab. The police called our central number and they put a call out to see who was in the area. I was nearby and able to be at his side in a few minutes.'

'That was lucky,' Tripp said.

'Not really. It didn't save him in the end, did it?' Maclure rubbed his temple. 'Our statistics are pretty good. Most people don't go through with the attempt, they just need to work out where they're at. Of those who do try, most suicides aren't successful, either because there's a sudden will to live that kicks in and sabotages the attempt, or through simple lack of research. There are about seven hundred suicides in Scotland every year, more men than women, the biggest group being Stephen's age category.'

'How did you talk him down?' Callanach asked.

'There was someone he cared about, a young woman. I'm afraid I can't remember her name now, but it's in my notes if you need it. Often, in the heat of the moment, the details get a bit blurry for me. They'd been in a serious relationship, though recently split. I was persuading him to call her. I find that making a meaningful contact often changes a person's mind about ending their life. He slipped on the railings before making the call, realised he didn't want to die in that moment and I was able to help him back up.'

Callanach felt the room slide, seeing Ava slipping through his arms again, certain he was going to drop her, already feeling the dreadful loss of her before she'd gone. The potential for grief had hit him with overwhelming force.

'Are you all right?' Maclure asked him.

'Yes, sorry. I was imagining how scary that must have been. For him and for you,' Callanach replied.

'We're simply trained to do the very best we can. If we took responsibility for everyone we came into contact with . . . well, you wouldn't last very long at this job. I was really pleased when he came down. Obviously, the police had to question him, but I gave a statement and spoke on his behalf, asked the police to consider not prosecuting for the knife. They said they'd refer the matter to get a decision quickly.'

'Why did he do it?' Callanach asked.

'Stephen was bipolar. His prescribed drugs weren't helping consistently, which is something many sufferers experience. All premature deaths are tragedies, but when they're caused by a neurotransmitter problem in the brain, how do you come to terms with that as a family member? We can put men on the moon but medicine isn't advanced enough to treat this. Such a waste.' Maclure shook his head, lacing his fingers behind his hair and giving the ceiling a long look. 'Sorry. You're here for help, not to listen to me moaning.'

'I think you're entitled,' Tripp said. 'I can't imagine how you do your job every day.'

'Trying to make a difference, same as you,' Maclure said. 'I still see a better side of humanity than if I worked in a bank. What else can I tell you?'

'What was your last contact with him?' Callanach asked.

'I saw him twice after the suicide attempt. The first time was two days afterwards. He came here to see me and thank me for what I did. I told him what we could offer, tried to persuade him to get counselling, but with bipolar disorder that feels like a drop in the ocean. To Stephen's credit, he agreed, although I realised he was reluctant. The last time I spoke to him, he phoned to say he'd changed his mind and didn't think the counselling would help. He cancelled the session.'

'Are there any notes?' Tripp asked.

'Yup, I'll get a copy for you. As he's deceased, confidentiality ceases to apply. I couldn't talk him into getting any more help. There's a limit to how pushy we can be, or we push people away from us at the time when they need us most. It's a fine line.'

Callanach bet it was. Trying to persuade people to open up to you, knowing it would initially at least be pouring salt on their wounds. Wanting to help people who wanted to be left alone.

'Did Stephen talk to you about any other problems in his life? Anything external to the bipolar disorder? Debts, addictions, conflicts, for example?' Callanach tried to make it sound casual, but there was no way of hiding the fact that they were digging.

'None, although I didn't have much time to explore that. He certainly didn't reveal anything to me. He seemed like a genuinely nice man, to be honest. Likeable, thoughtful. He left his donor card at the roadside in case anyone could be helped after his death.' Maclure smiled and Callanach was drawn to him.

Maclure had a gentleness about him that was all warmth and ease, which reminded him of Ava. The two of them would get on like a house on fire, Callanach thought. Maclure would be the perfect foil to her stresses, and Maclure would like Ava's natural intelligence, passion and empathy. Neither was the least bit bothered by social structure or setting out to impress. They did their jobs only to serve. Ava would like him.

As soon as the thought crossed Callanach's mind, another part of him objected. Ava meeting a man she might be drawn to would mean sharing her again, and Callanach had been looking to spend more time with her. While he'd been going out with Selina, it had been hard to invest in his friendship with Ava. Their evenings out watching old movies at the cinema, and eating and drinking at the city's lesser-known treasures, had kept him sane while he'd been settling into life in Scotland. He wasn't ready to let anyone else do those things with Ava yet. At least he could admit it to himself. More than that, Ava's private life was none of his business. He had no idea why he'd been thinking about her in the context of finding her a partner.

Tripp was handing over an email address for Maclure to send the notes relating to Stephen Berry and offering thanks for his assistance. Callanach stood up and shook his hand, noting the lack of wedding ring, and wishing he could erase the image of Ava and Rune Maclure together.

Callanach and Tripp made their way to the door, leaving Maclure to get back to work. As they were climbing into the car, there was a tap at the window. Tripp opened up.

'I meant to ask,' Maclure said. 'Would you let me know when the funeral is? I'm not sure how much social contact Stephen had. I'd like to pay my respects. He should have people there to say goodbye to him.'

'That's very thoughtful of you,' Callanach replied. 'I'll make sure you're notified, although it might not be for some time. There will have to be a fatal accident enquiry first.'

'You're not clear about what happened, then?' Maclure asked.

'Not yet. There are no witnesses and the forensics are difficult to interpret.' Callanach chose the most vague phrase he could.

'Poor Stephen. Still no peace for him. He was even mocked while he was contemplating suicide from the bridge. Can you believe some people? I worry about the human race.'

'Sorry, he was mocked how and by whom?' Callanach asked.

'There was a man in the crowd, laughing, while Stephen was struggling to get himself safe. The police officers were nearer than me. I'm not sure who it was. I could hear but not see who was responsible.'

'Thank you, Mr Maclure,' Callanach said. 'We'll be in touch about the funeral details when we have information.'

They drove away in silence, contemplating how the landscape of Stephen's death had shifted in the previous hour. The bipolar disorder provided a simple motive for suicide and the decision not to proceed with counselling might well have been confirmation that Stephen was still struggling.

'Phone the pathologist when we get back to the station, Tripp,' Callanach said. 'She'll need to get hold of Stephen Berry's medical records to check the bipolar disorder and hopefully that'll tell us what medication he was taking. And speak to the officers at the Queensferry Crossing incident. See if any of them remembers a man laughing and get a description. It's probably nothing, but the procurator fiscal will want it covered if there's to be an inquiry.'

Tripp's phone rang. Callanach drove on, cursing the traffic lights as Tripp answered it.

'Yes, ma'am,' Tripp muttered. 'We'll be back in quarter of an hour. Sure. I understand. Straight there.' He ended the call.

'What was that about?' Callanach asked.

'DCI Turner wants you back at the station as quickly as possible, sir. We're not to stop anywhere, she says, and don't talk to anyone else. Direct to her office. She sounded weird, to be honest.'

'Weird, how?' Callanach asked.

'Quiet and polite. As if she were at a tea party, you know?' Tripp said.

Or as if she'd spent too much time staring at her injuries from the previous night in the mirror and was trying to figure out why she'd taken such a massive risk, Callanach thought. Ava wasn't in the best place right now.

Chapter Six

4 March

Ava was standing at her office window when Callanach and Tripp entered. Arms crossed, face pinched, she was as defensive as Callanach had ever seen her.

'Thank you, DS Tripp, you can go now,' she dismissed.

Tripp glanced at Callanach but said nothing, exiting quietly.

'Ava, are you all right? I was worried about you,' Callanach said, crossing the room to her, ready to give whatever support she needed.

Instead, she took a step away from him.

'I had a call from Ailsa while you were out,' she said.

'Stephen Berry's tox results?' Callanach asked.

'New case, actually. Her deputy performed the postmortem early this morning. What looked like a natural death turns out to have been a suffocation.'

'Do you need me to get a squad to the scene?' Callanach asked.

'Scenes of Crime is already there with uniformed officers,'

Ava replied tersely. 'They're conducting preliminary interviews. I'm giving this one to Pax Graham.'

'You're putting him in charge of a murder investigation on his first day? I'm not sure he's even up to speed with MIT procedures yet. If it's handled wrongly, it could be fatal for the prosecution.'

'I'm aware of that,' Ava said. 'Where were you when I called you to meet me at the mortuary to see Stephen Berry's body?'

'I told you at the time, I was at my flat. I hadn't unpacked. I still haven't after last night . . .'

'Actually, you said you were at the gym, so I'm curious that it turns out you were at a nursing home visiting a man called Bruce Jenson.'

'Bruce Jenson?' Callanach paused. There was no way Ava could know anything about Jenson. They'd never discussed him or what he'd done to his mother. 'Sorry, I don't understand what you're asking me.'

'Are you denying that you lied to me about the gym?' She was breathing fast, her voice louder than the conversation warranted.

Ava was furious, Callanach realised, and it was about more than just being lied to.

'Fine, I wasn't at the gym. I had personal business that I didn't want to discuss. No big deal. What's going on, Ava?'

'I'm not Ava right now,' she said, her voice little more than a whisper. 'I'm DCI Turner. And once this conversation's over, I'm going to have to make up a formal statement recording what we both said. Technically speaking, I should probably have another officer in here as a witness, but you saved my life last night, so I'm giving you this, but I won't break procedure to any greater degree. Were you at the nursing home, yes or no?'

'Yes,' Callanach said.

Ava's folded arms flopped momentarily to her sides as if

defeated before she took control and landed them forcefully on her hips.

'And you lied to me because?'

'You needed me and I didn't want you to think you were disturbing me,' he said.

'You lied to me for my own sake?' Ava's voice was getting louder.

'I lied because I made the decision to get straight back on with work. I wasn't doing anything I couldn't walk away from. What exactly has happened that's so . . .'

'Bruce Jenson's dead,' Ava said abruptly, watching his face.

Callanach remained still.

'He had advanced dementia and death was apparently inevitable, the doctor said, but not expected any time soon. He had perhaps a year, maybe more left. His doctor hadn't seen him for a month and the nurses were happy with his condition, so they were surprised to find him deceased. In those circumstances, procedure is for there to be a postmortem and then . . .'

'Wait,' Callanach said. 'Just . . . give me a moment.'

It was Callanach's turn to walk to the window. He stared down at the rows of police cars parked below and at the brave pedestrians outside in the rain. Bruce Jenson was dead. He'd wished it on him every day since his mother had revealed the tragedy in her past, had so nearly lost his temper sufficiently to bring Jenson's life to an end himself, and now that it had happened he felt nothing. No relief, no pleasure, no sense that justice had been done.

In a bitter twist, Jenson had left him one single, poisonous inheritance. Callanach had been left to answer for his presence in Jenson's room just hours before the man had died. How absolutely fucking typical. Once fate had decided that you were an apt target, it was as persistent as chewing gum on the bottom of your shoe.

'How did he die?' Callanach asked quietly.

'Looks as if a cushion was held over his mouth. We won't have confirmation until the fibres in his mouth have been inspected under a microscope, but there are teeth marks against the inside of his upper lip, which suggests that pressure was applied, and there's no other obvious causes of death. No stroke, no cardiac event.'

Clear-cut murder then, and with the same cushion he'd been holding just a little while before. The possibility that it was a coincidence seemed ridiculous and yet the cushion was the most obvious weapon in the room. One that didn't require you to get your hands dirty and which offered a silent death.

For a second he wondered if he hadn't, perhaps, gone further than his memory was allowing him to recall. If he hadn't pressed the square of material and stuffing into the bastard's face and held it there just long enough for all the oxygen in Jenson's lungs to be depleted. He deserved it. No question about it. As far as Callanach was concerned, Jenson had deserved that and a whole lot more. But it hadn't happened at his hand. Callanach turned to look Ava straight in the eyes.

'I didn't do that to him,' he said.

'Of course you didn't, you bloody idiot. If I thought you did we'd be in an interview room with the tape running and I'd have handed the case over to a different team. So really, no bullshit: why did you lie to me? And what the hell were you doing there anyway?'

'Just visiting,' Callanach said.

'Yeah, well unfortunately for you, when the – and I quote – really, really good-looking French policeman goes for a visit somewhere, he doesn't exactly blend in. The nurse who allowed you access virtually gave the uniformed officers who took her statement your inner leg measurement.'

'It was a completely innocent visit . . .' he mumbled.

'Social?' Ava clarified.

'Yes,' Callanach said.

'That's what I assumed, only you used your police ID to gain access rather than signing the visitors' book, so it looks like official police business. Only for the life of me, given that you're in my command, I cannot think what case we have running that Mr Jenson is in any way involved in. Please say you can enlighten me.'

Callanach reached into his pocket and withdrew a pack of Gauloises cigarettes. Shaking one loose, he stuck it between his lips unlit, tasting France and his youth. Actually, lighting a cigarette was a line he hadn't crossed in years, but there were times he wished he wasn't quite so disciplined.

'I've got to tell you that's not quite the reassuring response I was hoping for,' Ava said. 'Oh, Luc, for God's sake, you're going to have to tell me everything. You were the last person save for medical staff with access to that room. Bruce Jenson has a son. He's demanding answers and is entitled to them. At the moment, there are only a handful of people who know what's going on, but that won't last long. You'll have to be formally interviewed, so if this was police business you'd better write up some notes pretty damned quickly.'

'It wasn't,' he said quietly. 'It was personal. I didn't want to leave my name in the visitors' book for his family to see.'

'So you lied to me about having been there and you lied to the nurse about the nature of your visit.'

'I guess,' Callanach said.

'The nurse also said that you broke a vase while you were there, that you cleaned up after yourself and put it in the bin. Will your fingerprints be on it?'

Callanach thought back. He'd put gloves on to pluck the hair from Jenson's head, but not to clean up the broken pottery. There hadn't been any reason to at the time.

'There'll be plenty of prints,' he said. 'It was an accident.'

'Think very carefully about this next question. Did you touch Bruce Jenson at all? Is there any possibility that you could have left skin cells or fingerprints on any part of his body?'

Callanach sat down, recalling the way he'd taken Jenson's chin in his hand to direct his attention towards the photograph of his parents. He nodded affirmation at Ava.

'Anywhere near his mouth?' Ava asked, her voice hoarse with emotion.

He nodded again.

'Holy shit,' Ava said. She tapped the desk and stared blankly at the wall. 'Okay, it's not that bad. No one's going to believe you were involved in a murder. You just need to present your reasons for being there and explain the sequence of events. They don't have any sort of motive for you to have hurt him and that's the most compelling evidence in cases like this. It's probably someone who has day-to-day contact with him.'

'You think it was a staff member who killed him?' Callanach asked.

'That would normally be the first consideration,' Ava said. 'It's hard work looking after dementia patients and carers have been known to break down, either from the stress of the job or from a desire to end the suffering quickly. We'll be checking the family too, of course . . .' Her voice trailed off.

'There's a but,' Callanach commented.

'Actually, the "but" is broken glass in the lower section of a patio door. Scenes of Crime think the glass was broken potentially to allow an intruder to reach up inside and unlock the door. It explains why no one apart from you or staff members was seen in the corridors during the evening. That's extremely helpful to you. Why risk being identified by the staff and then breaking the door? It makes no sense. Either that or it's genius deflection.' She gave a small smile.

'Ava . . .' Callanach whispered.

There was a knock at her door.

'Come in,' she called brusquely.

Pax Graham entered, keys in hand. 'Oh,' he said, looking from Ava to Callanach. 'Am I interrupting?'

'Not at all,' Ava replied, back to businesslike. 'I was just asking Callanach about the nursing home. He was there visiting Mr Jenson. I've asked him to go home now and write up a full statement to give you as much information as possible. Once that's done, you'll have to speak with him on a formal witness basis, of course. Usual procedures will apply. Make sure you keep a team with no overlap to DI Callanach on this matter. You can have DS Lively and DC Monroe. Let me know what other resources you'll require.'

Graham looked uncomfortable.

'Is something wrong, Detective Inspector?' Ava asked.

'Not that I'm unhappy about being given the case, ma'am, but should we not send this outside MIT? If there's any question about DI Callanach's involvement, it might be helpful for him to have it investigated and be cleared by an impartial team.'

'He's right,' Callanach said. 'You're going to have to suspend me for the duration of the investigation, too.'

'You're both overreacting,' Ava said. 'Callanach's a witness, nothing more. No one's suggesting that he was involved in the commission of an offence. There's been no complaint filed. It's not as if you tried to conceal your presence at the nursing home. Graham, you might have the best possible witness. I suspect it'll turn out to be extremely fortunate that a police officer was on the premises just before the murder happened. Callanach might well have noticed something that other people would have missed.'

Graham paused. 'Sure,' he said. 'That sounds right. I'll be getting on then. Luc, you'll forgive me if I don't chat to you very much during the investigation? I don't want anyone suggesting there was contamination.'

'I understand,' Callanach replied. 'Very sensible.'

Graham left without further conversation. Ava walked to a drawer and pulled out a bottle of whisky.

'We shouldn't,' Callanach said.

'You're damned right we shouldn't,' Ava said, 'but we're going to. I have about a thousand questions for you and this isn't the right time or place.' She pushed a measure of single malt into his hand. 'Down it.' She ordered. 'You look like hell, so pull yourself together before you leave this room. If you're not guilty, you'd best stop acting guilty.'

'I want you to suspend me,' Callanach said, putting the empty glass down on the desk.

'You've been suspended before, back at Interpol. You hadn't done anything wrong then and look what damage it did to your career. I've got your back, Luc, but I need the whole truth.'

'It's not that simple,' Callanach said.

'So find a version that is,' she replied, finishing her own drink and replacing the bottle cap. 'Now go home. I've got to head off this impending hurricane with Overbeck, then I'll join you. We're going to go through what happened second by second, until there's no possible space for misinterpretation. None at all.'

It was a nice idea, Callanach thought. The only problem was that the opposite was true and when Ava found out why he'd been there, even she would start to doubt his innocence. Though that wasn't what really bothered him. He knew perfectly well he hadn't killed Bruce Jenson. But someone had. Straight after his visit. Using a cushion he'd touched. Coming through a door he'd kicked. What he wanted to know was who and why.

Chapter Seven

4 March

It was well after 6 p.m. before Ava got away from the station and Edinburgh's traffic wasn't letting her go anywhere in a hurry. Fortunately, Detective Superintendent Overbeck had been out of the office all afternoon engaged in a bout of brass-kissing, so Ava wrote her a brief, bland email explaining that Callanach had been at a crime scene immediately before the event and that MIT was screening off that investigation from him. It was intellectually dishonest but technically correct, and that would have to do until Pax Graham and his team found a more appropriate suspect.

Resting her head on the steering wheel, Ava sat outside Callanach's apartment wondering what she was doing. She'd spent the night in his arms. Waking up and extricating themselves from one another had been more than just a little awkward, but he was one of her closest friends. She'd stared down death with Callanach at her side more than once, always knowing they wouldn't hesitate to protect one another.

But trouble followed him. It had found him at Interpol and seemed reluctant to leave his side now. He'd become the sort of partner most police officers would count as a blessing until she'd been promoted over him, and even then he'd bent the rules as needed to help her out. Whatever it took, she'd do the same for him now.

Her face was a thumping mess of pain and she suspected the wound on her leg might require a dose of antibiotics in spite of Callanach's admirable clean-up job, but all she really wanted was paracetamol and another hot bath. Climbing the few steps to Callanach's front door, reaching out to press the buzzer for his flat, she sighed as her mobile began to ring. Caller ID showed her DS Tripp was on the end of the line.

The day's events had wiped her mind blank and right now, she was supposed to be at the pub celebrating two of her team's promotions. If she took the call, she was going to have to make an excuse. She certainly couldn't reveal where she actually was and what she was there for. God, it never rained but it dumped an entire fucking ocean on you, she thought, ending the incoming call. She'd have concocted a proper excuse by morning, and there was every chance that both Tripp and Graham's hangovers would be painful enough that they wouldn't be talking much anyway.

Her phone began to ring again before she'd had a chance to put the mobile back in her bag. Ava stared at it. DS Tripp was perhaps the most sensible officer on her crew and when you combined that with his good manners, there was no way he'd call twice in rapid succession simply to remind her about a few swift ones after work. She gritted her teeth and answered, hoping beyond hope that Overbeck hadn't read her email and was demanding her presence back at the station for an update.

'Turner,' Ava said. 'What's up, Tripp?'

'Ma'am, you're needed at 278b Easter Road. There's a body.

I'm on my way there now. Apparently it's a bit chaotic,' Tripp said.

'Okay.' Ava was already pulling her car keys back out of her pocket. 'Where's DI Graham?'

'Still at the nursing home working with Scenes of Crime, trying to figure out which other patients, medics and visitors had access to the deceased's room. I've been trying to get in touch with DI Callanach but he's not responding at the moment.'

Ava looked up at the window above her and hoped Callanach was okay. He'd had a bad day and as someone who'd been accused of misconduct before, she wasn't sure how well he was going to handle a second incident.

'I'll find him,' Ava said. 'We'll both be there shortly.'

Finally, she got to press the buzzer. Callanach's answer was simply to allow her access. He was standing holding his flat door open by the time she got to the top of the stairs.

'I've made food,' he said. 'I assume you haven't eaten anything since leaving here this morning.'

'Will it keep? We're wanted at Easter Road. You can drive. My leg hurts like hell.'

'Are you kidding? I can't go. DI Graham was right. You have to suspend me, Ava. If Overbeck decides you broke protocol this could turn out worse for you than for me, and I don't want to be responsible for that.'

'Have you written up your statement as I asked?' Ava demanded.

'Yes, of course, but there are circumstances . . .'

'And have you taken part in any criminal activity or conspired to commit any crime in relation either to the crime scene or the victim?' she continued.

'Ava, you know I haven't . . .'

'Good. Then suspending you is simply going to create endless gossip and speculation. It'll go on your record and, frankly, I don't want to be without my most experienced DI at the moment. Now, someone's dead and we have a job to do, so let's go. Also, do you have any more paracetamol?' she added, softening her tone.

Callanach smiled at her. 'Sure,' he said, disappearing off in the direction of his kitchen and reappearing with pills and a bottle of water.

They made it in under ten minutes, leaving the car down the road, one side of which had been blocked off as a tent was erected to give some privacy at street level. Easter Road led out of the city towards Leith. The area was suffering a sad decline, and the three-storey housing featured sheets hung in place of curtains and window frames that had lost more paint than remained on them. The flat in question was on the second floor with a shared entrance hall.

Ava and Callanach donned white suits, shoe covers, gloves and hats, and prepared to enter. A sulphuric, metallic smell gave the situation away from the first-floor landing. The body had been there a while. The weather was so cold that unless the flat had been heated to an extreme, the smell would have taken a while to get so strong.

Ailsa Lambert appeared at the front door of the flat, talking brusquely to a member of her team and handing over a camera.

'You ready for us to come in and take a look?' Ava asked her.

'Go ahead,' Ailsa replied shortly.

Ava and Callanach shared a brief look. If Ailsa was out of sorts, then whatever was waiting for them had to be bad.

The bathroom was tiny and the forensics team cleared out to allow them access. Ava stood with her back against the window and Callanach spread his legs either side of the toilet so they could both look down into the bath. Tripp appeared in the doorway as they were taking stock.

'Who reported it?' Ava asked him.

'A neighbour,' Tripp replied. 'The smell had been getting worse over two weeks, so he finally called the police.'

'Two weeks?' Ava hissed. 'Are you kidding?'

'Afraid not. I suspect the neighbour might be selling some weed on an informal scale judging by the smell of his own apartment and the fact that while I was talking to him, his mobile rang repeatedly. He'd obviously just cleaned off every surface in his flat but neglected to cover up the scales on the floor in the corner.'

'So he didn't want the police in here until it got to the stage where the stench was actually affecting his clientele, is that it?'

'Something like that, ma'am,' Tripp replied. 'The pathologist confirmed the body's been here at least two weeks, more likely three. Judging by the photos on the walls, I'd say the deceased is the owner and resident, a Mrs Hawksmith.'

As one, they all looked down at the woman's body. Mrs Hawksmith was past middle age but not yet old. Each of her ankles was bound by a cable tie to a tap pipe, below the handle, at the end of the bath, leaving her legs splayed open, slightly bent, and flopped against the sides. Her wrists were bound with handcuffs over her stomach. A deep wound – Ava estimated three inches long – ran across the inner bend of her left elbow with another, shorter one, on the same wrist. Her head lolled against the side nearest them, eyes open, mouth agape, as if she were appealing for help.

The corpse was bloated, limbs swollen and hard, a dark red colour with brown patches. The putrefaction gases were appalling, even though the doors had been open for some time. She was a large woman but not obese. Her tattoos were visible but not clear through the discolouration of her skin and there were no other obvious wounds. The goriest of tidemarks was a muddy-crimson line around the rim of the tub and the plug remained in place.

'The bath was full when she bled out,' Ava said. 'The water must have leaked out slowly in the days that followed. Has anyone found the key to the handcuffs?' she asked Tripp, leaning over to take a closer look at the cuffs.

They weren't police or military issue, nor were they the joke shop sort with the button that could be pressed to spring them open. A key had to be fitted into a central slot to release the wearer, which would have been possible if the key was within grabbing distance.

'No key as yet,' Tripp said. 'You can get those sort of cuffs online or in sex shops. They're bondage-type regalia. Maybe she was tomming.'

'Okay, get asking the neighbours if there were men – or women, for that matter – coming to the flat at odd hours, or if Mrs Hawksmith was coming and going at unusual times. Does she have any previous convictions?'

'Still checking. We don't have a confirmed date of birth yet. She doesn't have a passport or driving licence here that we've found.'

'Do we know what the cut was made with?' Ava looked around the tiny bathroom.

'We haven't found a blade or a weapon,' Tripp said.

'Really?' Ava asked. 'Is there blood anywhere else in the property?' She tried to peer through the plastic sheeting beneath her feet. 'Blood on the bathroom floor, even?'

'None,' Ailsa said, appearing behind Tripp. 'Excuse me, young man.'

Tripp moved out of her way to let her stand over the body with a thermometer.

'Decomposition is advanced. Thank goodness it's not warm enough for the insects to be out in force yet, or this would be an even worse situation. As it is, my estimate of death won't be terribly precise. I don't know how long she spent in the water after passing, but I can tell you that her death would not have been immediate. There was little clotting around the wounds, so the water was warm and that kept the blood flowing.'

'How long would she have suffered?' Ava asked.

'Difficult to say, but this isn't the deepest of cuts. Keeping the ankles up above the buttocks would have kept the bleed more constant and her heart would have continued beating for possibly four hours, maybe longer. Eventually, her heart would have stopped. She might have gone into shock and died faster. I won't be able to give you exact figures.'

'Four hours? God Almighty!' Ava said. 'She'd have been screaming for help. I can't believe no one heard her.'

'The window was shut, the walls are thick – the property's got to be a hundred years old – and there's every chance people had music on or TVs playing. Or perhaps they were used to the sound of screams coming from this flat,' Callanach suggested.

'Could she have done this to herself, Ailsa?' Ava asked.

'She could easily have put the cable ties around her ankle and the taps, then run the bath. Logically, after that, she'd have had to have closed the cuffs around her left hand, made the two incisions on her inner arm, then got her right hand into the cuffs and snapped them shut.'

'Which leaves the question – where's the blade? Even if she'd thrown it out of the bath, it would still be somewhere in the bathroom,' Callanach said, looking around. He shifted his body forwards to give himself the flexibility to turn, then opened the toilet lid. 'One mystery solved. No blade, but the key to the handcuffs is at the bottom of the bowl.'

'Don't touch the water,' Ailsa instructed. 'If someone else was here recently, we might just get some cells from the seat or beneath the rim, possibly information about sexual diseases from any urine left in the bowl.'

Ava climbed past Ailsa to stare down into the toilet next to Callanach.

'Looks like the right key to me. Small round barrel, ornate bow at the top. It's obviously not meant for a door.'

'Everyone out of here, please,' Ailsa ordered. 'I'll need to get my team in to retrieve that and take samples.'

They left one by one, regrouping in the small lounge, where photos of cats and the late Mrs Hawksmith hung on the walls.

'Ailsa,' Ava said when the pathologist had finished giving instructions to her crew, 'is there anything she could have done to stop the bleeding? You said the victim probably had hours rather than minutes.'

'If she'd had her legs free, she could have pulled the plug chain with her toes and the bleeding would have stopped sooner, if she'd thought of that. The problem is that using her stomach muscles to sit up and fiddle with the taps and chain would have made her heart pump faster and the bleed rate would have increased. She would also have been scared, panicky, not made good decisions. It's possible she thought her screams would be heard, or perhaps she was expecting a visitor who might have helped. Tripp, how was the flat secured when police first attended?'

'Locked, but the chain wasn't across. Didn't require much effort to bash it open, ma'am. It's an old door.'

'Right, we'll let you get on, Ailsa,' Ava said. 'Looks like we'll be seeing you again in the morning. Could you have a preliminary assessment by 11 a.m.?'

'Certainly,' Ailsa said, stripping off her gloves and stepping forwards to press gentle fingers into Ava's forehead around the lump. 'What happened?'

'Tripp,' Ava said. 'I want officers canvassing the neighbourhood tonight, not tomorrow. And I want every bit of information on Mrs Hawksmith we can get. Focus on next of kin. It looks like she lived here alone, but there must be someone who'll want to be notified. I want a briefing ready for the squad by 1 p.m. tomorrow. You can go.'

Tripp disappeared out of the flat, looking happy to be away from Ailsa's disapproving glare.

'Are you going to answer me or should I guess?'

'Slipped at Tantallon, bumped myself. No big deal. I'm still standing,' Ava said, taking off her gloves and unzipping her overalls.

'You're limping more than standing. If you fell and bumped your head, how did you hurt your leg?'

'The leg *is* actually hurting a bit.'

Ava tried a brief grin. Ailsa didn't return it.

'Let me see,' Ailsa ordered. 'Come on, in the bedroom.'

'Ailsa, this is a crime scene, I can't just . . .'

'Bedroom, now,' Ailsa snapped. 'I've got better things to do than to argue with a stubborn girl who takes too many risks. Now move.'

Ava did as she was told, in part because Ailsa was an old friend of her mother's and generational correctness was an involuntary response, but also because her leg really was hurting and having someone qualified take a look at it felt like a good call. It was clear from Ailsa's sharp intake of breath that Ava's self-diagnosis was right.

'Is your tetanus shot up to date?' Ailsa asked.

'Ummm, should be. I'm sure I'd have been notified if it needed updating,' Ava murmured.

'You need antibiotics, straight away, strong ones.'

'I don't suppose you can . . .'

'I'm a pathologist, Ava. We've had this discussion before. I might have stitched you up in the past, but there's no reason for me to carry a prescription pad. And forget making an appointment with your doctor for next week sometime. You'll have to go to accident and emergency.'

'I've actually got quite a lot going on. Is there another option?'

'There is!' Ailsa replied brightly. 'You can decide not to do as I say, and get an infection that at best will result in you needing time off work and at worst will require surgical intervention.' She waited until Ava had done her jeans up again then called Callanach in. 'Luc, she's to go directly to the hospital. A & E. Prescription for antibiotics that you'll have to collect immediately thereafter. Do not let her drive, or change her mind, or fail to take the antibiotics. Who put the Steri-Strips on?'

'Callanach,' Ava told him. 'Don't be too hard on him. I thought he did a great job.'

'He did his best with a wound that should have been treated by a doctor immediately. You could have come to me when it happened as an alternative. You've done that before. Why not this time?'

Ava and Callanach stared silently at one another.

'So that's the way you two are going to play it. Ava Turner, your mother would have wanted me to take better care of you.'

Ava smiled and reached out an arm to hug the woman who'd been like a favourite aunt to her since she'd joined the police force.

'My mother can rest peacefully, Ailsa. You're taking perfectly good care of me and we're headed directly to the hospital, okay? Cross my heart.'

'Not that I don't believe you, but I expect you to produce the medication for me tomorrow morning. Understood?'

Ava and Callanach left, with Callanach extending a hand to help Ava to hobble down the narrow staircase.

'You'd think, now that I'm a detective chief inspector, Ailsa might have decided I'm a grown-up,' she grumbled.

'I'm not taking sides in that argument,' Callanach said. 'Ailsa's scarier than you.'

'Yeah, but I'm your boss, so you're duty bound to agree with me.' Ava winced as she climbed into the car and bent her leg. 'To the hospital then, but we'd better make it quick. We've still got a lot to do tonight.'

'Back to the station to start working on the Hawksmith case?' Callanach asked.

'Your place first. You can't avoid it, Luc. This thing with the nursing home isn't going to go away on its own. We're doing all we can for Mrs Hawksmith for now, God help the poor woman.'

They pulled away slowly, neither of them noticing the man who was watching from the window of the chippy across the road, clutching newspaper-wrapped cod that he had no intention of eating. You had to have a death wish to consume that much saturated fat and salt. He smiled at the irony of it and wondered what Mrs Hawksmith looked like now, three weeks after he'd last seen her.

Chapter Eight

4 March

The Royal Infirmary's emergency department was oddly quiet, but then there was a football match on. Most people would try to avoid serious injury until the pubs were kicking out. Callanach accompanied Ava to reception, knowing she'd play down the extent of the pain if left alone. She showed her badge and explained that time was limited. A nurse appeared immediately and showed them through to a cubicle.

'I'll give you some privacy to get undressed,' Callanach said.

'Not much point. You saw the wound last night and I'm guessing the sight of me in my underwear won't be hugely thrilling at the moment. Take a chair and turn your head away.' She unzipped her jeans and pulled them slowly down over the wound. 'Shit,' she muttered beneath her breath.

'Everything okay?' Callanach asked, keeping his focus on the sink in the corner.

'Not really. I should have shaved my legs a fortnight ago. I look like a bloody yeti, and now I'm going to be stitched up by a doctor who'll assume I'm some washed-up old maid whose idea of a good night is reruns of the TV series *The Book Group* while I sip vodka and Irn Bru, pretending it's a proper cocktail because I dropped a maraschino cherry in it.'

A slim, tanned hand appeared and gracefully drew back the curtain to reveal Dr Selina Vega, the only woman in the world who could make a white coat look sexier and more glamorous than a red-carpet gown.

'Selina,' Callanach said. 'That's a coincidence.'

'Not really. One of the reception staff recognised you and asked if I wanted to take the case,' she smiled. 'Hello, Ava. That's a nasty cut. Why don't you lie down so I can get a better look at it.'

'Er, sure . . . I think I probably just need a prescription for antibiotics, though. We're on the clock. It's good to see you again. You keeping well?' she asked, horribly aware of the tension between Callanach and his ex-girlfriend, and wondering if tea-party conversation was going to help or make things worse.

'I'm going to have to clean it out then stitch it. The butterfly stitches aren't pulling the sides together properly. Left like this you'll have a serious scar and the underlying tissue will be painful for life.'

'So it's a yes to the stitches, then,' Ava said. 'Luc, this could take a while. Did you want to go and get a coffee or something? Sorry, Selina, we've just come from a crime scene. It's been a long day.'

'Sure, I'll bring you back a tea. Selina, espresso?'

'Please,' she nodded, taking various implements from a drawer and pulling a light over the top of Ava's leg. 'You need me to anaesthetise you first?' she asked.

'Don't bother. It's so painful already that you sticking a needle in won't add much.'

Selina began peeling off the strip stitches and cleaning the wound. Ava watched her dexterous fingers work their magic and wondered how Callanach could have given up such a beautiful creature. They seemed to have so much in common.

'I was sorry to hear about you and Luc,' Ava said. 'Truly. I think you were good for him.'

'You'll need a shot of antibiotics to get on top of this infection. There were some small stones and dust stuck in the bottom of the gash. It won't start healing until the infection's dealt with. How did it happen?'

'Fell over late at night, checking out a potential crime at a castle, of all places. Thank God Luc was with me. He always seems to be in the right place at the right time. Fire away with the antibiotics. Needles don't bother me. Do you mind me asking what happened? I know it's none of my business, but Luc is so closed-off about his personal life and I worry about him.'

Selina withdrew the needle from Ava's leg and dropped it into the sharps bin.

'Are you asking as his boss or in some other capacity?'

'As his friend. You know, you stole my cinema buddy from me. No one else'll watch black-and-white movies with me at midnight on a Wednesday. Even so, I'd have continued making the sacrifice to see him happy. I was hoping things would work out between the two of you.'

Selina took a semicircular suture needle from a sterile packet and got ready to begin stitching.

'Luc's complicated,' she said. 'His past affects him every day. People have the wrong expectations of him and he feels the weight of that.'

Ava closed her eyes and laid her head back, gripping the sides of the bed. It was one thing being brave about needles, but only a fool wanted to watch one being weaved in and out of their own flesh.

'That's why I was so pleased when the two of you started dating. After all the trouble with Astrid Borde and the rape allegation, he needed someone he could really trust.'

She inhaled suddenly. The flesh around the wound was more tender than she'd realised and she'd been wrong to think that the pain couldn't get any worse.

'Did he talk to you about me much?' Selina asked quietly.

'Of course,' Ava rushed to reassure, trying to recall specific conversations when Callanach had described what they'd done at a weekend, or the sort of person Selina was. She came up blank. 'But it's hard given our job. Lots of people prefer to leave their private life at the door, so you can go home without a crossover. You understand. It must be the same for you.'

'Actually, I used to talk to my colleagues about Luc all the time,' Selina said, dabbing the wound dry to make the stitching easier. 'I was hoping we'd move in together this summer. He didn't tell you I'd suggested it?'

'I think he did say something about that, yes,' Ava lied, looking at the curtain and wondering how long Callanach was going to take with the drinks.

She was a bad liar and Selina was an intellectual match for anyone. Pretty soon, she was going to have make a clumsy attempt at changing the subject.

'Like you, I thought Luc was happy. We're both Europeans, immigrants to Scotland, we love active sports and sunshine, we understand the pressures of shiftwork. Perfect, right?'

Ava managed a small nod. The pain really was quite bad.

'So I keep asking myself, why did he decide it wouldn't work out? Am I not enough fun, not a good enough cook, do I take life too seriously? But you know what, I don't think it's anything to do with me. That might sound arrogant . . .'

'Not at all. My mate Natasha thinks you're a goddess,' Ava interjected.

'. . . but I work hard, play hard and I'm not in bad shape.'

It was all Ava could do not to roll her eyes.

'So I think there must be someone else.' Selina stopped stitching and sat upright, pausing to look Ava in the eyes. 'What do you think, Ava? Is there another woman in Luc's life I know nothing about?'

'Bloody hell, no. He was reclusive until he met you. There was a weird moment with his neighbour, Bunny, but that was her doing rather than his and it stopped before it got started. Apart from that, he's not had a single date since he moved to Scotland, as far as I'm aware.' Ava inspected the neat stitching along her leg as Selina stuck a gauze pad over it. 'Wow, great job. I'm really grateful.'

'You mean, except for all the dates with you, at the cinema, dinner, drinks, fishing . . .' Selina said as she cleared the debris from the operation.

'Well, neither of us would call those dates,' Ava laughed. 'A couple of work colleagues keeping each other company because they've got no one else to be with, maybe.'

'Do you know he wakes at night sometimes calling your name? He has this recurring nightmare. He told me it comes from a time when you were taken hostage and he was worried he'd reach you too late. That must have been terribly traumatic for you.' Selina stripped off her gloves and dropped them in a bin.

'It was,' Ava said quietly, reluctant to recall the events. Other women hadn't been as lucky as her. Not all of them had survived.

'Those sorts of traumas create a strong bond between people. Sometimes it felt as if he'd have been happier holding you after waking from those dreams. I was always just a substitute. I suppose it's better I figured that out sooner rather than later.' She stood up and took a prescription pad from her pocket.

'Sorry it took so long. Drinks at last,' Callanach said, kicking the curtain aside to enter and thrusting steaming paper cups at them both.

'Thank you,' Ava said quietly. 'Luc, could you wait outside while I get my jeans back on, please?'

'Oh, sure, just give me a shout if you need any help.'

He looked confused but exited anyway.

Ava took a deep breath and tried to compose a reply. Selina had obviously misjudged the situation between Callanach and her, and if that was what had split them up, she needed to put it right.

'Selina, Luc and I are just work colleagues. You know that, right? He sees me more like one of the guys than a woman he could ever be interested in. And it's not always easy between us. My God, when we argue it's like sailing through a storm.'

'I bet it is,' Selina smiled. 'Here's your prescription. You should get it filled immediately and start taking the antibiotics tonight. No alcohol until you finish all the tablets. Any problem with the leg, see a doctor immediately. Keep the stitches as dry as you can.'

Ava sat up and pulled her jeans back on gingerly.

'Thank you,' she said quietly, taking the piece of paper from Selina's hand.

'Don't hurt him, Ava,' Selina whispered. 'He may act tough but there's only so much one person can take. If you don't feel the same way about him as he feels about you, you should let him go.'

'But I . . .'

'With respect, stop playing dumb. It doesn't suit you,' Selina finished. 'I hope the leg heals soon.'

Ava sat on the edge of the bed, wondering if she should go after Selina, who'd either forgotten or abandoned her espresso. Not that there was anything else to say. She'd clearly made up her mind that there was something going on between Callanach and her, and as for the playing-dumb comment . . . that was a step too far. It was difficult to share someone like Callanach, she guessed. The good looks and French charm would make him a target for many women, so it was understandable that any girlfriend of his might get the odd pang of jealousy. And she and Callanach did work very closely together.

She slipped her feet back into her trainers. More than just closely, she had to admit. This morning she'd woken up in his bed shortly after he'd saved her life. That was what Selina was feeling. It was that co-dependency that police partners some-times developed, the sense that there was one person in all the world who'd never let you down. The knowledge that there was one human being who knew what you were thinking, who could anticipate your every action and decision, and who would catch you every single time you fell – physically, emotionally, professionally, personally – *every* single time.

Ava took a sip of her tea and bit her bottom lip, wondering if she should talk to Callanach about Selina's delusion. He might be a little shocked at first, but he'd see the funny side. Perhaps it would even allow Selina and him to have a conversation where they could mend the rift between them.

The talk of nightmares had shocked her. She'd pushed those awful days of her life as far back in her mind as she could and in doing so had assumed everyone else involved had done the same. Callanach had lived with the prospect of losing her to a deeply deranged psychopath and that must have been hard for him. She composed herself and wandered down the corridor, finding him reading a noticeboard and grimacing over his coffee.

'We can go,' she said softly.

'Great, that was quick. Where's Selina?'

'She got called to another cubicle,' Ava said, lying becoming a theme of the night. 'She said to tell you goodbye. You should call her soon. I'm sure she'd appreciate a drink when you're both less frantic.'

'Good idea,' he said, putting an arm around Ava's waist so she could lean on him and keep the pressure off her leg. 'What did you and Selina talk about when I was getting coffee?'

Ava barely paused. 'Spain,' she said. 'Would you mind driving me to a chemist next?'

'Whatever you need,' he said, opening the car door for her. 'I'm all yours.'

Chapter Nine

Before

As Ava waited for her prescription to be filled at the chemist, a man armed with nothing more lethal than a fish supper walked the streets of Edinburgh, peering into windows carelessly left uncurtained. Dr Selina Vega had offered to cover a shift for a colleague who'd called in sick, knowing she wouldn't get to sleep after seeing the man she loved and had lost. Pax Graham, sitting at his brand-new desk, read the statements taken from the staff at the nursing home and wondered how he was going to tell his boss on the second day of his new post that a colleague was the prime suspect in a murder case. And Mrs Fenella Hawksmith – Fenny to her bingo friends who'd been wondering where she was for the last three weeks – was being wheeled out in a body bag for transfer to the Edinburgh City Mortuary.

Fenny had assumed for the last three years of her life that death would be something of a relief. Losing her husband to cancer had been bad but fast. Unable to continue living in the house they'd shared, she'd taken the cheaper, anonymous one-bedroomed flat on Easter Road. What pained her more was the daughter she'd lost to drugs in Glasgow. Alice had run away twelve years earlier. Came back. Went to rehab. Relapsed. Ran away again. Lived on the streets. Came home. Stole from them. Ran away again. For the last five years, Fenny hadn't known if her precious girl was alive or dead. She couldn't even share the knowledge of her father's passing with her. There had been no one to hold her as she'd grieved, and no one for her to comfort and give her a reason to live.

Fenny's doctor had been sympathetic but overstretched, prescribing antidepressants on request when she'd described her feelings of hopelessness. Her husband's hospice had reached out to her, but there had been too many ladies in flowery dresses. 'Edinburgh posh', her own mother would have said, and a million miles away from the Glasgow poverty she'd grown up in. It wasn't that they were judging her, she just hadn't felt like she belonged.

Her first attempt at exiting the miserable world she'd found herself inhabiting had come to an abrupt end when she'd simply thrown up all the tablets she'd taken, together with the bottle of cheap red wine used to wash them down. The only lasting result had been a nasty stain on a beige carpet and a hangover that had lingered for days.

The next occasion had been better planned. Knowing better than to attempt the deed at home surrounded by photos of those she'd loved and lost, she'd spent a hundred quid of her savings, figuring she couldn't take it with her, and booked a hotel room. The irony of that expenditure was that if she'd simply locked herself in her own bathroom, the suicide might have been successful. As it was, a member of housekeeping had failed to deliver a full set of clean towels that morning, so the woman knocked on the door while Fenny was slitting her wrists and entered when no response came.

An ambulance had been called and Fenny had been whisked

away to a nearby hospital. A psychiatric consultant had been engaged and she'd spent the following four months as an inpatient at a unit where the staff wore pink, smiled a lot more than was normal, and insisted that she do a series of daily classes including yoga, meditation and mindfulness. By the end of it, Fenny had been such a flawless student that she was released with cake and good wishes.

They had no idea that she'd have done anything at all never to have to go back to yoga classes again, with a teacher who constantly talked in sing-song hushed tones and insisted that she should love her body and listen to it. Fenny's body, she was pretty sure, fucking hated her and she didn't want to listen to anything it had to say, but compliance had got her out of the unit, with a side-effect of making her truly angry. Angry that her husband had smoked forty a day and left her alone as she marched towards old age. Angry that the daughter she'd cried for every day for more than a decade was gone for no good reason at all. Angry at the neighbours who blasted rap music out day and night.

Anger, it turned out, was a cure in itself. She didn't want to die any more. Countering the rap music with Italian opera, she'd bought a speaker that would drown out a whole festival. She'd joined a bingo club because her husband had spent his life bitching about women who spent money on such frivolities. It had turned out to be rather good fun, too. And she'd stopped looking for her daughter through missing persons websites and family reunion agencies, accepting the reality that there was nothing she could do to bring someone back who was either dead or who wanted to remain lost. Let fate play its games, was her new philosophy. She would simply be carried along on the tide.

Then there'd been a knock at her door at noon one Tuesday. Who the hell worried about answering the door between elevenses and lunch? Nothing bad happened at that time of day, not on a Tuesday in your own home. It wasn't unusual for one of the other tenants simply to buzz people in without asking for so much as a name. The pizza delivery guy regularly just pressed any old button and worried about checking the flat number when he was indoors, out of the rain.

Fenny had answered the door hoping it hadn't been the Jehovah's back to talk her ear off again. She always felt guilty when she told them to get lost but the result of her not doing so was sometimes a thirty-minute polite conversation about how nicely printed their brochures were as she figured out an excuse to shut the door.

Instead, the man at her door was looking sombre and professional.

'Mrs Hawksmith,' he said, holding up a badge dangling from a brightly coloured lanyard. 'I'm from a family reintroduction charity. We have information about your daughter, Alice. Could we talk, if it's not a bad time?'

She hadn't given it a second thought. Thirty seconds later, she was brushing crumbs off her couch so he had somewhere to sit without ruining his smart trousers. Her head had been reeling. News of her daughter, after so long . . . So she wasn't dead. If she'd been dead, it would have been the polis at her door.

Standing in the middle of her tiny sitting room, Fenny had shifted from foot to foot, wanting to hear the news, dreading what it might be, clinging on to hope she'd long since forgotten existed.

'Is there anyone here who might support you or are you alone today?' the man had asked.

'No, it's just me . . .'

Fenny realised in her excitement that she hadn't even asked the man's name. Now she wasn't sure how to backtrack, not that she wanted to waste any time. There was news. It was suddenly worth every birthday and Christmas, every Mother's

Day, every morning when her daughter's bed hadn't been slept in. Finally, there was the prospect of something other than the void of loss.

'Just to clarify, you aren't cohabiting or flat-sharing at the present time. It's important to establish that any information we share with you will remain confidential, you see.'

'Yes, absolutely,' Fenny had gushed. 'It's just me here. If you have some news, I promise not to talk to anyone else about it.'

'Good,' he'd said reassuringly. 'That all sounds fine. Finally, I need to assess your current mental state. We often find that people have very strong reactions to being given news about loved ones who've been missing for a sustained period, and the process of attempting a reintroduction can be fraught with difficulties and disappointments. That's not a journey we recommend people embark upon unless they're in a good place emotionally.'

Reintroduction. She hadn't imagined it. He'd said the word. Her daughter was not just alive but was somewhere accessible and in a fit state to make contact. In that moment, she believed in everything. Karma, kismet, destiny, God, four-leafed clovers – the whole shebang. There was a reason she'd decided to blow money on a hotel room to end it all. There was a reason the housekeeping woman had come in at the worst – now the best – possible moment. The endless stretches in yoga had been worth every second of humiliation and fake smiles. The tranquillisers that had made her feel nauseous. The therapy where she'd poured out every sordid or boring detail of her life. They'd all led her here.

She crossed the room – just three steps, but her legs were jelly and she worried she might not make it – to pick up Alice's photo from the windowsill. In it, her precious seven-year-old had just won a drawing competition. She'd had a real talent, certainly not inherited from Fenny. Drawing faces was what she'd been best at, spending hours of her young life at a table, getting through notepad after notepad.

Fenny still had some of those drawings tucked away in an envelope, hidden in a box with her wedding photos and Mother's Day cards so dearly prized that she dared not take them out and handle them any more. Inside were the childish declarations of forever love that had become screams of hatred as drugs had made her daughter's world a place where the only warm arms she welcomed were delusions that came from plastic wraps, and where only handing her money was enough to induce her to profess love.

'Where is she?' Fenny had whispered, the muscles in her face rising to produce an unfamiliar picture.

Smiles had been absent from her outlook for so long that forming one was an alien sensation.

'I don't know,' the man said, 'do you think you deserve to see her?'

Fenny's smile drooped a little.

'Deserve?' she asked slowly. 'Yes, of course, why would I not deserve to see my baby?'

'Have you treasured your life, Fenella?'

'Of course I have. My husband's gone. He'd have done anything to have looked into our girl's eyes again. Now I'm the only one left and I'll have to do that for both of us. She doesn't even know her daddy's passed. I'm not sure how I'm going to break that to her.' Fenny's legs finally gave way and she lowered herself onto the sofa, taking deep breaths.

'Your husband couldn't have prevented his death though, could he? It was cancer that took him, if I'm not mistaken.'

'Um . . .' she stalled.

The last thing Fenny wanted was to be impolite to the man who was trying to help her, but she wasn't sure quite where he was getting his information. Alice would have had no way of knowing about the tragedy that had struck in her absence and Fenny didn't recall giving any of the reunification agencies the details of her husband's illness.

'Yes, lung cancer. I signed up with a few agencies when I was trying to find my daughter. I was a bit surprised when you turned up and I missed the name of the one you're from.'

'But you . . .' – he continued as if she hadn't said a word – 'have taken the gift of life for granted. You thought you could throw it away. You decided your need to be rid of the responsibilities that come with your place in this world was more important than valuing what you were given.'

'I'm not sure what you're talking about,' Fenny said. 'What does this have to do with my daughter?'

'Are you still taking your medication, or did you decide you knew better than the people who were trying to help you?' he asked.

Fenny put the photo of Alice that she'd been clutching down on the coffee table with a shaking hand.

'Who sent you?' she asked quietly. 'Was it someone from the hospital? Is this part of their follow-up regime? Am I being tested? Only if this is all just part of their scheme to make sure I'm still in recovery, then using the information I gave them about my daughter is . . .'

She couldn't finish the sentence. There was no phrase that was strong enough to express the disgust she felt at what was happening.

Fenny looked the man up and down. He didn't have a file with him. No papers at all. Surely if he'd come to talk about her daughter, he'd be making some notes, or asking her to sign a document, or even check her identity. Looking around the sitting room, she tried to recall where she'd left her glasses so she could read the awfully small print that was currently just a blurred mass on his ID badge.

'Fenella, we need to have a conversation and I need you to give me the right answers,' he said, standing up. 'You'll need to concentrate. I'm going to help you with that, okay? I'm going to make it all much easier for you.'

'I want to see my daughter,' Fenny said, looking at the bulge in the man's trouser pocket.

It certainly wasn't mobile phone-shaped and the broad curves suggested something other than a set of keys.

'Do you?' he asked. 'How much time do you spend actually thinking about her? Once a day? Does she even get that much from you? Isn't it more realistic that you think about her maybe once a week?'

Fenny stood up, closer to him than she was comfortable with, lifting her face several inches to look at him directly.

'There's not an hour of the day that goes by when I don't think of my girl,' she said, tears filling her eyes and rage tensing every muscle.

'Do you?' he smiled. 'Does a mother who actually loves her missing child really attempt suicide? I think not. I believe that you'd wait for her as long as it took, because if there was the most minuscule chance that your daughter might come home, or get arrested, might end up in a hospital and ask for you, you ought to be there for her. Why would you attempt to deprive that poor girl of her only surviving parent? That's just not right.'

He reached out and took hold of Fenny's left hand with his right. Something about his touch felt off, too cool, fake. She raised her hand in his grasp to get a better look.

Gloves. Whoever this man was, for some reason he was wearing clear plastic gloves.

As she opened her mouth to put the question she was thinking into words, she felt a thump that was punctuated by a metallic snap over her left wrist. The dangling handcuff was closed but not overly tight. Ridiculously, she wondered if he was police, after all – not there to notify her of her daughter's death but to arrest her for some parenting offence she hadn't even known she'd committed. The wrongness took a few seconds to sink in.

'What the fuck do you think you're up to? You've got to get out of my place right now. Do you hear me?'

The man laughed.

Fenny tugged at the handcuff. She didn't even want him to get the cuff off. That would mean him touching her again and she really didn't want that. Not with those creepy gloves on.

'You want me to leave already? But you haven't heard what I came to tell you about Alice yet,' he said.

'You're not here to talk to me about my daughter,' Fenny said. 'Now get the fuck out of my flat, you friggin' weirdo, or I'm calling the police.'

The man turned his attention to the speaker that dwarfed Fenny's room, switching it on and scrolling down the iPod that allowed Fenny to randomise music for hours at a time without bothering with it.

'You like opera, right? I've heard it through your door before,' he said. 'A couple of times it's been so loud that I could hear it from the street.' He hit a button and violins filled the air in a dramatic minor key. 'It's the one thing about you that impressed me. An appreciation for the arts is what separates us from the beasts.'

As Fenny screamed, the man simply turned the music louder. From the floor below came the retaliatory strains of an American rapper.

'Let's take this into the bathroom, Mrs Hawksmith, as that's your preferred location.'

He led her by the handcuff towards the bathroom and that was enough to break her from her shocked inaction. Fenny made a dash for her front door, ripping the handcuff through his fingers and sprinting. He'd been waiting for her to make a move. That was what she realised as she crashed to the floor, courtesy of him hooking an outstretched ankle between her legs and watching calmly as she greeted the carpet with her jaw.

'Fucker,' Fenny murmured.

He pulled her back up by her hair and tutted.

'That's right. Now you want to live. Now you've decided to stop being an ungrateful, whining little bitch and protect what you have. Only it's mine. You wanted to give it away and fortunately for you, I'm the one person who'll value that gift.'

'I never wanted to die,' Fenny shrieked. 'Not really. It was depression. I didn't know how to cope with it then, but I learned at the hospital. They helped me. Who are you? You're not from a charity. Who told you about me?'

'What do you think your poor dead husband would make of it? He contracted a terrible, inescapable disease and lost his life to it unwillingly. Then you decided to go and throw yours away, with no consideration at all for the beauty of it, for the power humans harness within their bodies. You treated your own life as disposable after his was stolen from him. You know what I think, Mrs Hawksmith? I think your husband would decide that you'd forfeited your right to live.'

He drew a gun from inside his jacket. Fenny had never seen a real gun before. It was smaller than she'd imagined but it unleashed evil into the atmosphere. Its very presence seeped poison.

'Take off your clothes,' the man ordered, 'and get into the bath.'

Fenny looked down into the porcelain whiteness and saw death waiting for her.

'I don't want to,' she sobbed.

'That's good. Not wanting to is good. It's the start of your healing process. Take your clothes off.'

A swarm of flies were buzzing inside Fenny's brain and she couldn't make the zipper of her trousers work, no matter how hard she tried.

'I have some jewellery,' she pleaded. 'And some money in my purse. My grandpa's war medals, too. They're worth something. You can have all of it. I don't care. Please don't kill me.' Somehow, she dropped her trousers to the floor. 'Remember, you said I needed to be here for Alice, and you were right. She could turn up any day. She might even have a wee baby she needs help with.' Her hands shook as she fussed with the buttons on her shirt. 'I could get more treatment, just to make sure I never do anything stupid again. I'll do whatever you want. Just . . . not this. I don't want to get into the bath.'

Fenny cried and he nodded appreciatively.

'Please don't make me. Please, please don't make me . . .'

'All of your clothes. Just like you did it before. I want to see it just the way it was.' He motioned with the gun for her to remove her knickers.

Fenny stared down the barrel, wondering if it was really loaded. The bullet would be faster than whatever he had in mind for her, she was certain of that. His eyes had all the warmth of a reptile. It was amazing that she hadn't seen it straight away at her front door. The smile was perfect, the clothes were neat and the talk was all reassurance, but if the eyes really were the windows to the soul then his revealed a sort of no-man's land, where life had long since given up the battle. Even the creepy-crawly things that normally thrived on death and decay had deserted that place. Inside this man was an endless echo of nothing.

Fenny knew right then that no amount of begging, crying, screaming or pleading would make a difference. It was the end. She stepped into the tub and followed the remainder of his instructions without a fight. It seemed easier that way.

Chapter Ten

5 March

Ava swallowed the first antibiotic capsule with a glass of orange juice and lifted her extremely sore leg up onto Callanach's couch. It was 12.30 a.m. and the city was remarkably quiet.

'You believe there's any chance Mrs Hawksmith committed suicide?' Ava asked.

'Physically, that would have been just about possible, but it doesn't feel real. Why stress yourself out with the cable ties around your ankles?'

'Maybe to make sure you can't change your mind,' Ava said. 'If it had just been the cable ties, I might have believed it. It was the handcuffs that did it for me. They gave the whole scene a sense that a tableau had been constructed. Someone had worked hard building that image in their mind. They'd seen how it would play out. Surely you don't plan a suicide like that. It's reactive, chaotic in most instances. I'm no expert, but I'd have said your natural instinct is to give yourself some sort of flexibility or an out clause. Also, an element of comfort or ease. No one wants their death to be that traumatic, no matter how depressed they are. You spoke to a witness from a suicide support group about the Stephen Berry killing, didn't you? Do you think he'd be willing to come in and talk to me about it? I reckon we'd benefit from having an expert to give a second opinion.'

Callanach thought about it, knowing Ava was right and that Rune Maclure would probably be more than happy to help. The idea that the two of them would be ideally suited struck him again. Maclure would make Ava laugh, he thought, and put her at ease. He was the right age for her and Callanach was pretty sure he hadn't been wearing a wedding ring. That didn't mean he was single, of course, but if he was . . . Callanach stopped himself there. He had no right to limit Ava's access to men who might be good for her, or bad for her, for that matter.

'Yeah, his name's Rune Maclure. I'll talk to him tomorrow,' he compromised. 'You go to the postmortem and get what you can from Ailsa. We can meet back at the station and debrief the team. It'll save time.'

'You'll have other things to think about tomorrow. Pax Graham's going to have to interview you about the nursing home death and the sooner we get that over with, the better. He needs an official statement on file in case you have any relevant facts that might assist and it'll ensure that we've followed proper procedure. What I still don't know is why you were there in the first place. Seems like a long time ago now, but that *is* the reason I came round earlier.'

'I'm going to need a drink for that conversation, even if you can't join me,' he said, walking to the kitchen to pour himself a glass of red wine.

'Do you have any beer?' Ava shouted after him.

'Yes, but you can't have it. Doctor's orders. How did Selina seem to you?'

Ava considered how to answer that. Selina had been a number of things. Upset, angry, bereft. Jealous. That was the word Ava was avoiding. Jealous of her and Callanach's relationship. She'd got the wrong impression, that much was clear, only how could she explain that without embarrassment. Natasha had teased her about Callanach plenty of times, but that was just ribbing. There was nothing behind it.

'I think she'll be okay and don't try changing the subject. I thought you didn't know anybody in Scotland apart from the MIT reprobates. I know the man in the nursing home wasn't part of a case before today. His name comes up blank on the system. You're going to have to explain it tomorrow, so you might as well have a practice run today.'

Callanach sat down next to her on the sofa, lifting her injured leg so that it rested on his thigh.

'Bruce Jenson was my father's boss, years ago,' he said. 'Back when my dad got his first real job working for a furniture company called Edinburgh Bespoke. In fact, it was before I was even born. I spent some of my holiday researching my family's history, asking my mother about it, so when I got back, I thought I'd look him up.'

'Bullshit.' Ava watched as Callanach drained half a glass of wine in one mouthful. 'Since when do you need to down that much wine to talk about historical research? What aren't you telling me?'

'Nothing,' he replied. 'No drama, no problem. Whatever happened to him today was coincidental. I'll hand DI Graham my statement in the morning, he can interview me about the forensics and that'll be the end of it.'

Ava stared at him. 'Fine, I'll play along. So Jenson was your father's boss thirty-odd years ago. Why go and see him?'

Callanach shrugged. 'Curiosity, I suppose. A desire to make a connection with the past.'

'All right. But when I told you he was dead, your face was blank. There was some shock when you realised you were the last person on record as seeing him alive, but you didn't express any sadness for him, or concern for his family.'

'I met the man once for fifteen minutes. How do you expect me to react?' Callanach asked, leaning his head back on the sofa and closing his eyes.

'I expect you to write your name in the visitors' book and not flash your badge when you have what seems like the most innocuous reason in the world for visiting an old man. Also, I hate it when you lie to me because it makes me feel like you don't trust me and that's kind of upsetting, it turns out.'

'Ava, don't do that,' Callanach whispered.

'I'm not doing anything,' she said, taking his glass from his hand and helping herself to a sip of wine.

'Yes, you are.' He rolled his head to the side to look at her. 'You're making it about emotions when I want to keep it simple.'

'You've already admitted to me that your DNA or finger-prints might be on Jenson's chin. Touching someone's face is either a loving or an angry gesture. Which was it?'

'How about he dribbled and I held his chin to wipe it away,' Callanach replied, reaching out to retrieve his glass.

'Is that what you wrote in your statement?'

'Yes,' he said.

'How did the vase get broken?'

'I knocked it with my elbow by accident,' he said, walking to a shelf to fetch a clean glass and fill it with wine, knowing Ava wasn't giving his back whatever the medical advice was.

'Funny. I've known you a while now and I've never, ever seen you be clumsy. You're very aware of your surroundings, especially in places like hospitals. Seems out of character to me.'

'You have to stop digging,' he said. 'For your sake and mine.'

'I said the same thing to you in previous cases and you've kept digging until there were no secrets left between us. You did that for me. What is it you don't want me to know? Come on, Luc. They'll get your DNA from his face and if the only other DNA is Jenson's, your dribble explanation isn't going to wash.'

'Shit,' he said. 'I hadn't thought about that.'

'About what?'

'My DNA being compared with his to make sure there's no contamination.' He lurched forwards, clutching his stomach, spilling his newly poured wine and trying not to vomit.

'I take back what I said about you not being clumsy.' She smiled gently, taking the glass from his hand. 'Luc, what's going on? If you didn't touch Jenson, whatever really did happen, you've got nothing to worry about.'

Ava hobbled to the kitchen to fetch a cloth. Kneeling on the floor, soaking up the worst of the spillage, she tried not to stare at her colleague. Depositing the sopping cloth in the sink, she washed her hands to give Callanach time to compose himself before returning to the sofa.

'Listen,' she said gently, sitting at his side, 'last night you saved my life when I took a risk I had no business taking. I climbed that wall knowing it was foolhardy, but it didn't occur to me that I could get really hurt, because you were there, holding me. You're always there when I need you. Let me do the same for you. Please.'

Callanach rubbed his eyes, his shoulders suddenly drooping. He turned sideways along the couch and Ava did the same. They faced one another, legs stretched side by side, and Ava waited for him to speak.

'When my mother came to Edinburgh last year, and you arranged for me to meet her in the hotel, she told me about a Christmas party, years earlier, at the factory where my father worked. They were young, struggling for money. Good jobs were hard to come by and she didn't speak great English, so my father was supporting them both. He was a supervisor at Edinburgh Bespoke, popular, with a wife so beautiful – and exotic, being French in those days – that I guess there was an amount of envy at work. When a truck broke down during the Christmas party, my father was sent out to fetch it. He could drive and hadn't been drinking as he was with my mother. He took his responsibilities as a husband very seriously. Ironically, if he'd been drinking that night, my mother would have been perfectly safe.'

Ava said nothing. She didn't need to. Any experienced police officer could have guessed what was coming.

'The company was run by two men. Gilroy Western and the late Bruce Jenson. While my father was out they offered my young, innocent mother a tour of the factory, including their offices, which were upstairs away from the music and rowdiness of the party.'

'Oh God . . .' Ava muttered.

'They got her into an office, shut the door, shoved a canvas bag over her head and one of them raped her. It was obvious they'd agreed what they were going to do in advance, no question about it. She had no way of defending herself and she'd had a couple of glasses to drink at the party. They told her if she reported them, they'd say she'd offered herself to them and her husband would be sacked.'

'And your father would have killed them. Quite literally, if he was anything like you,' Ava added.

'So there you go. That's the horrible truth about why I was there. I tried for such a long time to stay away from Jenson, but when I saw my mother in Paris, I realised that the passage of years hasn't dulled the pain they put her through. Not one bit.'

'You can't tell Pax Graham about this,' Ava said, her brain

already several steps ahead. 'With that sort of motive there's no way I could continue to keep you on active duty.'

'Then suspend me. I didn't do it, Ava. I wanted to. I held that bastard's face to make him look at a photo of my parents, but he was so far gone with the dementia that I might as well have been holding a corpse's chin. Bruce Jenson was already serving his sentence. That's what I realised while I was there.'

'The vase?' Ava asked.

'I lost my temper when I knew I wasn't going to get any answers from him. I cleaned up straight away and explained to the nurse that there'd been an accident.'

'What about the smashed glass in the patio door?'

'I kicked it in frustration, just with the tip of my boot so there won't be a print. There was a stress mark in the glass but it didn't break. I wasn't responsible for that,' Callanach explained.

Ava sighed. 'Which just leaves the issue of you having used your badge to gain access. What's your explanation for that going to be?'

Callanach ran a hand through his hair. 'The bigger problem might be the DNA.' He smiled at her. 'Depending on how carefully the lab checks the two samples, mine and his.'

'I don't understand,' Ava said.

'My mother never told my father about the rape and so that he didn't suspect anything, she continued having intimate relations with him as normal. The following month it became clear that she was pregnant.'

Ava took a few seconds to process the relevance. Her hand flew to her mouth.

'Oh no. Luc, I'm so sorry. He can't be . . .'

'Actually, there's a one in three chance that he is,' Callanach said. 'I don't have anything left of my father's to check the DNA, so all I have is a process of deduction. That's why I was there. I took a hair from his head and sent it away for testing.'

'But if he's your father, your DNA might look oddly similar to his when the Scenes of Crime forensics tests come back.'

'Yeah,' Callanach said.

'Which would easily be motive enough to put the case before a jury, with the rest of the evidence. Fuck.'

'Uh huh,' Callanach agreed.

'Fuck, fuck, fuck,' Ava finished. 'But that's only a one in three chance, like you said. Even if he does turn out to be . . .' – she chose not to say the actual words – 'the lab may not put two and two together from the sets of DNA, especially if they're already expecting to find yours on the corpse, so they won't be doing anything more than double-checking it against the sample of yours that's already on the database for exclusion.'

'Ava, whatever you're thinking, you have to stop. If we try to cover this up there'll be a disaster. Right now I have nothing to hide.'

'Are you kidding? Nothing to hide? You went to see a man who ended up dead, who at the very least conspired to rape your mother and who might be your father. What the hell do you think is going to happen if this goes to court? Were you angry? They'll point at the broken vase. Were you trying to conceal your identity? They'll say that's why you didn't sign the visitors' book . . .'

'I went through the front door and spoke to the nurses. Even I'm aware that I'm fairly recognisable. No one's going to believe that I'm stupid enough to kill a man then simply walk out as if nothing had happened. There's no way I'd have got away with it.'

'So you lost your temper when you were in there. Didn't plan on killing him, just got cross. It all went wrong, so you did the only thing you could do, which was to exit the same way you went in.'

'Are you on my side or not?' he frowned.

'I'm being a realist. You can't breathe a word of this. If the DNA similarities between the two of you are discovered, you'll have to plead ignorance.' She stopped, shutting her eyes, shaking her head. 'Oh God, Luc, is that why your mother disappeared when you were awaiting trial on the rape allegation?'

He nodded.

'And you've dealt with all this, without telling me any of it? Why? I could have helped you, just listened, something . . .'

'It wasn't that simple, Ava. It's taken me a long time to process. I thought that maybe I could let it go and move on. Now I wish I had.'

'Which begs the question, who actually killed Bruce Jenson and why?' Ava asked, emptying the remnants from the wine glass.

'I have no idea,' Callanach said. 'My money would be on a nurse or medical assistant who'd been looking for an opportunity to kill and saw the perfect chance. No one else came to Jenson's room while I was in there and it was late when I left. I doubt they'd have accepted any other visitors at that time. They'd have turned *me* away if I hadn't shown my police badge.'

'Do you know where Jenson's former partner is?' Ava asked.

'Western? The best information I have is that he's living in Spain, somewhere near Malaga. I haven't contacted him.'

'Thank God for that, so he'll have no reason to mention your name when he hears the news. What about Jenson's family? Would they recognise your name?'

'I can't imagine why. It's not the sort of thing you admit to your wife and child, is it — raping a young woman and then continuing to pay her husband's pay cheque for the next two years until he became terminally ill so you let him go?'

'You must hate them,' Ava said. 'I don't think I'd blame you if you had held that pillow over Jenson's face.'

Callanach paled.

'I'm sorry.' She shifted on the sofa, moving close enough to reach out for him, wrapping her arms around him and dropping her head on his shoulder. 'I'm so glad you told me. We're going to get through this. I won't let anything happen to you, I promise. You've already been through enough. The whole team knows there's no question that you're capable of something like this, no matter how bad it looks.'

'Not even Sergeant Lively?' Callanach attempted to lighten the atmosphere.

'Actually, now that we've drafted in Pax Graham, you're suddenly Lively's favourite detective inspector,' Ava laughed. 'Apparently, you're no longer the most eligible bachelor in MIT. Are you going to cope?'

'I'll try,' he smiled. 'So does that go for you as well? Has DI Graham caught your eye with the big shoulders, long hair and the Scots accent?'

'Would it be any of your business if I said yes?' Ava teased.

'Only that I'm pretty sure you shouldn't be forming personal associations with officers in your command,' he said.

'Oh, you mean like waking up in their bed?' she grinned. 'Yeah, you're right. That's definitely not okay.'

'Speaking of which,' Callanach said, 'looks like you're staying another night after drinking wine with your antibiotics. Come on.' He checked his watch. 'It's half past two. You may as well stay here again. No point going home now.'

Ava considered arguing then realised how stupid that was. She'd spent one night at Callanach's, so a second would make no difference at all. And she didn't want to leave him now, after what he'd revealed to her. There were times when no one should have to be alone.

Chapter Eleven

5 March

Ava made it home to shower and change before driving over to the Reach You charity. Tripp had phoned ahead for her and Rune Maclure was waiting when she pulled up. He held the front door open, stepping back to let her pass and motioning towards her leg.

'Been in the wars?' he asked.

'I got into a fight with a wall. Are you Mr Maclure?'

'Call me Rune. Given that my parents were so adventurous with their choice of name it always seems a shame not to use it.'

'Ava,' she returned, offering her hand. 'Did DS Tripp tell you why I wanted a word?'

'He did,' Maclure replied. 'Did your face get into a fight with the same wall or was that a separate incident, only from where I'm standing police work is starting to look pretty perilous.'

'Same wall. I think I'd have to concede that I lost.'

Maclure laughed. 'Let's sit down. There's fresh coffee on the table if you'd like it and one of our volunteers has even broken out the biscuits. They're normally reserved for people in distress, but given your apparent braveness in the face of vicious bricks and mortar, it seems fitting that we pump you full of sugar.' He poured as Ava got herself comfortable, wishing she'd taken double the recommended dose of paracetamol that morning. 'So ask away. Your colleagues wanted to know about Stephen Berry, but I gather this is a more general enquiry.'

'It is. I can't give you any details, you understand confidentiality in your line of work, but I need to comprehend the psychological process at the point of committing suicide. Not the day before or even the hour before, but when someone is actively in the process of taking their life.'

'That's a tough one, I'm afraid, because it depends on personality types. Some people have almost disassociated their mind from their body when they take final measures and it's almost mechanical in nature. They tie a perfect knot in a rope, make sure the stool is on a flat surface and won't wobble when they step up. They've taken painkillers an hour before to minimise their physical discomfort, have an email in drafts explaining what they've done to family or friends, ready to send with just seconds to go. It's extraordinary. And what we find out is that those people were usually equally organised in life. They're also the best at hiding both their intentions and their distress.

'Chaotic personality types, as you'll have guessed, fail more often because their attempt is less well organised. They often improvise at a very low moment and end up causing themselves life-changing injuries but without dying, or they succeed but leave a very distressing scene when they're found. Then there are truly spontaneous suicides and sometimes we never get to the bottom of those, which can be jumping in front of a train or driving a car into a river. Journeys, when people might be alone in their thoughts – in public but feeling as if no one in the world can see them – often result in the least predictable tragedies.'

Ava stirred her coffee and wondered how she could apply that to the Hawksmith death scene.

'That's not quite what you needed, am I right?' Maclure asked.

'Only because it doesn't quite fit with what happened at a scene we're dealing with at the moment. We have a victim who doesn't match any category you've described.'

'Can you tell me anything at all about it?' Mature raised his hands in the air. 'No names, no address, no identifying features, and if it helps, I regard my general work confidentiality as extending to this conversation.'

Ava smiled. 'Thank you,' she said. 'We have a female victim who restrained herself sufficiently that if she'd changed her mind and decided she wanted to survive, couldn't have done so. Also, the chronology of the self-binding was complex. If she'd got one thing out of order, she wouldn't have been able to do the next thing, etc. I suppose my question is, that seems fairly elaborate and incredibly disciplined. She chose a slow death. Is that normal? Only if it were me, and I was feeling that desperate, I'd want out as fast as possible.'

'Well, the first thing you have to recognise is that deci-sion-making immediately prior to an attempt isn't always logical, not what you'd deem logical anyway. There are people who'd rather extend death and deal with the psychological trauma of knowing what they were doing but thereby avoiding a dramatic impact. For example, taking sleeping tablets over a few hours to get a good build-up in their system. Ensuring there's no way to back out isn't unknown, particularly if a person has had failed attempts in their past; although I'd say human psychology usually tries to build in get-out clauses.

'If it were me, I'd make an attempt to find out more about your victim's personality in life and then see if the scene makes sense. You can't just look at a suicide as an event on its own. Every part of it is always intrinsically linked to the person's life.'

'That's good advice,' Ava said. 'How long have you been working in this area?'

'Fifteen years,' Maclure said. 'How about you? You're a detective chief inspector, so I'm guessing you've put in a few years on the job; although I wouldn't have thought you were old enough.'

'Some days it feels as if I've been in the police forever, and then I see another crime scene and realise the universe thinks I'm still a child who needs to be taught a lesson. I should go, but I'm really grateful for your time.'

'No problem. Take this . . .' He extended a blue business card. 'The number on there is my personal mobile, not my emergency work line. It's on most of the time. If you have any questions, day or night, please call me. I'd love to be able to help. Do you know if the information I gave your DI helped at all? There was somebody at the Queensferry Crossing scene they thought might have been of interest.'

'I haven't caught up with the ongoing enquiries yet, but I'm guessing DS Tripp who you met will be pursuing that.'

There was a knock at the door, and a stocky young woman with the palest of skin and gleaming ginger hair looked in, stifling a yawn.

'Rune, you've a walk-in. Seems fairly upset. Will you be much longer?'

'We're just finishing,' Maclure smiled. 'Get them a hot drink, talk to them about nothing for a few minutes and I'll be there, Vicki.'

Vicki Rosach plodded away.

'I'm keeping you,' Ava said. 'Go ahead.'

'It's all right. Vicki hasn't been here long and she still thinks everyone who walks through the door is secretly hiding a

107

weapon that they're about to turn on themselves. I try to discourage that sort of drama. A laid-back approach is usually more reassuring for the people I treat.'

Voices in the corridor beyond the closed door made both their heads turn at once.

'Can you tell me who's in there with him?' a man demanded.

'No idea. Some woman,' Vicki said.

'That's not terribly helpful, Vicki,' came the reply. 'Is he counselling, or is the meeting to do with something administrative?'

'I dunno, but she looked fine to me, except her face looks like she plays a bit rough.'

Ava couldn't help but raise her eyebrows at Rune Maclure at that. He stood up and went to the door.

'Charlie,' he said quietly. 'I'm dealing with a police enquiry in here and for the record, these doors don't do much in the way of soundproofing when you're right outside.'

'Maybe this isn't the appropriate place to be talking to the police considering the sensitive nature of what we do here,' Charlie said.

'I'm nearly finished. Give me a minute. We can discuss this later,' Maclure replied softly.

The door opened again and Maclure reappeared, rubbing his eyes.

'I'm so sorry. My colleague, Charlie Packham, doesn't suffer fools and he's rarely one to hold back from offering an opinion. He's a great counsellor, though. We see a lot of military personnel here and he's specially trained for that. Whatever he does for them, it works.' He smiled. 'Listen, I hope you don't think I'm taking advantage of you needing help in a difficult case, but the number on the card is there even if you don't have any other questions. You know, in case you ever just feel like chatting. I learned a long time ago not to wait until there's a good time to do something like ask someone out. It's a surefire way never to get another opportunity.'

'Oh,' Ava said. 'Thank you. Things are a bit difficult right now,' she added noncommitally.

'I get that,' he said. 'Just, you know, whenever.'

Ava returned to her car and stared at herself in the rear-view mirror. What the hell was happening? First, she took an insane risk out at Tantallon Castle, then she spent two nights in Callanach's bed, now she was giving out signals that had men she'd only just met handing out their mobile number to her. All when she was looking like she'd recently escaped an abusive relationship. Then there was the weird conversation with Selina at the hospital.

Perhaps it was an age thing and everyone around her was simply assuming it was now or never for settling down. Her track record with men showed a startling lack of good judgement. Most of the relationships she'd been in were either to please her mother or to reassure herself that she wasn't entirely married to her job. Ava sighed. Now wasn't the right time to be navel-gazing. A call to her best friend, Natasha, later on would sort out any personal issues, through the inevitable response of some high-grade piss-taking. Right now, she was late for Ailsa and that just wouldn't do.

The city mortuary was busy. Ava kept her head down and quietly made her way round the back of the group of three families who were there to see their loved ones. A drunken helium-inhaling session had left Edinburgh with teenagers to mourn. Every time she saw parents crying for their children, she was glad she'd gone down a different path than parenting. The fear it brought was terrifying.

Dr Ailsa Lambert waved her into the postmortem suite, the dark shadows under her eyes reflective of too little sleep and too many deaths. Edinburgh was unarguably one of the most beautiful cities in the world, but it saw its share of tragedies.

'Were you here all night?' Ava asked.

'Not by choice. Do people really need floaty balloons so badly that it's worth giving the general public access to pressurised helium canisters and the temptation of making funny voices? There was no need for a single one of those young people to die last night. It's not just a tragedy, it's an avoidable waste of human life.' Ailsa slammed a pen down onto a metal counter and composed herself.

'I'm sorry,' Ava said. 'I don't know how you cope with the pain of what you see day after day.'

'Someone has to,' Ailsa said. 'Now, Mrs Hawksmith. First name, Fenella, I've been notified. A friend of hers came in and identified her body this morning after seeing the police at her flat yesterday.' She pulled the sheet back from the body. 'I had to do a limited reveal. Didn't want to give the poor woman nightmares, but she was able to describe two tattoos in detail, as well as height, weight and eye colour. We're double-checking her fingerprints against the database following a drink-drive conviction some years ago.'

'All right, what else do we know?'

'Nothing good,' Ailsa said. She busied herself pulling the sheet down to reveal the whole body. 'Are you taking your antibiotics?'

'Yes, and Luc's been looking after me. He's so scared of you, he'll hardly leave my side.'

'That's got nothing to do with fear,' Ailsa said. 'Take a deep breath; this isn't what you were expecting. We've located the weapon that was used to make the incisions into Mrs Hawksmith's arm. It's a penknife, one of those multitool jobs, too. Expensive.' She looked disapproving. 'I've been able to match the precise width of the blade to the cuts, as well as blood on the blade itself, so I'm one hundred per cent certain that this is the weapon. Fingerprints on the blade match Mrs Hawksmith's and there are no other prints on it.'

'Okay,' Ava said slowly. Everything Ailsa said was making sense given the scene, but the pathologist seemed tense and angry. 'That indicates suicide. I saw an expert this morning who said that while an organised suicide scene might be unusual, it's far from impossible. So what are you not telling me?'

'It's not suicide,' Ailsa said. 'I've been doing this job thirty years and I've seen more people end their lives than I care to recall. This is something else, Ava, and while everything that happened to this poor woman might, technically speaking, possibly be self-inflicted, I refuse to believe it was.'

'Tell me.'

'The blade couldn't be found at the scene because it was inside her body,' Ailsa said. 'I found it while I was checking the body cavities. The blade had been folded back into the knife after the incisions were made and then it was inserted into her rectum, as high as it could be pushed using a digit.'

Ava stood silently. There weren't many things she heard in the mortuary that left her lost for words, but just occasionally she still found herself dumbstruck.

'Can I go back out, come in again and see if you give me different news?' Ava asked eventually.

'Only if I can come with you,' Ailsa said.

Either side of Fenella Hawksmith's body, they stared down at her. Ava shook her head.

'So either she cut herself, folded up the blade, inserted it into herself, then did up the handcuffs and waited to die . . .' Ailsa began.

'Or someone did all those things for her,' Ava finished the sentence.

'It's the latter, I believe. Look at this.' She turned the corpse's left arm outwards to display the incisions more clearly. 'The

111

callusing on Mrs Hawksmith's right hand is indicative of a right-hander. Over the years, the hardening of the skin on the ends of the fingers and the palm leaves its mark. Writing, cutting vegetables, picking things up, opening jars, you name it. Also, the muscles of the dominant hand are always fractionally more developed. Now look at the cuts.' Ailsa pulled a mobile light over the top and swung a magnifying glass to highlight the gashes. 'The deepest end of the cuts is on the inner elbow nearest the body, moving from the right side of the inner elbow to the left. When you compare the blade, it has a flat edge on one side and that flat edge was inserted closest to Mrs Hawksmith's core.'

'So the blade would have to have been pushed outwards rather than have been pulled towards her body,' Ava noted.

'Which isn't natural at all. You're taught to write pulling the pencil towards you. You cut food pulling rather than pushing. It's inconceivable to me that she started the cut on the inside of her arm and pushed to the outside, not least because she'd have been holding the knife with the blunt side of the blade inwards, which doesn't fit with a right-hander.'

'Someone else made the cuts,' Ava said.

Ailsa nodded. 'It's not that she couldn't have done all of this to herself, don't misunderstand me, but it makes no sense at all. None of it. And as for where the blade was found . . .'

'It's a debasement. Signs of sexual assault?' Ava queried.

'No evidence at all. Neither vaginal nor anal. There's no tearing or injury; although fluids might have disappeared, as she was sat in the water for so long before being found. We've taken swabs for DNA tests but I'm not expecting anything.'

'It's a very personal thing to do and I don't mean physically. It suggests anger at a deeply personal level, wanting to degrade a dying woman like that. There would have to be a specific motive,' Ava said.

'There's one last thing,' Ailsa said. 'There's a substantial amount of bruising beneath the handcuffs and cable ties. It's very area specific and wasn't apparent on the surface of the skin owing to discolouration of the corpse, but it appears that Mrs Hawksmith struggled. Now, playing devil's advocate, I could say that perhaps she made all these preparations then changed her mind too late, but the bathwater stayed in a long time. We know that because of the tidemark and because of the water inside the body. If she changed her mind, though, why not pull the plug at least, in the hope that her wounds might clot, buying her time until she was found?'

Ava thought back to the bathroom.

'The plug was between her feet, a normal rubber plug on a chain, right?'

Ailsa turned back to the counter behind her, picked up a large photo and handed it to Ava. In it, the plug was clearly visible still in the hole.

'Any physical reason why she couldn't have sat up to pull that plug out?' Ava queried.

'No. Mrs Hawksmith likely hadn't done any sit-ups for a couple of decades, but she could have pulled against the binding around her ankles. She was fit enough to have done that once and to have reached the plug, particularly given that her ankles were bound to each tap, leaving the necessary space between her legs.'

'So why didn't she?' Ava mused.

'That, my dear, is your question to answer.' Ailsa snapped off her gloves. 'Do I need to take another look at the wound on your leg, or can I trust that you're taking better care of yourself?'

'I am, I promise. I'm even eating five portions of fruit and vegetables a day,' Ava murmured, removing her own gloves and depositing them in a bin.

'Probably best to minimise the lying. It's not your strong point,' Ailsa reprimanded gently.

'I need to get back and brief the team.' Ava smiled and reached a hand out to touch Ailsa's shoulder.

'And I have families waiting for explanations that won't make them feel any better at all. Before you go, Stephen Berry. The tox results came back. He had high levels of selective serotonin reuptake inhibitors in his body.'

'In plain terms?'

'Antidepressant medication. If you block the reabsorption of serotonin into the brain, there's more available in the body. Keeps you feeling more positive and works against the depression. It's commonly prescribed for bipolar disorder and it's in line with the medical notes provided by his doctor. Given the fact that we now know he'd recently attempted suicide, I'm going to sign it off as a deliberate taking of his own life. Wherever the bruise on his middle finger came from, there's no corroborative evidence to suggest the death was suspicious.'

'All right, that makes sense,' Ava agreed, privately wishing she'd known that before climbing onto Tantallon's walls in her misguided fit of heroism.

'There's a girlfriend, lovely thing – came in to speak to me about Stephen. Rosa, if I remember correctly. Perhaps you could have a member of your team speak with her.'

'No problem,' Ava said, leaving Ailsa to get on with her day.

Sitting in her car, she took a couple of minutes out to text Natasha. Antibiotics or not, she was going to need a drink later.

Ditch the girlfriend for an evening and meet me, she typed.

Natasha replied immediately.

Thought you'd never ask. Whighams Wine Cellars 8 p.m. And change your clothes first. Cocktails are on me.

Exactly what was required, Ava decided. Cocktails with Natasha was usually a recipe for disaster, but the way she was feeling right now, it could only be an improvement. That was the theory, anyway.

Chapter Twelve

5 March

DI Pax Graham and DC Janet Monroe sat in the interview room opposite Callanach, each of them tense and awkwardly polite. Having handed in his statement first thing to give the investigating team time to peruse it, Callanach had made it clear he was happy to be interviewed formally, on tape.

Callanach ran through the history he'd discussed with Ava, leaving out any parts that gave him a potential motive for harming Bruce Jenson, then described his visit in brief terms.

'So the vase,' Graham asked. 'How did that come to get broken?'

'Mr Jenson had dribbled down his chin. It seemed overkill to ask a nurse to come and deal with it but callous to leave it as it was, so I walked round the room looking for a towel or tissue paper. In the process, I knocked the vase with my elbow and upset the contents onto the floor. The vase smashed and there were a few old flowers and a small amount of water to clear up. I wiped his chin first with a paper towel, then cleared up the floor and put the debris in the bin,' Callanach explained.

'Did you notice any problem with the glass in the patio door when you were in Mr Jenson's room?' Graham continued.

Callanach gave it a moment, drawing his eyebrows together as if concentrating.

'I didn't notice anything wrong.'

'It was smashed when the nurse found Mr Jenson dead,' Graham said. 'It would have been easy for an intruder to have reached in and unlocked the door to gain entry. There was glass found on the floor inside the room, suggesting that it had been kicked in from the outside.'

Callanach hid his surprise.

'There wasn't any glass on the floor when I was in there. I would have noticed, especially given the fact that I cleared up the broken vase.'

His shoulders relaxed a few centimetres. No one had told him about the glass. Whatever had happened to Bruce Jenson was nothing to do with his visit. It was just unfortunate timing. Even if he had put a crack in the glass, that didn't make him responsible for Jenson's death. Except that he'd left the room more easily accessible to would-be burglars. Cracked glass didn't require much force to break.

'Was anything taken?'

'Mr Jenson's son says not,' Janet Monroe answered.

DI Graham shot her a look that made it clear she should have kept quiet.

'Did you know Mr Jenson was suffering from dementia before you visited?' Graham asked.

'Yes. It was a nursing home, so I knew there were health problems, but not how advanced it was. Had I known, there would have been no point going.'

'So, what was it exactly that you wanted to talk to Mr Jenson about? I understand your father used to work for him, but was there something specific you were pursuing?'

'No, I was just curious about my father's history. I suppose I wanted to know if Jenson remembered my father. Being back in Scotland has made me curious about my past and my family. I was looking for more of a connection with Edinburgh.'

'But you used your police badge,' Graham noted. 'You didn't sign in. The nurse you spoke to got the impression you were there in an official capacity.'

'My fault. I was somewhere between being lazy and being on autopilot. I'm so used to walking into places in Scotland and just showing the badge to gain access, I didn't give it a second thought. Also, I'm pretty recognisable here. To my knowledge, I'm the only French officer in Police Scotland, so there was no way I was deceiving her about who I was. It was just quicker. I fully accept it was the wrong way to go about it, but she saw my name and would have been able to identify me just the same as if I'd signed the visitors' book.'

Pax Graham flicked through a sheet of notes.

'There will obviously be extensive forensic testing, both of the body and items in the room. Can you confirm what you recall touching, so we know where to expect to find your DNA.'

'Sure. Door handles, the bin, the surface where the vase and paper towels were, the floor. I wiped his chin, so also Mr Jenson's face. I leaned on the chair as I did that, so maybe the cushions, too. I also picked up the couple of photos that were on the bedside table, looking to see if any of them were older and might have gone back to the days of the factory, but they were all modern pictures of his family, I assumed.'

'Why would you think the photos might have been of the old factory?' Graham asked. 'Isn't that unlikely?'

Callanach was ready for it.

'I was aware that with dementia patients, it's good to remind them of their past, keep memories alive. I thought there was a chance the family might have been trying to give Mr Jenson a sense of who he was at times that were important in his history.'

He hated the real reason he'd picked those photos up. Looking to see if there was any family resemblance between you and the children of the man who might have raped your mother wasn't something Callanach wanted to think about too hard.

'There was also a severe injury to the victim's testicles,' Graham added. He rubbed his eyes, keeping them closed. 'Anything you can tell me about that?'

'What the fuck?' Callanach leaned forwards, hands on the desk.

'We have to ask all the questions, you know the procedure. If there's any possibility that these injuries were caused by accident or innocently . . . well, we need to clarify the picture,' Graham said.

Callanach sat back in his chair, grateful that DI Graham had mistaken his reaction for insult rather than shock. Who the hell would want to injure the groin of a man already in the grip of dementia that was going to prove fatal anyway? The only person it could be relevant to was him. The possibility that Jenson's death was a coincidence was starting to fade and the truth – that he was being set up – was sinking in.

'No,' he said. 'I don't know anything about an injury to his testicles. Not by accident or any other way. When I left Mr Jenson he was fine. Still breathing and completely uninjured. I didn't see anyone else enter his room. I apologised for breaking the vase, asked if I could pay for a replacement, said goodbye to the nurse then left. After that I received a call from DCI Turner and attended the city mortuary regarding Stephen Berry's death. I was with her all night.'

'All night?' Graham asked. 'Literally all night?' His tone was suddenly confrontational.

'DCI Turner got injured while we were investigating up at Tantallon Castle. She required medical assistance and after that we were formulating a plan of action for the Berry investigation.'

'At the station?' Graham persisted.

'No. My apartment,' Callanach replied, wary of providing grist to the ever-ready rumour mill but knowing he couldn't lie about such trivial details.

That was when stories started unravelling. There was every chance DI Graham would double-check his movements with Ava and their stories had to match. He knew it didn't look good, them going to his place rather than to the hospital or the police station, but they'd done nothing wrong. Which was why it was strange that he felt so guilty about it.

'We were both tired, cold and hungry, and DCI Turner needed someone to keep an eye on her given the head injury she'd sustained.'

'I see. Well, I think we're finished here. Obviously, if there are any more questions once all the forensic testing is completed, we'll ask for a further interview. PC Monroe, could you give DI Callanach and me a moment please? I'm turning off the tapes. It's not related to the investigation.'

'Sure,' she said. 'Can I get either of you a coffee? You've both been working flat out.'

Callanach smiled. Monroe was astute and a peacemaker. He liked her.

'Thank you, I'd appreciate that,' Callanach replied.

'Nothing for me,' Graham said, crossing his arms.

Monroe left.

'You're putting DCI Turner in a difficult position. I recognise that this is awkward. I've been in MIT and at your rank for just a couple of days, but I have to speak my mind. You should accept a voluntary suspension while the investigation continues.'

'I have nothing to hide,' Callanach said. 'And yes, it is awkward. DCI Turner can take care of herself. She's made her decision.'

'Really? Has she thought through the impact of you making statements on tape that you spent the night together at your flat? Don't play games with her career.'

'You're that concerned about her after just two days? It seems to me that I'm not the one being unprofessional here.'

'Meaning?' Graham asked, the muscles in his jaw flexing.

'You know what? Let's not do this. We're going to have to work together in MIT for the foreseeable future, so we'll let Ava make the decisions. I'll make myself available to answer any questions you have and if at any time you have reason to believe I'm an active suspect, then I'm sure I'll be suspended immediately.'

Callanach stood and made his way to the door.

'You called her Ava,' Graham said. 'Is MIT's chain of command really that informal?'

Callanach could have kicked himself.

'I've got work to do,' he said. 'Good luck with the case.'

Chapter Thirteen

5 March

Ava broke the news to the assembled MIT squad that they were treating Fenella Hawksmith's death as suspicious, sharing the disturbing details from the postmortem.

'At the moment, knowing it would have been possible for her to have pulled the plug from the bath, I'm assuming that whoever inflicted the injuries on her stayed for the duration to watch her bleed to death, or at least until she'd passed out, to ensure that the water remained in the bath, preventing the wounds from clotting.'

'But that could have been hours, right?' Tripp asked.

'Yes,' Ava confirmed.

'We're looking for someone who could have tied her up, inflicted the wounds, debased the victim by inserting the knife inside her, who then watched her bleed out that slowly?' a constable asked, sounding incredulous.

'Aye, otherwise known as the hunt for another sick fuck,' Lively chimed in.

Ava had made the decision to bring Lively back onto the Hawksmith case. Once the details hit the press, there was going to be uproar and she needed the most experienced team she could put together.

'Tripp, do we have a family background?' Ava asked.

'Husband deceased, natural causes,' he read from his notes. 'Daughter is missing, or so a friend of the victim confirms. Long-term drug addict, who Mrs Hawksmith had spent years trying to reconnect with. We have no idea where the daughter is, or if she's alive or dead. We're gathering details on her right now.'

'Put out a national alert. If the daughter is still alive, she either needs to be informed of her mother's death or treated as a suspect. We'll also need her known associates if she's still involved in the drug scene. It's possible Fenella Hawksmith was tortured to get money out of her. That would explain the bindings.'

'There was also an ongoing dispute with neighbours about noise. Apparently, Mrs Hawksmith was in something of a community war, countering constant loud rap music by playing opera.'

'Unlikely, but check it anyway,' Ava said. 'If this was murder, it was perpetrated by someone conscience-free and extremely well prepared. Neighbour disputes don't usually fit that description. Door-to-doors in her area. I want all of her close friends or associates spoken to. Check her recent communications. And find the daughter as a priority.'

Callanach caught Ava in the corridor.

'We should talk,' he said quietly.

'In your office then,' she replied, detouring through a doorway. Callanach closed it behind himself.

'DI Graham interviewed me this morning. I had to explain that I was with you after I left the nursing home.' He paused. 'All night.'

'We should have seen that coming. Don't worry about it. We were working on the Berry case. Speaking of which, Ailsa has concluded that was either accident or suicide. He was taking an antidepressant, high levels of it in his blood. Backs up what Rune Maclure said about him being bipolar. Anything else?'

'I was going to ask what you're doing tonight. I thought we could both do with a diversion. Is there anything on at the cinema you want to watch?'

'Actually, I'm going out with Natasha. You must be fed up with me by now. I've crashed at yours for the last two nights.' She ran a hand through her hair. 'I shouldn't have stayed last night. I feel bad about it.'

'Don't.'

'But I do. You need your own space and it's not healthy, working together and being such good friends. I could have taken a taxi home last night,' she smiled. 'I should've done. Let's not talk about it again. I'll cover it with DI Graham. Was everything okay between the two of you?'

'Sure,' Callanach lied. 'So you met Rune Maclure. Did you like him?'

'Yes, I did. Not so sure about his assistant, though. There's something about getting a disapproving stare from a twenty-year-old that makes my blood boil,' she laughed. 'And I think that possibly Maclure gave me his number for non-professional reasons. I wasn't sure how to handle it, to be honest, it's been that long since anyone was interested in me.'

'Are you going to call him?' Callanach asked before he could stop himself. 'I thought you two might hit it off.'

'No, I'm not,' Ava declared. 'As if I haven't got enough on my plate. We've got two active investigations, with new team members to train, and I look worse than I can ever remember.'

'That obviously didn't bother Maclure,' Callanach noted.

'Then the man's an idiot and however attractive he might

be, I don't date idiots. Right, I need to update the queen of profanity. Wish me luck. I'll take a raincheck on the cinema. *The Prime of Miss Jean Brodie* is playing from tomorrow as part of the midnight classics run up at York Place.'

'Would I enjoy it?' Callanach asked.

'No, but I would. I've got to go. Organise the squad. We're already three weeks behind whoever did this, so we'll need to move fast.'

Callanach watched her go, wondering where she got her energy from. They hadn't fallen asleep until 2 a.m., and she was up again at six to get home and change. He should have spoken to her about his concerns over the Jenson murder, but Ava had enough on her plate already.

Opening his laptop, he sat down to write an email that was long overdue since his vacation. His mother had a right to know that Bruce Jenson was dead, but he didn't want her concerned over him being implicated. He decided to keep it short and simple.

> *Maman,*
> *I'm writing to let you know that when I returned to England I decided to find Jenson and Western. I didn't tell you before because I knew it would be upsetting for you. I hope it will help you to know that Bruce Jenson is dead. He had advanced dementia and died in a nursing home. I have no news on Gilroy Western. Busy here again, so forgive me if I don't call in the next couple of weeks.*
> *All my love,*
> *Luc.*

Hitting send, he realised how much he also needed to get out. Ava was going to be spending the evening with Natasha and contacting Selina was too complicated, so he texted Lance

Proudfoot, a local journalist who'd proved to be not only a useful contact, but also a good friend over the previous year. Brighter than most people on their sharpest day, and more persistent than a salmon jumping upstream, Lance was semi-retired and writing his own news blog, when he wasn't helping Callanach out and getting injured in the course of semi-official police business.

They met up at seven in Sandy Bell's on Forrest Hill, a new bar to Callanach, but Lance had made it easy to find, with its bright blue facade and the music that was issuing forth onto the street. Already at the bar and talking whisky, Lance was in his element. Callanach stood and watched him from the doorway for a few moments, noting that his friend was in his biking leathers, looking fit and well. He greeted Lance with a slap on the back.

'Is there a pub in this city where they don't know your name?' Callanach asked.

Lance turned, hugging him warmly. 'Not one worth spending your hard-earned in, I guarantee you that. Luc Callanach, you look like you haven't slept for a month. You'll ruin those boyish, European good looks if you don't start taking care of yourself.'

In the corner, a folk band entertained the early crowd, strumming guitars and singing harmoniously about some long-lost sailor. The bar looked like a sanctuary for rare single malts and every seat was taken. Lance had saved a couple of bar stools for them by leaving his helmet on one and his gloves on another, which he shifted to the floor so they could sit.

'Your ears must have been burning when you texted me,' Lance said. 'I was just talking about you.'

'Good or bad?' Callanach asked.

'You're too cynical, man!' Lance bellowed. 'Good, obviously. I was telling my neighbour how much more interesting my life has been since meeting you.'

'Interesting perhaps, but you've also spent a lot more time at the hospital,' Callanach grinned. 'Have you been keeping out of trouble lately?'

'Ach, the secret to life, Luc, is that it's getting in trouble that keeps you young. My son finally moved out and got his own place, so I no longer have to listen to his girlfriend and him either rowing or doing God knows what else in my spare room. I love the boy, but there comes a time when you want to be able to watch the rugby, cook a curry and listen to the Beatles without anyone else criticising your choices. So what about you? How was your holiday?'

'Complicated,' Callanach replied. 'Good to be back in Paris, though. I stayed away from France too long.'

'Paris is always a good idea. Damn, what movie's that from?' Lance took a sip of whisky. '*Sabrina* – Bogart and Hepburn – that's it.'

'Not you as well. Ava's obsessed with old films.'

'Speaking of Edinburgh's loveliest detective chief inspector, how is she?'

'Infuriating, unstoppable and funny. Same as ever,' Callanach said. 'But I need to talk about something other than work. What have you been up to recently?'

'Sticking my nose into other people's business and hoping the rest of the world wants to read what I have to say about it. Now that I've got you here, what's the story with the body on Easter Road a couple of days ago? The street was cordoned off for hours and the flat still has crime-scene tape around it.'

'Suspicious death, can't say more than that.'

'Come on, off the record, and I won't release it until the formalities are completed. The city's been remarkably quiet this month. Give me something,' Lance complained.

Callanach considered it. They needed to find Alice Hawksmith and after a day's research, MIT had come up with nothing.

Fenella's daughter had a string of old convictions but had gone off the radar six years ago and not been heard of since. No benefit claims, no doctor on record, no income or tax payments. She wasn't just going to turn up without a push.

'All right. You can have this. I'm in charge of the investigation, so you can quote me. We'll do it officially. We'd like to speak to a woman called Alice Hawksmith, now twenty-nine years of age, on a witness-only basis. She was last known to be living in the Aberdeen area. The body is her mother's – that's Fenella Hawksmith – and the daughter is believed to be her only living relative.'

Lance had his mobile out and was typing notes onto the screen.

'If you're in charge, it's an MIT case,' he said. 'So this must be a murder, right? You're not just looking for a relative to inform. What's the real story?'

'You can't publish the rest of it,' Callanach said. 'So you're probably better off not hearing it.'

'This is me. I stood in the basement of a Glasgow pub with you, convinced we were both about to die, covering for a former colleague of yours who'd stolen from the mob, and I still didn't write about it. Just how much more loyalty do you need me to show before you believe you can trust me?' Lance grinned.

It was a fair comment. Lance had broken the law *with* him and *for* him. If ever a man knew how to keep a secret, it was him.

'Nothing concrete yet. It's a very disturbing set of circumstances, with shades of suicide, but much more abusive than you'd expect to see. The body had been there three weeks.'

'Three weeks? That can't have been easy to look at. Do you have any suspects?'

'I can't say at this stage. We can't keep it quiet much longer, anyway. Officers were out making door-to-door enquiries today. Perhaps if you run the story and name the victim, it might trigger a memory and someone will come forwards.'

'Cause of death?' Lance asked.

'I want to keep some of the details quiet for now, to separate useful information from the inevitable bullshit. My feeling is that it was someone who knew the victim. There were . . . personal elements to it.'

'So if you could get a good picture of her life, that would help. Friends and known associates, the places she frequented, where she shopped regularly, that sort of thing?'

'Exactly. We need to know who saw her last, if she was in any trouble, you know the form.'

'Got it,' Lance said. 'I'll get a piece out tomorrow morning. So come on, spill the beans. How's the gorgeous doctor and why have I still not been allowed to meet her yet?'

'You're too late. The gorgeous doctor is back on the singles scene. And she's too young for you, so don't get any ideas.'

'Hey, some women appreciate the substantial benefits that come with dating an older man. We're better at DIY, know how to stack a dishwasher properly, understand the perils of failing to pick up our dirty socks and most of us only have the energy for sex once a fortnight.'

'You're not selling the ageing process to me,' Callanach laughed.

'What happened?' Lance asked.

'Wasn't working for me. It wasn't fair on her to keep pretending it was. She deserved better.'

'Do you need some advice?' Lance asked, slipping an arm across Callanach's shoulders and gripping the far shoulder.

'No,' Callanach replied, downing his whisky.

'Sex is all in the mind. It's not about perfect legs or shapely breasts. It's about finding the person who presses that button

128

in your head. Usually that's also someone who makes you crazy and who thinks you're a total idiot. Perhaps the doctor was just too into you.'

'You remember the part where I said no to the offer of advice?'

'This is a bar. I'm a Scot drinking single malt. You've split up with your girlfriend. What did you think was going to happen? If I hadn't offered you useless advice, we'd have broken every pub tradition in the book.'

By the time eight thirty rolled around they were both past the legal point of driving and headed for either a long walk or a taxi ride home.

Natasha was late, which was usually Ava's thing. By the time she sashayed into Whighams Wine Cellars on the corner of Hope Street and Charlotte Square, Ava was on her second cocktail and had already ordered food for them both. The rustic chic, bare brickwork and intimate cellar booths made Whighams the perfect place for a first date. It was Natasha's go-to for seducing new partners, but Ava just wanted the sense of other-world idyll she got there.

A jazz band produced good enough quality music that Ava had been able close her eyes for a few minutes and lose herself in it. There would be no fights, no bloodshed. No weapon would suddenly appear from a pocket in a moment of drunken idiocy. In Whighams, Ava could pretend to be in any good restaurant in any city in the world. Not that she wanted to be anywhere other than Edinburgh, but sometimes the fantasy was pleasing and right now, a fantasy was the only thing on the cards with her annual leave still three months away.

'Bloody hell, tell me there's an explanation so titillating behind what's happened to your face that I can sell the story to the gutter press for enough money to buy myself a sports car!' Natasha beamed as she threw herself into Ava's arms, hugging her then prodding the reducing bump on her forehead.

'Ow! Could you not? And why are you so late?' Ava moaned.

'I was having my legs waxed and the beautician was delayed. Stop changing the subject. Why are you sitting so awkwardly?' she demanded.

Ava pulled up the trouser leg to display the gash complete with stitches.

'Oh my imaginary fucking deity,' Natasha whistled. 'I thought my legs were hairy. You look like you've been living wild for the last five years.'

'Thanks for that,' Ava laughed. 'My boss recently compared me to an extra in a zombie movie. I'm feeling all the love this week.'

A waiter appeared with two tall glasses full of rainbow liquid and ice. Ava took hers and drained half of it before Natasha could gear up with another insult.

'Seriously, the injuries. Line of duty or something more entertaining?'

Ava sat back, hugging her glass. 'Officially? Line of duty. But I took a stupid risk, Tash, and I have no idea why. If Luc hadn't been there, I'd have been mashed potato at the base of Tantallon Castle.'

'What were you doing out at Tantallon?' Natasha asked.

'Looking for evidence at a potential crime scene, which proved not to be, before it disappeared overnight in a storm. It made more sense at the time.'

'I'd hope so. You went up on the walls in the dark? Have you completely lost your marbles?'

'Guilty as charged and paying for it. I hope you're hungry, because I ordered half the menu.' Ava said, waving at the waiter to order more cocktails.

'And you were up there with Luc, who saved the day. That

sounds exciting,' Natasha said, pulling a cocktail cherry from her glass and running it to and fro over her bottom lip.

'A bit too exciting for us both. I nearly squashed him when he pulled me back over the wall, then he spent the night patching me back up. My leg bled all over his bedsheets, so I owe him a new set to add insult to injury, and now he's going through . . .'

'Overnight? In his bed? Just the two of you?' Natasha raised her eyebrows. 'Two champagne cocktails, please,' she directed at the approaching waiter.

'Don't start,' Ava warned her.

'My oldest friend spent the night in bed with the best-looking man in Scotland – although he doesn't do anything for me, so I'm taking everyone else's word for that – and I'm not even allowed to ask about it? Does the delicious Spanish doctor know what the two of you have been getting up to?'

'Selina and Luc aren't together any more. And no, I'm not giving you her number.'

'Damn, when did that happen? How am I so out of the loop? Hold on . . .' Natasha continued before Ava could answer any of her questions, 'you and Luc spent a whole night cuddled up in bed together and you're both currently single? Wait, don't tell me anything else until I have a drink in my hand, and take it really slowly. I want a blow-by-blow account. Hopefully literally. You have no idea how relieved I am. I was starting to think you'd taken some sort of vow of celibacy.'

'Would you stop? Sorry to disappoint, but my night with Luc was completely platonic. Both nights, in fact. Believe it or not, we're grown-up enough to be able to offer each other support without getting so carried away that we end up naked as soon as we're alone together.'

Natasha stared at her, frowning. 'Both nights?'

'Listen before you put two and two together and come up

with the answer to what's beyond the limits of the known universe. Give me a chance to explain. The first night I was badly injured and in shock after my near fall. Then last night, we'd come back from a crime scene and needed to talk. We had a few drinks and it was really late. I'd just had the stitches put in my leg, so it was easier to stay.'

'Easier to stay? Be still my beating heart. So are you telling me you both kept all of your clothes on, both nights, and neither one of you touched the other?' Natasha let her head fall heavily to the table, banging her forehead up and down three times. 'You know, you were a lot more fun when you were sixteen. At least when you were still a virgin, you thought sex was something to look forward to.'

'Tasha!' Ava reprimanded. The waiter put two glasses on the table and she picked one up to taste the contents. 'That's so good.'

'Did you at least see Luc naked?' Natasha giggled.

'I hate to be the one to remind you, but you're a lesbian. Why the sudden interest in male anatomy?'

'Humour me,' Natasha said. 'Details, please – less dull than you're currently making it sound.'

'I'm not doing this. I'm Luc's commanding officer. It's not appropriate for me to . . .'

'That's such bollocks!' Natasha laughed, spraying champagne across her lap. 'You spent the last two nights in his bed. Were you worried about chain of command, then? Plus, Luc's my friend, too. I'm not asking you for any details I wouldn't be perfectly happy to demand from him if he were here.'

'I can't argue that point. You're shameless, do you know that?' Ava rolled her eyes.

'Stop. There's method to my madness. I want to prove a point – you know I love that. Think of it as a real-life example of a philosophical argument. I'm offering you my expertise for free. Now, finish your drink and give it up.'

132

Ava did as she was told.

'Okay,' she began, 'as I have nothing to hide, and neither does Luc, I can tell you every boring detail. I was a mess from the injury and wet through from the storm. Luc needed to see my leg to clean the wound and apply butterfly stitches. I had a bath, then I got into his bed – for the record, he stayed on top of the covers – and we fell asleep. It was late. We got three, four hours, then got up. He went for a shower as I got dressed and we drove to work.'

'So you were naked, after your bath . . .'

'Logic dictates I would have been,' Ava sighed.

'And did Luc take his clothes off?' she grinned.

'Oh! come on, Natasha, what is this?'

'I'm just asking. Have you seen him naked?'

Ava attempted to drain non-existent remnants from her glass before answering.

'Yes, I have seen Luc naked, for your information, but only during an argument ages ago when he was making a point in a very childish way. The low-down, as you're going this low, is that he's physically perfect, as you might expect given the face. Six-pack, those nice little dimples between each hip and the curve of his butt cheek as he walks. His skin's more than just tanned; it's quite a smokey colour on his body. Good chest and nice arms, not excessively built up but well defined. You can see the different layers of muscles. Strong thighs, broad and flat at the top. And that line of hair that goes up from groin to the base of the stomach, like an invitation. You know?' She smiled into her empty glass.

'Waiter!' Natasha called. 'Bring us four more of these, please.' She pointed at the empty glasses on the table. 'That's quite the picture. Thank you.'

'You did ask,' Ava said smugly.

'I did, and your answer confirms everything I thought. You've thought about every inch of him. In detail. You've run it through your mind. No hesitation, no uncertainty. It's all flattering. Some of it was actually quite nauseating. Did you stop to wonder how he felt about having you in bed with him?'

Ava considered it.

'It was his idea that I stayed. There was no point either of us sleeping on the couch, so it seemed like the natural thing to do to share the bed. He's just got out of a relationship with a goddess, so it's pretty obvious the only emotion he'd have had looking at me would have been pity.'

'God, you're stupid!' Natasha said. 'I mean, I love you, you know that, but you are outstandingly dense when it comes to your personal life. How the hell did you ever become a detective?'

'Excuse me?'

'You haven't noticed the way he looks at you? How possessive he is around you? How angry he gets when you're in danger? I'm willing to bet quite a lot of money on the fact that he didn't sleep at all. I reckon he just lay there staring at you all night, maybe stroking your hair a bit, or . . .'

'That's enough! Did the leg waxing also strip out your intellect? Luc has never made a pass at me. He's never implied that he's interested in me. After two nights in his bed, I can tell you that he didn't lay a finger on me. If we weren't such good friends, I might actually have been insulted; although, to be fair, I'm not looking my best . . .'

'Well, the leg forest would have put me off, too.'

'Fuck you,' Ava said, taking the next drink off the tray before the waiter could set it on the table.

Natasha burst out laughing. 'Listen, you don't have to answer this question out loud, but at least answer it honestly inside your own head. Can you genuinely say you've never looked at Luc – either fully clothed or naked – and not felt that fizz, low in the pit of your stomach? That liquid warmth spread through you? Because I've seen it in his eyes when he looks at you and I think you two may need to have a conversation about it.'

Ava raised her eyebrows. 'Are you done?'

'Yup,' Natasha said, sitting upright and pulling her shoulders back.

'Good, thank you. Now, let's change the subject.'

'Okay. I know what I know.'

'How's your new girlfriend?'

'Needy. Were you aware that your pupils dilated when I asked if you'd ever got turned on by Luc?' Natasha leaned forwards and peered into Ava's eyes.

'It's dark in here. Of course my pupils are dilated. Needy in what way?'

'Too many phone calls and texts. Too much "hold me until I fall asleep". Just so we're clear, it's not that dark in here and your pupils were just fine earlier.'

The food arrived, distracting them with its beauty and smell. Ava had ordered Natasha the Scottish rib-eye, just barely touched down onto the pan, and herself the Shetland mussels. At last, Natasha stopped talking.

Chapter Fourteen

6 March

Osaki Shozo pressed the buzzer and stood back, waiting to see if he could be saved, wondering if he should let himself be saved. He'd found the card for the helpline on a board in the job centre, which was presumably a last resort. Can't get a job? Try not to kill yourself. Here are some people who might be able to help. It was either genius or cruel.

'Yes, hello?' a dull voice rattled through the tinny speaker.

'I was hoping to see someone. I need . . . help. Can you help me?'

'I'll come and open up,' the reply came.

Osaki stepped back and waited for the door to open. He had no idea why he was here. The people inside wouldn't be able to change anything.

A red-headed young woman opened up, looked Osaki up and down, then stood aside and gestured for him to enter.

'Follow me; there's a lounge where you can wait. I've a form for you to fill in, but you're not obliged to answer any questions if you don't want to.'

The tone of her voice suggested differently, Osaki thought. It seemed rude to refuse to complete the form and Osaki was never rude. That was part of the problem.

'My name's Vicki. I can get you tea, coffee or water. Here's the form and a pen. Our next available counsellor will see you. It'll either be Mr Packham or Mr Maclure, as the other counsellors are busy. It should only be a few minutes, anyway. Are you carrying a weapon? Only I'm supposed to ask. Also, if you're currently under the influence of either drugs or alcohol?'

She handed Osaki a clipboard and visibly sniffed the air. Checking for alcohol fumes, Osaki guessed, and not subtly. It was like being back at home with his parents in Tokyo. He bowed his head, realising Vicki was still waiting for a response.

'No alcohol. No drugs,' he said, 'and no weapons. You can check if you need to.'

'That's not part of my job,' Vicki replied. 'You can hand the form to the counsellor when they come to get you.'

Vicki had reached into her pocket and was reading text messages before Osaki had even begun reading through the form. It was all standard questions. Name, address, date of birth, doctor, current medication, addictions, next of kin – all clearly prefaced with the fact that no information at all needed to be given for Reach You to provide assistance. Osaki began writing his name, looking up when he heard voices from the other side of the door.

'Vicki, I have asked you not to use your mobile while you're at work. It's really important that we focus on the people we're trying to help and there's a confidentiality issue, as you know,' a deep voice rumbled.

'I was just texting my mate. I didn't realise I couldn't even do that,' Vicki responded. 'And I've already added this file to Mr Packham's list, so maybe we should just leave it for him.'

'If someone's waiting, we just get on with it. Take the file back off Charlie's pile. It's not a big deal.'

'No, but Charlie hasn't seen that many people today. I thought I'd share the cases out a bit better.'

'Vicki,' Maclure said patiently. 'We're not on commission. It's about not keeping people waiting. Now, what's happening?'

'He's filling in the form.'

'It's helpful if you stay with people until one of us can get to them, to set them at ease and offer a friendly face. You know that.'

'I was just getting him a coffee,' Vicki replied.

Osaki couldn't remember asking for coffee. Presumably it was a mistake. It sounded to him as if Vicki was new on the job. At least she had a job. Osaki would have given anything to have been offered work. Perhaps then his wife would have become less dissatisfied with him.

'All right. I think there's some paperwork in the office that needs filing, if you don't mind. We'll run over our meet-and-greet policy again later. Thank you.'

Vicki had obviously been dismissed. Osaki stood up, anxious not to appear disrespectful to the man he hoped would have answers for him. The door opened.

A good-looking black man with designer stubble and a broad smile offered his hand to shake.

'I'm Rune Maclure,' he said. 'Come on through to my room, it's more private. I gather Vicki's bringing you coffee. She'll find us.'

Osaki followed Maclure up a short staircase and into a room full of photos of grand-scale landscapes and comfortable furniture. There was no desk, no office chairs, only bookshelves, plants and soft furnishings. He sank slowly onto a sofa and tried to put together a coherent explanation for why he was there.

'It's okay,' Maclure said quietly. 'The first few sentences are the hardest, so why don't you let me start. Everything you say to me is confidential. We maintain notes, but they're kept securely, the same as if you'd seen a doctor. If you don't want to give your name, the notes simply record the time and date of your visit, and often they're only referred to for internal training. It takes a lot to walk through this door, so whatever you're going through, know that you've already been brave and helped yourself. Do you feel able to tell me what's going on?'

Osaki nodded, lacing his fingers together on his lap and sitting upright, fighting the natural recline of the seat to do so.

'I have failed,' he said abruptly.

Maclure gave him a few moments to expand on the statement. When nothing more was said, he offered encouragement.

'Failure's subjective. It depends on the standards we set ourselves. If you judge yourself too harshly, almost anything can constitute a failure.'

'If I had not failed, my wife would not have left me. I could not get a job or support her. She has to work long hours. It is not the life I promised her.'

He kept his eyes on his knees and spoke in a level tone. He'd already let himself down badly enough by crying in front of his wife. He couldn't shame himself in front of the stranger, too.

'Do you mind my asking how old you are?' Maclure asked.

'Twenty-five,' Osaki replied.

'And it sounds as if this is your second language, by your pronunciation, not your grammar. It's impressive. Learning another language fluently is very demanding.'

'I met my wife when she came to Japan on a student exchange three years ago. I could already speak English, but I made sure I was fluent before I came here when we were married.'

'I see. That's a long way to come for someone else and it's

difficult to start a new life in a foreign country. It can't have been easy, job hunting here.'

Osaki thought of all the job interviews. It wasn't just the language that was different, it was the use of facial expressions, the manners and formality, not to mention the customs. The feedback he'd had from those few potential employers who'd bothered to give any was that he was too uptight and direct for them. That wasn't even limited to positions where he might have come into contact with the public. Corporations were looking for 'team players' or 'good communicators' and 'inspiring colleagues who understood how to bond with their peers'. It hadn't mattered that he'd been willing to work as many hours as he could get, or for minimum wage, or to perform tasks well below the expectations he'd had on getting his degree in systems management.

'Japanese and Scottish cultures are different,' he said simply.

'I'm sure they are,' Maclure said. 'So how are things between you and your wife now?'

'She is dissatisfied. There is another man who is providing her with comfort.'

'In an intimate way?' Maclure asked gently.

Osaki nodded.

'So you've been unable to get a job, you're away from your home and family, and your wife is having an affair. That's a lot for anyone to deal with and it doesn't sound to me as if you've failed. It seems to me that you've been very brave and need extra time and support to adjust to life here.'

The door opened yet again, and Vicki entered carrying a tray with two mugs of coffee and a plate of biscuits. Maclure gave her a tense smile.

'Thanks, Vicki. That'll be fine on the table. Perhaps try knocking first, just in case it's a bad moment.'

Vicki gave a slight sigh before issuing a curt apology and exiting.

'She's new,' Maclure commented. 'It can be a strange place to work until you're familiar with it. So tell me what effect it's having on you, this perception of failure.'

'Not perception. It is real. If I go home, my parents will know I have failed them, too. They told me not to come. They said Kylie was wrong for me. I told them I knew better. I was rude to my parents. I have no right to take my deficiency back to them.'

'That's a big burden to be carrying and I understand there are cultural differences that I may be less then adequately equipped to advise on, but I can say that most parents forgive quickly and easily. Love makes us want nothing but the best, even in the worst circumstances. Have you tried talking to your family about what's happening?'

'I cannot. My wife brings another man to our flat, even when I am there. She laughs at me when I ask her not to. She says . . . she says personal things about my body and tells me if I was a proper man, she would not have to. I am ashamed. My parents should not have to bear that.'

Maclure picked up the form that remained only half-completed.

'It's Osaki, right? Tell me if I mispronounced that. I, too, am guilty of not being as worldly as I should be. As a counsellor, I try never to take a path where I demonise a partner or take sides. There's always a lot left unsaid both between couples and between us in here, but all partnerships are based on mutual respect. If you know in your heart that you've been properly respectful to your wife, then you're entitled to be shown an equal amount of respect in return. Perhaps it's not you who's dishonouring your marriage. I understand that your culture puts a different emphasis on the roles within a marriage, but I think it's a universal truth that an inequality between two people in an intimate relationship almost always spells disaster.'

'The cause no longer matters. I cannot find work. I cannot pay the rent. I cannot even satisfy my wife. I have disobeyed my parents and brought shame on myself. I am here because death is the only path I can see to redeem myself.'

'All right, let's think about that for a moment,' Maclure said. 'Did you want to try the coffee? It's not great, but I've seen so many cups get cold if we don't take a break from talking. Did you want yours?'

'Thank you, no. I don't like coffee.' Osaki commented.

His head was bowed so low Maclure could hardly hear him.

'Did you ask Vicki for tea or water, then? I can get you something else.'

'No, I did not ask for anything, but the offer is appreciated.'

Maclure looked towards the door where Vicki had exited, wondering how their newest recruit was managing to get even the simplest of tasks wrong, given her impressive CV and references. At the very least, she was going to have to learn to leave her mobile alone during work hours. Nothing told people they were worthless like someone fiddling with a phone when they needed attention.

'You mentioned death,' Maclure said matter-of-factly. 'Is that an option you've been actively considering?'

'It is inevitable. There is no other possibility,' Osaki announced.

'Well, let's agree to disagree on that point just for now. Suicide prevents you from redeeming yourself. You can't make things better with your parents, or plan a new life. It causes as much pain as it resolves. And it's not always successful. There can be terrible non-fatal consequences.'

'I have planned everything,' Osaki said. 'I do not wish to be any further burden to my family.'

'But you're here. I'm glad you are, because it tells me that you still have hope, you're still open to the idea that there might be another way to proceed. Can we explore that?'

Osaki didn't answer.

'You know, I see a lot of people at many different stages in

142

this process. I've come to believe over the years that it takes more courage to ask for help than it does to do the deed. You risk not being believed, or thought hysterical or attention-seeking. I can understand that your concerns about the state of your life are real and valid. I believe they would affect anyone, not just you. Where we differ is in the extent to which you are culpable.'

'Culpable?' Osaki asked.

'Responsible. Accountable. It sounds as if there's an element of racism in your failure to find jobs. Perhaps not overt or even deliberate, but it's possible that potential employers have been unable to move past cultural differences and find ways to bridge the gap. You're obviously intelligent and qualified. I see from the form that your degree is in systems management and you're bilingual. I think perhaps you're looking in the wrong place for employment. You need to embrace the differences rather than ignore them. Try the university or colleges, perhaps teaching Japanese. What about travel companies, or translation services?'

'Say I get work. What about my wife? I don't know what to do about that even if my situation improves.'

'That's really up to you. Only you know if you want to save the relationship, but you both have to agree on the way forwards. It won't be easy getting the trust back, but you should also ask yourself if you're not owed more. Marriage should be about getting through the tough times together, not just the easy parts of the journey. Can you see your wife at your side long term?'

'But what would I tell my parents? They do not believe in divorce.'

'Here's the thing. Japan is very far from Scotland. You can tell your parents whatever you want to. You're a grown man. This is your life and you have one shot at it. I respect your sense of family and tradition. I think it's essential for society to have structure and generational respect, but it cannot be at the cost of moving forwards how you want to.'

'I cannot lie to them,' Osaki said sternly. 'That would only bring more shame. If they find out that my wife put another man in our bed . . . I might as well be dead already. They will never want to see me again. My father thought I was weak for coming to Scotland. He said I should have insisted that we remained in Tokyo. I hate that he was right.'

'Your father wanted to keep you close, to help you. I can't imagine how hard it must be for a parent to accept that their child is ready to live independently. There are plenty of ways to skin a cat, though,' Maclure said.

Osaki looked horrified. 'Skin a cat?'

'It's a saying. I didn't mean literally. Think about it. You could tell your parents that you discovered your wife couldn't have children and that it caused a divide between you. Or that there weren't enough jobs available in Edinburgh and you opted to return to Tokyo, and that your wife felt unable to leave her family. Or even just that you missed them so much, you were willing to sacrifice the marriage to go back to your home country.

'They might wonder about the details, but that would be enough to justify returning home. You could get work, start a new relationship. The divorce here would be relatively simple as she's committed adultery. No death involved.'

'It is still a deception.'

'Reality is whatever we make it,' Maclure said. 'Don't lose your life to pride or principle.'

'It is not pride,' Osaki countered. 'It is humiliation. My wife calls me names. She says my . . .' He looked up at Maclure, the cracks beneath the surface starting to show. 'My penis is too small. If I argue, she threatens to email my parents and tell them I prefer men and will not have sex with her. I would rather die than have to explain what is really happening to my mother and father. They are very traditional. They will not understand.'

'It sounds to me as if you're trapped in a very abusive

relationship. Too many people think that only women are victims of abuse. Psychological violence is still violence. It leaves wounds not visible to the eye but no less real. It's hard for men to talk about it, because society portrays males as needing to be tough guys. It's all bullshit. I look at it this way: if you saw your sister in an abusive relationship, you'd do everything in your power to get her out of it, right? You wouldn't tell her she was weak or foolish, or that she should have been able to handle it herself.'

Osaki stood. 'Thank you. You have helped very much.'

Maclure followed suit.

'You don't have to go. There are lots of options. We have information about places you can go, free legal advice, help sorting out your finances, even assistance getting employment. Sometimes it's just about taking back control. Feeling as if your life is spiralling can be daunting. Let me put you in touch with . . .'

'My decision has to be a rational one, based on research. You have been kind and I appreciate it. Now I must go.'

Maclure looked disheartened but extended a hand to shake Osaki's.

'There's someone here twenty-four hours a day, or you can phone us. We even have an online chat facility now, if that's easier.'

'Mr Maclure,' Osaki said warmly. 'You are not responsible for me or for anything I choose to do. I did not mean to make another person feel sad.'

'You haven't,' Maclure said. 'You made me hopeful as soon as you walked through the door. I just want you to take some positivity back out with you.'

They shook hands. Osaki showed himself out. It was how he'd always handled difficult decisions in his life. With careful thought and deliberation, taking objective counsel. Except for his choice of a wife. That had been all raging hormones and overactive ego when the visiting Scottish girl, who all his friends had competed for, had chosen him. Now, as his father had predicted, he'd come to regret acting on impulse. He wouldn't do so again, even when it came to making a life-ending decision. Rune Maclure had helped him more than he could possibly have known.

Vicki walked him to the door, a stack of neatly labelled files tucked under one arm, telling him distractedly to have a good day. She really did need some additional training, Osaki thought as he avoided another man heading down the path towards him.

'You just ring the blue buzzer to the left of the door handle,' Osaki told him.

'I'm not here to get help,' the male responded gruffly, offence written plainly on his face. 'I'm meeting a friend.'

'Apologies.'

Osaki inclined his head slightly as Vicki stepped out, fastening her jacket, pausing when she saw Osaki still there.

'I haven't got long,' the offended man said.

Vicki joined him and together they walked along the path towards the pavement.

'What was he in for?' he half whispered, still easily loud enough for Osaki to hear.

'Would you shut it?' Vicki hissed.

Osaki waited for them to choose a direction then went the opposite way. He didn't need to hear any more of their conversation to know what the offended man thought of him. It was obvious by his response. Seeking help was weak. Pathetic. He might as well have labelled himself a loser, that was the popular phrase, and how appropriate to him. He'd lost everything. His country, his family, his culture. His pride. It was time to do something about it, sooner rather than later. He had made a decision. All that remained was to put it in place.

Osaki set off for the nearest hardware store.

Chapter Fifteen

6 March

Since Callanach's journalist friend, Lance Proudfoot, had published his online article, the phone lines had been alive with callers offering information about both Fenella Hawksmith and her daughter, Alice. Ava was all too aware that most of it would turn out to be a diversion rather than substance, but they had to start somewhere.

She'd just reviewed Pax Graham's report on the nursing home murder, noting with dismay the additional evidence that Bruce Jenson's genitalia had been damaged in the attack. There was no doubt about Callanach in her mind, though. He'd proved himself to her time and again. There was nothing hidden between the two of them, no lies. She'd be willing to bet her life on that, so she was more than happy to bet her career on it.

Callanach had texted her at 7 a.m. to warn her that he'd set up the online article, trying to push for results in the Hawksmith case, while she'd been busy swallowing painkillers for her head and hoping the alcohol hadn't invalidated the benefits of the antibiotics completely.

'How was Natasha?' Callanach asked before Ava had time to look up as her half-open door received a brief single knock.

'On her usual electrifying form,' Ava grinned. 'She asked after you.'

'I miss Natasha. Why don't you both come to dinner at my apartment next week?'

'She's a bit busy with the latest conquest,' Ava dissembled. There was absolutely no prospect of her putting Natasha and Callanach in the same room while Tasha was so intrigued by their misconstrued nights together. 'Good call asking Lance Proudfoot to release the article. Looks like it's been shared successfully. There's information flying in.'

'That's why I'm here,' Callanach said. 'Fenella Hawksmith's medical notes just arrived. She had a history of suicide attempts, including a period when she was committed to a hospital for her own safety.'

'Was she still taking medication?' Ava asked.

'Not any that was prescribed; although it's possible she was taking non-prescription drugs. The tox screen will give us more details. I've checked with the Scenes of Crime team. There was no medication, legal or otherwise, found at the flat, other than standard over-the-counter stuff, and they were out of date with some still in the pack.'

'So no sign of addiction, then.'

'None,' Callanach agreed.

They stared at one another across the desk. Ava studied her fingernails, still ragged from clutching the wall at Tantallon, and wondered who was going to say it first. Callanach let her do the honours.

'You don't think . . .' she said slowly.

'It has to be a coincidence,' he replied. 'Because otherwise you and I are going back to Tantallon, and back up on that fucking wall.'

'It's rained almost non-stop since the night Stephen Berry died. The chances of us picking up anything useful now is slim, but I think we have to try.'

'Ava, we already have one victim from the nursing home and Fenella Hawksmith. Are you sure about this?'

'Stephen Berry attempted suicide a few weeks ago, now he's dead following a long drop from a castle wall in the middle of the night. Think about it. The chemicals in his body that showed up on the tox screen confirmed that he hadn't gone off his meds. He was doing what his doctor had instructed him to do. There should have been enough serotonin in him to keep him steady, if not what you and I would think of as happy. He had a girlfriend, right?'

'Ex,' Callanach confirmed.

'So let's talk to her, confirm his movements and moods between the attempt from the Queensferry Crossing and his trip to Tantallon.'

'I'll get Tripp on it,' Callanach said. 'Anything concrete regarding Mrs Hawksmith's daughter yet?'

'No death certificate,' Ava said. 'So either she's still alive, is dead but wasn't identified, or is dead but hasn't been found.'

'How are you going to persuade Overbeck that we need to investigate the Berry death as a possible murder?'

'I'm not,' Ava said. 'I shall be engaging a secret weapon. You don't need to worry about it.'

'You've got a secret weapon you're not prepared to share with me? That's hardly fair.'

'Believe me, you don't want any part of it. And in case you're wondering, Pax Graham's team are proceeding on the assumption that the Bruce Jenson killing was committed by a staff member. Forensics has shown the initial blow to the glass door was from the inside and that afterwards someone hit the fractured area from the outside. They've concluded it was an attempt to make it look like an intruder.'

'Motive?' Callanach asked.

'Nursing home killings often come from a build-up of frustration or work stress. Occasionally, there's an underlying condition like Munchausen's by proxy or angel-of-death syndrome that attracts carers into the profession in the first place.'

'If that were the case, I'd expect there to have been other unexplained deaths there.'

'Because we don't have enough to deal with at the moment?' Ava raised her eyebrows. 'It could have been a new staff member, a temp. Other deaths could have been expected but just hastened, meaning there'd have been no postmortem. A lack of evidence doesn't mean this is an isolated incident. It's the hardest possible environment to make sure all deaths are natural. I'm only telling you so you can relax about it a bit. Graham's a good detective. He'll figure it out.'

Callanach nodded. 'Okay,' he conceded. 'I'll start sifting through the Hawksmith information. Good luck with Overbeck.'

Back at his desk, he checked his emails. There were a few from Lance — responses to his article that should have gone straight to MIT but that had gone to him. There were a few adverts that had escaped the trash folder and some online bills. Below that was a bounce back from the email he'd sent his mother. He felt suddenly sick. The last time an email to his mother had bounced back was when she'd disappeared from his life while he was fighting the rape allegation. That time it had been deliberate. She'd needed to get away from the whole dreadful situation and the memories it was dragging up. But in Paris she'd seemed fine. They'd undone most of the damage and reclaimed the close relationship they'd enjoyed before. Now this . . .

Callanach read his original email, checking the address he'd entered carefully for typos. There were none. Hitting resend, he doubled it up with a text to her, explaining that he'd tried to contact her but failed, hoping there was nothing more serious going on. It was difficult enough to bring up the subject of Bruce Jenson's death without worrying that his mother wasn't coping again.

Sergeant Lively's face resembled a punctured beach ball. Ava pointed at the empty chair opposite her desk as she finished typing a note requesting extended funding for forensic testing at Tantallon. It was a low trick to get Lively to request it for her, but it wasn't as if Detective Superintendent Overbeck could complain publicly about it.

'I need you to use your considerable influence with the super to get a full crime scene workout at Tantallon Castle,' Ava smiled at him. 'I'm just finishing my notes, then I'll hand this straightforward administrative task over to you.'

'The Tantallon file's closed,' Lively said. 'Dr Lambert decided it was suicide gone badly wrong, but nonetheless suicide.'

'Yeah, only that would make two in a row,' Ava replied quietly.

'Now hold on. The Berry case bears no resemblance to the Hawksmith case. The evil Overlord is going to be having none of that. I'm not going upstairs bearing that bouquet of poisoned ivy, thank you very much,' Lively grumbled.

'You don't need to link the two cases unless she asks. I'm about to phone the pathologist and have that discussion with her, and I'm sure she'll agree that we need to consider the similarities between the two cases.'

'Similarities? One man, one woman, different ages. The first was a fall and the second was deliberate cutting in a warm bath.'

'You're starting to sound like her,' Ava quipped.

'With respect, ma'am, you can do one.'

'I'm giving you a pass for that, Sergeant, but it's the last one you'll get. I've got two bodies that seem superficially like suicides, but neither is quite that simple.'

'Two's a coincidence, three's a pattern. The superintendent won't like it,' Lively said. 'And with respect, it's not fair of you to use me like this.'

'Is that your social conscience speaking out, only you've given your colleagues more crap over the years than any other officer I've known. It didn't bother you before.'

'I never used an officer who was in a relationship to try to gain an advantage,' Lively said quietly. 'You wouldn't be asking if I were female.'

Ava stood up, hands on hips. 'Are you accusing me of sexism?'

Lively took a deep breath. 'Aye, I suppose I am. If your new constable, Janet Monroe, were seeing a man higher up the chain of command than you, you'd sooner poke out your own eyes than abuse her position with him to get what you wanted.'

'Shit,' Ava muttered. 'I didn't think of it like that. I'm sorry. Truly. Forget it, I'll see Overbeck myself. For what it's worth, you're right. I wouldn't have done that to a woman. It just didn't occur to me . . .' She wasn't sure how to end the sentence.

'That I might have feelings? Thanks for that, ma'am. I'll be in the incident room if you need me for anything that actually constitutes my duties.'

He left without actually slamming the door, but Ava felt the impact as if he had.

Grabbing her notes, she strode to the stairs and did her best to run to Overbeck's office, choosing action rather than considering how badly she'd misjudged Lively's reaction, not to mention her own culpability. She'd expected Lively to give her some grief, complain about the assignment, but not considered the ethics of asking him in the first place. Police Scotland was a hotbed of ribbing and political incorrectness, but none of it was meant. When push came to shove, she was as sure as she could be that every one of the officers under her command had each other's back. Lively had given out vastly more abuse than he'd ever had to take, which was why she hadn't considered the appropriateness of her request. If anything, it had seemed light-hearted and trivial. Now, she saw it for what it was – an abuse of the knowledge of his relationship.

Detective Superintendent Overbeck was exiting her office as Ava approached.

'If you want me, you'll have to walk with me to my car,' she said.

Ava turned on her heel and did so.

'Give me the good news.'

'It's not good news, I'm afraid,' Ava said.

'Sarcasm failure, Turner. Of course it's not good fucking news. You're coming to see me holding a file. Get on with it, then.'

'I need to open a crime scene in a public place. Tantallon Castle, in fact, which will mean closing the castle to the public.'

'Tantallon? I love it there.' Overbeck smiled wistfully. 'High fall, right? If I'm not mistaken, that case has been closed. Why are you seeking to reopen it?'

Ava explained as concisely as she could given the time constraints and Overbeck's dislike of long speeches.

'All right,' the superintendent concluded. 'You can have complete forensics from the scene, interview Stephen Berry's nearest and dearest, and see if you can establish any other link between Berry and Hawksmith, but no other follies, got it? This is tenuous. Don't start taking the piss.'

'Yes. Speaking of which,' Ava said as they approached Overbeck's car, 'I did something I shouldn't have.'

'That's unusually exciting of you,' Overbeck laughed. 'Come

on then, shock me.' She unlocked her car and slid into the driver's seat.

'I asked DS Lively to approach you to extend the funding. He quite rightly refused. He also . . . well, he accused me of sexism, and I'm afraid he was right. I wanted you to hear it from me rather than him. I've apologised.'

Overbeck's face contorted, her mouth pursed, then she gave a huge guffaw, clutching the steering wheel as she got her laughter under control.

'Chief Inspector, the only shocking thing about that is that it's exactly what I'd have done in your shoes. Don't get your knickers in a twist about it. It may be the first thing you've ever done that's made me respect you, you devious little cow.'

Ava stared at her open-mouthed.

'And he accused you of sexism, did he? He has been a bit snippy lately. If he were a woman, I'd think he was due his period.'

'Oh God,' Ava murmured.

'Don't worry about it, Turner. He'll get over it. It's me he's pissed at, not you.'

'I'm sorry about that,' Ava said, and she meant it.

It was becoming increasingly obvious that her obnoxious but loyal sergeant had fallen very much in love with the super-intendent.

'He wants me to file for divorce. The problem is that I feel rather sentimental about my husband, blithering idiot that he is. I'm not sure I'm ready to take the next step. Isn't that what the popular media calls it? Why on earth can't men be happy with a quick shag? If I had a pound for every string that got attached, I sure as shit wouldn't be doing this job.' Overbeck closed her door but lowered the window. 'And what's happening on the other murder? That nursing home job.'

'Most likely a member of staff,' Ava said, wishing Overbeck would just get going.

'Fine. Now, be a good girl and don't upset any other MIT squad members with that nasty sexism of yours.'

She wheel-spun away, cackling at her own hilarity, leaving Ava feeling both relieved and upset. DS Lively was obviously at a low point, which made her attempt to use him all the more unfortunate.

Chapter Sixteen

8 March

Gilroy Western was weighing up the pros and cons of having an affair. At his age, the very use of the term 'affair' was a euphemism and he knew it. Not in the marital sense. That was pretty clear. He'd left his wife, in her sixties, at home in their apartment in Spain with her golfing buddies for company and with the endless consolation of the multitude of expat bars nearby. Sleeping with anyone else naturally constituted an affair, only this was more of a professional arrangement and he knew it.

The woman half his age who obliged him with sex in positions his wife had decided years ago hurt her back, and with the blowjobs his wife had never deemed appetising, would inevitably find herself too busy to see him on his return were he not so generous with his purchasing of jewellery, clothing and fine wines. A prostitute in all but name and he knew it. He also didn't care. When you paid a fair price for a service, no one had any complaints, and that was how he liked his life.

He'd touched down at Edinburgh Airport the previous evening, had driven home to Moray Place, and was now just half an hour away from the warm, wet bliss of oral sex. His lover was expecting him and would hopefully be wearing some of the outrageously expensive lingerie he'd purchased for her during his last visit. He wasn't due to be back in Scotland for long, having only returned when he'd been notified that his old business partner, Bruce Jenson, was dead.

They'd had limited contact for the last decade, but Bruce had apparently harboured some affection for him, having named him in his will. Western had been more than a little surprised. They'd sold Edinburgh Bespoke for a good price to a company that had filled half their factory with machines that could make furniture in a fraction of the time and at half the cost. Then they'd made some serious money letting their remaining industrial units go to developers who'd demolished and replaced them with luxury flats.

It was annoying that Bruce Jenson had opted for one of those horribly old-fashioned will readings with all the family gathered, mainly because it meant Western couldn't reasonably avoid attending the memorial service later that day. The email from the solicitors had been vague about the cause of death, but Western was well aware that his former partner's health had been failing for several years. To be brutally honest, the signs of dementia had been there long before the diagnosis. His memory had gone first. You had to have every conversation with him three times, and Jenson had never been good with names and faces.

The memorial service had been billed as a celebration of Jenson's life and Western was grateful that there was no suggestion he should attend a burial or cremation. It was bad enough reaching the stage of life when every headache rang with the possibility of a brain tumour and the slightest bowel problem made him question the sense of having skipped his standard colonoscopy. The last thing he wanted was to watch yet another of his peers hitting the dirt. Recognising your own mortality was no fun at all.

He sat in his hire car and checked his watch. His lover didn't like him to appear early. She'd made it clear on previous occasions that she considered it rude. He knew why but pretended he didn't. She had more than just one 'gentleman caller', as they were laughingly labelled in the old days. Good for her. Gilroy Western wasn't a happily-ever-after kind of man. His primary fantasy on the plane over had been that the diamond earrings he'd purchased as a gift for her might be just enough to persuade her to swallow for once.

He still had ten minutes to kill before he could leave. Staring up at his beautiful five-storey townhouse, he wondered how much it was worth at current market value. Part of a curve of terraced period properties, it defined classic Edinburgh architecture with its brown brick, arched ground-floor windows, wrought-iron balconies at the first floor and the basement flat he rented out.

In reality, he didn't spend enough time in his home city to justify keeping a house there. Hotels when he visited would be cheaper, but there was something to be said for maintaining one's investments. Property prices in the city were continuing to rise and Edinburgh was as popular with tourists as it had always been. It would be something to leave his daughter eventually and he was proud of his nationality.

Spain was all well and good, but Malaga had none of the cosmopolitan chic of Barcelona, nor the historic grandeur of Madrid. Edinburgh, in spite of the cold, the rain and the American-owned golf courses, was still home. He had enough cash to last him another ten years without dipping into any stocks or selling any of his properties. Enough to maintain his other 'girlfriend' he visited once a week in Spain and more than enough to buy his wife the trinkets that kept her from asking too many questions about what he got up to in his spare time.

All in all, life had treated him very nicely indeed. He'd earned it, too. Made tough decisions, been ruthless – which was what business required – made good calls when it came to buying in and selling out, which was why having a conscience about enjoying himself was foolish. What his wife didn't know couldn't hurt her, just as long as he avoided catching anything that required strong doses of antibiotics, or the regular application of unpleasant-smelling medicated creams.

He checked his watch again. That was enough waiting.

The engine turned over nicely, unaffected by the wet weather, and he set off humming to himself, imagining what awaited at the other end of his journey. He was hard before he'd even got out onto Doune Terrace, wondering exactly what Bruce Jenson had left him in his will. Jenson hadn't done as well as him since they'd sold the business, but then his former partner had never been interested in long-term investments. He hoped to God Jenson hadn't bequeathed him the collection of furniture he'd insisted on taking when they closed down Edinburgh Bespoke, accompanied by lengthy monologues about how the company had contributed to the city's history of fine craftsmanship. Imagine the bonfire that would be needed to burn all those memories before he could get back on the plane to Malaga . . .

Western took a left onto Gloucester Street, revelling in the unusual lack of traffic. Even the rain had stopped for his well-deserved pre-memorial service fuckathon, aided by a hefty dose of Viagra that was handed out like sweeties by the expat community doctors. He'd be banging like an angry teenager on his first drum kit in no time at all.

Gathering pace down the narrow hill, he squeezed the brakes gently. There was a hollow thud as the pedal hit the floor, but no mechanical response from the brake pads. Lifting his right foot, he tried again, seeing the cyclist who came hurtling out from India Place just in time to swerve and avoid him. Western pumped the brakes again. He was up to forty-five miles an hour now, the gradient steep enough to be propelling him at an increasing speed.

Grabbing for the handbrake and losing his grip on the steering wheel, he veered left and hit the pavement. The car spun. He abandoned the handbrake to turn into the skid, straightening up, seeing traffic approaching at the Kerr Street intersection below. Fifty-five miles per hour. Bloody hire car. Why the hell did he bother coming back to Edinburgh? Sixty-five miles per hour and there was a woman with a pram crossing Kerr Street to his left where he needed to turn. Why fucking now? He grappled with the handbrake again, but his palms were slick with sweat and the car was moving erratically.

Kerr Street went downwards to his left and uphill to the right. Aiming for the right to kill the acceleration and avoid the pram, Western flew over a corner of pavement, lifting the driver's side wheels off the ground. Another car clipped the end of his as it tried to brake, creating a seventy-mile-an-hour spin that threw the world into a slow-motion, anti-gravity cartwheel.

There was screaming. It sounded female but seemed to be coming from his own throat. Then he was falling. The whoosh-whomp of the airbag sounded simultaneously with an impact that was hard enough to leave his jowls struggling to keep up with his bone structure as his face rushed forwards.

When the back end of the car caught up with the front, there was a tipping movement normally reserved for roller coasters, and from Western's left came the sound of ripping metal and exploding glass. He'd hit a building. He saw, from his vantage point of the airbag, that had his neck turned ninety degrees. The rest of the car concertinaed, attempting to bend his back in half, the wrong way.

The driver's door was nowhere to be seen as arrows of glass aimed their fury at him. As they struck his vulnerable face, neck, arm and leg, the surprise was how hot they felt entering his flesh. For some reason he'd expected them to be cold. Then came the stench – overwhelming, pungent, sickly. Cheese. Why on earth would his car smell of cheese?

The windscreen glowed red and there was something sticky in his eyes. He had time to register the fact that his daughter was going to be inheriting the stunning Moray Place property much sooner than he'd anticipated. His wife would become a rich woman, and waste all that hard-earned cash on golf clubs, cocktails and shoes she'd wear only once. Perhaps Bruce Jenson was going to be waiting for him on the other side.

He couldn't breathe. Gilroy Western saw his mother's face, smiling, then felt the slap of his father's belt. He heard his daughter's first cry as she was handed to him outside the delivery room. He remembered the first time he'd had sex with an American girl at university who'd liked his Scot's accent and who'd giggled when he'd whispered endless rubbish in her ear. And that brought back something dimmer a distant memory he'd squashed and changed and added unfair blame to. Another woman, another night.

There had been a party. Too much booze. Had it been Bruce Jenson's idea or his? He wanted to blame Jenson but knew it wasn't the truth.

His brain processed the relevance of the odour and he realised his car had crashed into the cheesemongers across the Kerr Street junction.

The woman Jenson had held down for him had screamed and begged them to stop.

161

Brie, he thought, trying to distract himself. He'd always loved cheese. Camembert, Stilton, Gouda. But the memory overpowered even the most aromatic of the dairy produce.

A larger shard hit his jugular.

He saw Bruce Jenson pinning the woman to the floor and wondered why he couldn't understand what she was saying. She'd been French, that was it. Beautiful, too, truly breath-taking. He'd wanted her from the second she'd walked into the party.

Everything was black now and there was a droning in his ears. Even the smell of the cheese had faded.

The woman had sobbed as he'd entered her. He'd felt so powerful, king of the world, taking another man's prize, stealing, violating, knowing she wouldn't – couldn't – say anything.

Western tasted blood in his mouth, felt it trickle from his ears.

He saw her face as they'd taken the bag from her head and thrown her back out into the corridor. But she wasn't crying now. And although she seemed to be speaking French, a language he had no grasp of at all, he could understand perfectly well what she was saying now.

Chapter Seventeen

10 March

DI Graham sat at the desk of the interview room, looking entirely at ease compared to the man opposite him, who was openly attempting murder by glaring, and the female solicitor sat at his side, who was tapping her nails on the desk and intermittently patting the glaring man's arm. DC Janet Monroe perched on the edge of her chair next to Graham, pen poised to take notes. DCI Ava Turner, invited late to the party that morning after Andrew Jenson had been brought in for questioning, opted to stand in the corner, leaning against the wall.

'At the present time, you are being interviewed voluntarily, as a witness. You are free to leave at any time, but I should warn you that we are pursuing an active line in this investigation and if you're unwilling to answer our questions, it's possible at a later date that you could be arrested and brought in for formal questioning. Do you understand?'

'It's not rocket science,' Andrew Jenson retorted.

'Do you consent to us recording this interview?' Graham asked.

'Yes, we know the form. Let's make it quick, shall we?' Jenson's solicitor sniped.

'As you wish,' Graham said. 'Mr Jenson, where were you during the evening of March the third when your father was murdered?'

'At home, with my wife, watching TV,' Andrew said.

'And you didn't leave your home all evening?'

'Nope. My wife will back me up.'

'Are there any other witnesses who might be able to confirm that?' Graham asked.

'In my house? It was just the two of us,' Andrew said.

His face was an unattractive shade of purple and there was a single bead of sweat forming between his eyebrows.

'What time did you get home?'

'Nine thirty. After work I went to get a takeaway. My wife avoids cooking whenever possible.'

'So what time did you leave work then?' Graham clarified.

'I'm not exactly sure. It was a frustrating evening. There was a long queue at the curry house and the staff were taking bloody ages to get the orders right.'

'Roughly what time do you think you left?' Graham persisted.

'I'd have to check.'

Graham looked over to Janet Monroe, who flicked through a couple of pages in the file and scanned a page, pointing out a line of text.

'You work for Borderline Airways, right?' Andrew nodded. 'CCTV there shows your car exiting the car park at 7 p.m. Does that sound about right?'

The solicitor leaned across and whispered in Andrew Jenson's ear.

'Yes,' Andrew agreed.

'So getting a takeaway and making it home took two and a half hours, then?'

No reply.

'Which restaurant was it that you got the takeaway from?'

'Prashant's on Main Street.'

'You know it?' Graham asked Monroe.

'I do. Spent many an unpleasant Friday night after chucking-out time getting a load of verbal from customers who didn't like their korma and thought the situation could be resolved by throwing it at the owner. That's why they have 24-hour camera surveillance now, both inside and out,' Monroe noted, keeping her eyes on her notepad.

'What did you order?' Graham asked Andrew.

'Do you want to keep this relevant? If not, we can leave,' the solicitor said.

'I'm just wondering if the details will help Mr Jenson remember how long it took to place his order and for it to be cooked, only your client's recollection was that there was some delay.'

'I had a jalfrezi, and the wife had cod and chips.'

'So your memory's pretty good, then,' Graham noted. 'That's great. How long do you think you were in Prashant's from entering to leaving?'

Andrew Jenson cast a sideways look at his lawyer. 'Twenty minutes, maybe more,' he said.

'Let's see,' Graham said, waiting for Monroe to flick through the file again and locate a different page. 'Yes, here we go. You arrived there at 8.55 p.m. and left at nine ten. You parked right outside, got back in your vehicle and presumably went straight home.'

'If you knew which takeaway I went to, why did you ask?' Andrew asked though gritted teeth.

'Let me handle this,' his solicitor cut in. 'Are you trying to back my client into a corner, Detective Inspector? You know the rules. You're supposed to summarise what evidence you've got in advance of an interview.'

'I'm not interviewing a suspect though, am I? This is a voluntary witness account we're taking here.'

The solicitor swallowed, looked across the room to Ava, who returned her gaze steadily, then the lawyer appeared to smile. It wasn't friendly.

'All right. Carry on,' the solicitor said.

'The thing is, Mr Jenson, you gave a statement the day after your father was found dead. In it you claimed to have arrived home rather earlier from work and there was no mention of the takeaway. Those details came later from your wife's statement.'

'So what? I'd just been told that my father was dead, murdered. You think I was worried about a bloody curry under those circumstances?'

'Which is why we're asking you again today, now that you've had a chance to think more clearly about the sequence of events. In your written statement given to uniformed officers you claimed you'd left work late, at about 8 p.m., and had arrived home at about eight thirty. The problem is that we now have a period of almost two hours that are unaccounted for, give or take some driving time.'

'I'm not having this. I've done nothing wrong. He was my dad, for Christ's sake. Why the hell would I kill him?'

'Because we now know that you've instructed your solicitors to contest his will. Your father, for reasons that are not yet clear, left his whole estate to a rape crisis charity. That's the proceeds of sale from his home, some stocks and shares, one classic car that's in storage and any cash left in his accounts. We don't have a figure on the cash yet, but our best estimate for the estate is that it's worth £800,000. Without the bequest to the rape crisis charity, you'd have been the sole heir. It seems reasonable to think you might have been more than just a little angry about that.'

In the corner, grateful that neither Graham nor Monroe could see her face, Ava tried to keep her breathing steady. The investigation had stumbled across a perfectly legitimate issue that could provide a motive for Bruce Jenson's murder, yet she was unable to pass on the information she had about why Jenson had an interest in a rape charity without immediately implicating Callanach as a suspect. If she did that, and she knew she should, it would become clear that crucial information about Callanach's reasons for visiting the nursing home had been withheld from the start. It didn't matter that she was convinced Callanach had nothing to do with Bruce Jenson's death. This was about something more fundamental. Honesty, openness and legal procedures.

'That's my money. I'm entitled to it and I'm allowed to have my lawyers challenge the will. It doesn't mean I've done anything wrong,' Andrew snarled.

'You're right, it doesn't, but when we found out about it, we had cause to re-examine the timeline you'd given. So now we need to know where you were between leaving work and arriving at Prashant's,' Graham explained calmly.

'None of your fucking business,' Andrew shouted.

Ava studied Andrew's body language. His arms were tightly crossed, high over his chest, almost a self-hug. His shoulders were hunched inwards. He was as far back in the chair as he could get, away from Graham, but bolt upright. Ready to flee if the fight got too much for him in evolutionary terms. His jaw was switching from left to right, like a swing boat beneath his face.

'Okay, you can pass on any question you like while you're not under arrest. Let me move to a different subject. Do you have any idea why your father was prepared to be so supportive of a rape charity?'

'Of course I don't. It makes no sense at all. He had dementia, imagined all sorts of things. He never gave to charity his whole life, not a penny that I saw. Then, when he got really ill, when he knew he didn't have much time left, he decided to change his will. He'd get upset, rant, would bang his head against the table or the wall, anything he could find. That's why I'm challenging the will. He had no idea what he was doing when he cut me out of it.'

'Did you discuss it with him?'

'I tried. He just got really upset, said I had a good job and more than I already needed. Told me if I wanted extra I could work for it like he had. Said there were other people who needed it more. Then he got so upset, I had to let the subject go. I didn't try again after that. He went downhill really fast and I knew that I could take the matter to the courts once he was gone.'

'So you were just waiting for him to die?' DC Monroe interjected.

'It wasn't like that,' Andrew said quietly.

'But you were angry with him,' Graham said.

'He was demented!' Andrew Jenson stood up, leaning over the table, furious.

'Except that he wasn't. He had his solicitor and two independent witnesses for the amendments to his will, and they'd taken the precautions of getting a consultant psychiatrist to certify that at the time of making the changes he was of sound mind,' Graham read from a statement in the file.

'That's ridiculous. Why would my father suddenly decide to leave that much money to a rape crisis centre?'

'Perhaps something had happened to someone he loved?' Monroe offered.

'Yeah, and perhaps he'd watched five minutes of a documentary, got upset and managed to persuade the lawyer he was paying by the hour, and the psychiatrist he was also paying, to say what he wanted them to say. The symptoms of dementia aren't always obvious. My father could seem lucid and then have no memory of the conversation he'd had five minutes later.'

'All right,' Graham said. 'We can leave it there, but I'm urging you to tell us where you were during the period when your father was killed.'

'Do you have evidence that my client was involved?' the solicitor asked.

'No,' Graham replied honestly. 'But our job is to investigate all possible suspects and it makes our job a lot easier when people are forthcoming. If you weren't involved in any way, Mr Jenson, if you have an alibi for the hours in question, then the sooner you tell us everything, the sooner we can get on with finding the person responsible.'

Graham waited until Andrew Jenson and his solicitor had left the room before turning to Ava.

'What do you think?' he asked her.

'I think the man's an idiot, but he looked angry rather than scared. Do we have any idea what he's hiding?'

'We're checking the public CCTV for the evening, trying to follow his car route. His wife gave us more accurate, detailed information, so I'm sure she's no part of it. There's motive, for sure, though. Leaving his whole estate to a charity was always going to cause a problem,' Graham said, standing up.

'Yes, but Andrew Jenson already knew he could challenge the will in court and he's got a reasonable chance of winning, even with the psychiatric report,' Ava said, doing her best not to comment on the rape charity issue itself. 'Find out where he was and what he was doing. That's the fastest way to exclude him from the investigation and shift the resources to where we'll get results. Good work, both of you.'

Ava left, trying to keep her pace normal, knowing discussing the case with Callanach was inevitable. The real question, though, was not how Callanach was going to react to the news, but what she was going to do with the knowledge she had.

Chapter Eighteen

10 March

Callanach handed Rosa Macmillan a box of tissues.

'I'm not sure which is worse,' she sniffed. 'I know that sounds awful, but he seemed to be going through a good period, so when I was told Stephen had killed himself, I started doubting everything I thought I knew about him. Then when I was told that somebody might have killed him . . . why would they? He was struggling enough just to survive.'

'Did Tantallon Castle have any particular meaning for Stephen?' Callanach asked.

'Not that I was aware. I'm sure he said he'd been there, probably a school trip or something like that, but not recently. And as for going there at night when it was closed, that was totally out of character.'

'He waved a knife around in the taxi on the way to Queensferry,' Callanach reminded her. 'So would it be fair to say his behaviour was becoming more erratic and unpredictable?'

'Not as far as I was concerned. He was back on his medication.

I know he felt terrible about what he'd done in that taxi, and he was worried about whether or not he was going to be prosecuted, but he was ready to take responsibility for it and his doctor had agreed to write a medical report if needed.

'Stephen and I were talking regularly, seeing each other occasionally. I wasn't ever going to be his girlfriend again, it was all too painful for me, but he'd let me back into his life. For the first time, he was thinking about his future, maybe getting some new qualifications, booking a holiday with one of those tours that takes groups of people to South America or Australia trekking. There were real signs of improvement.'

'When did you last see him?'

'The night before he died. We grabbed a coffee, talked about how he was doing, and he was able to ask me about work and my parents, which was always a good thing. When he was at his low points he couldn't ask about anyone else, or think outside his own head. I spoke to him the day he died, too. I called his mobile and we arranged to have dinner the following week. Just pizza, nothing fancy, but I could tell he was looking forward to it. That's why when the news came that he was . . . I just couldn't believe it.'

'Had he talked to you about his suicide attempt? It must have taken some time to recover from the incident on the bridge.'

Callanach refilled Rosa's coffee cup and handed it to her, just to give her something to hold.

'A lot, but not in the way you might think. As traumatic as it was, he said he realised at the very end how badly he wanted to live. He was angry, really raging, about a man in the crowd he'd heard laughing at him. Stephen said he was determined not to die after that, not to give the crowd what they were waiting for. He said he'd felt like a sideshow freak.'

'I heard about that,' Callanach said. 'The gathering crowd is an unfortunate side effect of public suicide attempts. I'm sorry.'

'I'm not, or at least I wasn't. If being angry was what it took to get him down, then the insensitive moron who thought encouraging someone to end their life was a good laugh can be there every time someone does the same.'

'Were you aware of any injury to Stephen's right hand, specifically his middle finger?' Callanach asked.

'When we were having coffee the evening before, I held both of his hands in mine. They were perfect. Why?'

'Just below his fingernail, it looks as if there's part of a boot tread print and the finger was fractured. He didn't mention any accident when you spoke to him on the phone?'

'No, he was upbeat, said he'd had a good day,' Rosa replied, beginning to cry again and folding a tissue daintily to press against her cheeks.

'One last thing. We haven't been able to find Stephen's mobile. It wasn't at Tantallon Castle, in his car or at his flat.'

'The guy who helped him at the Queensferry Crossing – I can't remember his name – was holding it to try to call me when Stephen slipped. He grabbed Stephen's hand but dropped the mobile. We'd been speaking on the landline. He hadn't got a new one.'

'That explains it,' Callanach said, making a note. 'I'm very sorry for your loss and I apologise for asking you to come to the station to speak with us. I know it's the last thing you'll have wanted.'

'Actually, it's good to talk about him. Because we'd already split up, some of my friends and family have been telling me how lucky I was to get out of the relationship and how much better off I am. None of them seem to understand that I left him because I couldn't stand the idea that he might kill himself. Now, I spend every day wondering how I could have stopped it. If it was a murder, at least I can be sure there's nothing I could have done.'

'Whichever it was, there's nothing you could have done. You're not responsible. We all walk a thin line between coping with life and it becoming too much for us. Stephen sounds like a good man. The last thing he'd want is to think he'd left you feeling guilty about his death, however it happened.'

'You're right,' she smiled vaguely. 'Thank you for saying that.'

'I'll find an officer to show you out,' he said. 'When there's an update, we'll be in touch, whatever our conclusion.'

He walked to the door and opened it just as Ava appeared on the other side.

'Hey,' she said. 'If you're done, we need to talk.'

'I am,' he said. 'Your office or mine?'

'Neither,' Ava said. 'We're going out to lunch. I'll meet you at Pret on Shandwick Place in an hour, okay?'

'Okay,' he said, wondering why she looked so pale.

Lack of sleep, he suspected. Ava never had been very good at looking after herself. He asked Tripp to take care of Rosa then made his way back to his office to write up his notes. His laptop showed new emails in his personal account. One was from Lance, the other from his mother. He started with Lance's.

Luc, a food bank in Inverness has been in touch, reporting a woman who matches Alice Hawksmith's description as being a regular visitor. She has the Saltire flag tattoo on her left shoulder as shown in the photo you gave me. I've forwarded their email, below. Hope this is what you were looking for. Also, I understand Tantallon Castle has been closed to the public and is being treated as a crime scene. Anything you can share with me?

Callanach scrolled down to read the email from the food bank then picked up the phone to Inverness police and gave them the details. They'd have to station an undercover officer

173

in the area until they could talk with Alice Hawksmith. If nothing else, she needed to know what had happened to her mother.

Taking a deep breath, he opened the email from his mother, half expecting her to ask for more space and time before he contacted her again. However much he understood why she'd disappeared from his life, the bruise still hurt when he pressed it.

'Luc, darling,' he translated. She always wrote to him in French even though she spoke fluent English.

Sorry for the email confusion. Just a mistake. I had an email saying my account was insecure, but I was unable to change the password. I received no emails for a few days, but it seems to be working again now and your email finally reached me this morning.

Callanach sighed, happy to have had an explanation, suddenly ashamed he'd doubted his mother without cause.

I know I should be more forgiving, but the truth is I'm happy that Bruce Jenson is dead. It means I don't have to think about him any more. Please don't go looking for Gilroy Western. It will end badly, my darling, and you've suffered enough. It was a long time ago and while it's still sometimes painful, the memories are diminished. Get on with your life. I so enjoyed spending time with you in Paris. Promise you'll visit me in Monaco soon.
  All my love,
  Maman
  x.

Lively put his face around Callanach's office door.
'Got a minute?' he asked casually.

174

'A couple,' Callanach said. 'What do you need?'

'We've had a call from the vehicle investigation unit. A car crashed into the cheesemongers on Kerr Street, one fatality. The vehicle was a hire car. Turns out its brakes had been cut. They're asking us to take over the investigation. I said I'd go down and go over their findings before opening an MIT file. Can you spare me? We're not making a lot of progress on the Hawksmith case and the forensics from Tantallon Castle won't be back for a couple more days.'

'Certainly,' Callanach said. 'You cover the car crash, leave Tripp in charge of the Hawksmith investigation and I'd appreciate it if you'd leave a message for Superintendent Overbeck about the new case. She'll want to know if we're about to add another murder to our current caseload.'

'You taking the piss?' Lively demanded.

Callanach stared at him, confused.

'What exactly did DCI Turner tell you?' Lively asked.

'Sergeant, I have no idea what you're talking about. What did DCI Turner tell me about what?'

Lively frowned, paused, dug his hands hard into his pockets.

'Sorry. I might have misunderstood. I'll get right on it.'

'Are you sure everything's all right?' Callanach checked as Lively made his way to the door.

'Nothing you'd understand,' Lively muttered. 'I'll check in later.'

Shaking his head, Callanach grabbed his jacket and car keys. It wouldn't have done any good to force an explanation from Lively. The man wasn't exactly a sharer on his best days and when he decided to be stubborn, he could run a masterclass for spoiled sixteen-year-old girls denied a shopping trip. Better to ask Ava what was going on, he decided, especially given that she was already waiting to talk to him.

Chapter Nineteen

10 March

It wasn't Osaki Shozo's day. He'd woken up in the morning to find his wife and her lover sleeping on the couch, contemplated throwing a bowl of cold water over them both, then decided he didn't want to make a scene. They would write that on his tombstone, but not any time soon. Instead, he was going off the grid.

Further research had revealed that his wife would be able to file for divorce on the grounds of desertion after two years. There weren't any assets to make the financial settlement bothersome. No joint bank account, no loans. His parents would have to put up with him disappearing from their life rather than him ending his. It was a compromise of sorts for the dishonour he'd brought upon them.

He'd showered, shopped for lunch and returned home, by which time his wife and her close friend had vacated the apartment. He managed to resist the temptation to pick up the couch cushions that were scattered across the floor. A week ago he was still cleaning up after them, washing their coffee mugs and putting down the toilet seat when it had been left up.

At first, it had hurt that she'd chosen to go with the sort of man who couldn't even put the seat down. Now, Osaki had decided she was getting exactly what she deserved. Sooner or later, the honeymoon period would wear off and then she'd realise what she'd lost. Or maybe not, but by then he'd be far enough away that he could believe whatever he liked.

Finding systems-based work in Edinburgh had been impossible, but getting a position on a fishing trawler setting sail for Iceland had proved incredibly easy. He wasn't there to fish, the captain had laughed at him when he'd asked to join the crew for those purposes, but they'd needed what amounted to a housekeeper on board. He'd be cooking, cleaning, washing and doing the lowest of chores for the rest of the crew, who needed to eat, sleep and haul the catch from the sea into the hold, and not be bothered by anything else.

His cooking skills were good enough that he could cater for twelve and what he didn't know he'd learn. The one issue the rest of the crew would grapple with was precisely the reason Osaki had agreed to go. Not coming into close contact with a female for the next four months was no hardship at all.

The trawler left in three days. He could take one large bag of clothes and personal effects, so whatever was left after he'd packed, he was planning to take to a charity shop. Then he had to empty what little was left in his bank account and close that down. His final task was to spend some time reading recipes and figuring out what sort of things he should be cooking. It all seemed fairly obvious: pies, casseroles and pasta looked to be the easiest way to feed a dozen ravenous men. Keep them full of protein and carbs.

He had a library card from his days attending workshops to get his CV up to scratch and had contemplated taking out a selection of cookery books, then his overactive conscience had kicked in and he'd been unable to proceed, knowing he'd never return them. Certainly not in a fit state for anyone else to read after months surrounded by stinking fish and stinking men who wouldn't think twice about using the books as coasters for wet-bottomed mugs.

Osaki hung his head. Some day, good manners would do more than just lose him a wife and make him a laughing stock. On a fishing trawler with a bunch of claustrophobic, testosterone-laden men, they might actually get him killed.

First, he took out the new spanner and washer he'd bought from the hardware store. He'd promised to mend the leaking kitchen tap and such maintenance was required under the lease. It only took a few minutes and he was pleased with the job he did. Making good was satisfying. He couldn't mend his marriage, or be less disappointing as a son, but he could leave the flat in the state it was when they'd moved in. What his wife did with it once he'd gone was a matter for her.

After that, he decided which clothes he'd take and which would go to charity, not that there was a vast amount to be given away. He'd arrived in Scotland with three suitcases, so one full bin liner was all that was needed to be delivered to the hospice shop around the corner. Its contents were clean and neatly folded, and he'd attached a small label providing collar, waist and leg sizes to make life easier for the people who'd have to sort and rack the items. He was depositing the bin bag next to his front door, when a knock came from the outside. Osaki opened up.

The fist slammed hard and fast into the centre of his nose, then there was blood pouring down his throat and his eyes were on fire. He didn't remember staggering backwards, but he found himself on the floor in the middle of the lounge area, spluttering as he tried to draw breath and coughing blood onto the rug his wife had so desperately wanted. Osaki wasn't the only thing she'd grown tired of.

'Lean your head forwards,' the man instructed, providing assistance by taking Osaki by the hair and pushing his face until it nearly touched the floor. 'Now, spit out as much blood as you can.'

Osaki did so, more by instinct than willingly.

A strip of gaffer tape was slapped hard across his mouth.

'You'll need to stay in that position, or you'll choke on your own blood. Stay still while I help you out a little.'

He pushed scissors towards Osaki's mouth and snipped a tiny hole in the tape, just enough to allow an additional whistle of air through, but not enough to allow his mouth to open and issue sound.

'We're going to make this quick, before your lovely wife comes back. Not that I reckon she'd stop me. What do you think? Do you think she'd make a run for it, try to alert the police, or would she secretly be pleased by what she found?'

Osaki stayed on his knees, forehead balanced on the rug, the room spinning. The man's words were unclear. The air entering his lungs was wet. Nothing made sense. Gloved hands were rolling him onto his side, pulling his hands behind his back. He could no longer move his arms, connected at the wrists by a painfully thin thread of plastic. He breathed in what oxygen he could through the slit in the tape then blew hard from his nose. A stream of thick blood spattered the lower section of the sofa, but it did the trick. He breathed more freely, blinking hard.

His attacker's back was turned and he was fiddling with a bag. Osaki seized the moment, thrashing like a fish out of water towards the nearest wall, knowing if he could only bang on it hard enough with his feet, his constantly irate neighbour would be hammering his door in seconds. It had been a curse since they'd moved in. Now, it was a lifeline. One thump was all he managed before he was hauled back into the middle of the room.

'No, you don't,' he was admonished. 'Bravery doesn't suit you. You don't deserve it. Too little, too late. You're weak.'

Osaki nodded unenthusiastically.

'But I'm not.'

He pulled a box from the bag and ripped it open, his gloves slowing the process slightly but not enough to give Osaki hope. What came out was a gleaming new toaster, not a smudge on it. The man set it down on the floor.

'I'm going to take what you were willing to throw away. I'm going to use it and feed it, and relish it.' He leaned across to the nearest socket and pushed the plug into the wall, switching the power to live. 'Do you know what I think of men who contemplate suicide? You can't speak, I know, so I'm going to tell you anyway.' He grinned. 'I think they aren't men at all. They're . . . sorry to use such a demeaning word – feminists hate this – but they're pussies. You know what I mean? Limp-dicked little whiners without the backbone to survive the shit life throws at us all.'

He moved down to take hold of Osaki's ankles and bind them together like his wrists, then dragged the heavy old armchair across to wedge his legs between the chair and the sofa. If Osaki's brain had been working slowly at first, now it was on overdrive. He foresaw endless possibilities for pain, none of which ended well. Picking up his head, he tried banging it on the floor, but a carefully slid cushion put paid to that.

'You stay there quietly. No running away.' The man grinned.

A tap ran in the kitchen for a few seconds and Osaki had time to wonder if it was the cold tap he'd fixed earlier. There were few ironies as poignant as having potentially made your murder run slightly more smoothly than it otherwise might have done. He had time to regret not leaving for the boat earlier and time to wish he'd stood up to his wife. Even so, he was still sorry she'd have to return to their flat to find him dead. As a child, he'd found his grandfather after a stroke, his face a contortion of pain, and the image had haunted him for years. His wife, he assumed, would make a speedier recovery.

The man returned carrying a full jug and humming the theme tune from a 1970s TV programme he'd seen reruns of, about American army doctors during the Korean War. He couldn't remember the name of it now. And he couldn't feel his legs, or his face. Everything was suddenly cold, as if he were outside in winter. His legs were wet.

'Well, look at that, I went out to get some water in case you couldn't do what I needed and you've gone and done it before I even asked. If you'd just applied that sort of enthusiasm to the rest of your life, I'd never have had to visit you today.'

He pulled on heavy-duty black rubber gloves before kneeling down and undoing Osaki's trousers, sliding them down, along with his underwear, to leave his genitalia bare.

'I thought long and hard about how to do this and it seemed to me that as you've effectively neutered yourself, the most fitting ending would be to represent that in the flesh. It'll be quick, I promise. Faster than anything you'd have done to yourself. Any last words? Don't worry, I can imagine them. That way you won't embarrass yourself by begging. Are you ready?'

He positioned Osaki's body exactly as he needed it, emptying the jug of water from head to foot then stepping away and drying the gloves on his jeans. He stretched his arms in the air, taking several deep breaths as if about to attempt some Olympic feat. The man looked towards the ceiling, palms upwards, taking a moment.

Osaki watched him, mesmerised. It was as if an audience of

thousands was watching and he was about to pull off the greatest magic trick of the century.

Finally, he took a thick wooden stick from his bag and held it directly over the toaster lever. As he pushed it down, allowing a lethal amount of electricity to flow, not a moment too soon, Osaki Shozo passed out.

Chapter Twenty

10 March

'So, Bruce Jenson left all of his money – every penny of it – to a charity supporting victims of sexual violence. His son said he has no idea why, and I believe him. He's instructed solicitors to challenge the will; although Jenson had the presence of mind to get a psychiatrist to declare he was of sound mind at the date of the alteration.'

'The money should go to the charity,' Callanach said, pushing his lunch away and nursing a black coffee instead.

'I'm guessing it would help the charity if your mother stepped forwards and explained that the bequest was purposeful. The only problem is that it would create an additional link between you and Jenson, including a motive to have murdered him. It would be in the public domain, too. No possibility of keeping it quiet,' Ava said, abandoning her own lunch out of sympathy.

'I should have told the truth in the first place,' Callanach said. 'Now I've dragged you into it and the prospect of helping a charity that deserves financial support has become a question of them or me. How did it all get so complicated?'

Ava covered his hand with her own. 'What will your mother want to do?'

'She's been fiercely private about the rape for so long, I think it'd hurt her to have to go into the details now, but she'll want to help other victims and survivors. I'll talk to her about it. If she wants to tell her side of it, I'll explain the history to DI Graham and take the suspension while he investigates.'

'God, Luc, this is my fault, too. I feel as if I persuaded you to stay silent at the start. Now, you'll be in more trouble for failing to disclose the rape than if you'd just admitted the whole thing. We'll see the superintendent together. This is as much my problem as yours.'

'Are you kidding? What would be the point? It won't make things any better for you to be suspended with me. In fact, I suspect you'd just make me watch endless black-and-white movies and eat takeaway. I'm not sure how much of that I could take. This is my problem, Ava. You did nothing more than have faith in me and try to protect my reputation. You don't need to fall on any ill-conceived sword.'

'It's just so unfair. Your poor mother will have to relive it all if she wants to ensure the money goes where it should and your career will get put on hold again while the investigation runs its course. Where's the justice?'

Callanach picked up her hand and kissed the back of her knuckles so lightly Ava barely felt it. She blinked at him.

'The justice,' he said, 'is that unlike the last time I was falsely suspected of a crime, this time I have one friend who I know will stand by me, no matter what. That means more to me than you could possibly know.'

Ava smiled gently, squeezing his fingers then sighing as her mobile began to ring. Callanach's followed suit seconds later.

They each answered, ducking their heads for quiet against the backdrop of noisy lunchers. One look at each other was all it took to have them both running for the door.

The Leamington Road flat boasted a short walking distance from the city centre but little else. The top-floor apartment was made up of just four rooms – kitchen, bathroom, bedroom and lounge – and two of those could only fit one person in at a time. Ava and Callanach had made it there before both Dr Ailsa Lambert and the Scenes of Crime officers, and their first job was to stop the firemen who'd found the body from destroying all the potential evidence.

'Who called it in?' Ava asked.

'Neighbour below smelled burning and called us. He ran up and knocked on the door, but no one answered,' a fire officer explained.

'I'll need anyone who entered the flat to make a statement and retrace their steps to avoid DNA or tissue contamination,' she instructed. 'Can you describe the scene from when you arrived?'

'Sure, we were pretty certain there was no active fire, as there wasn't any smoke coming out into the hallway, but even from the floor below, there was a coppery, sulphuric smell, which was very strong when we were at the flat door.'

'Indicating?' Ava asked.

'The sulphuric smell often comes from burning human hair. It's the chemical that keratin gives off when it burns. The coppery odour can also come from burning meat if it's very bloody, but if it's been in a kitchen, the smell is usually contained.

'We knocked on the door hard and then took the decision to break it down when there was no response. We found the male lying on the lounge floor. He hasn't been moved, as it was obvious he was dead as soon as we saw him. All my officers did was turn off the electricity and unplug the toaster, then we checked the rest of the flat for people or other fire sources. As soon as it was secure, we called you.'

Ailsa Lambert strode in, issuing a barrage of orders to clear the scene immediately. She started photographing the body within seconds, addressing Ava without looking over to her.

'Just when I thought I'd seen everything, human beings stoop to new lows. This man's been dead no more than an hour, rather less, I'd think.'

She got down on her knees and took a close-up shot of the cable tie that held his wrists together, then looked into the digital camera's viewfinder screen, enlarging the shot.

'Ava, you have a problem,' Ailsa declared.

'I take it by your tone that you mean a greater problem than a semi-naked man lying tied up and dead on the floor?'

'I absolutely do. It'll take more detailed investigations, but judging by the product mark, and the manufacturing groove in the nylon, there's a good chance these cable ties came from the same batch used in the Fenella Hawksmith murder.'

'Show me,' Ava said, bending down next to her.

'Here,' Ailsa said, 'on the square section the tail is threaded through, there's a diagonal nick where the nylon is lifted away from the production line. It's at the same angle and the same length as the other cable ties, and the product code is B80, same as before.'

'There must be millions of them in circulation,' Ava said.

'Of course, but two of them have turned up attached to bodies in this city, restraining victims prior to death. How likely is that?'

Ava ran her hands through her hair.

'No you don't, not in my crime scene. I don't need any more hairs on this floor. Hands down and hood up.'

'Sorry,' Ava said, pulling her crime-scene suit hood up

immediately. 'I was just hoping against hope that the two deaths had nothing to do with one another.'

'Bursting your bubble there,' Ailsa said. 'High levels of psychological torture involved in both. They'd each have known what was coming. This man would have died substantially faster. He'd have been rendered unconscious as soon as the electricity went through him, but still, that's no way to go.'

Callanach finished his conversation with some other fire officers and joined them.

'Fuck . . .' he muttered.

Ailsa gave him one of her looks reserved for particularly bad language, which she discouraged at her crime scenes.

'Ah, yes!' she said. 'Men always react badly to the disfigurement of male genitalia. This one is especially shocking, I'll give you that.' She stood up and leaned over the corpse. 'So our victim is, I believe, Japanese by race, between twenty-five and thirty years of age at first assessment – visual only – and I'd estimate five foot ten tall. His clothing was unbuttoned and unzipped to allow for exposure of his genitalia and chest.

'There's a jug thrown onto the sofa, which we'll take for fingerprinting once it's been photographed in situ, but my guess is that it was used to pour water over the body to maximise electrical conductivity. What's left of this man's penis' – she took an implement from her bag and hooked it under the blackened inches of flesh – 'was originally inserted into the toaster before the current was switched to live. With the water, it was easily enough to have killed him. The burns are in line with death by electrocution, as is the splitting of the skin up the groin. His legs were trapped between items of furniture to prevent him from jerking away from the toaster. The other burn points on the body aren't separate injuries, just a side effect of the electricity trying to leave his body.'

Callanach walked to the door of the flat, and inspected the locks and surfaces.

'No damage,' he said. 'Just like at Fenella Hawksmith's place. Whoever did this was let in without a fight.'

One of the tech officers handed Ailsa a passport.

'Here we go. Looks like the victim is Osaki Shozo, twenty-six years of age. He's wearing a wedding ring and I noticed two pairs of women's shoes in the corner. We'll need his wife to attend the mortuary to formally identify the body.'

'I'll get straight on it,' Ava said.

'You'd better,' Ailsa said. 'Whoever killed Mr Shozo here is terribly disturbed. This, and what happened to Fenella Hawksmith, is the work of a deeply psychotic mind.'

'The deaths are close together,' Callanach noted. 'Usually there's a longer recovery or planning period, or at least a greater time span when the offender's feeding off reliving the event.'

'Psychopaths need constant stimulation. The more disturbed the mind, the less gratification the perpetrator will take from each violent act,' Ailsa contributed.

'It's about more than that, though,' Ava said. 'Serial killers refine their technique with each murder. They think up new mechanisms to try out. Most criminally active psychopaths regard the murders they commit as a work in progress. A new victim is a blank canvas. Osaki Shozo was an experiment as much as he was an expression of the murderer's vision and capabilities. The question is, what exactly is our killer trying to show off about himself?

'The Fenella Hawksmith scene was emotionally complex. The bindings were not only a practical method of restraint, but they also took away more than the physical ability to fight. It was like an additional punishment, a sign of what was to come. When you render a victim physically helpless, the offender is also expressing their own power.'

'And the toaster?' Callanach asked.

'It's not about the toaster, it's about his penis,' Ava said. 'He's been emasculated, reducing the victim to something less than male.'

'Could it be retributive, maybe following a sexual assault?' Callanach suggested.

'Worth considering, although vigilante beatings are usually marked by a high level of out-of-control violence, typically resulting in multiple punches and kicks. There's one punch to his face but that's it. Overall, this is very controlled, hands-off violence. It's structured.'

'True, but there are cases of women waiting until their partner's asleep or passed-out drunk before cutting off their penis. This could just be a more imaginative version of that,' Callanach said.

'Only the victim died, which negates the point of rendering his penis useless. Women who commit forceful penectomies usually want their victim to be aware of what's happened to him. The payoff is in the emotional damage suffered, as much as the physical loss. It would have been obvious to whoever did this that the victim was likely to die.'

'Penectomy?' Callanach asked.

'Yes. There's actually a word for it,' Ailsa said, shifting position to the victim's head, peeling the tape off his mouth and sealing it in an evidence bag, then prising open his jaws. A chunk of bloodied meat fell out. 'New evidence bag for human tissue,' the pathologist called to a passing tech officer. 'He bit through his tongue. Not uncommon but it's cut clean off. The shock must have been sudden and massive. His heart would have stopped immediately.'

'Which meant the killer chose a method that enabled him or her to enter, do what they wanted and get out fast. Why such a different scenario to Fenella Hawksmith?' Ava mused.

189

'He or she is adaptable. Mrs Hawksmith lived alone. Lock the door, don't answer, they were never going to be disturbed. Here, there was the possibility that the wife might come home for an unforeseen reason,' Callanach said.

'It's my fuckin' flat. You can't tell me I'm not allowed to go in!'

A woman pushed between two officers, tripping on a tech bag and literally falling into the lounge.

Ava and Callanach both lurched forwards in an effort to shield the woman from the charred body on the floor, but too late. She was screaming before Ava could reach out a hand to her. Ailsa grabbed a sterile sheet from a quick-thinking SOCO and covered Osaki Shozo's shocking state.

'Oh my God!' she screeched. 'Osaki? Oh! Holy fuck, that can't be real. What happened to my husband?'

A man burst through, all bulging biceps and amateur tattoos.

'Kylie? Let me see my girlfriend!' he shouted into the face of the uniformed officer attempting unsuccessfully to restrain him.

'It's a crime scene,' Ailsa sighed softly in Ava's direction.

'Everyone out except SOCOs,' Ava shouted. 'Ma'am, I appreciate you're distressed. We're going to move you to somewhere we can talk.'

She nodded to the team of officers, who were now crowded at the flat entrance, suddenly in the vicinity, having been nowhere useful when the entrance to the flat should have been under guard. It took three of them to remove the posturing male, and another two to get the sobbing woman to her feet and out into the corridor.

'If that's the wife, then why is another man calling her his girlfriend?' Callanach asked Ava.

'Maybe the marriage was part of a cash-for-immigration-papers deal,' Ava offered.

'Perhaps, but her reaction was more personal than professional.

If that was a business deal, she'd have been off the hook with a dead pseudo-husband and free to offer her services elsewhere.'

'Could you two continue this outside, do you think?' Ailsa cut in. 'We now have additional scene processing to undertake and it's time we made the deceased more comfortable.'

Ava and Callanach obliged. They found the woman in a police van outside the entrance to the flat. Her boyfriend – the need to follow proper procedure having finally occurred to the uniformed officers – was being held separately. Ava introduced herself and asked the woman's name.

'Kylie Shozo,' she sniffed, accepting the bundle of tissues being offered by a policewoman.

'Can you confirm who the deceased is?'

'That's my husband, Osaki. What in the name of Christ happened to him?' She blew her nose noisily and dropped the tissues to the floor of the van.

'Osaki Shozo?' Ava clarified.

'Obviously,' Kylie replied with an open-mouthed frown. 'Was it an accident?'

'That seems unlikely, I'm afraid. When did you last see your husband?'

'He was here this morning when we left. Everything was normal. Who did that to him?'

'We don't know yet. I was hoping you might be able to tell us if your husband was in any trouble or had enemies?'

'Osaki?' She laughed then sobbed. 'Not likely. He never said boo to a bloody goose. Am I going to lose my flat over this? Will I get kicked out because he's gone and died?'

Ava folded her arms and made herself count to five.

'Mrs Shozo, your husband is the victim of a crime. There will need to be a postmortem. The body will be released to you for burial when a criminal investigation has been success-fully completed.'

'Oh, that's just great. I can't afford to pay for his funeral. That stuff's expensive. I didn't ask for any of . . .'

'Who were you referring to when you said "we" left this morning?' Ava cut in.

Kylie stuck her chin in the air. 'Beef.'

'Presumably Beef is the gentleman who entered the flat after you?'

'That's right. And my private life's none of your business, you snooty bitch.' Kylie took a pack of cigarettes from her pocket and shoved a stick in her mouth.

'You can't light that in a police van, but you're at liberty to smoke it outside,' Ava told her. 'Did you have a conversation with your husband before you and Beef left this morning?'

'No. He was in the bedroom.'

'Can you describe your current relationship with your husband?'

'Are you stupid?' Kylie laughed.

'Apparently,' Ava mumbled. 'Look, Mrs Shozo, we'll need to take you and – sorry, does Beef have a real name?'

'Sheldon,' Kylie said quietly.

That explained the use of the nickname then, Ava thought.

'You and Sheldon will have to come to the police station, give statements, and provide fingerprints and DNA samples to be excluded from other evidence at the crime scene if you've both been at the flat recently. We'll also need to establish your movements yesterday and today. We'll need contact details for his family, too.'

'Tokyo. I'm not phoning to tell them about this.' She lit the cigarette anyway.

Ava opened the van door to release the smoke.

'That's fine. We'll contact the Japanese embassy. So, help me understand. Very briefly, you and your husband were separated but still sharing a flat. How did he feel about that?'

'He just frigging cried. Not in front of me, mind, but I heard him locked in the bathroom. For a while he tried to persuade me to stick with it, you know, but he couldn't get work. We never went out or had any fun. He's some sort of computer geek, yeah? When I first met him, I thought he'd be able to get a good job here that'd pay a ton. No point marrying someone who isn't going to pay the bills, right? So I said yes when he proposed, got him a bloody visa and what happened? I ended up forkin' out for all the rent, the bills and basically looking after him. Can you believe that?'

'It must have been difficult for you both,' was the most diplomacy Ava could muster. 'So, how did you meet Beef?'

'He's the captain of the darts team at my local. Beef's in construction. Should've stuck to my own from the start. Serves me right for trying something new, I guess.'

Ava moved to exit the van.

'I did love Osaki, for a while, anyway.'

Ava paused to listen.

'When we first met, you know? He was kind and sweet, sort of exotic. I loved listening to him talk in Japanese. Did you never meet anyone like that? Who just seemed so completely different to anyone else you'd ever known that you just got carried away with it all?'

Ava didn't have an answer for that.

'Will you be able to tell me if he had life insurance?' Kylie finished.

Ava left uniformed officers to deal with the appalling Kylie. She'd thought it impossible to feel any more sympathy for Osaki Shozo than when she'd first seen his body, but the real-isation that his life must have been just as miserable as his horrific death was gutting.

Chapter Twenty-One

11 March

Five fifty-four in the morning and he hadn't slept a wink. He never did after a kill. His body was thrumming, laid on sweat-stained sheets and a mattress that had accommodated increasing amounts of solitary celebration, so much so that its owner was planning on purchasing himself a new one directly following his next salvage operation.

He was the ultimate recycler, the embodiment of green energy, taking the life source of people who'd squandered it and recharging himself, coming out stronger, enhanced from the process.

A crow outside his window shattered the peace. A couple of minutes later a different window opened, accompanied by some colourful cursing. An object was thrown. It landed with a hollow metallic twang, suggesting an empty can. The crow was silent for a moment before recommencing its cawing, laughing at the ridiculous attempt to silence it. Predatory by nature, its feeding and hunting patterns were no different than foxes. Crows would eat eggs and nestlings, even adult birds given half a chance, soaking up the life force of their prey, consuming them, merging with them. It was the circularity of nature.

Life. Not death. He loved animals. Animals fought to survive. They strove to mate, to eat and to protect their young. They never gave in. Not like humans. People were self-obsessed, victims of their own evolution, inward-looking. He wondered exactly when homo sapiens had stopped responding to their environment and started living inside their own heads. They ate pity for breakfast, lunch and dinner. They dissected their emotions as if they were living on the set of a reality TV show. They valued the gift of a life so little that throwing it away had become a nothing. An Internet challenge. A modern-media bedpost notch. Those weak souls were aberrations.

He rose and went to the window. The crow, perched on the top of a tree that was never going to sprout new leaves, no matter how well spring progressed, cawed again, flapping its wings grandly. Swivelling a glassy, soulless eye, it stared back in through the window. There was a moment of connection. A revelation.

He and the crow were one.

Shuffling sideways to a cupboard, careful not to disturb the bird from its perch − not that it seemed likely the crow would fly away, they shared too much natural courage for that − he took out a pellet gun. It was already loaded. You couldn't be too careful living in a city. The gun had an impressive sight mounted on it, even though the power of it didn't justify the expense, but now the lens came into its own.

Raising the gun slowly, sliding it into the hollow between his shoulder and collarbone, he took aim. The bird's head was too small a target, but its breast would work, too. Breathing in, holding the air in his lungs, he let himself relax slowly, blowing out and counting five seconds in his head.

The crow opened its beak to disturb the peace but no sound was released. Instead, there was a soft wallop as the pellet forced the bird off its perch. It tumbled, hitting three or four other branches as it dropped, coming to rest on an abandoned fast-food box on the ground. No fuss. It was a dignified ending, the man thought, realising he needed to get dressed before he could retrieve the body. Time was of the essence.

Throwing on jeans and a hoodie, he took the stairs down past the other apartments and entered the shared garden quietly. He was always careful not to attract attention from the neighbours and being spotted removing the carcass of a dead bird from the garden wouldn't be a good way to start. He still had the cover of some darkness though, ruined as it was by light pollution from nearby buildings and roads.

Slipping the crow into a plastic bag, he shook his head sadly for the benefit of anyone who might be watching and curious. He'd gone out to see what had happened, he rehearsed to himself, and found the bird, taking it indoors to care for it, wrongly believing it to be stunned not dead. He practised versions of events all the time. You never knew when the unexpected was going to strike and he was taking greater risks these days. Greater risks, greater rewards. Greater power.

Taking the stairs silently – he'd practised that, too – he locked his door and unwrapped the crow in his kitchen. It was a thing of beauty. The ultimate in design, made for flight and hunting, the bird sang louder to him now than it ever could have done in life.

He ran his forefinger along the beak, checking its sharpness, admiring the aerodynamics that started at its tip and ran the length of the body. He held it until the last of the warmth seeped from the carcass into his hands, then he began to pluck it – a longer and more complex procedure than he'd imagined. It was lucky he had the day off.

Wings and tail first, the easy bits, then the back and stomach, which was more difficult in such a small bird. He wanted it all, would have preferred it intact, but in the end he had to compromise with the head. Removing it with a single chop from a kitchen knife, he sat the bird's watchful skull on top of the cactus on his kitchen windowsill. Perhaps the bird had a right to see what was happening.

Slitting from throat to belly, he removed the entrails then took off the legs. After that, he heated butter, sea salt and garlic in a frying pan, dropping the crow in once it was good and hot.

Cooking it took no time at all. Arranging it on a plate so he could still make out the shape of the creature, he sat cross-legged on the sanded floorboards and breathed deeply of the same air the crow had breathed until only an hour earlier. He looked through the window at the same sky the crow had flown. He listened to the wind in the tree the crow had used for a perch.

The first bite was ecstasy. It didn't matter that the meat was stringy, or that the taste was unsettlingly like goat's cheese. It was life. Life so recently being lived that he could feel its essence sliding down inside him. His transition to crow was complete. He was the crow, and every life it had ever consumed.

All the tiny birds fluttered inside him.

He was evolving at superspeed. He understood the very nature of nature.

That made him laugh. Then laugh again. Laugh so long and hard his sides hurt. He felt lighter than air, as if he could fly. He was a predator. A hunter. But not without purpose. He would consume only to improve his own strength, to live longer and become the best possible version of himself. He understood how precious life was. It wasn't wrong to punish the people who toyed with it and took it for granted. It was justice. More than that. It was necessary to exterminate them.

Now that he'd found himself in the crow and become one with the world, he'd be an unstoppable force in upholding nature's laws.

Chapter Twenty-Two

11 March

Ava stared at the screen. There were few classic films that she couldn't enjoy, but being out of the station on enforced down-time, knowing the best she could hope for was to lie in bed staring at the ceiling while her clock ticked the minutes away, was far worse than the exhaustion she was feeling.

Fenella Hawksmith was dead. Her daughter had been located and she had an airtight alibi. They had no leads.

Osaki Shozo was dead. His wife and her companion, Beef, were off the hook, their every minute having been accounted for by a variety of witnesses. The only caveat was if they'd paid for a hitman, but to no purpose. Kylie Shozo stood to make no money from her husband's death and it wasn't as if he'd been limiting her movements. Quite the opposite, given that the only information they'd discovered was that Osaki was due to disappear on board a fishing trawler. The wife's reaction, however disgusting Ava may have found it, was also completely genuine. No doubt about that.

Then there was the quandary of Stephen Berry's death, just that one tiny boot print on his finger. No obvious link to the other two. No real evidence of foul play. Yet, Ava just couldn't get it out of her head – three bodies, no answers.

Then there was the Pax Graham investigation and Luc still hadn't got an answer from his mother about what she intended to do regarding the inheritance Bruce Jenson had left to the rape charity. The victim's son, Andrew, had finally produced video evidence from a casino proving he'd spent his previously unaccounted for hours there, trying to win back some of the vast amounts of money he owed the house. That was him off the hook, and there were no other suspects in sight.

Ava sighed. A single decent lead in either case would have been nice. But no. The days were piling up and the issues were getting murkier. Ava was becoming more and more culpable for failing to reveal Luc's interest in the Jenson killing. Now, she'd dragged Luc to a film that was even boring her. It was 10.30 p.m. and the only thing she could contemplate eating was popcorn. So much for promising Ailsa that she'd take care of herself.

'Did anything happen yet?' Callanach asked as he sat down and passed Ava a paper bowl brimming with hot, buttery corn.

'Nothing that's going to make cinematic history.'

A woman several rows in front shushed them dramatically.

'Sorry!' Ava called to her breezily.

'Want to get out of here?' Callanach asked.

'Do I get to bring my popcorn?'

'Back to my place? Only if you promise not to spill it like you usually do halfway through a film.'

'You're no fun. We could get hotdogs as we leave. Make a real night of it,' she grinned.

'How are you so thin?'

He put her coat over her shoulders as she struggled to get up holding the massive carton.

'Stress,' she replied. 'And the lack of an intimate relationship. Being single means I don't have to go through the ups and downs of arguments that lead to unhappiness eating, post-row eating, pre-separation eating, reunification eating. These days my life's very simple. Microwave meals or anything from the deli counter, seven days a week. No man means no snacking. My body is a temple.'

'But what's the point if there's no one worshipping there?'

'Ha ha!' Ava poked him in the ribs.

One viewer, sat alone, not the least bit interested in classic movies, turned away from the screen to watch them go.

They exited onto the street. The cinema in York Place was only a five-minute walk from Callanach's apartment and they wandered slowly across Picardy Place roundabout with Ava waving nonchalantly at the cars that beeped them.

'Have you been stealing cocaine from the evidence room?' Callanach watched her drift casually along the pavement.

'Not yet, but it's an option. I never thought I'd walk into a crime scene where a man had had his penis jammed into a toaster and been electrocuted through it. It's like we're in the twilight zone. It's almost Shakespearean in its drama. The Fenella Hawksmith scene was bad enough, the whole slow death set-up and the violation with the knife. It's all so bizarre, it doesn't seem real. And we're nowhere with it.'

'We've had tough cases before. What's really bothering you about this one?'

Ava stopped, threw her popcorn untouched into a nearby bin and planted her hands on her hips, middle of the pavement, causing several less than sober men singing loudly in bad Italian to find a path around her.

'That,' she pointed after them. 'I don't know if they're friends, or brothers, or members of a football team, but they're connected. Usually we have to avoid family members knocking down our door to demand answers, a prosecution, justice. If not the families then the press is there waiting on every new clue, ratcheting up the tension, stirring public emotion. And yay for us, we've kept the crazy down to a reasonable level this time. The media has yet to link the Hawksmith case with Osaki Shozo, but the cynic in me wonders if they'll be all that bothered.

'Fenella Hawksmith's daughter didn't want to be found and was remarkably blasé about her mother's murder. The lovely Kylie Shozo, who was accommodating both husband and lover in a one-bedroomed flat, was deeply worried by how the murder might affect her tenancy. Does society have victim stereotypes, do you think? Does the public need victim sympathy to come wrapped in the body of a twenty-something woman with smiling photos on social media, with the standard "a life cut short", or "so much potential unfulfilled" bylines? Replace that with an ageing, overweight widow and a Japanese immigrant, and who gives a fuck?

'I worry, Luc. I really worry that bodies don't count as victims unless their skin colour and dress size matches our atrociously low bloody standards.'

Her voice was raised as she finished her sentence.

Callanach waited until she'd taken a breath, then stepped forwards to hug her, holding her tightly for half a minute until he felt her relax in his arms.

'Do you want me to get the popcorn back out of the bin for you?' Callanach asked.

Ava let out a small laugh, dropped her forehead onto his shoulder, then laughed again.

'Am I still standing on my soapbox?' she asked.

'I think you broke it, actually. Come on,' he said, releasing her but taking one of her hands in his and pulling her gently along the street. 'If it's worth anything at all, Rosa – Stephen Berry's former partner – is very concerned indeed. She cares, and one person is just as important as a thousand. Doing justice isn't about crowd-pleasing.'

He slid his key in the communal door and stepped back to let Ava take the stairs first. She waited for him outside his apartment, her back against the wall, fighting tears.

'I know this is going to sound pathetic of me, but it made me wonder who'd miss me.'

Callanach took her by the hand again and pulled her inside.

'Well, anyone who's a massive fan of incredibly high-level self-pity would hold a week-long wake in your honour, but other than that particular cult, then, no, you're probably right. Absolutely no one.'

'Luc, I'm serious. My family decided I was married to the police years ago. These days they ask what's wrong if I turn up at any of their houses. The squad looks at me with a mixture of suspicion and resignation when I walk into the incident room. Sooner or later, Natasha's going to hook up with some gorgeous woman who'll both make her laugh and put up with her terrible taste in music, and then she won't have any use for me at all. And you. . .' Callanach took her coat from her shoulders and threw it on the dining table. 'I'm pretty sure one day soon you'll sod off back to France. You'll recover from the trauma you went through and know you can't really be happy anywhere else. You'll long for the sunshine and the vineyards, and you'll pack your bags and leave me. What am I going to do without you?'

'Ava, I'm not going anywhere. Here, I'll prove it to you.' He unwound the door key from his own keyring, took Ava's from her coat pocket and slid it on there instead. 'Have I convinced you now?'

'Idiot,' she laughed. 'I don't need your key.'

'Keep it anyway. Unlike you, I actually know where my spare is. It's not like you ever take no for an answer when you decide you're coming round. Seriously, why would you think I'm going to leave?'

He took two glasses from a shelf and opened the bottle of Balvenie whisky he'd been saving for one of her visits.

'Why would you stay? It's cold. You hate the cold. And it rains so much, the Scots have evolved to be almost amphibious. Then there's Bruce Jenson's death. Just when you thought you'd left all the horrors of your past behind, it crops up again. I haven't been the best of friends, either. I've interfered in your life . . .'

'Trying to do what you thought was right,' Callanach added.

'I've cut you out of my life without explaining why . . .'

'Trying to protect me,' he said.

'And I've been jealous rather than supportive. I'm ashamed of myself. Maybe if I'd been more grown-up about Selina, you two would still be together. She was good for you and I couldn't bring myself to spend so much as a single evening with the two of you. I'm so sorry.'

Ava slumped back on the couch, frowning uncharacteristically. Callanach sat on the arm, swirling half an inch of whisky around the bottom of his glass.

'Jealous?' he asked. 'Of what, exactly?'

'I don't know. Of Selina having you all to herself. I suppose I'd started to think of you as mine. That's ridiculous, right? We work together all day, I spend more hours with you than most married couples, and yet those evenings when we walked away from work and were just friends kept me going. Having dinner, spending hours talking rubbish over coffee on a Saturday morning, watching films at 2 a.m. Then suddenly there was someone else in your life, and I hated it. God, this is dreadful. Apparently, feeling morbid also makes me horribly honest. I intend to get drunk. Call me a cab before 2 a.m., okay?'

'Why didn't you talk to me about it before now? We've always been able to discuss anything.'

'Oh, right, silly me. I should have just called you into my office, forgetting the uncomfortable fact that I'm your boss, and said, "Hey, Luc, could you ditch the beautiful, leggy Spanish doctor. I'm feeling a bit put out by her." Because that would have been an easy conversation to have had.'

'Does it help for me to tell you I felt the same when you were with Joe? I hated him from the start and that had virtually nothing to do with the fact that he was a pretentious, arrogant bastard. All I could see was that he took you away from me.'

Ava tossed back the whisky, pushed the glass onto the coffee table and covered her face with her hands.

'Really? You had to bring up Joe? What was I thinking? That just proves the point – my private life really is an unmitigated disaster. Always has been. Catch a vicious psychopath? Sure, no problem. Find a decent man to wake up with in the morning? Fails the course, last in her class, displays no natural aptitude.'

'I think you're being a bit hard on yourself,' he laughed.

'Make up your mind. I thought my speciality was self-pity.' Ava poured herself another measure of Balvenie.

They sat in silence, appreciating the skill that went into blending the Scotch, glancing at one another occasionally.

Callanach sighed deeply then smiled. 'You want some painful honesty? I can beat you hands down. I never slept with Selina. Not once, in all the months we were together.'

Ava stopped her glass halfway to her mouth, staring at it as if it were alive.

'I'm sorry, what?' she asked eventually.

'It's true. I mean, we did other stuff, I'm no monk, but there was no – I forget the English word – consume?'

'Consummation,' Ava corrected him.

He reached into his trouser pocket and pulled out the crumpled pack of Gauloises cigarettes he carried with him everywhere as a testament to his smoking days. Ava smiled as he shoved an unlit stick into his mouth, tasting tobacco without the satisfaction – or danger – of breathing smoke in and out.

'Why not?' Ava asked.

'One of the things I like best about you is how you say whatever's on your mind,' Callanach grinned.

'You mean I have no filter,' Ava smiled back.

'I mean you're exactly who you seem to be. No pretence, no show. You wouldn't know how to be deceitful if your life depended on it. I, on the other hand, have learned to lie. First to myself, then to the people I love.' He lowered himself off the arm of the sofa and down next to Ava, propping his feet on the coffee table. 'I'm impotent, Ava. I have been since Astrid accused me of rape. I've tried therapy, medication and a gorgeous, leggy Spanish doctor. I'm broken. You're the only person who makes me forget about it. No stress or pressure when I'm with you. Just reality, true emotion, open conversation. So no, I'm not thinking about going back to France, where all this began. The only place I want to be is right here, with you.'

Ava turned to face him, arms folded.

'What the genuine fuck?' she rebuked. 'You've been going through this since the day I met you and you didn't let me in?'

'Ava!' Callanach said, incredulous. 'How could I possibly have . . .'

'You really are a bloody idiot,' Ava told him, taking his face in both of her hands and leaning forwards, pressing her lips against his, letting her body slide into his chest.

She pulled away thirty seconds later, red-faced and breathless.

'Um, I'm not sure what to say. I shouldn't have done that. Listen, I'm leaving, and I'll understand if tomorrow you . . .'

Callanach reached one arm around her waist and slid his free hand around her neck.

'Shut up,' he said softly, lifting her from where she sat and onto his lap, pulling her face back down to meet his, parting Ava's lips with his own.

She pushed her fingers into his dark, curly hair, pressing her body against him, feeling his warmth as she let her tongue drift slowly along his lower lip before pulling away slightly to stare into his eyes.

'Seriously?' she asked quietly. 'Of all the women you could have, why would you want me?'

'Because if I can't have you, I don't want anyone at all. Seriously.'

He pulled her hair back slowly to expose her throat, running his tongue from the dip at the base of her throat between her collarbones and up the soft underside of her jaw, before releasing her so she could meet his kiss once more.

Ava grinned, exploring his body beneath his shirt, feeling his tensed muscles moving in waves beneath her hands, tendons flexing and releasing. She ran her short, ever-practical nails over the hills and valleys of his upper body, delighted with herself as he arched and breathed out heavily.

'Ava, are you sure about this? I don't want you to regret it,' he mumbled, undoing the top buttons of her shirt and kissing the smooth skin between her breasts.

'I trust you more than I've ever trusted any man in my life, and regret is a word male politicians use when they get caught cheating on their wives. Could you finish taking my shirt off now, please? It's getting a bit hot in here.'

Callanach did as she asked, sitting back to look at her

appreciatively while she fumbled with his buttons, balancing on the edge of the couch and kissing at the same time.

'This isn't working,' Callanach said.

'What? I thought . . .'

'Not enough space on the couch was all I meant,' Callanach clarified, sliding his hands beneath her buttocks and lifting her up with him as he stood and walked towards the bedroom, banging his shins on the coffee table then grazing Ava's back on the doorframe.

'Are you always this clumsy?' she laughed.

'Only when I'm carrying a woman who won't stay still and is in my line of vision. Watch out!'

He dropped her unceremoniously onto his bed and watched her roll about on his duvet.

'God, this is the best duvet ever. It's like landing in clouds. How is it possible that you have a six-pack, TV hair and also the best bedding in the universe? You're never staying over at my place. In fact, I may have to kill you and take over your apartment.'

'Or you could just stay here with me and never bother to go home again,' he suggested, climbing onto the bed beside her and stretching out. 'You're so beautiful. You don't even realise it, do you?'

'Knock it off, poster boy. There's only room for one super-model inside MIT and you win that prize.'

Callanach rolled on top of her, brushing hair from her eyes and smiling down at her.

'Well then, you won't be able to resist me, will you?'

'Resist you? What exactly did you have in mind?' Ava raised her eyebrows.

He slid a hand beneath her back and under her bra, slipping it from her shoulders.

'Why don't you relax and let me show you?' he whispered,

letting his hand drift down her stomach, his thumb circling the soft skin directly above the button of her jeans. 'Explain to me why we waited so long to do this.'

'That's easy,' Ava said, lacing her fingers beneath her head and sighing happily. 'It's because I'm worth waiting for.'

'I'm not going to disagree with that,' he grinned, flicking the button open and kissing her again, teasing her lips with his teeth as he ran a warm hand over her breasts. 'But I'm glad you didn't make me wait any longer. I wasn't sure my sanity was going to hold out.'

Moving down, he ran his tongue along the vertical pathway over her stomach, pulling her body up to meet his. Ava let her head fall backwards, loving the heat of his mouth on her body. Millimetre by millimetre, he pulled her jeans over her hips, exposing simple black cotton panties and the whiteness of her thighs. Throwing the denim to the floor, he man-oeuvred himself between her legs, gently nibbling the sculpted hipbones that defined her sides, running his fingertips back and forth over her thighs. Ava relaxed back onto the bed, her neck tipped upwards, her right hand playing in Callanach's hair.

'I suppose I should ask if you'll still respect me in the morning, or something like that,' she murmured.

Callanach replied in French – something incomprehensible but Ava got the general idea – as he slipped her panties down and tossed them aside.

'Thank God. Did I finally get you to stop talking?' he asked, running his tongue up the inside of her leg.

'That's kind of rude of you,' Ava laughed.

'You think that was rude? Give me another minute.'

Ava gasped as Callanach's fingers found the most tender part of her, playing gently between her legs, circling up and around her clitoris, keeping his touch silky and light as he maintained the pressure enough to have her melting back into the bed. He followed his fingers with his tongue.

'Oh my God,' Ava groaned. 'Don't ever stop.'

'Not even to take my jeans off?' Callanach asked, getting to his feet, hands on hips, staring down at her naked body.

'Okay, I'll accept you stopping to take the rest of your clothes off,' Ava smiled. 'Just don't be long.'

'Other than that,' he said, 'I don't think I ever want to leave this apartment again. Not as long as you're here with me, anyway.' He climbed onto the bed, one knee between her legs, the other to the side. 'Say you'll stay.'

'The night?' Ava grinned.

'You know I mean for longer than that,' he replied, kissing her neck and lying on his side next to her. 'Promise me.'

'Hey, you know what?' Ava stared into his eyes as her fingers made a trail down the ripples of his stomach. 'That problem you thought you had? I honestly don't think you have to worry about it any more.'

She wrapped her hand around his penis, gripping the hard length of it, pulling gently, leaving him breathless, gritting his teeth to control his reaction to the long overdue pleasure.

'It was you I was waiting for,' Callanach said. 'Ava, I've imagined this so many times. I just never thought it was going to happen.'

'Don't admit that!' she grinned. 'What happened to your cool, collected, sexy man-of-mystery routine?'

He kissed her gently, parting her lips, taking his hand back down between her legs, slipping his fingers gently inside her as she rolled over, thrusting towards him.

'I met you,' he said, pulling away from her lips to stare into her eyes. 'That's what happened.'

Sliding his free arm beneath her neck, he pushed her onto her back, covering her with his body, every inch of his skin caressing hers, pressing, pulsating together.

Ava pushed back, taking her time lifting herself upwards, forcing him onto his back, sitting astride him, watching his face as she explored his body.

'Sorry to break the moment,' she said softly, 'but given that it's been – oh God – longer than I can even remember since I had sex, I'm not on the pill. Do you have anything?'

'If it helps, it's been even longer for me.'

'Sorry, that was insensitive of me,' she smiled.

'No problem. And I do. Apparently, I never gave up hope. They're on the very bottom shelf of my bathroom cupboard underneath the sink. Let me get them . . .'

'You'll stay right there,' Ava said. 'Exactly where I want you.'

'Okay, but I'm only giving you sixty seconds. Any longer than that and I'm coming to get you.'

Ava leaned over and kissed him playfully before bounding into the bathroom, the smile on her face testament to the unforeseen joy of finally allowing herself to both accept and acknowledge how she felt about Callanach. The last time she'd used his en suite, she could still kid herself that what she'd felt was purely platonic. Natasha's stirring had given her pause, though, and while before she'd always been able to laugh it off, she knew something had changed.

When Callanach had split up with Selina, Ava had felt something close to relief. When he'd saved her life and they'd spent the night together in his bed, it had been like coming home. Not just to his comfortable apartment, but to the warmth of him and the ease she felt around him. Largely ease. There had always been flashes of something else that she'd been careful to leave unexplored in her imagination. Moments when he'd put his arms around her and she hadn't wanted him to let go. Times when they'd been thrown together in danger and yet it had never really occurred to her that anything bad would happen when Callanach was there.

Pausing, Ava looked at herself in his bathroom mirror, running a hand through her messy hair and trying to calm the grin that seemed utterly childlike. Hard for anyone else to realise in the middle of investigations, where every day brought new talk of death and violence, that you had to go home and live. Really live. When you were witness to so much loss, the only antidote was to fill every moment with value.

'Do you need a map?' Callanach shouted.

'Hey, I'm worth waiting for!' she laughed.

'White cupboard, bottom shelf beneath the sink. If you're much longer I'll fall asleep.'

'It'll be your loss if you do,' she said, pulling both cupboard doors open and dropping to her knees, unable to make out what was what for the towels, bottles and boxes of toiletries packed in there. 'At least now I know why this place seems so tidy. It's because you've shoved literally every piece of rubbish into this cupboard. Are you sure they're here?'

As she ran a hand underneath the pile of towels, Ava's fingertips grazed a rough, cold surface. Curious, without thinking, she grabbed and pulled.

For a few moments she sat in silence, unmoving. Even in the dim light, she recognised what she was holding immediately.

'Ava, did you find them?' Callanach called.

She opened her mouth to reply, but words were suddenly too complex to form. In the bedroom, she could hear him shifting on the bed, his feet hitting the floor. Additional light spilled into the bathroom, illuminating the child's prayer slate she was holding.

On the circular grey slate, six or so inches in diameter, a traditional Celtic prayer had been painted in a beautiful swirling calligraphy. The prayer was one she'd whispered before sleep for as long as she'd been able to read. Regardless of the fact that puberty had seen the rejection of her parents' chosen

211

church, the slate had remained in her bedside table throughout her adult life. A fragment of comfort, of simplicity, memories of an easier time.

It had registered in the back of her mind that she hadn't seen it for . . . what? Months, years? But life was too busy to spend time looking for stray items that would inevitably have been pushed to the back of a cupboard. It had never occurred to her that it might have been taken without her knowledge.

'Seriously, let a woman into your bathroom and she won't come out for hours. I knew I should have gone to look for them myse. . .'

The end of the word died on the lips that had been kissing her just minutes ago. The lips she'd thought would never issue lies. The man she'd trusted, always, since the day they'd met. Until now.

'This is mine,' she whispered. 'What's it doing in your bathroom, hidden?'

'Ava, damn, I'm so sorry, I meant to give that back to you ages ago, I just didn't know how,' Callanach said, getting to his knees next to her and putting an arm across her shoulders.

She pulled a few inches away. 'I assumed I'd misplaced it. I thought I was just disorganised. You know me. I can catch a killer but never find the pair of shoes I'm looking for. It never dawned on me that anyone would take something so incredibly personal. Something obviously from my childhood. Why would you do that?'

Running her fingers over the rough surface of the slate, she recalled her father's face when he'd given it to her. It was a sweet gift, innocent. The very definition of a treasure.

'Ava, it all happened such a long time ago. When I first joined Police Scotland and you got me into line, forced me to accept a friend. Then you were abducted with the other women and I had no idea if you were alive or dead. I felt responsible.

I was a wreck. I visited your house to make sure we hadn't missed something or to see if there were signs of a struggle. While I was there, I accepted the truth about what had happened to you. I was at a low point. The squad was making no progress with the case. We had no way of knowing where you'd been taken. The items I took were just a way of maintaining emotional contact, of figuring out where you might be. . .'

'What do you mean?' Ava frowned at him.

'There was a void in me after I left France – it was hard to feel anything at all – so I suppose I was looking for an attachment . . .'

'No, not that. I get that's how you're justifying this, but you said items. Plural.'

Callanach stared at the bottom shelf of his bathroom cupboard. The day Ava was kidnapped during a case the previous year could have been yesterday. Still just as raw. When he'd taken the slate from her flat, it was meant to be a temporary thing. Even then he wasn't sure why he'd done it.

Ava leaned forwards, pulling any remaining items in her way from the shelf onto the floor. A couple of bottles smashed and cotton buds stuck in the viscous liquid spreading around her knees. Finally, reaching to the very back, she drew out a paperweight and a globe keyring.

'These had better not be what I think they are,' Ava said, her voice pitched at a dangerous level of quiet.

'You don't understand.'

'You sound surprised about that. You think I should be more understanding about what I'm holding in my hands? Psychopaths take trophies, Luc, not police officers. These things belong to victims, women who were kidnapped and tortured. What exactly did this paperweight tell you about the crime and how to solve it?' She stood up, still naked, hands on hips, purple-faced.

'I'm not going to pretend it made sense. Please, come back to bed, let's talk about this calmly.'

'Are you fucking kidding? You want to talk about this calmly? Do you have any idea how badly you've invaded my privacy and broken my trust?'

'While you were being held captive, it was the closest I could get . . .'

'How many times have you been to my house since then? You've had endless opportunities to return it to me.'

'It wasn't that easy.'

'Yes, it was!' she thundered, grabbing a towel from the rail and wrapping it around herself. 'Even if it was hard giving it back, why the hell are you still in possession of the other items? Do you take them out and look at them? Do you think about what happened to us? Reginald King killed at least three women and ruined the lives of the two who survived, and here you are with mine and their possessions secreted in the bottom of your bathroom cabinet. It's like you want to be able to remind yourself of it.'

'You know that's not true.'

'Honestly, I have no idea what to think. Ten minutes ago I'd have sworn I knew you as well as I know myself. I'd have staked my career on you being as honest and straightforward as anyone I've ever met. God, I am literally currently staking my career on that! Even if I could accept your relationship with me as an explanation for having the slate, the other two women were taken first. Why take their belongings? Mine was just a continuation of the pattern. It's just . . . I don't even know what it is. Fucking creepy, if I'm honest.'

'Don't do this, you know you can trust me . . .'

'What did you do with it, my slate?' she asked softly.

'Come on, Ava, this is out of context.'

'I'm serious. Has it been in here the whole time?'

'That's insane. I didn't know what I was doing when I took those things. They're shoved in the bottom of a cupboard because I was trying to forget I ever took them. You know it's standard procedure to go through a missing person's belongings when they're taken.'

'Bullshit,' she said. 'You knew who'd kidnapped me. If there was any doubt about it, relevant items would have been put into evidence, not sneaked back here to your bedroom without any authority at all. Is this part of some bizarre fantasy where you play the hero? You rescue me, know everything about me, making it easier to seduce me?'

'That's not fair. I didn't plan this and you know it, and I sure as hell didn't target you. You're here willingly, remember? It's not like I dragged you through the front door.'

'Of course not. You're Luc Callanach. You don't have to drag women anywhere. They throw themselves at you like mindless bloody dolls. Well, apologies for being so predictable and pathetic.'

She barged past him and strode into the bedroom, gathering clothes as she went before marching into the lounge to get dressed.

'Don't leave. We have to sort this out, Ava, not least because we still have to work together and we're in the middle of an investigation.'

'I'm professional enough to be able to work with you without being overcome by my feelings and turning to jelly every time you walk into a room, so I'll be fine.'

'What about me? Do you really not care at all how I feel?' he asked, arms folded, still naked, leaning against the doorframe as she dragged on her boots.

'I'm going to pretend you didn't just say that,' she said. 'Those other items need to be returned to the women you took them from. Do you want me to do that, or are you going to sort out your own crap?'

'I'll do it first thing in the morning,' he said. 'Listen, you can't drive. I'll sleep on the couch, you can take the bed. Tomorrow, we can try to put this right . . .'

'Tomorrow, I'll have my head straight and I'll be at my desk trying to solve five different murders. I suggest you do the same.' She switched on her mobile. 'I'm calling a cab. Thanks for the legal advice. I can wait for it just fine outside.'

Snatching up her slate from the floor, she shoved it in her coat pocket and made for the door.

'Ava,' Callanach said quietly. 'This can't be over. I made a mistake. A huge mistake that looks weird, I know, but really it's just reflective of the crisis I was going through when I arrived in Scotland. I'm hoping you'll see it for what it really is when you're less angry.'

'You don't get it, do you? Trust is *everything* to me and of all the people who should get that, it's you. We weren't just colleagues. I thought we were friends. We had each other's backs. Natasha might have known me longer than anyone else, but you. . . I let you see every vulnerable part of myself. I held nothing back from you, Luc. Nothing. And I find you're keeping secrets like this . . .

'You think this just looks superficially weird? I'm a fucking expert in weird. I deal with it every day at work. I looked it in the eyes when I was held captive. You know what I don't need? I don't need even more goddamn weird in my personal life when I'm in the bedroom of a man who I thought was my rock, when I'm looking for condoms – condoms, of all frigging things! – in the bathroom cabinet of the man I thought that maybe I was in love with!'

She turned, ripped the door opened and slammed it closed behind her.

Chapter Twenty-Three

12 March

Callanach rose early and boxed the objects Ava had discovered in his bathroom cabinet. He left the paperweight at Elaine Buxton's parents' house, where she'd returned to live after her kidnapping ordeal had left her law career in tatters and her confidence destroyed. The globe keyring was small enough to slip through the Reverend Jayne Magee's letter box in an envelope. She'd managed to return to work a few weeks after Luc had found Elaine, Ava and her locked in a secret basement.

Other women had died. The memories – and the thought of what would have happened if he hadn't got there when he did – still left him feeling nauseous. Slipping a note into each box, he'd white-lied about the evidence store finding a few items that had slipped the net after the investigation. It wasn't great, but it would have to do.

It was still only 8 a.m. He would have to make his way into the station sooner or later, but right then later seemed like the preferable option. Lance rang as he was sitting in his car, sipping espresso and contemplating the fact that at least his day couldn't get any worse.

'Just catching up,' was Lance's opener. 'How're you doing?'

'I screwed up,' Callanach said.

'Everyone screws up. Anything specific?'

Callanach sighed. 'Yes, but nothing that I want to talk about now.'

'I could cook you dinner tonight, 7 p.m. at mine? I know it's fashionable to eat later but at my age, eating late in the evening is about as comfortable as having sex when your mother-in-law's visiting.'

'I don't think so, Lance. I'm not in the mood to socialise. Was there anything else?'

'Isn't there always? Raincheck on dinner then, but I still need to call in one of those many favours you owe me. A young Japanese man died under strange circumstances, only there's not been much information released to the press yet, at least not by the police. The man's widow, however, possibly less than sober, decided to make an impromptu statement during a lock-in at her local pub at about midnight last night. Her version of events is disturbing, to say the least. I was wondering if you could maybe shed some light on what she's claiming?'

'Oh hell.' Callanach crumpled his empty cup and wondered if Ava had found out yet. She would be at her desk by now – 8 a.m. was late by her usual working standards. 'What did Mrs Shozo say?'

'From what I could gather, she was hoping to raise funds to cover the expenses she was incurring by being locked out of her flat which is still a crime scene and then she elaborated with a few almost unintelligible sentences about her husband being killed with a toaster. Most of what she said made little sense, but she managed to get her account details correct several times while she was speaking. She also referred any questions about how people could help, to someone she called her manager; although it looked to me as if his management style was at the personal rather than professional end of the spectrum.'

'Would that be someone called Beef by any chance?' Callanach asked.

'So, you're up to date with the case. Fortunately, in spite of the not terribly grief-stricken Mrs Shozo bombarding every media outlet with an invitation, very few of Edinburgh's finest journalists bothered to attend at the pub last night, but there were at least four of us who were serious about getting the details and the rest will have picked up the story by now. So, why the radio silence from the police if this was a murder?'

'It's off the record, Lance. You'll have to go through the media liaison officer if you want something you can print,' Callanach said, starting the engine. It was freezing and the inside of the windows were misting over.

'Just give me something I can follow up and pretend it was through my own genius deduction,' Lance joked.

'Shozo had no known enemies. No debts that we're aware of. No criminal history or dubious acquaintances. In fact, he had a job offer and was about to leave the mainland for a while.'

'That pretty much reflects what his widow said last night. So you could do with some help, right? Anyone who knew him, or who could give you a better idea about his last movements, how he might have attracted the attention of the wrong person.'

'Yes, but you'll have to be careful. Mrs Shozo is obviously more interested in talking to the press than she was in talking to us. If you can get hold of her again, see if she'll give you a one-on-one interview – maybe you could use it to do a bigger feature. And as for the toaster, I'm not confirming anything.'

'You're not denying it,' Lance commented.

'I wouldn't recommend that tactic given the day I'm having,' Callanach cautioned him. 'I'll see you soon, okay?'

'That's what you always say. Stay well, Luc. Call if you need me.'

The station was buzzing when Callanach got there at 8.30 a.m. Ava had already issued a document redefining priorities to assess links between Fenella Hawksmith and Osaki Shozo. Tripp was overseeing witnesses on the Shozo case, including door-to-doors in the vicinity of the flat, and trying to trace the purchase of what had turned out to be a brand-new toaster. Superintendent Overbeck had taken over managing public relations, an inevitable task since the merry widow Shozo, had decided to go on a fundraising bender, presumably to finance her new life with Beef. And Callanach had no idea what he was supposed to do. As much as Ava wouldn't want to see him, at some point they were going to have to talk.

He knocked on her office door, waiting to be called in, recognising Sergeant Lively's less than dulcet tones on the other side. It was DI Graham who opened it after a few seconds, moving his huge bulk out of the way to allow Callanach access. Ava stood the other side of her desk, gripping the wood with her fingertips, her teeth clenched so hard Callanach could see the veins standing out in her neck.

'Should I come back later?' Callanach asked.

Ava glared at him.

'Actually, we just came to see the boss about that brake-cutting I told you about,' Lively said, eyes shining, voice booming, completely missing the invisible daggers flying from Ava's side of the room to Callanach's. 'Turns out the driver who'd hired the vehicle was in town for a memorial service. Here's the interesting thing. He'd flown all the way from Spain to pay his respects to another recent victim of crime.'

'Bruce Jenson.' Pax Graham filled in the punch line.

Lively looked deflated.

Callanach glanced at Ava, who was keeping her eyes firmly fixed on Graham.

'What was his name?' Callanach asked.

'Gilroy Western,' Lively said, not to be outdone. 'That car crash was no accident. Brakes cut clean through – not a particularly professional job, though. The amazing thing was that Western got as far as he did and that no one else died.'

Callanach took a deep breath to counteract the sense that there wasn't quite enough oxygen in the room. Jenson and Western both dead. Both murdered, he self-corrected. His mother was in France and no more capable of cold-blooded murder than an innocent child. The thought occurred to him that perhaps there had been other rape victims, other employees' wives. Odd that he'd never considered that possibility before, but now it seemed entirely plausible. How many parties must there have been at the factory in two decades of operating? Jenson and Western had worked together to subdue and assault his mother, after all. What were the chances they hadn't planned such a scheme before or, having got away it, tried it again afterwards?

'Did you know him?' Pax Graham asked quickly.

No time to prepare and that was the way he'd intended it, Callanach thought.

'I spoke to his widow in Spain. She says Western was Bruce Jenson's old business partner,' Graham persisted.

'I knew his name, but I'd never met him myself,' Callanach said.

Pax Graham was looking at Ava as Callanach responded. However oblivious Lively might have been to the atmosphere in the room, Graham was right on it, Callanach realised.

'That's not the best bit,' Lively continued. 'Every other case we've got running might be fucked up right now, but this time whoever cut those brakes also cut themselves. We've got the bastard's blood. If they're on the system, we'll have them in custody within the week.'

Pax Graham wasn't looking quite so jubilant.

'But it's a hire car, so any number of people might be looking under the bonnet on a regular basis. I'm guessing if we swabbed the whole engine we'd get several different DNA samples turning up. We still need to find someone with cause to want both of these men dead. The curious thing is that they've had no contact with one another for years. They're not exactly close friends any more. So whatever links them is from some time in their mutual past.'

'What's the plan moving forward?' Ava asked.

'We're going to interview Gilroy Western's family over the telephone tomorrow and they've already given us permission to search his recent communications, both from his mobile and emails. Apparently, he didn't use social media. There were no witnesses to the brakes being tampered with, which must have been overnight so not entirely unexpected. No CCTV cameras in the street as it's residential, and it was raining. Most people out on neighbouring commercial streets had umbrellas or hoods up, so we won't get an ID that way.'

'Let me know when the DNA result comes in,' Ava said. 'Lively, as you're up to speed on the Gilroy Western case, you can continue to work with DI Graham. I'm transferring Janet Monroe back to the Fenella Hawksmith and Osaki Shozo murders. Agreed?'

Lively and Graham nodded.

'Unless there's anything else, we should all be getting back to work,' Ava added.

'I need a minute,' Callanach said.

'Not a good time. I need to prepare a statement for the

press,' Ava said, sitting down and pulling a notepad out from a drawer.

'It's all right, ma'am, the Evil Overlord is covering that one for you,' Lively grinned.

'Fine. One minute,' Ava said.

'I'd appreciate it if you'd write an addendum statement, just to confirm you never met Gilroy Western,' Graham said quietly as he passed Callanach. 'Crossing the t's given the link to Jenson.'

'Absolutely,' Callanach agreed, meeting Graham's fierce gaze. He was more intelligent than his bulk suggested. The size of him provided almost perfect cover for his acuity. Graham was well aware there was more going on than he was being told. 'I'll do that for you this morning.'

Lively and Graham disappeared, talking tactics and forensics. Ava waited until the door was firmly shut.

'Before you speak, think very carefully,' Ava said, fiddling with her watchstrap. 'You said you knew nothing about Bruce Jenson's murder, even though you were in attendance at the murder scene just before it took place. I know you have a vested interest in getting revenge on Western. So if this was nothing to do with you, why the hell are they both dead in this city, lying side by side in the sodding mortuary?'

'I have no idea,' Callanach replied, sitting down.

'Stand up,' Ava hissed. 'We're not going to be having a cosy, informal little chat.'

'Ava . . .'

'Detective Chief Inspector,' she corrected him. 'That's what I am to you, and we're going to address one another formally from now on.'

'If that's what you need,' he said.

'It is, but what I need more is to be sure, really fucking sure, that you didn't take out a contract on the men who conspired to rape your mother.'

Callanach breathed in deeply and walked to the window, staring out into the spring drizzle dampening the grey street. Edinburgh had rarely looked so cold. Even the depths of winter had seen more welcoming days. Here he was, in a city he'd had no attachment to a couple of years earlier, a place that had held almost everything he'd wanted just twelve hours before, and now it was a ghost town.

'I didn't arrange to have either of those men killed. I didn't suggest to anyone that it was what I wanted. I haven't discussed the situation with anyone at all, save for my mother and you. I'm not involved in any crime at any level. Is that what you needed to hear, Detective Chief Inspector?'

'Don't sound so petulant. This has gone so far beyond anything I anticipated that you and I are both going to get fired if the real reason you were at Bruce Jenson's nursing home gets out.'

'And that's the only reason you're pissed off with me, right?' Callanach asked.

'It's the only reason I want to think about right now, but as you raised it, what I found last night more than justifies my being concerned about your mental state.'

'I'd try to convince you otherwise, only I know that look on your face, so I won't waste my time,' he said, walking to her door.

Ava stood. 'You should know, I'm considering suspending you from duty until Pax Graham has a suspect in custody. I think it'd be better for everyone involved.'

'You mean easier for you not to have me around.'

'I mean better for MIT to be seen to have done the right thing if the shit hits the bloody propeller. Write up the additional statement DI Graham asked for, then make sure DS Tripp is completely up to date with all aspects of the Hawksmith–Shozo investigation.'

'And how exactly are you going to justify that decision given that I continued working after Jenson's death?' he asked.

'Quite easily, in fact. Jenson might have been a one-off, not connected with you at all. Now we have two victims, both linked to you, a pattern has been established that I can no longer ignore. You know it makes sense,' she added more gently.

'I know we make sense,' Callanach said.

Ava looked at him, her face blank, her body completely still.

'There is no we,' she said. 'Close the door on your way out.'

Rune Maclure walked in as Callanach was exiting, offering them both a solemn smile with a warm good morning.

'That was quick, thanks for making contact,' Ava said, motioning towards a chair and waiting for Callanach to shut the door before proceeding.

'I'm amazed you could see me so soon. You must be rushed off your feet,' Maclure said. 'I won't take up much of your time, but I read an online news blog this morning. I gather there's been another death under suspicious circumstances.'

'That sounds more vague than it really is, I'm afraid. It's definitely a murder.'

'And I gather the victim's name is Osaki Shozo, a Japanese national who settled here after his marriage?'

'That's right,' Ava confirmed.

'Then you should know that Mr Shozo came to our offices a few days ago. I'd say he was suicidal, only not like I've seen with other people,' he paused. 'More as if he was weighing up his options. That sounds cold and calculating, which isn't the impression I got of him at all. If anything, suicide was a cultural option he felt obliged to consider. I did my best to persuade him otherwise, I had hoped with some success.'

'I can assure you, Mr Maclure, that whatever advice you gave had no bearing whatsoever on Mr Shozo's death. Far from it, in fact.'

'May I ask how?'

'Electrocution,' Ava said. 'Is there anything in particular you remember about your discussion with the victim?'

'A sense of regret towards his family in Japan, of having let them down. There were issues within his marriage that he didn't feel equipped to deal with. If I had to sum up the real problem, it was that Mr Shozo wasn't at all prepared for conflict, to the point where he was letting himself be treated very badly. I should add that I've only heard one side of the story – I obviously had no contact with Mrs Shozo – but Osaki seemed genuine and he wasn't dramatising more than was necessary. He didn't seem to want either sympathy or support. Just facts and a sounding board. Like I said, it was a session that I felt was unusual in nature.'

'I appreciate you letting me know,' Ava said. 'We're in the process of trying to reconstruct Mr Shozo's final few days and that information fills in a blank.'

'You don't think, so soon after Stephen Berry's death . . . is it possible they're linked? I appreciate you probably can't tell me much, but I had this sick feeling this morning, as soon as I heard the name. That's two people the agency have helped in a short period and now they're both . . .'

Ava let the pause do its work as she considered how to reply.

'We're not sure how or why Stephen Berry died, Mr Maclure. The two deaths are likely unrelated, although I can see how it would be troubling and upsetting for you. May I ask, who allocates the cases to you as counsellors?'

'At the office, it's a question of a walk-in being met at the door and presented to the next available counsellor. There are four of us there every day, two doing outside visits and two others off duty. If more than one of us is free, whoever does the meet-and-greet makes an ad hoc decision. Sometimes if it's a female patient, she'll specifically request a woman counsellor, so there are some variables. With a phone-in situation, a suicide attempt in progress, it's about whoever's geographically closest and able to attend. Very much up to fate and who happens to have their mobile on.'

'That's helpful, thank you. Could I ask, does the name Fenella Hawksmith mean anything to you?'

'I'm afraid not, and it's one that would stand out. That's the woman who was found dead recently in the city, right?' Maclure leaned forwards, head resting on his upturned palms, elbows on his knees.

'It is. I wonder if we could send an officer over to check your walk-in records?' Ava asked. Not that she needed permission, but it was always better to operate with goodwill than court orders.

'Absolutely, as soon as you like. Our records are brief, basic identification information, together with a couple of lines' summary from the counsellor. Also, walk-ins aren't obliged to give any information at all. Some fill in the form with false information. Obviously, our priority is simply to see anyone who needs to talk. I guess it's like emergency medicine. Filling in forms is the least important part of the process. It's an odd fact in today's society that both feeling suicidal and asking for help to prevent suicide can be viewed as rather embarrassing or abnormal. It's one of the reasons we find it so difficult to reach the people who need us.'

'I understand. In that case, perhaps we could also bring photos of all three of the deceased to show staff members, see if anyone recalls any contact with them, in addition to those you've reported. Would that be all right?'

'That sounds sensible,' Maclure said. 'We have a fairly hefty rota, as some of our counsellors do home visits or are on call to hospitals and prisons, so we travel widely. I'll provide you with a complete staff list. That way your officers can get round to everyone more promptly.'

'I appreciate that. You've been very helpful, Mr Maclure.'

'Rune, please,' he reminded her. 'And forgive me for taking advantage of the most ghoulish of circumstances, but the offer of coffee or tea – or something stronger – is still on the table, so to speak. I'm hoping that even during a case this serious you still have to leave the police station once in a while.'

'Actually, it's difficult right now,' Ava sighed. 'My time's not really my own mid-investigation.'

Maclure smiled. 'And the look on your face is telling me that being asked out on a date isn't what you need right now, case or no case.'

'You should have chosen a career in the police with powers of observation like that,' Ava replied gently, managing a half-smile.

'Oh no, I talk people out of acts of violence. Can't stand the sight of blood myself, but I'm in awe of people like you who do what's necessary. It must entail sacrifices the rest of us simply cannot comprehend,' he said, standing. 'At least give me permission to ask you out again, in a couple of months' time, when hopefully things are simpler. Early summer, maybe? Things always seem brighter when the sun shows herself.'

'How do you know you'll still want to go for coffee with me by then?' Ava asked honestly, no flirtation, no agenda. She was all played out of games.

'Because all good things take patience,' Maclure said. 'I'm old enough at least to be able to recognise those things when they cross my path.'

Ava nodded. 'No promises,' she said. 'But you can ask me.'

'Good,' he said gently. 'I'll get all the information you need about staff. Let me know when your officers can attend to go through our records. Will it be DI Callanach attending?'

'More likely it'll be Detective Sergeant Tripp,' Ava said, walking him to the door. 'Callanach's about to go on leave.'

She had no idea when she'd made the decision, but it was suddenly clear in her mind and inevitable. Callanach simply couldn't continue working inside MIT while both Jenson's and Western's murders remained unsolved.

Rune Maclure reached out his hand to shake hers. 'I wish we could have met in almost any other situation than this. It feels like a terribly guilty pleasure coming to see you today.'

Ava watched him leave, considering his final words and realising that for the previous decade she'd only ever met men courtesy of investigating violent crimes. Small wonder every relationship she had went wrong. She picked up the phone and dialled Callanach's number.

Chapter Twenty-Four

13 March

Ava was watching the clock in MIT's briefing room. As it flicked to 8 a.m., she stood and began to speak, ignoring the squad members still filing in and the conversations still taking place noisily in the background. The quiet didn't so much settle across the room as drop like a rock. The latecomers hustled into corners and raised eyebrows were exchanged.

'As of yesterday afternoon, having checked the records of a national suicide prevention charity called Reach You, we're officially treating the death of Stephen Berry as probable murder. The crime scene at Tantallon Castle offered us no evidence at all, but that was expected after the storm that followed the discovery of the body. However, both victims were spoken to by a counsellor from the charity who works in the Edinburgh branch, Rune Maclure. Mr Maclure came forward and raised his concerns with us after seeing Osaki Shozo's name in a news article.'

'What about Fenella Hawksmith? Any link there?' Janet Monroe asked.

'There's no link at all to Reach You – teams checked that extensively yesterday – but her medical records show that she received treatment for severe depression and previous suicide attempts from other agencies, and she spent time in at least one hospital unit having been committed by her GP.'

'So is this some sort of quasi-medical psychopathy? Does the killer think he's putting these people out of their misery?' was Monroe's follow-up question.

Ava liked Janet Monroe. She paused to consider the question.

'It's possible, but unlikely. You're suggesting something like "angel of death" syndrome and typically in those cases the victims are killed by medication or without extreme violence. These deaths have all been traumatic to an extreme.'

'More like a punishment,' DS Tripp contributed. 'These feel more like hate crimes.'

'I agree,' Ava said. 'So I want to go back to Stephen Berry's death and see what we missed. The forensics has given us little to go on. Stephen previously made a very public suicide attempt on the Queensferry Crossing that was shared widely on social media. There was a large crowd on the bridge, and we know that both photos and videos were taken. There was a man laughing there. That information came from Mr Maclure, who talked Stephen Berry down, and it was confirmed by several officers at the scene. Our priority is to find that man. I want the identities of all the people at the scene. We should be able to get car registrations for those vehicles that were stopped behind the police line during the incident and drivers should be able to account for who was in their vehicle.'

'That won't prove who the person laughing was,' someone added from the back.

'No, it won't, but we'll be able to ask those present for any photos or video footage taken and maybe that'll get us a step closer. Stephen Berry was likely the first victim, so it's possible that someone at the scene took a lasting interest and seeing him attempting to jump was some sort of trigger for them.'

'But how would they have found out about Fenella Hawksmith?' Tripp asked.

'Check media reports at the time. Speak with Mrs Hawksmith's doctor, see if there was any public suicide attempt that might have got into the papers. Look at her medical records, find out the circumstances of her committal. I've already requested that uniformed units take statements from staff members at Reach You detailing their contacts with both Berry and Shozo, including their movements and whereabouts when all three crimes were committed.'

'The murderer's ramping it up, though, right?' Janet Monroe said. 'Three killings in three weeks, each more extreme than the last. We're going to need to be more proactive to catch him or her before anyone else dies.'

'What are you suggesting?' Ava asked.

'An attempt to attract the killer's attention?' Monroe suggested.

'I don't think so. It'd be difficult to set something like that up convincingly, not to mention dangerous, and a spate of public suicides can lead other vulnerable people to follow the same path. We know that from the online teenage suicide pacts. The last thing we need is to contribute to a pattern. If we do that, and other people follow suit, we may well end up focusing the killer's attention on the wrong person and unwittingly end up helping him or her find his next victim.'

Monroe nodded.

'So, DS Tripp'll be in charge of day-to day operations, answerable directly to me. I want all hands on today and we're not stopping until we have something to work with.'

'What's DI Supermodel working on, then?' Lively called out.

Ava hadn't realised he was in the room. She took a deep

breath. She hadn't been intending to break the news to the squad so brutally or so soon, but now that they were all gathered, it seemed the easiest course.

'DI Callanach's on leave at the moment. A conflict with the Jenson and Western investigations has come to light and he's had to step away from an investigative role until that matter's settled.'

Lively stepped forwards. 'The Gilroy–Western brake-cutting is my case. How come I wasn't told about this?'

'The decision was made late last night for the good of everyone involved. It won't affect your investigation; in fact, I'm hoping it'll make for a cleaner resolution,' Ava said, picking up her file and readying to leave.

Lively was having none of it.

'It might not affect my investigation, but you've got a triple murder on your hands that Callanach was heading up. You don't think MIT might need its most experienced detective inspector at the moment? No disrespect, Max,' he directed at Tripp.

'None taken,' Tripp said quietly. 'For what it's worth, ma'am, I agree. This isn't a good time to be losing the DI.'

'Thank you all for your opinions,' Ava said. 'My decision has been agreed with the detective superintendent and is not reversible for legal reasons. I'm sure DI Callanach would be pleased to know that he has so much support from the unit, particularly from some people he might not have anticipated.' She gave Lively a brief glance, knowing as she did that the bitchiness was beneath her. 'I'm sure you'll be seeing your DI again very soon. That'll be all.'

'What's the point of suspending Callanach from duty, if you don't mind me asking, ma'am? There's no way he was involved in the murders of either Jenson or Western. You know that and every person here knows that. This is bullshit,' Lively said.

Absolute silence – a rarely observed quality within one of

Police Scotland's occupied buildings – stretched gulf-like between Ava and Lively.

Eventually, with leaden legs and a thumping head, Ava walked across the room clutching her files in front of her like a bullet-proof vest, stopping directly in front of her detective sergeant.

'I said, that will be all. You have work to do.'

Forcing herself to pause en route to her office to make coffee, rather than being perceived to have bolted and hidden, Ava could imagine the conversation happening behind her. That her promotion had finally gone to her head, that she'd lost her judgement, that Luc Callanach was being unfairly treated and was suddenly – in spite of all the ribbing and grief he'd received since joining Police Scotland – something close to a local hero.

She stirred her coffee slowly, inexplicably adding sugar, tasting it and promptly dumping it in the sink before returning miserably to her office. Delivering the news to Callanach of his full-pay, non-disciplinary, temporary suspension the previous evening had been stilted at the start and entirely one way by the end. Utterly confused by what she was feeling, Ava had ended the call coldly before weeping furiously, alone in her office.

She'd returned to her own home only long enough to shower and change. Sleep, at least that part of it that required you to lie quietly trying to relax with only your thoughts for company, was the enemy she was avoiding at all costs.

Callanach had accepted his fate without complaint and Ava had known he wasn't thinking about either Bruce Jenson or Gilroy Western but trying to keep a lid on the memory of his previous suspension in Lyon, France, when he'd been not only removed from duty, but also arrested for a rape he didn't commit. In spite of the harshness of her words with him, she was sure about that one thing: Callanach was no rapist. Still, the deaths MIT were investigating bothered her. If two men conspired to rape a woman she cared about, her own now-deceased mother in her thoughts, Ava knew she'd have stopped at nothing – absolutely nothing, consequences notwithstanding – to have destroyed them. If Callanach had managed to show the restraint he'd claimed in Bruce Jenson's presence, it would have been a miracle.

Her desk phone rang and Ava picked it up absent-mindedly.

'Turner, it's Overbeck. Are you there?' she snapped.

'Yes,' Ava mumbled. 'Sorry, trying to do too much at once.'

'That's all right,' Overbeck said. 'It'll come as no surprise to you that I've just had a visit from DS Lively. I thought he might really have a heart attack this time.'

'I was hard on him,' Ava said. 'I can understand why he's angry. I'll apologise.'

'Stupid girl. I'm not phoning to discipline you. You're his superior officer and he had no right to challenge you in that manner, particularly in front of the rest of the squad. If you hadn't given him such short shrift, you'd have been in for an absolute bollocking from me. How did Callanach take the news last night?'

'Quietly,' Ava said.

'Hmmm,' Overbeck drawled. 'Hierarchical relationships are complex little buggers. I don't think Lively's going to be gracing me with his after-hours company for a while.'

'I'm sorry,' Ava said awkwardly. Overbeck's relationship with Lively was always the elephant in the room.

'Don't be. Lively and I both knew what we were getting in to. You've done the right thing, Turner. Can't have Callanach fucking up the investigation. When we arrest a suspect, we'll have defence counsel crawling all over us if there's an active member of the investigating team involved as a witness.'

'Thank you,' Ava said. 'Does DS Lively understand that or do I need to speak with him?'

'You most certainly do not. I told him it was my decision and that you'd argued against it. He'll probably turn up clutching a packet of chocolate Hobnobs by way of an apology any minute.'

'You didn't have to do that, ma'am,' Ava said, disliking the sensation that the world had turned on its head. She and Overbeck on one side, Callanach and Lively on the other. Who the hell could have foreseen that turn of events?

'Yes, I did. Comes with the territory. And before you get all teary-eyed and mushy on me, you should know that this is how it works. You have to control those officers and while they need to respect you, they also have to want to follow your commands. I take the shit from them on your behalf and when I get shit from the top brass, I likewise pass it on to you, because I need to keep a good relationship with them. I always did say you were a bit slow with the office politics. Now, get off your self-pitying arse – and please don't deny it, I can hear it in your voice. You'll feel much better when you've got someone in custody. Or at least I'll feel better and that's pretty much the same thing.'

'Yes, ma'am,' Ava said. 'And could I just say I really appreciate the support . . .'

She was talking to a dead line. Overbeck's speciality, she remembered.

Pax Graham knocked and entered as she was actively working to pull herself together. Overbeck, as harsh as she was, was right. Lively trooped in at Graham's rear clutching a packet of biscuits. In spite of everything, Ava had to fight not to laugh when she saw the chocolate digestives in his hand.

'I forgot the coffee,' Lively said, depositing the biscuits on Ava's desk and staring at them, evidently stuck for where to go next.

'Doesn't matter. Thank you,' Ava replied, reaching out and

drawing the biscuits a few inches closer towards her, peace made over baked goods as only Lively could. 'I take it there's an update.'

'There is,' Graham said, perching on the edge of Ava's desk as Lively took the seat. 'Gilroy Western's wife says he travelled here at Jenson's solicitor's request as there was to be a reading of the will after the memorial service and he'd been left a bequest. The email didn't say what, only that he should attend.'

'I take it there's a but,' Ava added.

'There's a "butt" even bigger than mine,' Lively said gruffly. 'The memorial service date and time was given correctly, but there was never going to be a will reading, as Jenson's entire estate has been left to the rape crisis charity.'

'So, if he checked the memorial service details online, for example, he would have had verification, but it was the promise of getting something in return for travelling that made sure he'd come?' Ava asked.

'That and the added temptation of what his wife says was a long-term liaison he had in Edinburgh. Looks like he was headed to see a lady friend when his car crashed. He had a pair of diamond earrings nicely wrapped and ribboned in the car with him. According to the wife, she wasn't supposed to know about any of it, but knew when to put up and shut up. She doesn't have the woman's name but is pretty sure we'll get the details from Mr Western's phone. I think the term she used was a cheap piece of street-corner decoration,' Lively said.

'High-end prostitute?' Ava asked. 'Trace her and speak to her. See where she was the night before Western died and if she'd ever had any contact with Bruce Jenson. Prostitutes get raped more than any other sector of society.'

'You think there's a link to Bruce Jenson's final monumental decision about where to leave his money?' Graham asked.

'I think we should check and see if Gilroy Western had made any recent changes to his will,' Ava said. 'He was a businessman who must have had plenty of contact with lawyers over the years, so how did he fall for a fake email?'

'It was good. Whoever had sent it had gone to the trouble of setting up a false email address, including the law partnership's name. They used all the company details and reproduced the logo. They'd signed it from Jenson's personal lawyer. It was no botch job. Left nothing to chance.' Lively checked his watch. 'I'd best go. We've got the tech nerds checking the mobile phone and I'm hoping they can give me some answers. Am I allowed to speak with DI Callanach at all, just as a mate?'

'You're mates now, are you? Was I in a coma when that happened?' Ava folded her arms.

'All right, I shouldn't have faced you down in the briefing, but it's . . .'

'Sergeant, I've already forgotten about that, but you can't contact Callanach. He's on administrative leave for a reason. You're involved in an investigation that Callanach needs to be protected from. Getting in touch with him right now would be the worst thing you could do.'

'I get that,' he mumbled. 'It's just that, well, he and I haven't always got along. I just wanted him to know that the team's going to support him.'

'He doesn't need the team's support, or anyone else's, given that he's not implicated in any way, but the sentiment would be appreciated, I'm sure. I'll pass it on.'

'Right, I'll be off, then. I, er, bumped into the superintendent earlier,' Lively mumbled, his eyes darting to Graham and back.

Lively was about as good at subterfuge as he was at dieting.

'I spoke to her, too,' Ava said. 'She's got MIT's back, Sergeant. You should probably give her more credit.'

'Aye. Maybe,' he said glumly as he left.

Graham waited until Lively was well down the corridor before asking the inevitable.

'You all right? Seems like you're having a tough day.'

'I'll survive. What's your gut instinct on the Jenson–Western case right now?'

'I think it goes way back. It's either something both men were implicated in or it's an unresolved issue between them. Western's wife was clear they've had no dealings for a decade,' Graham said.

'You're sure the two deaths are linked?'

'I'm not sure of anything right now, but the email enticing Western to come for Jenson's funeral is too much of a coincidence. Otherwise, why not just fly out to Spain and cut Western's brakes at his own home?'

'Maybe there was too great a risk of killing another family member,' Ava offered.

'Or maybe travelling abroad risked leaving a trail – passports, tickets, credit cards.'

'All right, see what you can turn up, but let me know quickly. Now that Callanach's on enforced leave, we'll have to resolve it without delay.'

'Must be difficult. You two were colleagues before you got promoted. I can't imagine how hard that conversation was. Let me know if you need anything, won't you? And we never got that drink, not that anyone was in the mood for celebrating promotions with bodies piling up. Remind me, I owe you a pint still when this is over.'

'I'll hold you to that,' Ava said, attempting a smile, aware that it was strained.

Graham wandered out of her office, remarkably lithe in spite of his frame, carrying his height well. So many tall people stooped, but Pax Graham seemed content to fill the entire corridor. He was a good man. Observant. Perhaps a little too observant for her right now. As for the offers of coffee and drinks, it was hard to remember a time when she'd been so popular. The truth was that the last thing she wanted was to encourage advances from either Rune Maclure or Pax Graham, as attractive and intelligent as they both were. There was only one man she could think about and if she'd been able to wipe her memory clean of all they'd done two nights before, she'd have pressed that button with no hesitation at all.

Callanach picked up the glass of red wine he'd failed to finish the previous night and knocked it back, staring into the empty glassware before sending it flying to connect with the door into his kitchen. The resulting shards flew and skittered into every corner of the lounge. After Ava's phone call, he'd immediately changed into joggers and a T-shirt, and hit Edinburgh's streets at a pace that had left every muscle torn to shreds. The pain this morning was a welcome distraction from the fact that he had nowhere to go and nothing to do, except wait for other people to do their jobs so that he could get back to his.

It didn't help that Ava was right. Continuing to work when there was an active investigation in which he was involved – even as a peripheral witness – was asking for trouble and Ava had found a means to get him out that avoided having to declare his deep loathing of both Jenson and Western. Still, his anger was barely controllable. It seemed that however hard he fought, fate was determined to slap him back down. As if leaving his former life in France wasn't enough, not to mention his prized career at Interpol, now he had another question mark over his head. There were only so many times your colleagues would accept you were innocent in the face of scandal. Sooner or later it stuck. The worst of it was, his career wasn't the loss he really cared about any more. He'd screwed up something of much greater value to him.

Retreating to his bathroom, he crashed to the floor and stared into the cupboard where he'd previously hidden Ava's slate, untouched and largely forgotten. In spite of his attempt to explain what had been going through his mind when he'd taken it, he was only guessing at his motivation. To say he'd been an emotional wreck back then was an understatement.

He'd regretted his decision to join Police Scotland almost as soon as he'd signed on the dotted line. Only the knowledge that he had to fill his time with something positive or spiral into depression had made him board the plane to Edinburgh. That, and the sense that if he didn't continue to do some sort of police work, then he'd have let his accuser, Astrid, take absolutely everything from him.

Then he'd found Ava in MIT, tried to keep her at arm's-length, realised she was way too strong and decent a woman to tolerate that, and given himself permission to make a friend. Just as quickly, she'd been taken from him by a man who was capable of the most grotesque acts of torture and violence.

Taking a personal item from her home had been wrong, but it was the only thing that had given him any comfort at the time. As for the other items, he'd simply been searching for a way to make the victims matter to him, in spite of the emotional void in his life. Not returning the victims' personal belongings when the investigation had come to an end had been part denial, part shame.

He stared at the towels still littering the floor that had covered the possessions he'd taken. Like most things in his life, his stupidity had been born of fast living. Use a towel, wash it, put it back on the top of the pile. And at the bottom, the objects he'd taken from three different victims of crime had sat untouched, until now.

It was a disaster. Ava, finally in his arms, and now she couldn't bear to look at him. Trying to rationalise what he'd done would do no good. She might be the most level-headed woman in the world when it came to an investigation, but her heart ruled her brain in her personal life.

Slowly, folding carefully as he went, he rebuilt the stack of towels and put them away, closing the cupboard doors behind them. Then he stood and tidied the surfaces in the bathroom. After that, he turned his attention to his bedroom, straightening the covers on his bed, remembering the celebrated recent quote that if you wanted to change the world you had to start off by making your bed. Such a trivial activity, but the sense of it resonated with him.

He couldn't afford to feel sorry for himself the way he'd slid into introspection after Astrid Borde had accused him of rape. True, the implications of his current predicament were nowhere near as grave, but he wasn't going to run away this time. It had taken all his strength to establish himself in Edinburgh and only a fool would let so much effort go to waste.

In the lounge, he brushed up the broken glass and made sure there were no outward signs of the chaos in his head. By then, it was lunchtime. The easiest option by far was coffee and toast, but he forced himself to grill some fish and prepare a salad to go with it.

Then he did the one thing he really didn't want to do. He got in touch with his friend, Lance, arranged to join him for dinner and prepared to tell him everything. Absolutely everything, missing none of the details of what he'd been through before and what he was going through now. It was the final hurdle, learning to trust again, and he couldn't lay it all at Ava's door. He had to find some balance in his life, that careful layering of family, friends, colleagues and lovers.

As he stacked the dishwasher, Ava's final words came back

to him, as they had every few minutes since she'd left his flat, echoing with so much pain that he'd thought he might never be able to hear anything else. The man she'd thought she'd fallen in love with, she'd said. He wondered how much she regretted that now.

Chapter Twenty-Five

14 March

The Crow didn't have to use either ingenuity, force or persuasion to get into the farmhouse and he felt cheated. Folks out at East Saltoun were old-style, apparently, leaving their doors unlocked until late into the evening. He stepped inside, taking a deep breath and catching a strong waft of manure from a pair of discarded boots before tasting the unmistakeable sweetness of an apple pie baked with a generous helping of cinnamon as it wafted from the oven.

The resident farmer was presumably seated in front of the television, where he'd been during each of The Crow's previous visits, although on those occasions he'd restricted himself to peering through the windows. The main concern with a farmhouse was dogs, but with no sheep, the owner kept only one mutt for company and that appeared to sleep in front of the fire almost constantly. His assumption that it was half deaf had been borne out by its complete lack of reaction to an intruder.

He took his time and was careful in spite of the fact that

by now he was surely invincible. His strength was increasing daily and since he'd consumed the original feathered version of himself, he'd noticed a substantial improvement in both his eyesight and his balance, real – not imagined – in spite of what others would say if he told them.

The world was limitless. Those people who thought science had uncovered all the secrets of the world were blind to potential and cut off from the mysteries of the universe. The Crow was an open mind. He could accept and therefore receive the benefits the natural world had to offer him. He'd evolved into a focal point of natural power.

Those who'd call him insane – the small people – had had their senses dulled by electronic gadgets, screens, machines to keep them fit, machines to measure their fitness, machines to read books from, the list was endless. He was raw, real and untainted. He had a mobile phone, of course – sometimes you had to adopt common necessities to function and fit in – but he saw such accessories for what they really were: a conductor that drained humankind's base energy.

Better armed this time, The Crow had a handgun in one pocket and doubled up by taking a butcher's knife from the block in the kitchen. The farmer might be in his mid-sixties, but he'd spent a lifetime working on the land and was still likely to be strong and, perhaps more of a threat, unafraid. The farmer's shotgun was in a cabinet in the hallway, stupidly visible from the lounge window; although he did at least bother to keep it locked.

A bang from upstairs took him by surprise. He froze, tipping his head to get a better location on the noise, summoning all his considerable new senses, sniffing the air for anything he might have missed. A scent that seemed not to fit, items abandoned that indicated the presence of a person other than the farmer, who wasn't married and had no children, the reason for that as plain as the hideous scarring on the farmer's face. Also, he suspected, the reason the farmer had attempted to flee this world before his allotted time on many occasions in the past.

Burn victims were cruelly treated by society. The staring, constant rejection, the polarisation between everything society plugged as perfect and the reality of looking in the mirror. The Crow could understand how hard it was, but not forgive. Animals didn't sit around feeling sorry for themselves, wishing they could die. They foraged, hunted, killed, fed, mated, irrespective of how they felt at any given moment.

They strove. That was the right word.

Satisfied that the noise from the upper floor was nothing more than a door slamming in the breeze, he began, drawing the gun from his pocket and disengaging the safety catch. It wasn't that he needed the weapon – he had no doubts whatsoever about his physical prowess – but it was going to make controlling the farmer substantially easier. The point was that the evening had to go exactly as he'd played it in his head. That was the surest way that the farmer's life force would transfer to him. There had to be circularity and meaning to the death, otherwise he was simply committing murder and that would be a trivialisation of his work.

Walking into the lounge, it took a few moments before the farmer even noticed him. The old man huffed loudly, then picked up his remote control and flicked off the television.

'I paid my frigging taxes. I don't care if you've got a bloody court order, I called the sheriff's office myself and made sure my file was closed. So go on then.' He gave a wave of his hand. 'Bugger right off and close the door behind yerself.'

'I'm not here about your taxes,' The Crow said. 'And I'm not a sheriff.'

'Well, you're not polis. Polis have to announce themselves

before they come in. Are you one of those new immigration bastards? I told you, I've got nothing to hide.'

He stood up now, in full finger-pointing flow, anger compensating for a blossoming confusion. No fear yet, but that would come.

'Are you carrying a gun?' he asked, peering at the small black object, largely concealed in The Crow's hand and currently pointed at the threadbare carpet.

'I am,' he replied, levelling it at the farmer's gut. 'I know you have one, too; although at present it's in its case, like the law-abiding citizen I'm sure you are.'

The farmer glanced through the doorway and into the hall where his gun cabinet stood beside the staircase.

'That's the one, just out there. All I need you to do is give me the keys.'

'Like hell I will, you daft wee prick. What're you gonna do, shoot me over a knackered auld shotgun?'

'That's exactly what I'll do if you don't hand it over. Just that, then I'll be on my way,' The Crow said calmly.

The farmer glanced into the hallway again. He was about to give in. The Crow felt it as certainly as he could smell that the pie had begun to burn, the former sweetness rolling into charcoaled bitter.

'Then you'll go? That's all you came for?' the farmer double-checked.

The Crow gave what appeared to be a related shrug of his shoulders. What the farmer couldn't see − invisible to mortals who'd not become anything greater than their human selves − were the huge wings The Crow felt on his back. He gave them a flutter and in his mind they filled the back wall of the poky lounge. He felt the breeze they created ruffle his hair.

'Sure,' he said.

The farmer dug deep into his pocket and pulled out a rusty

keyring holding just four or five keys. The smallest he took between his thumb and forefinger as he walked slowly to the gun cabinet.

'I'll do that,' The Crow instructed, holding his hand out, keeping the gun aimed at the farmer's chest.

Keys in hand, he walked to the cabinet, motioning for his hostage to stand in the far corner. He wasn't worried about the man making a run for it. The farmhouse was a good mile from any other buildings and if he had to fire a shot to persuade him to stop running, it wouldn't be such a surprising sound in a farming community well used to controlling fox and badger populations when the need arose. The Crow pulled the gun from the cabinet, checked it was loaded. It was, which was sloppy gun care, but useful for him.

'Thank you,' he said. 'Before I go, do you have a downstairs toilet?'

'You're no using ma fuckin' cludgie as well as taking my gun. Get screwed,' the farmer said, braver now that his intruder had what he'd come for.

The Crow ignored the insults. He was above that. He opened two doors before the third produced what he wanted.

'Come and stand here,' he told the farmer, whose face was a deep burgundy in the half-lit hall, the reflections of firelight on his face a cruel parody of the injury he'd already suffered. He wouldn't need to worry about that much longer. The Crow helped to persuade his hostage to move by pointing both guns at him at once. It worked.

'You're locking me in so I cannae call the filth while you go, is that it? I can save you the trouble. I don't want the polis here any more than you, so you just be on your way,' the farmer tried.

The Crow ignored him and gave a one-way nod with his head. The farmer walked into the tiny privy that hadn't been decorated for an age but that was as clean as a whistle, give the man his dues.

'I just want you to stand there and look into the mirror,' The Crow said. 'You can lean on the basin if it helps.'

'What are you playing at? Don't you get any twisted ideas about touching me, you sick wanker.'

'No danger of that. No one's wanted to touch you for the longest time, have they? Does it still hurt? I bet it pains you at night. How long were you burning before someone rescued you? You must have thought you were going to die. I know you've spent a lot of time since then wishing you had.'

'How do you know that?' the farmer asked The Crow's image in the mirror. 'Who are you?'

'I'm everything,' The Crow replied. 'Now, what I need you to do is push the barrel of the shotgun into the side of your neck. Here, let me help.' Keeping his handgun pressed into the small of the farmer's back, he used his right hand to elevate the shotgun. 'You just put your finger on the trigger. I'll take the weight.'

The farmer made the mistake of looking him in the eyes before making his move. The Crow was only surprised he left it as late as he did and he was ready when the farmer pushed backwards, away from the sink, trying to bring a heavy fist round and into his face. The Crow let off a single shot, carefully aimed to be non-fatal but ensure compliance, through the left shoulder. It was a shame the mirror got shattered, ruining the setting, but it couldn't be helped.

'I don't think you'd enjoy a slow death,' The Crow whispered as the farmer staggered against the sink clutching his shoulder.

A steady scarlet stream was running down his chest and dripping into the sink. The metallic odour hit the air, sharp and reeking of endings.

'So, let's try again.'

The farmer was crying now – that was unexpected. The tears took a winding path down his cheeks, over the roughened skin, rivulets splitting off and leaving his face a glittering rocky terrain. Raising the gun once more, The Crow had no choice but to hold his fingers over the trigger. The farmer's were shaking too badly to leave him to make his final move unaided.

Another bang came from upstairs. The farmer and The Crow both looked at the ceiling at the same moment. The Crow wasn't afraid, but it was only sensible to ensure he didn't lose what was in his hands after so much preparation. The farmer was slipping now, the blood loss and shock taking its toll.

With one arm around the man's waist and the other over his trigger finger, The Crow made sure the barrel wasn't pointed in his own direction, then squeezed. The sound in that tiny room was overwhelming. The Crow's ear drums popped painfully and for one panicked moment, he thought they might both have burst. The farmer dropped to the floor, his head flopping lifelessly over his chest, his ending illustrated perfectly on the newly reddened wall to their left.

The man left staring in what zigzags remained of the mirror was less than human, raw, a creature still maturing. Flecks of the farmer's skin peppered his face. The look was carnivorous. Untameable. The Crow loved it. He wanted to remain there, staring at his image, until the remnants of the farmer were absorbed into his own flesh, becoming one, but there was a loose end. An unanticipated complication.

Grudgingly, he left the fractured reflection and took the stairs two at a time. The upper floor of the property consisted of four rooms: three bedrooms and a bathroom, he guessed. He opened the door to his left first, kicking it open, keeping his left hand free and his right hand on his gun. That was the bathroom, shower curtain pinned helpfully back, the only cupboards too small for even a young child to fit into.

250

The next door was hiding a room used to store boxes, suit-cases, old chairs and a fake Christmas tree, still bedecked with tinsel that had long since lost its lustre. The Crow moved swiftly to the wardrobe and pulled its doors open. Ageing clothes tumbled out onto him before falling to the floor. He let out a small, high laugh that sounded nothing like his normal self. It was a nervous laugh and he hated it.

Striding to the next room, he stood still in the open doorway and looked around himself. The bedspread was floral and neatly arranged. There were flowers on the windowsill. Not one single dirty item of clothing was strewn on the floor. Not one. And there was a mirror on the far wall, opposite the bedhead.

That was wrong. What use would a man with such life-changing scarring have with a mirror, last thing at night, first thing in the morning, always reminding him? Unless The Crow had failed to do his work properly this time, and that was unthinkable. Perhaps the slammed door he'd heard wasn't the wind. Perhaps there really had been someone here, listening to his voice. Had she crept downstairs and seen his face? Had she already called the police? This bedroom, the whole house, he realised too late, had a woman's touch all over it. From the flowery bedspread to the apple pie, from the sparkling bathroom to the mirror on the wall.

'Come out, come out, wherever you are,' he sang, opening the door to the built-in cupboard and grinning into the void.

Sure enough, there amid the thick jumpers and winter coats were a few women's shirts and jeans. Stepping inside, he ripped at the hanging clothes and dashed the folded items from the shelves. Nothing. He checked under the bed and was finally convinced. Not so much as a stray sock or a ball of dust. This was not the farmer's handiwork.

That left one last room.

The Crow steeled himself for a confrontation he hadn't

foreseen. That was both troubling and a potential benefit. A second life force in one single event would render him stronger than he'd ever felt in one night, but it wasn't part of his plan. Taking a life that might have been valued, that nature had planted and nurtured, might upset his evolution.

Then again, were there really *any* accidents in nature? Predators hunted when and where they could. They took whatever crossed their paths. They didn't waste their time evaluating and philosophising. He breathed hard, once, twice, three times, and stepped into the last bedroom.

It was a guest room, with a double bed against the wall in the corner, and a rug providing the only colour. Another built-in wardrobe was set into the wall. The Crow listened for a moment, checking the small window for flashing blue lights, admitting to himself for the first time that he may have underestimated the situation. There was no way of knowing how much time he had left to get out if the police had already been called.

Tearing at the wardrobe door, he growled as he thrust his gun hand inside. It was a bedding cupboard, filled with towels, a spare duvet, clean sheets and blankets, piled everywhere. Other than that, nothing.

He had imagined it. The banging door was no more than the wind. The look on the farmer's face as he'd stared up at the ceiling . . . The flowery bedspread might be no more than the touch of a housekeeper who came in once a week. And why couldn't a man have put an apple pie in the oven? It was probably shop-bought and straight out of the freezer. Still, he wouldn't stay. The event had been tainted for him. Spoiled. A hot flash of resentment washed over him as he stood dripping secondhand blood onto the carpet.

Back downstairs, he had one final task. The farmer's face was still completely intact. That element of his visit had gone smoothly, at least. Laying the body on its back, he reached into his trouser pockets and gently pulled out the prized objects. Arranging them was easier than he'd imagined.

He left the house in darkness, turning off all the downstairs lights and thoughtfully turning off the oven. The police would discover the body soon enough. No point attracting them too soon with billowing smoke. Much better that they had only a vague timeline to go by. So far, they were proving remarkably incompetent, and that was just the way The Crow liked it.

Mariam had waited on the top landing of the farmhouse almost too long. The intruder was light on his feet. From the time he'd left the staircase, she hadn't been able to tell which room he was going into. To avoid making noise and ensuring discovery, she'd stayed in the cubbyhole in the base of the guest room wardrobe until she was certain the house was empty again. After that, she'd opened the old upper barn door to the external wall of the converted house and braved the ladder to the ground.

It was well hidden from the eye by ivy growth, but the rungs were easy enough to feel with her feet. She reached solid earth, whispering a prayer. The farmer had made sure she knew how to get out should the need ever arise, not that either of them had honestly believed it would, and then all they were concerned about was an immigration raid.

Sprinting for the new barn, she took another ladder to the upper floor, where thirteen more immigrants were already asleep. Mariam shook them awake one by one, cautioning them to be quiet even though the intruder's car was gone. If there was one thing she'd learned in her native Mali, it was that danger was never truly past and that the second you relaxed would be the moment your soul flew to heaven.

The farmer had treated them well enough. It wasn't exactly slavery. They were given food and drink, warm sleeping bags and appropriate clothes for the weather. In return, they worked his land, and Mariam had been chosen to keep house for him. She was the one with the best English, not to mention the best figure. There were other things she'd had to tolerate to keep her children safe, but compared to the persecution and poverty she'd faced in her home country, she regarded it as a price worth paying.

The farmer wasn't a bad man. Just lonely, desperate and willing to take advantage of others' misfortunes when the opportunity arose. Him and several other billion people across the world. She hadn't enjoyed the sex, but it had earned her a place in a proper bed and decent meals. Most of the time she was also able to sneak extra food to her son and daughter. She'd have put up with a lot worse to see them safe.

Now, the farmer was dead and they had to leave. She hadn't needed to hear the gunshot to know that blood had been spilled. Mariam had been witness to too much death over the years not to recognise its black stench. She whispered long and low to the small band of illegal immigrants, who spent every day dreading this news but had prepared for it nonetheless. In four minutes, all of their worldly possessions were packed. They took a path over the farmer's land away from the main roads, sticking to the trees where they could, walking spaced in groups of two or three so as not to draw too much attention if they were seen.

Mariam had gone back into the farmhouse only once before they'd set off. Standing well back from the man whose bed she'd shared for nearly a year, she said goodbye, filled a knapsack with all the food that would travel, emptied his wallet – certain he wouldn't have objected under the circumstances, they were all owed some pay – and picked up his ancient mobile.

In spite of her lack of options, the sex partnership she'd entered into only under duress and all the other advantages taken of her, she was sad to be going. The next step was an unknown. If they had to steal to eat, they'd be discovered sooner or later, and then it was anyone's guess what would happen. Incarceration was the best option. A forcible return to Mali – to disease, unemployment, to constant violence of one degree or another – was unthinkable.

They walked for hours before finding an abandoned set of greenhouses, in which they could rest until dark, and only then did she make the call, keeping it as brief as possible. Not to the police. They recorded their calls. People often made the mistake of thinking illegal immigrants were stupid. The truth was that she'd had to be resourceful in ways hard even to contemplate, to get her family to safety and find a man willing to take them in. She didn't have the luxury of keeping the word 'stupid' in her vocabulary. Instead, she phoned the local pub, one of the few numbers the farmer kept in his contacts list.

'Morning, Baldie,' a voice answered. 'What can I do you for so early in the day?'

'He's dead,' Mariam said plainly, doing her best to keep any recognisable accent from her voice. 'Call the police to the farmhouse.'

She broke the call off, taking the SIM card from the back of the phone and crushing it beneath her boot. The pub land-lady was a good person, or so she'd gathered from the things the farmer had said about her. Mariam could do no more than that. Common sense dictated that she not make the call, but there was wrong and there was right, and the two rarely had much overlap. The thought of him lying there with his head half off, after whatever it was the man had done to him – she hadn't been able to face taking a closer look – that was wrong.

The killer was out there somewhere and what sort of person would she be if she let him go simply to protect her own liberty? A man who could kill like that would kill again. Her

255

own husband had been shot in the head at the hands of robbers when he'd refused to hand over his only pair of shoes. Mariam was damned if she would let such people walk free. The police in Mali had merely shrugged, overwhelmed and under-resourced, too worried about their own families to do much more than make a note of the event. This was Scotland, though. This was a world where something could and would be done. Mariam prayed her own children wouldn't have to suffer in the process.

Chapter Twenty-Six

15 March

By the time Ava arrived at the farmhouse, forensic investigations were in full swing. Dr Ailsa Lambert had come and gone, and the body was due to be moved as soon as MIT had seen it in situ. The victim, subject to official identification, was the land-owner Jon Moffat, as notified to them by the person who'd called the crime in from the local pub. Uniformed officers were already there taking a full statement, and thirty additional officers had been mobilised from across the city to secure the scene and set up road blocks out of the area, questioning all those coming and going about their movements.

DS Max Tripp's sharp intake of breath when he saw the body was all the warning Ava needed before she rounded the corner to see it for herself.

'Do you want to wait outside?' Ava asked him.

'It's all right, ma'am. I've seen plenty of bodies before. I'll get a grip in a moment,' Tripp replied, gulping air, not that it was likely to help given the smell of the place.

'No one should have to see bodies in this state, Sergeant, and the day you get used to it will be the day I start to worry about you. There'll be more than enough photos later on. Go and see what else they've found. I've got this.'

Tripp went off without speaking. It was no indictment on the young officer that he hadn't the stomach for the corpse. Ava reminded herself that she'd find a way to sleep at some point in the future – she always did – and made herself take a proper look, kneeling down next to the crumpled body.

The man's face was badly burned, a long time ago from the look of it, and his throat was gone. His head remained attached to his torso by the spine. That wasn't what was going to give Max Tripp and anyone else working the scene nightmares, though. Inserted into each eye was a long, shiny black feather. A viscous fluid, mingling with blood, had leaked down each cheek, giving the impression that the victim had wept over his fate, as Ava would later. It didn't matter how hardened she became. There were always a few tears to spare for victims who'd suffered so appallingly. She got Ailsa on the phone, dispensing with small talk.

'Was he shot first, or were the feathers put into his eyes while he was still alive?'

'I'm confident he was shot and that the damage to the eyes was done postmortem. I'll have the feathers sent to an ornithologist as soon as we've removed them at the mortuary and taken any trace evidence from them.'

'How long has he been dead?' Ava asked.

'Twelve hours is my best estimate. Now, why don't you ask me the question that's really on your mind.'

'We should swap jobs,' Ava said. 'Not that I'm qualified to do yours.'

'Never!' Ailsa exclaimed. 'I only have to deal with people I feel sympathy for. You have to sit in small rooms with the men and women who commit these evil acts. I prefer to spend my time with the dead, thank you very much.'

'You've got a point. And all right, if you're going to make me say it: Is this the work of the same person who killed Fenella Hawksmith and Osaki Shozo?'

'What do you think?' Ailsa asked.

'My gut says yes, but I have no good evidence for that. New method of killing. I know nothing about the victim except that at some point in his past he was badly burned. No cable ties this time. But the level of violence, the force of destruction, that feels the same. I don't understand the feathers, though. If it's the same killer, why haven't we seen those before? Do you think it's the same perpetrator?'

'I do, for all the reasons you just stated. I can't give you anything to go on scientifically speaking yet, but the simplest explanation is usually correct. You have a serial killer in the area who's ramping up. Truth be told, we were all waiting for the next victim. Until we have DNA, prints or reliable witnesses you can't be certain, but this is a level of violence and degradation that few people are capable of. I seriously hope, for all our sakes, that it's just one killer. The thought of having two such psychotic individuals active at the same time in this city is unbearable.'

Ava rang off and went to find DS Tripp. She located him in a new-looking barn a couple of fields away, where officers were hastily erecting floodlights and removing articles in evidence bags.

Taking the ladder to the upper area of the barn, Ava went to see what all the fuss was about. A couple of bin bags filled with food wrappers and general debris had been cut open for inspection and four large water canisters were stacked in a corner, mostly empty. A few tatty blankets had been left, together with shoes that were more holes than leather, and clothes certainly not designed for Scottish weather.

'Several people living here for some time, we reckon,' Tripp said, appearing behind her.

'The farmer must have known. Most likely they were getting shelter in return for cheap labour,' Ava said.

'So it's either the homeless, kids or people who've fallen on hard times, maybe criminals with nowhere to go and no other offers of work . . .'

'Or illegal immigrants,' she finished for him. 'We'll need DNA from all the items to identify the people who were here. There's no dust settled on any of this, and no spider's webs either, so it looks like they left recently and in a hurry.'

'Do you suppose one of them's responsible, ma'am?' Tripp asked.

'Anything's possible, Sergeant. What I need to establish right now is a motive. The body's been removed to the mortuary. Thought you might want to do a walk-through of the rest of the property with me.'

They retraced their steps back to the house, avoiding the units checking every inch of the dirt track for fresh tyre prints.

Ava tried the front door. It was locked and bolted from the inside. All downstairs windows were intact and also locked.

'So the killer came in through the back door, but there's no evidence of force being used. Either the victim let him in, or he just walked straight in when it was unlocked,' Tripp said. 'No gun in the cabinet, so we're assuming the one that was found on the floor next to the body belonged to the farmer.' Tripp's phone rang. 'Excuse me, I should take this,' he said, moving into the lounge.

Ava took the stairs slowly, keeping her gloved hands off the bannister to avoid smudging any prints, looking at the carpet as she went. Here and there were dark red drips, but the only violence seemed to have taken place downstairs. What cause did the killer have to go upstairs after the event? Surely he'd want to exit the house as quickly as possible. The gunshot could have been heard from quite a distance at night. He was also contaminating the scene more than was necessary, something he'd been careful not to do at the other crime scenes, if – and she accepted it was a big if – he was the same man who'd killed the other victims.

At the top of the stairs, she paused. Either the killer had been looking for something, although robbery was clearly not the primary motive given the feathers, or he'd been spooked. It was an old house and entirely possible that squeaking floorboards had got the better of his imagination, but then there'd been a burned apple pie that the forensics team had put on the kitchen table. A large one. Too large for one man to eat alone. The farmer hadn't been skinny but he was far from obese. Certainly not a whole-pie-in-one-evening kind of figure.

Ava took the rooms one by one, clockwise from the top of the stairs, checking each cupboard, looking for signs of inhabitants. In the main bedroom she noticed the flowery bedspread and something else in a bedside cabinet. Tucked in the drawer along with a fly-fishing magazine and a torch was a half-used pack of condoms. Someone had been here, regularly enough for Jon Moffat to have planned for sexual encounters. She squashed the memory of when she'd last been looking for the same items, and the flash of pain that took her unawares with it, and got on with the job in hand. Nothing like a brutal murder to help get priorities straight, she thought.

In the final room, Ava opened the built-in wardrobe, noting the bloody handprint inside the door and calling down to the Scenes of Crime officers to come and photograph it. Stepping inside and to the very back, she heard a hollow thud beneath her foot.

'Tripp,' she called, kicking the bedding out of the way. 'Guest bedroom, now!'

She banged hard on the floor. In spite of the carpeting, the hollow sound of it was obvious compared to the solidity of the rest of the area. Running her finger around the edge of the carpet, she hit a loop of electrical wire. Clever. Hard to notice. Would have looked like a stray lead to anyone not looking for it.

Tucking her fingers into the loop, Ava pulled upwards. The floorboards had been nailed together and a trapdoor cut, carpet and all. Beneath it was darkness. Ava took the steep steps, one after the other, which seemed, ridiculously, to be leading to the outer wall of the house.

'What is it?' Tripp shouted from the hallway.

'Trapdoor. Come into the wardrobe,' Ava shouted. 'A sort of hidey-hole; although this type of property wouldn't have needed one, historically speaking, and this was made recently enough to stick modern carpet to it. It doesn't seem to lead anywhere . . .'

'Ma'am!' Tripp shouted as her last word turned into a scream he heard half from within the bedroom and half though the open window.

Jumping down into the hole, he found her hanging out of a miniature door that opened into the cold clear air. Tripp pulled her back and she landed roughly on top of him, at the base of the steps.

'You all right?' he asked, panting.

'I'd be better if I could stop nearly falling off high walls,' she puffed. 'What in God's name is this?'

'Stay there and hold on,' Tripp said. 'Wait until you hear my voice to open that door again.'

By the time Ava had recovered her breath, Tripp was shouting for her to open the door. She did so tentatively, pushing it with her feet and keeping well away from the edge.

'There's a lot of latticework with ivy all over it,' he shouted up. 'But I think there's a proper structure beneath, more like a ladder.'

'So the farmer was expecting company at some point,' Ava said. 'Which explains why our killer went upstairs after finishing his business with Mr Moffat. If he heard footsteps, he'd have had to make sure there was no one else in the house. By the time he got up here, our potential witness was already in this hole and ready to climb the ladder.'

'And they'd been trained to climb it. We walked right next to it to get in the back door and didn't notice it. No one could have found this by chance.'

'There was a packet of condoms in the bedroom,' Ava said. 'Our victim might have been unmarried, but I don't think he was entirely single.'

'Makes sense,' Tripp confirmed. 'I just got off the phone with the local pub landlady. She got a call early this morning from the farmer's mobile, knew the number as the caller ID came up on her phone. It was a woman's voice telling her Mr Moffat was dead and here's the interesting thing . . . The accent was definitely not Scottish or English. When pushed, the best she could say was that it sounded like an African accent; although the caller said few words then rang off.'

'We've got a witness,' Ava said. 'About bloody time.'

A couple of hours later, the incident room was packed. Ava let Tripp handle the briefing then took questions.

'Why are we assuming it's the work of the Hawksmith–Shozo murderer?' was the inevitable first line of questioning.

'Because the latest victim's doctor has just confirmed he received long-term treatment for depression, including several periods when he was considered to be an active suicide risk. We're currently awaiting a breakdown of the resources Jon

Moffat accessed and the date of his most recent contact with psychiatric services. Mr Moffat was badly burned in a fire in his parents' barn in his early twenties.

'He recovered physically after several surgeries, but it's fair to say his life was changed forever. The resulting depression was something doctors foresaw, but his mental health deteriorated over a period of years when he found it difficult – impossible, in fact – to find a partner. Until now.'

'No known enemies?' DC Janet Monroe queried.

'We haven't had enough time to check that thoroughly, but the local landlady says he kept himself to himself, was popular enough when he went in there for a quiet beer,' Tripp said. 'His bank account was in credit. No mortgage on the farm. No red flags.'

'What's the deal with the feathers?' someone else asked.

'Might be a personal reference to do with the farmer himself,' Ava suggested. 'Or a progression, something in the killer's psyche, maybe living out a fantasy. We'll take another look at that once the ornithologist has identified the feathers for us. There were no other feathers found in the house or any of the barns, though, so it looks as though they were taken to the house deliberately. It's highly deranged behaviour by someone who's not bothered by getting up close and personal with another body, very much the same as in the previous cases.'

'So we have to wait until we locate the witness who called in the crime to the landlady?' Monroe asked.

'That's one line of enquiry,' Ava replied.

'What if the caller just happened to find the body but has no useful information about the murderer? At the rate these killings are happening we could easily have another victim by the time we locate the caller,' Monroe said. 'We have to draw the murderer – him or her – out.'

'There was a bloody hand mark on the inside wall of the cupboard in he farmhouse and the size of it suggests the perpetrator was male. It was Moffat's blood but the killer was wearing gloves so we don't have any prints.'

'Him, then,' Monroe continued. 'I said it before, but his behaviour's escalating at an unprecedented rate. I think we should be more proactive.'

'I'm listening,' Ava said.

'It needs to be something public and we'll let the media get hold of it organically, keep it as credible as possible. Martello Court would be a good location. It's the highest residential building in Edinburgh: twenty-three floors, two hundred and ten feet high. We stage it as a suicide threat in progress, drag it out, put cameras in place and wait to see who turns up. We've already got a lot of social media from the Stephen Berry attempted suicide. Maybe we'll find an overlap, or the same interested professionals.'

'We'd need a volunteer and they'd have to be willing to be monitored to protect their safety until we had a definite suspect in play. It would be a substantial intrusion involving possible danger.' Ava looked around the room for raised hands.

'I wouldn't have suggested it if I weren't willing to volunteer myself,' Janet Monroe said quickly. 'It makes sense. I'm the newest member of the team. I've never been involved in any police media work, plus I've been on the Jenson–Western investigation until now, so I haven't been out to any crime scenes or spoken to any witnesses. I can talk about having a young baby and pretend I'm a single mother, so all sorts of potential for assuming I'm under pressure, compounded by being in a racial minority in Scotland, like Osaki Shozo. Gives me loads to say to whoever comes to my aid.'

Ava sighed. Janet Monroe was undoubtedly intellectually equipped to pull it off, but there was something unsettling about using a mother with a baby still not old enough to walk as bait.

'Don't even think about it,' Monroe said directly.

'What?' Ava asked.

'If I were male, would you have a problem with me volunteering?'

'I need more time to think about it,' Ava deflected. 'It might be better to use an undercover specialist from a different area.'

'You'll have to brief them and get them up to date. I know what I'm looking for. I've read the file on every victim and I'm more than aware of the risks. My partner'll take our baby out of the flat. He has family in Edinburgh. Let me do this,' Monroe insisted.

Ava looked at her. Monroe could handle herself and Ava knew it. She was a good officer with great instincts.

'All right. Tripp, Monroe, my office in ten minutes. We'll need to complete risk assessments and set up surveillance. And I'll need the superintendent to greenlight it. Confidential liaison with fire and paramedic units so they're on standby. Armed police to confirm they can be stationed outside your property on a rotating shift basis. Let's move.'

Pax Graham caught her as she was striding towards her office.

'Ma'am, quick update. The blood we found inside Gilroy Western's engine where the brakes had been cut. We're still working up a full DNA profile, but we've had confirmation from the lab that it's from a woman.'

'Gilroy Western's escort?' Ava asked.

'Lively's traced her through the number we found on Mr Western's phone. He's bringing her in as a person of interest now. We'll ask her for a DNA sample to exclude her from enquiries.'

'Well done,' Ava said. 'Update me tonight? I'm expecting to

266

be out on an operation all afternoon, but I'll text you when I'm free.'

Back in her office, Ava let herself fall into her chair. It occurred to her that she could let Callanach know straight away that the perpetrator might be Gilroy Western's well-paid euphemistically termed 'girlfriend', but decided it would be better to wait until she had more definite news. Between them, Graham and Lively would get a sense for whether or not the woman had anything to do with it. She could call Callanach later. And if that was an excuse to delay a task she wasn't feeling up to, then who could blame her?

Chapter Twenty-Seven

15 March

Janet Monroe stood on the top of what locals had affectionately dubbed Terror Tower several years earlier, when Muirhouse was the go-to area for scoring drugs, selecting your weapon of choice, or slipping a dubious man a bundle of tens to beat up the bastard your girl was seeing behind your back. Monroe had taken a hammer and broken the locks that would otherwise have prevented her from accessing the roof, making sure she was wearing trainers she could stand in for a lengthy period before her feet were screaming at her. She was careful to make herself seen from the ground without risking a tumble in the wind.

Nothing else was faked. The police were not to attend, at least not publicly, until a bona fide concerned member of the public made the call. After that, paramedics would be made aware and suicide prevention services would be brought in. By the time the first police car pulled up, a small crowd had gathered and was staring up at the building.

Ava and Tripp were in a parallel residence, looking out over the growing crowd, checking that the cameras stationed at six different points wouldn't miss a single onlooker. Plainclothes officers were to join the crowd at timed intervals, all wearing wires and recording conversations. Monroe herself had a more discreet transmission unit sewn into a hoodie under her coat.

'She must be freezing,' Ava muttered. 'I can't believe the super signed off on this.'

'First media van arriving now,' Tripp said. 'They'll have to be broadcasting with a time delay in case Janet actually jumps – I mean, not that she'll jump, but if this was real – it would only be a thirty-second buffer. The images should be all over the Internet shortly and we'll be just in time to catch the local evening news.'

'We've been avoiding the press with this story,' Ava said as she scanned the front of the building with binoculars. 'All suicides run the risk of encouraging others to do the same thing. Why is that? Wouldn't you think other people would look and say to themselves, I really don't want that to be me next? I need to get help, change my situation, see my doctor, anything but that.'

'That's logic talking, ma'am,' Tripp said. 'Mental health isn't logical. Depression doesn't follow rules. Misery loves company is a much more realistic way of looking at this. I can see how it would be comforting to know someone else was feeling just as bad as you, and seeing what they'd decided to do about it could be kind of . . . inspiring, I guess.'

'You're not making me feel any more positive about this operation, Sergeant,' Ava said, picking up a radio and buzzing through to the uniformed officer with overall ground control. 'Move the onlookers further back from the building's perimeter. I want a larger safe zone and I need the prople spread thinner so we can get a clear shot of every single face in the crowd.'

269

The result was instantaneous – four monitors in Ava's surveillance room immediately filled with clearer shots of individuals. Most were displaying the normal, expected human emotions. Hands were being pressed to mouths, there were tears, parents were shielding the eyes of children – although it would have been better still if the children had been removed entirely from the vicinity – and there was concerned speculation being exchanged.

Then there were the amateur photographers, taking stills, even footage, presumably in the hope of catching those last fateful moments. Wouldn't that be something to show your mates at the pub in the evening? A few of the better-prepared onlookers were standing around with cans of beer, settling in for the long haul. There was grinning, chatting, and some money was changing hands with a man who was writing slips of paper in return.

'What the fuck . . . are they laying bets?' Ava screeched. 'Tripp, get a camera on that piece of shit in the brown coat with the orange scarf. I want him under arrest before this is over. I don't care what else happens today, no one in the city is going to profit from running the odds on whether or not a young woman kills herself.'

'Can't do it, ma'am. They'll know we were watching and word gets round here almost as fast as a dose of the clap.'

'Jesus, Tripp, you've been spending way too much time with DS Lively,' Ava muttered. 'Fine. I want an ID made, though. I expect to see that bastard picked up on something in the next month. I don't care if it's just having insufficient tread on his tyres.'

'Movement on the top floor, ma'am. Officers have let another person onto the roof.'

Ava turned on the speaker connected with Monroe's wire.

'Stay away from me,' Janet Monroe sobbed, her voice wavering with emotion, her Latina accent more pronounced as she fought the wind to be heard.

'Not a problem,' a man replied.

'Who was that? The voice is familiar,' Ava said.

'Looks like the counsellor's arrived. Middle-aged, I reckon.' Tripp scribbled notes as he spoke. 'Edinburgh accent.'

'I won't come near you until you say I can. Please don't think I'm here to make things worse. My name's Charlie Packham. Can I ask yours?'

'No point,' Monroe replied.

Ava wished she wasn't making quite such an authentic job of sounding desperate. She turned the volume down on their conversation.

'I've met Packham. He works for Reach You with a specialisation in military counselling. Not afraid of being blunt, if memory serves, but he'll have been fully vetted before being allowed to work in mental health units.'

'We've traced the path through the system, which shows that emergency services sent paramedics who requested specialist assistance. The call goes out to whoever the duty agency is in the city and they send their closest counsellor. It seems random. I can run Charlie Packham's name through the police database anyway to see if we get any red flags.'

'Sure. No other faces we recognise in the crowd?'

'Two, actually, but not in connection with this. Uniforms have identified one male who failed to attend court last week on a robbery charge and a woman who's in breach of a probation order. They'll both be followed and arrested later. Other than that, I'm surprised at just how much of a crowd has gathered. There must be two hundred people at the base of the building and that's not considering how many are watching from the windows of adjacent blocks.'

'Here you go, results are in. Charlie Packham has no previous convictions, not even a driving charge. He's completely clean. Google reports that he's a former Marine who works for both Reach You and at the Royal Infirmary on an ad hoc basis.'

A sudden movement of heads in the crowd, mouths opening, reminded Ava of the synchronisation of a flock of birds. She directed her binoculars back up to the top of the tower block. Janet Monroe had taken it up a notch and was suddenly much closer to the edge of the building, leaning over. For a moment, Ava saw herself up there, pushing her luck to its limits at Tantallon Castle.

There were two more camera crews recording footage now and Monroe was fully engaged in conversation with Charlie Packham. Ava picked up her radio again.

'Unit Six, you're go,' she said.

Outside, one of the undercover officers was about to start a rumour that Janet Monroe was a neighbour of his. He would reveal limited information, give a different surname for her, but make sure the TV crew got sufficient for any interested party to be able to pursue her. Sure enough, the media began closing in on one particular area of the crowd. The officer would refuse to give an on-camera interview, purportedly out of 'respect' for his neighbour, but the details he gave would signal the beginning of the end of the operation.

'Check the online newsfeeds, Tripp,' Ava said. 'Let's make sure the information we've planted is filtering through, then we can move Janet on to being talked down.'

It took another ten minutes before the first updates came through online, but the undercover officer had done a good job. Janet Vargas – her maiden name – had been depressed ever since splitting from her partner. She lived a few roads away from Pennywell Gardens, probably in flats she could see from where she stood right now. The reports had already labelled her vulnerable and distressed. Impressive, given that not one journalist had spoken to her directly.

Through the radio, Ava gave the final order.

'Signal end to Monroe then move in.'

Holding her breath as she watched, Ava could see Monroe flailing her arms. The agreement had been that she never got within tripping distance of the edge. Enough lives had been lost in the previous month without Monroe adding hers to the total.

'Please,' Ava could hear the counsellor saying, 'I really don't want anyone to get hurt. Think about your baby. She needs to grow up knowing her mother.'

'She'll be better off without me,' Monroe cried.

'No. No, she won't. There's never going to be a replacement for you. Just take my hand,' the counsellor implored. 'No tricks, I promise. Just let me reach out to you.'

On top of the building, Janet Monroe swayed dangerously near the edge.

'Get back,' Ava ordered her, uselessly.

There were gasps from the crowd. Someone screamed, another began praying loudly and, above it all, Ava could hear laughter.

'Who is that?' she demanded.

'Can't find him. Definitely a male voice,' Tripp said, flicking from camera to camera. 'The crowd's too large now. Whoever's laughing is right in the middle and they're shielded from our viewpoints.'

'You make sure she gets down safely and as quickly as possible,' Ava said. 'I'm going out to find him.'

'You'll have to cover your face, ma'am. You're too recognisable, especially to some of the people who live round here. You've arrested a fair few of them.'

'Give me your coat,' Ava said, taking Tripp's hooded winter jacket and pulling it around her face.

'You don't know that whoever's laughing is the same person

who was on the bridge with Stephen Berry,' Tripp reminded her.

'Sounds the same to me,' Ava said. 'And this might be our last chance to catch him before someone else dies.'

She slipped out through the door, keeping her head down and following the sound of laughter. Pushing past one of the camera crews, she spotted the bookie who'd been taking bets on the outcome of the drama. By the time she got to him, making sure she got a good look at his face for later retribution, the laughing man had moved away, but the noise he was making continued, if anything higher-pitched and more aggressive. Above them, Janet Monroe was continuing her Oscar-worthy performance. The crowd closed around Ava, pushing forwards, desperate to watch, unable to look away.

'Go on, do it!' a man shouted from behind her.

By the time Ava had turned to catch a glimpse of his face, he'd gone quiet.

Someone in the crowd booed him and another shouted for him to shut up. Ava appreciated the community spirit but at that moment in time she just wanted everyone to be quiet so she could hear when he shouted again. She did a three-sixty, pulling her hood down so her ears could pick up the sound and direction better.

The laughing began again. It had a hysterical edge to it. All broken glass and chalkboard. Ava tried to make her way between several onlookers, one of whom was trying to climb onto her boyfriend's shoulders.

'Just wait a moment, would you, love?' the man asked her.

'I need to get through,' Ava insisted.

'You're gonna knock her off. What the fuck's your problem?' He pushed his face just inches from Ava's.

She instinctively reached into her pocket for her ID, then held herself in check, knowing all Monroe's hard work would be for nothing if she revealed the plainclothes police presence in the crowd. Making herself count to ten, she waited until the girlfriend was safely up in the air and waving like a reality-TV wannabe at the nearest camera operator.

A cheer went up from the crowd as the counsellor took Janet Monroe's hand and pulled her away from the edge. Uniformed police officers surrounded her, then there was nothing left to see at all.

Ava thrust herself between the bodies, heading for the back of the crowd. The laughing man hadn't got what he'd wanted again today and she doubted he'd hang around to watch the crowd's delight at the averted crisis.

Bursting through the rear line of spectators, Ava knew she was already too late. People were drifting away in all directions. Short of ordering that every one of them be detained pending details being taken, there was little she could do, and then there would be no chance at all of their murderer coming for Monroe and walking into their arms.

'You were here,' Ava whispered to the shifting crowd.

As the laughing man walked away, just ten feet from where DCI Ava Turner was standing, nails jammed into her palms, he sent a single line of text.

'Thanks for the heads up.'

Chapter Twenty-Eight

15 March

Callanach had spent more time at his gym than in his own apartment since Ava had decided it would be better for him to stay away from MIT. He'd run, walked, worked out and eaten at the gym, spent time in the sauna and the pool, then hung around the bar until it was finally time to escape to Lance Proudfoot's for dinner. The next day was a repeat of the same. It was only when he started to attract attention from women that he had to forego the gym and retreat home. He usually managed to avoid talking to anyone when he was working out. He'd learned not to make eye contact, not to engage in conversation. Better to appear rude than to look like he was open to socialising, and the very last thing on his agenda at the moment was hooking up with another female.

His key slipped smoothly into the lock and he let himself into his apartment. The air smelled floral and sweet. His neighbour, Bunny, regularly flooded their floor with the scents of perfume and beauty products when her clients came to have parts of themselves waxed, sprayed or dyed. He didn't mind, but all he wanted at the moment was the sense that he was entirely alone. It seemed there were women all around him, except the one he really wanted.

Logging into his emails, he realised he was both dreading and longing for contact from Ava. He knew better than to get in touch with her first. If he pushed too hard, it would only take longer to work things out. There was nothing. No emails at all. He checked his Wi-Fi connection then restarted his machine, finally making sure his email provider wasn't experiencing difficulties. Apparently, no one at all wanted to get in touch with him.

It was startlingly similar to when he'd been suspended from work pending trial after Astrid's false accusation. Then, in spite of the evidence she'd falsified, he was also innocent and he'd had the benefit of never doubting himself. This time he was treading on thinner ice. He might have played no active part in either Bruce Jenson or Gilroy Western's deaths, but he was guilty of withholding relevant information from a police investigation and he certainly hadn't answered Pax Graham's questions fully. He did have a motive. No doubt about that.

The other difference between then and now was that his emails had been full of requests from his lawyers, approaches from the press and official notifications from Interpol about his employment status. This period of administrative leave was so unofficial that he'd literally just drifted quietly away from the police station without so much as a conversation with anyone and since then he'd heard nothing. No human resources standard letter. No 'right to appeal the decision' conversations. Not one single email from any other member of the team asking how he was. No one owed him anything, and to expect it was just self-pity and vanity. But still. He'd thought that if no one else, Max Tripp might have been in touch.

He walked through his bedroom, into the bathroom and climbed into the shower, washing away the sweat from hours of working out and the sense that he was so unclean no one wanted to be near him. Turning on a fan to freshen the air from the smell of perfume, he settled onto his bed to read, a dent still in his pillow where he'd apparently been too distracted to follow his usual routine and make his bed properly that morning. He tried to read, to distract his brain from the on-repeat image of Ava finding her slate in his bathroom cabinet.

Other things came flooding back, unbidden, unwanted, too. Ava being taken hostage by a madman. Astrid Borde, so obsessed that she'd followed him to Scotland, stalking him and inadvertently making herself the only witness to Ava's abduction. Ava's best friend, Natasha, who'd provided the vital missing link to where Ava was being held. A young woman dead, whose life might have been saved if they'd arrived just an hour earlier. Other victims whose lives had been forever changed, even though they'd survived. Astrid disappearing into his past and allowing him to build a future. And beyond all that, the question he still had no answer for: Why had he never returned Ava's childhood prayer slate?

He remembered wanting to protect her. He still wanted to protect her. When she'd nearly fallen from the walls of Tantallon Castle, his world had collapsed in on itself for an infinitesimal, endless moment in time. But she'd clung to him. He'd felt her trust through the grip of their fingers. They'd shared something both terrifying and extraordinary. Something no one else could ever be a part of.

Callanach knew he hadn't given up the slate in case he never had anything else. It hadn't been a conscious decision, but the sense of not wanting to lose her before he could be sure he really had her was logical now. In trying to keep her close, he'd lost her forever. There was no point fighting it.

In the morning he'd book a ticket to France. He'd enjoyed Paris. Perhaps it was time to be brave and revisit Lyon, to walk the streets that had suddenly seemed like enemy territory while he was awaiting trial. Going home for a while had been Lance's idea and at first Callanach had protested that there was nothing left there for him. But that wasn't true. There were ghosts to be laid to rest. There were old friends to look up, to forgive for abandoning him. It was time to see what had happened through their eyes.

Astrid Borde's evidence against him had been both compelling and damning. She had all the injuries of a classic violent rape. Her neighbours had been witness to a row between the two of them, with Callanach swearing at her and her sobbing in the background. He'd been set up to perfection by a woman who'd done everything in her power to attract him, then anything to make him pay when he'd rejected her. Obsessive behaviour like that didn't just appear from nowhere.

Perhaps he'd been too used to women falling at his feet when he worked at Interpol, taken it for granted. He'd never been without a beautiful woman at his side for holidays or parties, and often they'd called him cold-hearted and disrespectful when he'd moved on to someone else. Everyone assumed it was his looks that made him careless in long-term relationships, but it was something far simpler than that. Callanach had just never met anyone who could hold his interest for more than a few weeks, months at best.

Going back to France would put some distance between Ava and him, and hopefully add some perspective. They'd gone from not even acknowledging they had feelings for one another to the bust-up of the century, bypassing the entire relationship phase. Some time to consider how to move forwards was definitely required.

He finally managed to concentrate on the book, unaware that the hunt for Jenson and Western's killer was another step closer to resolution.

Chapter Twenty-Nine

15 March

Maisy Gunnach was looking at Pax Graham with eyes that suggested she didn't mind being interviewed by him in the least and that she'd be quite happy to continue the conversation somewhere rather more private later that evening.

DS Lively folded his arms and rested them on his ample stomach. Women didn't look at him like that, at least they hadn't until he'd discovered Detective Superintendent Overbeck's softer side. He and his wife had called it a day a while ago. Policing wasn't the ideal profession for those who liked their relationships stable and long-lasting. Daisy Overbeck – not that he had ever or would ever call her by the given name she hated so much – was an enigma. The sort of woman he'd spent his life avoiding. Bossy, snooty and overbearing, she was perhaps the only woman who'd ever fully understood him. She didn't tolerate his bullshit, she was aware of his underlying faith – which he found so hard to talk about openly – and she appeared to desire him physically.

Pax Graham would never have to worry about that, Lively thought. As sickening as it was, the new detective inspector seemed to be turning it substantially to their advantage.

'I know this is private, Maisy,' Graham said gently. 'It must be difficult to be asked to discuss your personal life – and remember, you're not under arrest – but we just need a bit of help understanding Gilroy Western's lifestyle. What plans did the two of you have for that day?'

'It's no trouble at all,' Maisy smiled, all wide-eyed and breathless.

She reached out a hand and touched Graham's forearm quickly, as if he might burn her. Lively forced himself not to tut out loud.

'Gilroy was coming over to mine for a catch-up. He hadn't been back to Scotland for a few months. We're old friends. He visits me every time he comes back. We'd have stayed at mine for a couple of hours, had a drink, chatted. Then he had to go to a memorial service and see some lawyer. He was hoping to get back to mine and take me out to dinner by about 9 p.m.'

'That's really helpful,' Graham said warmly. 'You're doing great.'

Maisy giggled.

'I should have asked your age before we started. Just for the record.'

At that, Maisy looked slightly less delighted, but she leaned forwards conspiratorially to deliver the news.

'Promise you won't tell?' she asked.

'Nope, our lips are sealed, right, Sergeant Lively?'

'Okay, well, I tell people I'm thirty-four, but actually I'm forty-two. Thank God for moisturiser and vitamin pills, or I'd never get away with it.'

And boob jobs, Lively thought. Maisy was sporting the sort

of chest usually seen in lingerie adverts starring twenty–year-olds.

'How long had you been a close friend of Mr Western?' Graham continued without adding any false compliments to the already sickly conversation.

Lively was grateful for that small mercy.

'Ten years, give or take.'

'I don't suppose you know or have ever met a man called Bruce Jenson?' Graham asked.

'I know the name. He's the poor soul whose funeral Gilroy was supposed to attend. I never met him, but I understand he was in a bad state even before what happened to him.'

'He was, I'm afraid. Who told you?'

'Gilroy mentioned it. Said Mr Jenson was probably better off dead given the dementia. That's no way to go, is it, unable to recognise your own family? I'd rather be put out of my misery.' She looked up at Graham, reddening slightly.

'That's okay,' he reassured her. 'I'm sure lots of people would agree with you. We did find an item in Mr Western's car – a pair of diamond earrings, gift-wrapped but not labelled – do you know anything about them?'

A slow smile spread across Maisy's face. 'They'd have been for me,' she said. 'He always brings me jewellery, and diamonds are my favourite. I wondered what he was bringing me this time. He promised it would be something wonderful.'

'I see. So what sort of gifts has he brought you in the past?' Graham asked casually.

'Last time he took me out clothes shopping. It was mainly lingerie – I prefer real silk – but also some shoes, a handbag and a couple of dresses. I told him I was expecting something shinier this time. Sounds as if he obliged.'

'Did he ever give you cash?'

She gave a slight cough. 'He's helped me out with my rent

in the past and car payments, things like that. Like friends do. I'm no good at managing money. It just flows through my hands!'

Maisy gave brittle laugh and Lively realised she was still trying to pretend she was something other than a prostitute. Fair enough, he thought. When he looked in the mirror he still tried to pretend he had the body of a stunt double and wasn't the wrong side of middle age. Everyone lied to themselves about something.

'Miss Gunnach, we need to establish where all parties who were closely attached to Mr Western were the night before he died. I don't suppose you'd be able to recall what you were doing from 6 p.m. the night before he was due to see you. I know it's difficult to account for such a lengthy period of time, but . . .'

'Actually, it's not,' Maisy said quietly. 'I know exactly where I was.'

'That was easy,' Lively interrupted. 'Are you sure about this, because we'll need to check out whatever you tell us. Just to give fair warning.'

Maisy gave him the same look that his wife had just before she'd packed her bags for the final time. That look said, 'You are nothing to me.' It was an interesting shift from the sweetness and charm with which she'd answered Pax Graham.

'I can't give you his name,' she said, acid apparent below the superficial sugar of her voice. 'My friends don't like it when I give out information about the time I spend with them.'

Pax Graham sat back in his chair, giving Lively the smallest of nods. He could take it from there. Enough beating around the bush.

'Any friend of mine would be happy to help me out when I needed it, so I'm not sure what the problem would be. If, on the other hand, we're talking about clients who might not like their name taken in connection with yours because of the nature of your relationship, I could understand the reticence. Who were you with?'

'Really, I'm not doing this. You said I was under no obligation to answer questions. I think in the circumstances, when I'm grieving, you might be more sensitive,' she said, turning on a little sadness to water down the obvious irritability.

'We need the name, I'm afraid,' Graham confirmed. 'It would avoid having to make this a more formal interview.'

'Or what?' Maisy asked. 'I have an awful lot of friends, you know, and some of them wouldn't like you asking me questions at all. Maybe I should make some calls.'

'Maybe you should,' Graham said. 'Only then you'd have to explain the context and it would only be fair to explain that the person who killed Gilroy Western was a woman. We've also had confirmation in the last hour that a member of staff saw a female running away from Bruce Jenson's care home room at about the same time he was killed.'

Maisy looked from Graham to Lively and back to Graham again.

'Well, it wasn't me. If you must know, I was tied up for half the fucking night. I had bruises on my wrists the next day to prove it. I hate that. Puts my other friends right off.'

'So you won't mind giving a DNA sample to exclude you from the investigation,' Lively said. 'But we still need the name of the man you were with. We'll be discreet, provided we get information without a fight. Of course, if you don't provide us with what we need, we might remember that all the gifts you receive are reportable in your tax returns. I'm guessing you don't have a job and you're not claiming benefits, so the taxman might have a few question about the income you use to pay your rent. They can go back an awful lot of years. It would be unfortunate . . .'

'Motherfucker,' Maisy hissed at him, looking all her forty-two years and then some, boob job or not.

'The name,' Lively said.

'Dennis Mulanney.'

'Dennis Mulanney, the politician?' Graham qualified.

'Exactly,' Maisy replied smugly. 'We were at his flat near Holyrood. We had dinner in, watched a movie – his tastes run to some fairly extreme woman-on-woman action – then he got out the handcuffs. He indulges in some imaginative role play. Good luck asking him for confirmation.'

'He'll cooperate,' Lively said lazily. 'Most people do when they have the option to answer difficult questions quickly and without publicity, or at home when their wife is present. The other option is someone leaking the details to the press.'

'You really are scum, aren't you?' she said, standing. 'I'm done here.'

'We'll need that DNA sample first,' Graham reminded her.

'I'll need those diamond earrings,' she replied. 'They were mine – you'd already figured that out – and the receipt for them, if it was still in his wallet.'

'Those are all exhibits. They won't be released until the investigation has been concluded, even longer if they're needed for a trial,' Graham explained.

'They belong to me,' she snarled, leaning over the table. 'Do you have any idea what I go through to get paid?'

'Some idea, I think,' Graham smiled. 'But those earrings belong to the person named in Mr Western's will. They hadn't been handed to you at the time when he died, so you hadn't legally taken possession of them. Mrs Western is the rightful owner, and I suspect she'll be returning them and asking for the money back.'

'You bastards,' Maisy replied. 'Gilroy Western hated his wife. She has no right to them.'

'Then it was Mr Western's responsibility to change his will. Nothing we can do about it,' Graham said coolly, going up a couple of notches in Lively's estimation.

'Yeah, well, whoever killed Gilroy Western, good luck to her. He was a deviant little shite, so there you go. Whoever finished him off probably did the world a favour.'

Maisy Gunnach walked out, followed by the uniformed officer who'd been standing outside the interview room door, ready to take a cheek cell swab from her.

'I guess that's where the phrase high maintenance comes from,' Graham said to Lively when he was sure Maisy was out of earshot. 'What did the witness from the care home say? I didn't get a chance to read the statement before coming in here.'

'It was a male orderly. He was stood outside smoking while on duty, under the cover of a couple of trees in the garden. Smoking on the grounds is banned and during a shift it's a sackable offence. It took a while for him to decide it would be better to get sacked than to withhold information from us, not that it's very detailed. A female figure emerged through Bruce Jenson's patio door and ran through the gardens to the road. No hair or eye colour as it was so dark. No description of clothing other than tight-fitting trousers and a coat, not bulky. Tallish, slim, her figure gave the gender away.'

Graham sighed. 'Fits with the female DNA found in Western's car. Can you get hold of Dennis Mulanney tonight and confirm the alibi?'

'That would be my pleasure,' Lively said drily. 'What're your next steps?'

'Updating the DCI,' Graham said. 'Tomorrow, I'd like to talk

287

to Gilroy Western's daughter. I know we've established that his wife was in Spain when he died, but that doesn't mean his daughter was.'

'Strikes me you're getting the better end of this deal,' Lively said. 'Privileges of bloody rank.'

Chapter Thirty

16 March

Lance Proudfoot had arrived at the scene of Janet Monroe's dramatic non-suicide later than the other attending press vultures – he was under no illusion as to how they were thought of in the collective – after the story online sent multiple alerts pinging to his phone. In truth, he hadn't wanted to go. The prospect of potentially seeing a body fall from so great a height was grisly, but it was news and that was what he did.

The most impressive aspect of it would inevitably prove to be how the woman in question got access to the roof space in the first place. In an area that no tourist was ever going to visit, not willingly anyway, where poverty was the norm, and where it was easier to get drugs than an appointment with a doctor, the roof of one of Edinburgh's tallest buildings had long since been carefully secured.

Careful to keep his distance from the remaining press pack, Lance took up position further away from the base of the building between two rows of parked cars, assessing the scene from a distance. Much as he hated the thought of taking photos under such distressing circumstances, the professional in him inevitably won over. He focused on the tiny people at the top of the tower block, his high-powered lens offering a view of a distressed woman he very much hoped he wouldn't see descending at speed past the faces peering at the crowd through the windows.

That was enough. He put his camera away and took out his mobile. Speaking quietly into his phone's dictation app, he'd described the scene: the pack mentality of the crowd, reacting to one another as much as to the tragedy of the human condition taking place above them. The apparent calm of the emergency services as they constructed perimeters and prepared for the worst while maintaining an impressive air of assuming that nothing bad was actually going to happen. And the occasional chilling wail from the poor woman suffering so terribly above.

Then a man had pushed through the crowd, laughing. Lance didn't catch his face, but the body language was all arrogance and youth. In his twenties, swaggering with the lack of realisation that he, too, would die someday. And that before that – if he was lucky – he'd live through the steady decline of his body, the weakening bladder, clicking knees and eyes that only focused on the small print with your arms held out straight in front of you, as if you were driving some imaginary cartoon car.

The laughing male pulled his hoodie up as Lance turned round to share some advice about common decency with him that would inevitably fall on deaf ears, but sometimes in life the attempt to do the right thing was worth more than the realistic prospects of success. Laughing Boy was a little over six foot but thin and his clothes were a brand currently worn by every social media-obsessed youth. In his hand he clutched his mobile, the picture on the screen changing as he walked, and Lance realised the man's camera was on.

So that was the game. Attend at a possible suicide. Make sure you're ready to catch all the action. Then presumably post it on some site with no responsible policing at all and wait to see the hits roll in. Other Internet stars had sought to get followers under similar dubious circumstances and ended up in trouble for it, but not before their fame had reached what for them must have seemed dizzying heights. Not too difficult to comprehend how you could be tempted to the dark side by the thought of all that adulation. The problem was natural justice. At some point, you had to grow up, and the idea of spending the remainder of your days knowing you'd livestreamed a suicide would get more painful with each passing year.

As the male disappeared and Lance also decided he'd had enough – some stories you paid too high a price to report on – a woman thrust her way through the sea of bodies, staring after the would-be Internet star. It was her body language that caught Lance's attention first, a coiled spring, all tension and energy. Then he'd seen her face. Ava Turner, dressed to blend in, not a hint of police officer about her, was in pursuit. Not overtly, though. She didn't want to be recognised.

Lance slipped his phone into his pocket and followed his instinct that the real story was slipping away behind him. He knew better than to call out to her. If a detective chief inspector was on the ground and working a scene in person, it was serious. Making contact with her now would inevitably blow her cover and, given what he knew about the amount of work stress she was under – not to mention her personal life – that would end badly.

He wondered where Callanach was as he trailed Ava at a distance. They'd had dinner together two nights earlier and Luc had opened up more than ever before. He'd explained about the disastrous evening with the woman ahead of him in the crowd and the traumatic events that had led him to make the mistake that might well cost him the woman he so obviously loved.

Lance had been able to see both sides and privately thought there might be something at work on more of a subconscious level. He'd been there himself. Whenever he'd stood at the threshold of something he'd really wanted in life, he'd been struck with a certainty that it was never destined to work out. A sort of pre-emptive destruction that avoided no end of disappointment.

Callanach, for all the damage he'd taken, had hit his all time low a couple of years ago and had been ready for his happily ever after. Ava Turner was more of an enigma. Finding the prayer slate Callanach had taken from her was, in the grand scheme of things and after a cooling-off period, a transgression that might have been forgiven, but only if you weren't already waiting for things to go wrong. Or thinking you didn't deserve happiness. Or that perhaps it was easier to deny yourself happiness at the outset than to have it for a while, only to lose it later on. That revelation was what Lance had taken away from Callanach's disaster story. A woman who was protecting herself, by denying herself anything that might hurt her. She would be neither the first nor the last.

At the edge of the crowd, Ava Turner had halted, studying the various people who were walking away. He considered approaching her gently to see if he could help, then decided against it. Ava knew what she was doing and she wouldn't be there without backup. He left her alone, returning to his car within view of the building's main exit, from where the roof was only partially visible and was thus crowd-free.

Sitting in his car, on the street, he took the time to contemplate life. He'd be lying if he denied having moments when life had seemed to be made almost entirely of pain. When his son had a concussion that left him unconscious for long enough to be concerned about the state he'd be in when he woke up. When his wife had left him. Having to watch his mother – the least complaining, most jovial woman he'd ever met – die slowly of a cancer that had no purpose, nothing to gain from her, but which took her just because it could. But he'd never been close to suicide. The thought of it left him bereft. Unless you'd been there, it was inconceivable.

He hadn't really thought about the scale of the problem until he'd helped Callanach to find Fenella Hawksmith's daughter. That poor woman had a history of suicide attempts, too. Then there was the lad who'd tried to jump from the Queensferry Crossing only a month earlier.

Lance's head began to ache. He opened the car window to let in some fresh air. Luc had said that Fenella Hawksmith's body had been in her flat for about three weeks. Then Stephen Berry had died out at Tantallon Castle. Not long after that the poor Japanese lad had been murdered. Only hadn't his wife, that piece of work with the boyfriend affectionately named after a form of protein, said something about him being suicidal, too? Osaki Shozo, that was it. The old grey matter was still just about functioning.

A man wearing jeans made smarter by the addition of a striped shirt and an official-looking lanyard walked out of the building, accompanied by paramedics, police officers, and a dark-haired woman in leggings and a tatty coat. The latter looked absolutely exhausted. No doubt he was seeing the thankfully uninjured person whose pain had been so publicly aired. The more professionally attired male gave the potential jumper a brief hug, then paramedics walked her slowly to the back of a waiting ambulance.

Berry, Hawksmith, Shozo, he thought. All with a history of

suicidal thoughts if not actual attempts. All now dead. Now Ava Turner was roaming the crowd at another potential suicide, watching not the actual events but the onlookers themselves. Waiting for someone to reveal themselves? Lance wanted to be wrong. To go home, write up his story – one with a happy ending – for his news blog. But he knew he wasn't. Coincidences happened when you were holidaying on a different continent and you bumped into your best friend from junior school on an otherwise deserted beach. Coincidences and dead bodies, though, rarely – if ever – had anything to do with one another.

He started his engine and followed the ambulance at a respectful distance, making sure he wasn't spotted. The police would no doubt be doing the same. He'd have to be careful not to make himself a suspect, but it was pretty obvious that the police thought they might catch a serial killer in the crowd. It was a story he couldn't have walked away from if he'd wanted to.

Toying with the idea of calling Callanach for confirmation, he decided against it. His friend was supposed to be removing himself from active duty and the last thing Callanach needed was to have someone take advantage of his insider knowledge when he couldn't be a part of the action. That was all right. Lance could wait and watch. A lifetime of journalism had made him patient.

The ambulance failed to head for the nearest hospital as Lance had expected, instead, after taking a circuitous route, opening its doors in Kimmerghame Drive. Janet Vargas – the name had popped up online in spite of the fact that Lance would have considered it improper to give identifying information – was escorted indoors by the two paramedics.

They must have made sure someone was at home to look after her, Lance thought. No psych evaluation. No prescription. Of course, it was possible Janet had all the medication she needed waiting for her in her flat, but that just begged the question: why hadn't she taken it, or why it hadn't worked? The seed of the story, already firmly planted in Lance's mind, sprouted and did its best to reach for a light source. Too soon for that.

He identified a sufficiently inconspicuous parking space, checked his emergency car stash of drinks and packs of crisps – bugger the low-fat diet – and settled down to watch Janet Vargas' building for no other reason than because that's what his gut was telling him to do. In an hour or so, he'd wander in, grab one of the pieces of junk mail that would have been dropped on the floor somewhere and stick it under a door on the top floor. Give himself what looked like a reason for being inside while he got the lay of the land.

If the police were watching and they got suspicious of him, he'd use Callanach's name to clarify who he was. At least it would be confirmation of the bigger picture: that those attempting suicide in the city were prey to a ruthless murderer who saw them as bait. And that Janet Vargas, so recently saved from taking her own life, might soon be wishing she'd gone through with it, compared to the horrors that Hawksmith and Shozo had been subjected to.

Lance waited an hour, considered going home but didn't. Some habits you just couldn't break. He had no idea at all what, or who, he was looking for, but the journalist – and perhaps, he acknowledged, the egotist in him – assured him he'd know it when he saw it.

Chapter Thirty-One

17 March

The briefing room was full to capacity with members of both investigative teams. Pax Graham stood up to speak first.

'We still have no suspect,' he began. 'Gilroy Western's long-time escort has an alibi for the entire period and after some pressure was applied, the gentleman she was with has confirmed her version of events. Suffice to say, if she was lying there's no way he'd have put his political career on the line for her. Likewise Western's daughter and wife, while having potential motives for wanting Western dead, were both in Spain at the time. That leaves someone who hasn't yet figured into our investigation, or the possibility that someone ordered a hit on Jenson and Western.

'The DNA found on the engine of Western's car isn't in the police national database, but the same DNA has also been identified on the cushion used to kill Bruce Jenson. What we do have, though, courtesy of the staff member who finally came forward to say a female figure ran through the gardens while he was having a cigarette, is CCTV footage from the security camera of the industrial building opposite the care home.'

He turned around and hit a few buttons on a laptop while someone killed the lights. A large screen flickered into half-life, showing little other than darkened blurs with the occasional car headlights flashing past. The roof of the care home was visible in the top section but shrouded by trees and vegetation at the front. Large gates looked like an impressive enough security measure, fixed to sections of wall than ran for several metres either side.

Graham fast-forwarded the footage by a few minutes once the audience had found their focus. There was movement in the bottom right-hand corner of the screen, leaves and branches displaced in ill-defined shades of grey, then a patch of darkness appeared where the bush had been. A figure stepped through and out onto the pavement: slim, graceful, unmistakably female, even with only a shaky silhouette on view. The hair was either short or tied back and the line of her neck was clear. She leaned down.

'We think she's brushing off debris from the hedge,' Graham said as the figure straightened again. 'And here, she does something with both hands then reaches into her coat. It seems likely that she's removing gloves and putting them in her jacket pockets to avoid looking suspicious. That night wasn't exactly warm but it wasn't necessarily gloves weather. She exits down the street and we lose sight of her. After that we were unable to catch her on any other CCTV on nearby roads, so we assume she got into a vehicle at some point, or even called a cab.'

Ava stared at the screen as if the woman might reappear. In spite of the darkness and the horrible pixellation of the footage, there was something about the woman that struck a chord with her. A familiarity, something to do with the way she moved. How she'd cocked her head to one side and smoothed her hair before walking off down the road. She closed her eyes and tried to catch the threads of her subconscious mind that were already slipping away.

'If she was wearing gloves, how did her DNA get onto the cushion?' someone asked.

'We think from her saliva, possibly from the effort of pushing the cushion over his face, or from spittle flying as she spoke to him during the event,' Graham replied. 'Full DNA results from all the Bruce Jenson exhibits only came back this morning. It's possible we might be able to tell a bit more about her, in generic terms, in a few more days.'

He nodded at Ava, ceding the floor.

'DS Tripp has made some headway in the Berry case. The male on the Queensferry Bridge we've been referring to was captured on another onlooker's mobile phone. We don't have a clear facial view. He was wearing winter clothes, hood up, scarf on, but we've got the outline of his head. You'll see from this footage' – she took Graham's former place at the laptop and selected a file – 'that there's a man shown in a rear view. He shouts encouragement at Stephen Berry to jump – we see his mobile phone held up at one point – and then he begins to laugh. Although we only have the rear view, the movement of his head matching the shouting of words and laughing makes us certain enough that this is the man we've been looking for.'

She closed the file and opened another one. An audio track began to play as the camera panned across a crowd. The words, 'Go on, do it!' could be heard clearly above the background noise, then a break, then laughter.

'We had a speech recognition expert compare the two over-night. She's confirmed that it's the same man. We can't place him at a crime scene, not yet, but we're putting all of our efforts into identifying him. Tripp, I want your team pursuing media outlets to see what footage was posted of Janet Monroe yesterday.

'We know the laughing man was filming, so let's see if we can't trace him through that. We'll be able to exclude any innocent parties easily now that we have the speech pattern. We estimate that he's in his twenties, roughly six feet tall. I saw him in the crowd yesterday but was unable to follow.

'Assume he's local and has a vested interest in potential suicides. It can't be a coincidence that he appeared at two events in progress, so he's either watching the media, or he has a contact — emergency services, possibly — who's notifying him when a possible suicide is called in. Find him. Notify all progress to me immediately.

'In the meantime, I'll be showing the footage to Rune Maclure, the counsellor who assisted Stephen Berry on the bridge. I'd like results by the end of the day. If we can't do this quietly, we may be forced to ask the TV stations to broadcast the footage to see if anyone'll call in with a name, but that's a last resort. If we do that, it's a sure thing he'll run.'

Ava closed the laptop lid and picked it up, making for the door. Pax Graham caught her as she went.

'Could I have a word, chief?'

'Can it wait? I've got Maclure waiting in my office and I know he's got appointments to get to.' She began to walk.

Graham fell into step at her side.

'It won't take long,' he said.

Ava hoped he wasn't going to ask her for a drink again. He'd called to update her on the case the previous evening, inviting her to meet for a face-to-face chat at a pub, asking if she'd eaten. She'd claimed tiredness, which although not a lie, wasn't the reason she didn't want to see him. Pax Graham was single, attractive and much too attentive, which she needed in her life like she needed the measles.

'You've got two minutes,' she said.

'All right.' He paused, taking several strides before continuing.

'When the forensic results came back from the cushion used to kill Bruce Jenson, we didn't just find Gilroy Western's killer's DNA on there. Not unexpectedly, we found several different sources. One of them, though, was DI Callanach.'

Ava kept walking, reminding herself to breathe.

'Callanach placed himself at the scene and admitted he made physical contact both with Mr Jenson and the cushion. I'm not surprised his DNA came up. It's one of the reasons he's on administrative leave – to keep the investigation untainted.'

'I agree, but the DNA wasn't from skin cells or sweat, which I was expecting.'

Ava stopped walking.

'There was blood on the cushion, almost invisible to the naked eye, the droplet was so small.'

'He told us he broke a vase. He reported it to the nurse on duty. It's possible he nicked his skin then.'

'It is, but Callanach said he knocked over the vase looking for a towel to wipe Jenson's chin. His chronology is that it was only later he went back to clean up the broken vase. He didn't say anything about going back to Jenson again after that.'

Ava smiled and nodded. 'You're absolutely right,' she said. 'It needs clarifying. Thanks for letting me know first. Have DI Callanach come in and deal with it.'

'No need at the moment,' Graham said. 'It's not as if he's a suspect. I just wanted to give you advance notice, in case it comes up when the file gets passed over to the procurator fiscal for trial and that's not going to happen until we catch whoever's responsible. I'll let you get on.'

'Sure. Thanks,' Ava said quietly.

She still hadn't notified Callanach that it was a woman they were looking for in connection with the two murders. Things were too hectic and even if they weren't, passing on information about the investigation was just another breach of protocol.

If push came to shove, he'd have to come up with an explanation for his blood ending up on Jenson's cushion. That was Callanach's problem, not hers. She had enough to deal with.

Rune Maclure was waiting in her office, chatting with Superintendent Overbeck, when Ava entered. Overbeck was stirring a cup of coffee slowly, all eyes, in a manner that made Ava glad she hadn't brought DS Lively to the meeting with her. The sergeant was feeling insecure enough without watching the woman he was inexplicably drawn to flirting with a man as charming as Maclure. Overbeck, on the other hand, had called for coffee to be delivered in cups with saucers that actually matched and which weren't even chipped, something of a miracle in a police station. Ava steeled herself for the usual onslaught of insults.

'Ava, we've been waiting for you,' Overbeck purred.

So it was all first names and smiles, then. Overbeck must have been massively overselling herself, Ava decided.

'Mr Maclure, apologies for keeping you. Detective Superintendent, I can update you later. We just need to view an exhibit. It shouldn't take long. I can come to your office immediately afterwards.'

'Not at all,' Overbeck said. 'You know I prefer a hands-on approach. Why don't I stay and work through this with you? I might be of assistance.'

Ava tried not to sigh audibly. If Overbeck couldn't see how laughable the use of the phrase 'hands-on' was, with cerise nails that could easily be classified an offensive weapon, then she really was operating police command from a different planet.

'I'd really appreciate that, ma'am,' she said. 'Let me just set up the laptop.'

'So, how long have you lived in Edinburgh, Rune?' Overbeck continued.

'All my adult life,' Maclure said. 'It gets into your blood, I think. You can travel the world, but if you're from Scotland, she calls you back sooner or later.'

'I couldn't agree more. Where did you get your degree?'

'St Andrews,' Maclure smiled, catching Ava's eye-roll as Overbeck was taking a sip of coffee.

Overbeck was forgetting she was dealing with a psychotherapist. Her body language alone was enough to send any sensible man running.

'Here we go,' Ava said quickly. 'You said there was a man laughing on the bridge when you were with Stephen Berry. It took a while, but we managed to trace other people on the bridge by their car registration plates. Someone was filming from behind this male.' She brought the footage up on the screen. 'He filmed the laughter and some shouting. Can you confirm that this is the voice you heard?'

Ava pressed play. Maclure watched it once, asked to replay it and listened again, leaning in to study the screen.

'Yes, absolutely, that's what I heard; although I was some distance away and the wind was muffling it. Can I just ask—'

'Sorry, one moment, while it's fresh in your mind,' Ava said. 'I'd like you to look at another clip. There was a suicide threat in the city yesterday. Police attended to secure the area and assist the emergency services, and a camera happened to catch this from general footage of the crowd.'

She pressed play. The camera panned across heads. Almost manic laughing erupted and a man yelled. A view of his head, face almost entirely obscured by his hood, came and went, slightly blurred, as he turned his back and began weaving through the bodies around him.

'Take it back,' Maclure said. 'Let me see it again.'

Ava scrolled along the timeline.

'You should know we've had an expert consider both voice patterns. She's concluded it's the same man.'

302

Maclure didn't respond but pulled the laptop closer to himself, increasing the screen brightness as the clip began to play again. At the end, he sat back and crossed his arms, frowning.

'If that's our suspect, we're going to have to get a much better picture than that before we release details to the public,' Overbeck said. 'Have the techies tried to enhance it or whatever they do in that little cave of theirs?'

'You can't enhance it. If we increase the size, it'll just get blurrier,' Ava said, wishing Overbeck would just leave her to it.

'I don't think you'll need to,' Maclure said softly. 'God, I hope my office isn't responsible for any of these deaths, but . . .'

Ava gave him time.

'I have an idea who this is. I'm not definite, and I have no reason to believe he's the sort of person who'd ever be violent, but there's been a young man hanging around the drop-in centre recently who fits this description.'

'Do you have a name?' Ava asked.

'I don't, but I've seen him with one of our administrative assistants, the girl who does our filing and makes coffee for visitors if there's a delay getting them in to see a counsellor. Her name's Vicki Rosach.'

'Does Vicki have access to the personal details of the people you help?' Overbeck took over.

'They're all held in our files; although she's instructed not to open the files or access the information. It's in her contract.' Maclure put his head in his hands. 'I'm sorry, I was so certain this wouldn't come back on us. We're there to help people when they need it most. If we lose the public's trust, people won't feel able to come to us when they need us most. It'll be devastating.'

Overbeck laid a manicured claw on Maclure's forearm, squeezing gently.

'You're obviously doing a marvellous job. Please don't blame yourself.'

'I need Vicki Rosach's personal details,' Ava said. 'Don't alert your office. It's important Vicki has no idea anything's wrong. Do you know if she's at work now?'

'I think so,' Maclure said. 'If I call in to check, it's likely to be her who picks up the phone.'

'Don't do that,' Ava said quickly. 'Brief description?'

'About twenty, ginger hair, pale skin.'

'I remember her,' Ava said.

'She's not great at her job, to be honest. Perhaps I should have got rid of her, but I always thought of her as distracted or a bit thoughtless and I like to give people a proper chance. It never occurred to me there might be anything more suspicious going on.'

'We're not certain yet that Vicki's got anything to do with it,' Ava said, shutting her laptop and picking up her coat. 'We'll bring her in and ask about her associates. If we move forwards, I'll need you to attend and identify the man you think you recognised.'

'I'll help in any way I can, especially given that my office is responsible.'

Ava paused on the way out of her office.

'Mr Maclure, if I've learned anything in the police, it's that psychopaths always find a way. There's an inevitability about what they do. A determination that beats any barrier put in their path. Your organisation isn't to blame here. All we can do now is make sure there are no more victims.'

Chapter Thirty-Two

17 March

Whatever computer glitch had been keeping his emails from him was suddenly mended. Callanach opened his laptop to find forty-two messages he hadn't yet read. He started at the top.

Good morning, sir.

Tripp had messaged, no less formal in email than he was in the flesh.

I heard from DCI Turner that you're on administrative leave. I hope it's all right emailing, but I wanted to let you know that we're making good progress with the cases here. If you need anything, please call my mobile. I hope you're well.

Callanach smiled. His newly promoted detective sergeant was understandably formal, but the message was well-intentioned.

Tripp was nothing if not loyal and together they'd made an unlikely but successful team. Until now.

Callanach opened the next email, which was from his bank, then one reminding his about a dental appointment – at least he had plenty of time for that sort of thing now – before deciding to get himself a coffee. No point using up all his distractions at once when his days were so long and uneventful.

Returning to his desk, he ran his eyes down the emails to figure out where he'd got to in the list. That should've been obvious and easy, only every email on the page was marked as read. He tried to remember if they'd been like that when they'd popped up, or only since he'd been reading them, but he couldn't recall it clearly. Picking up his phone, he sent himself an email, with the word 'Coffee' on the subject line, and hit send. A minute later it came through in bold, marked as unread, no problem at all.

Scrolling back to emails from months ago, the ones that had slipped through his junk filter and sat unread in his inbox, he found several still marked as unread. So his computer was functioning properly, and his emails were sending and receiving properly.

He stared at the screen before typing in his mother's name and opening up her recent emails to him. He found what he'd been looking for in an email dated 10 March. His mother, too, had received no emails for a few days, then hers had made a remarkable appearance. She hadn't said whether they'd been marked as read or not, but there was a good chance it was something she might not have noticed. The emails from Callanach to his mother had named Jenson and Western specifically. They created a clear path from him to the dead men and Callanach was as sure as he could be that someone else had read them.

That left two possibilities: one was that someone with a grievance had been looking for a weak point and was intent on setting him up for the murders. If that was the case, the list was endless. He'd crossed too many gang members, crime bosses and corporate criminals – any of whom could have organised a hacking – to be able to point to a single one who might want vengeance. The other option, and a far more disturbing one, was that Pax Graham had moved from simply being suspicious of him to deciding to dig deeper into his story, thereby obtaining a court order to look at his emails.

Callanach considered taking a sip of his coffee, but his stomach was making it clear it would be rejected. If DS Graham had his emails, it could only be because Ava had approved the application.

She wouldn't, Callanach thought. Or at least she wouldn't have before. Right now, she was so angry . . . it didn't bear thinking about. The only thing was that Ava already knew about his emails to his mother. Handing those emails over to Graham would also implicate her. So perhaps Ava wasn't involved. She wasn't the only superior officer who could approve the application. Detective Superintendent Overbeck could have done that, and with Ava wrapped up in the Hawksmith and Shozo investigations, it was entirely possible that Graham had gone straight to his boss's boss. Overbeck would be quite happy to see him crushed. She'd made it perfectly clear he wasn't her choice for a new detective inspector when he'd joined Police Scotland. That didn't explain who'd killed Jenson and Western, though.

The next email was from DS Lively. Callanach clicked it open, hoping it would contain a case update.

Are you taking up modelling again, now that you're on a long holiday? it began. No 'sir' or pleasantries. Typical Lively.

We can all get to the mirror in the gents now that you're not here, and I've taken that chair you like and moved it to my

desk. Some wee bastard's still killing people. Guess you're
seeing that on the news. The Chief's got a bug up her arse, so
you should probably come back soon and help us out. There's
a beer on me if you fancy it.
  Lively.

In spite of everything, Callanach smiled. Lively was the last
person he'd have assumed was concerned about him. Frankly,
he'd doubted Lively even knew what his email login was, but
he'd made the effort to get in contact. The beer he'd take with
a pinch of salt. Lively wasn't known for getting his wallet out,
but the thought was a kind one and sufficiently out of character
that Callanach wondered if he ought to be worried.

His mobile rang and for a second Callanach thought it would
be his larger-than-life, rougher-than-sandpaper sergeant
following up. Instead, DS Graham's softer accent came through.

'What can I do for you?' Callanach asked.

'We need an additional statement for clarity. Just a procedural
matter relating to the forensics we've got back. Would tomorrow
morning suit?' Graham asked.

'Sure, I'll come into the station,' Callanach said.

'Best not in the circumstances. We'll come to you.'

As much as Callanach wanted to ask what it was about, he
knew the strategies too well to show any level of concern. Best
to be completely laid-back about it.

'Sure. Whatever you need. Is 9 a.m. okay?'

'That would be great,' Graham said. 'I don't suppose DCI
Turner's been in touch today, has she?'

'No, not at all,' Callanach said.

It wasn't a lie, so he wasn't sure why he felt as if it was.
Probably because it struck him that Graham wasn't just checking
up on him. He was checking up on Ava, too.

'Should she have?'

'No, I just lost track of her. Lots going on here. See you tomorrow.'

Callanach rang off. Graham's voice had been friendly and relaxed, but he was nobody's fool. Lively's email had confirmed that Ava wasn't happy at the moment. She was inevitably having to deal with every update on the Jenson–Western case and each time it was discussed, she'd be reminded what had happened between them. Perhaps it was time they talked. Hopefully by now she'd been able to put what he'd done into context.

He checked his watch. It was mid-afternoon. Right now she'd be in the middle of briefings, and up to her neck in forensics reports and witness statements. Phoning would only make things worse. He texted instead, keeping it light and brief, making sure he didn't reference work.

Hi, wondering if you have time to get a coffee? No rush but this week would be good.
Luc.

For the hour that followed he checked his phone every few minutes for a response, then forced himself to put it on a shelf. Eventually, he grew so fed up with his own desperation that he turned it off altogether.

Chapter Thirty-Three

17 March

By the time Ava arrived at the Reach You drop-in centre, a perimeter had already been formed around the building. She hoped there was no one inside the building right now getting help who'd be distressed by what they were about to do. Officers stood backs to the walls either side of the front door as she rang the buzzer. Someone buzzed back, presumably looking at a screen inside, judging by the camera, then the door was opened.

'Police,' Ava announced, raising her ID into the face of the young woman who was, without a doubt, Vicki Rosach.

'What the hell?' she mumbled, more sullen than scared, reaching into her pocket.

'Don't move!' Ava ordered. 'Raise your hands above your head and turn round.'

Then there were bodies everywhere. Uniformed officers took her to the floor, careful to ensure she was unharmed, even more careful to make sure they didn't damage her mobile, which Ava had made clear was a priority.

'I don't understand,' Vicki sobbed as she was handcuffed and assisted to stand. 'What are you doing with my phone?'

The officer who'd removed it from her pocket bagged and labelled it.

A mixture of other people filled the halls, all speaking at once, some counsellors, some patients, and there was a fair amount of crying. Ava could understand that. It was distressing, the sense of being invaded, of having the place where you worked and did a job you believed in suddenly raided. It was something of a violation. Just not as much of a violation as having someone enter your home and shove your penis in a toaster.

'We're taking all the computers as well as the hard copies of both staff and patient files,' Ava announced to the staff members once Vicki had been removed into a police van.

'You can't do that. You need a court order,' a man declared.

'You're Charlie Packham, right?' Ava clarified.

She'd only heard his voice before, first outside the door when she'd been talking to Rune Maclure, then again when he'd been talking Janet Monroe down from the top of the tower block. He was tall and skinny, arms crossed over his chest. However good a counsellor he might be, she thought, he had little natural charm about him.

'I have Rune Maclure's consent,' Ava assured him. 'I'll need you all to remain here until you've given statements to these officers. After that, please do not leave the city without notifying the police first.'

'Are we in trouble?' Packham asked.

'Not at all,' Ava reassured the group, the angry, unprofessional part of her wanting to say the opposite. That they'd been careless with the information they kept on patients. That a bunch of psychotherapists, of all people, had so badly misjudged the character of someone they'd employed that they'd rendered already vulnerable people prey to a vicious killer. 'But you may have information you don't even realise yet that'll help us to fill in some blanks. We just need you to be contactable, that's all.'

'Can we continue our work, away from the drop-in centre?' a female asked.

'Yes, of course,' Ava said. 'But you'll need to find a more secure way to keep patient information from now on.' That last one she couldn't resist.

'Rune Maclure doesn't have the authority to speak for all of us. This charity's run by a committee. Maclure's just one member of it,' Packham chimed in again. 'I'll be consulting a lawyer. I don't accept that the police can just read sensitive documentation without the authority of a judge.'

'And I don't understand why anyone would want us not to when it might save lives. After all, isn't that what your charity was set up for?' Ava bit back. 'But feel free to consult a lawyer, if you really think that would be the best use of your time and the charity's funds.'

Packham managed to stay silent, opting instead for giving her an unpleasant smile then checking his watch, reminding Ava that she was on borrowed time.

Lights and sirens ensured that she was back at the police station just as they were finishing booking Vicki Rosach in. Ava and Tripp would speak with her together, they'd decided, under caution. A duty lawyer had been waiting to represent her. All bases were covered. She let Tripp do the talking. Her temper was already frayed.

Having dealt with the legal formalities, Tripp began. Voice soft, low-key, all apologies for how bad the tea was and how uncomfortable the chair was, even the lawyer seemed to like the young detective sergeant.

'So, Vicki . . . sorry, can I call you by your first name?' Tripp asked.

'Um, yeah, whatever.' Her chin was on her chest, shoulders hunched.

'Vicki, we need some information from you and your assistance at this early stage should ensure that we can do our best to keep any charges against you at a sensible level.'

The lawyer raised his eyebrows and Ava could understand why. Tripp, a veritable fluffy bunny among Police Scotland sergeants although no less good a detective for it, was doing a great job of indicating best-case scenario while promising nothing that would ensure that outcome for the twenty-something in the hot seat.

'Perhaps just explain what the case is against my client and let us know what you want by way of information,' the lawyer said drily.

'Great idea, I can do that,' Tripp said. 'Thanks for being so direct. So, Vicki, I'd like to show you a couple of video clips and ask you to listen carefully to the audio. Would that be all right?'

Vicki nodded and Tripp hit play on the laptop that was kept on a separate table, just in case there was a sudden rise in hostilities and Vicki decided she needed something to use as a weapon. Looking at the young woman's face, Ava decided that wasn't going to be necessary. The first clip was enough to have her in tears.

The sight and sound of the laughing man had Vicki reaching across to hold her lawyer's hand. The lawyer did his best to wriggle free.

'Do you know that man, Vicki?'

'Uh huh,' Vicki responded, wiping her nose on her sleeve.

Ava reached behind her for the pile of tissues kept for such emergencies, knowing Tripp was a closet germaphobe. He and the lawyer both, by the look of it.

'One more clip,' Tripp persisted. 'Perhaps have a sip of that tea, help calm you down, before I ask you any more questions.'

Ava had a growing sense of admiration. Any other officer would have gone in with a sledgehammer. Tripp wasn't even pretending, though. Naturally sweet, he was a secret weapon. Callanach had seen the quiet brilliance in him before anyone else, encouraging him to go for promotion, knowing Tripp would excel. For a moment she wished Callanach were here, seeing the junior officer he'd help to train come into his own. It was the first moment her anger with him had been replaced by a more positive emotion. She squashed it and watched Vicki's response as the second film clip came to an end.

'Vicki, do you know that man?' Tripp asked.

She nodded, her eyes unable to settle in a single spot in the small room.

'Did you give him information about patients from the drop-in centre?' Tripp continued.

'Hold on a moment,' the lawyer interjected. 'I'd like to know what that young man is supposed to have done before my client answers that question. Sharing patient information in the circumstances might not be a criminal offence, but you can lay your cards on the table if you want anything more.'

'What's his name?' Tripp asked, ignoring the lawyer and looking straight into Vicki's eyes.

'RJ,' Vicki said.

'This interview ends here until you provide some initial disclosure. This is a fishing expedition,' the lawyer said.

Tripp looked at Ava, who pulled her chair forwards a couple of inches, all business, ignoring Vicki and addressing only the lawyer.

'The male on the clip – this RJ – was at the scene of an attempted suicide. It was the Reach You charity that took the call to send out an emergency counsellor. We know from the records that it was Vicki who took the call and assigned Rune Maclure to the case. It was a different counsellor – Charlie

Packham – who attended another suicide attempt yesterday in Pennywell Gardens, but your client took that call also. Sure enough, RJ was present at that scene, too.

'Given that we have your client's mobile phone and a court order to obtain her telecoms records, she might like to be transparent with us about her communications with RJ and explain why her friend is so interested in suicide attempts.'

'I didn't even think about it,' Vicki said quietly. 'At first, you know, RJ was just really interested in my work, like it was important and he respected me because of it.'

'Go on,' Tripp encouraged.

'He said he wanted to attend one – an attempt, I mean. Not to watch it happen, he said, but to see how the counsellors do it, you know, talk people down. He made out as if they were heroic. I suppose I wanted it to seem like my job was more important than it was, so I said I'd tell him next time I got a call.'

'Did you phone RJ to let him know when an attempt was happening?' Tripp clarified.

'I sent a text,' Vicki said quietly.

She'd stopped crying but her head was hanging so low it was difficult to hear.

'Did you give him any other details after that?' Tripp asked.

'Yeah, the Pennywell one yesterday. I didn't want to. By then I'd realised there was something else going on,' she muttered.

'What's RJ's surname?' Ava cut in.

'I dunno.' Vicki looked panicked.

'How do you know him, if you don't know his surname?' she continued.

'Five-a-side footie every Wednesday night. Mixed teams. Not a lot of women play, though. You just turn up and get put into a team. I don't make friends easily, especially not other girls, but I was always good at footie, so it seemed like

315

a way to meet people.' She hugged herself self-consciously. 'The team ended up going down the pub together each week. RJ and me got talking regularly, exchanged numbers. I thought he was cool. He's kind of loud and funny. He told me he was a YouTuber. I thought that maybe . . . you know. I liked him.'

Ava got it. It was hard enough being a tomboy at school. Excluded by the pretty girls, laughed at by the boys. The real world was supposed to be kinder, but it wasn't. Girls with broad frames, better suited to loose-fitting jeans and chunky trainers than tight skirts and stilettos, never seemed to fit in. People made assumptions about them. Trying to find a boyfriend at a football club was smart under the circumstances.

'You were hoping RJ was going to ask you out?' Ava clarified.

Vicki turned scarlet as she nodded.

'So his number's in your phone's contact list, then?' Tripp asked.

'Aye, under RJ football,' Vicki confirmed. 'That second time, he'd already figured out I'd be in the shit if anyone found out I'd given him the Queensferry Crossing details. Said if I didn't do the same again, he'd get me sacked.'

'Did he tell you what he wanted the details for on that occasion?' Tripp asked gently.

'Yes, I knew what he was up to by then,' Vicki sniffed.

'Well I don't, so does someone want to enlighten me?' the lawyer asked loftily.

'He told me he wanted to stream the events live, and get people betting on who'd actually kill themselves and who'd survive. Only when I saw what he'd put online, it was nasty stuff. Really awful, about how long it would take for them to die or if they'd be killed outright. He'd contacted a bookie, I know that.'

Fuck, Ava thought. Her instinct had told her to arrest the bookie straight away. At least they had a crystal-clear shot of his face on camera.

'Website name?' Tripp asked.

'CheaperReaper.com. I only logged in once then I never went back. It's gross,' Vicki replied, chewing a nail. 'RJ started asking me for details of the deaths I'd heard about at work. He wanted to know if I had access to any photos or pathologist reports. I told him I didn't, but he wouldn't take no for an answer and a few times he turned up at the drop-in centre to wait for me when he knew I had a break for lunch or was about to finish my shift. I had to pretend it was all normal, like we were still mates. I thought that maybe giving him the call yesterday might mean he'd leave me alone.'

'That's all?' Tripp asked.

'Yes, I know it's bad and I'll lose my job, but I had no idea what I was getting into. I'm such a fucking idiot.'

'Do you know RJ's address?' Tripp asked.

'No, but he's got a car, a knackered old silver BMW. Thinks he's God's gift in it.'

'Miss Rosach, I'm going to give you some names and I want you to tell us if you gave RJ information about any of these people, or if he asked you about them, or spoke about them. It's very important, both for you and for us, that your answers are accurate. Do you understand me?' Ava asked.

'Sure,' she whispered.

'Jon Moffat,' she began.

Vicki shook her head.

'Fenella Hawksmith.'

'Sorry, isn't she the woman who . . .' The lawyer suddenly sounded more interested.

Ava shut him up with a single piercing look.

'Osaki Shozo,' she finished.

Vicki actually looked relieved.

'Oh yeah, I remember that one,' she said as if she was finally about to be told well done.

'Remember him?' Ava asked.

'He came to the drop-in centre when I was working. Different to most people who came in. Quite calm and direct. I thought he was a bit freaky, to be honest.'

'Did you give his details to RJ?'

'No, I lied and said I knew nothing about him. He was being really pushy by then, asking me things right outside the office where other people could hear. I knew better than to get myself in that sort of trouble.'

'If you said you knew nothing about Mr Shozo, how did RJ come to ask you about him?' Tripp asked.

'He saw him,' Vicki said. 'One of the days when he came to meet me at work that Shozo bloke was coming out the same time RJ turned up. Why?'

Vicki looked at Tripp, then at Ava, and finally to her lawyer, who was already rubbing his hands over his eyes.

'Do you not read any news at all or watch the TV, Vicki?' Tripp asked, doing his best – and only just failing – to keep the incredulity from his voice.

'Naw, I bloody hate all that. Really depressing. I like reality TV, action films and sport. I don't bother with the rest of it,' she said.

Ava took a deep breath. 'So you've not heard about the murders happening in the city at the moment, then?'

'Obviously I've heard a bit, but I've not read anything, like,' she replied.

'So you're unaware that Stephen Berry, from the Queensferry Crossing, ended up dead at the base of Tantallon Castle and that Osaki Shozo was killed in his flat. At the moment, the only link between those two deaths is you and your friend, RJ.'

Vicki's hands went to her eyes first, then to her mouth.

'You're shitting me,' she said. 'You've got to be. I can't have done that.'

'We'll let you know,' Ava told her, 'just as soon as we've had a chat with your pal.'

'Rufus Jacob Bott,' Tripp announced to the waiting squad. 'To be fair, if that were my name, I might have reinvented myself as RJ, too. His phone contract provider has given his address and we've already confirmed that he has a silver BMW registered to him. He's twenty-four years of age and lives in a flat in the north-west of the city.'

'Good work,' Ava said. 'Have we got anywhere on how he might have got details on Hawksmith and Moffat?'

'Nothing so far, but I believed Vicki. I don't think she'd ever heard the other names you gave him. He managed to get information from Vicki, though, so it's possible RJ approached other mental health workers or support charities and got the information elsewhere.'

'I agree,' Ava said. 'We're ready to mobilise, just waiting on an armed unit to confirm they can provide backup, then we'll enter his flat and see what we get. Pull all units working on this from everywhere in the city. No mistakes picking him up. I don't want any hostage situations, no escape routes. Do we know if RJ has a job?'

'Not as such,' Tripp said, 'but it looks like Vicki was right about this guy posting nasty stuff online. I can't get into the website yet. It's members only, not fancy security but enough to keep the Internet team busy until we get back here. What I have seen, though, is that RJ was trying to build a name for himself as a video blogger. Lots about death, seems to be a big fan of some other dick who made a video visiting places known for suicides across the world. Also, he's offering money to anyone who can provide footage of people dying, doesn't matter if it's natural causes or not.'

'Someone notify Janet Monroe that we have a suspect and will be moving in on him shortly. And tell her good job for suggesting the bait operation,' Ava said. 'Let's get moving. There are units already on route to secure a one-street circular perimeter around his home and to ensure his car doesn't leave in the meantime. Five minutes until we go.'

She waited until the crowd had dispersed.

'Is it wrong to want the armed units to mishear a signal and just shoot him straight away?' Ava whispered quietly to Tripp.

'Just as long as you don't actually suggest it to anyone, I think you're allowed to wish for whatever you want, ma'am,' Tripp said.

Chapter Thirty-Four

17 March

The Crow wasn't at home. He'd been there until half an hour earlier, waiting for the light to fade from the sky. Now, he was sitting outside a block of flats, looking up at the third floor, trying to figure out which windows belonged to Janet Vargas. He was pumped, physically and metaphorically.

It had been a strange sort of day, with a variety of demands on his time, but he'd found thirty minutes to lift weights. He could see the changes in his body since he'd consumed the bird. He was more wiry, every muscle and vein defined as if he were an anatomical pencil sketch of himself.

The power he held within was more impressive still. His mind was working with an energy and precision he'd never experienced before. Making decisions was easy, reading other people and staying a step ahead of them had become second nature. But the need for more, to consume more and become more, was like a chain dragging him by the guts onwards. It was an insatiable appetite. If he didn't feed it, it would start to consume him instead. So Janet Vargas was a risk, but one he was certain he could afford to take. Not carelessly, though.

He waited in his car, watching for people approaching the flats. A single male went by, and that wasn't right. Then an elderly lady, but she was already looking like thunder. Approaching her would be like setting off an alarm.

It took another hour before exactly the right set of circumstances presented themselves. A young mother walked down the street looking hassled, with two kids in tow and another in a pram. The Crow put on his biggest smile and his most relaxed but reassuring voice, keeping his keys in his right hand and filling his other arm with a bag of grocery shopping from the nearest supermarket.

Since he'd become The Crow, little details like that had become more obvious to him. Want to look unthreatening? Fill a shopping bag with some cheap-brand nappies, chocolate breakfast cereal, washing-up liquid, teabags, oven chips and a bunch of nice but inexpensive flowers from the bucket at the supermarket door.

He opened his car door just as the woman was wandering past, making a show of trying to avoid her children and using the 'excuse me' as a way to start a conversation.

'Pauline, for goodness' sake, would ye get out o' the man's way, girl!' the woman chided.

'Aw, don't worry yerself,' he replied good-naturedly. 'I've two myself. They threatened to start screaming if I didn't make sure we had their favourite breakfast cereal for tomorrow morning.' He nodded ruefully at the bag of shopping for good measure. 'Me and the wife only moved in a few weeks ago. Takes a while to get to know a place, doesn't it?'

'That it does,' she replied. 'Where've you come from?'

He fell into step next to her, keeping his pace slow to match the pram, smiling down at the children.

'Fraserburgh,' he said. 'How old's your wee one? I wish mine would sleep so peacefully. I don't think we've had a break from the screaming since the little love arrived in the world.'

'Three months, and take it from me, he's just having a good ten minutes. When he wakes up hungry, you'd be able to hear him even if you still lived in Fraserburgh!'

The Crow laughed appreciatively, showing sharp teeth to the children, who were staring at the curious man walking so close to their mother. The boy moved forwards, taking a place at his mother's side, staring at each adult in turn. Didn't every boy get jealous when another male got their mother's attention? Good lad, The Crow decided. Protect what's yours. Just don't get in my way.

Continuing down the road, ever closer to the flats, she began fumbling in her handbag as she walked.

'I'm surprised I haven't bumped into you before,' he said. 'Usually you get to know the pram brigade before anyone else. It's kind of reassuring to know other people are going through all the same stages as you. Which floor do you live on?'

'Second,' she said. 'Damn, I can never find my keys in this bag.'

'Here, let me push the pram for you a second,' he offered.

'I'll do it,' the boy said, pushing forwards and grabbing at the handle.

The Crow got there just ahead of him.

'Naw, you're all right,' he laughed. 'I've clocked up enough hours behind a pram to be a safe driver for your wee baby here.'

The woman laughed, pulling out her purse and the baby's dummy.

'Don't fuss,' she told the boy. 'I'll just be a sec.'

A couple of minutes later, she pulled out a set of keys that wouldn't have looked out of place on the belt of a night security guard. The Crow carried on pushing for another minute as she zipped her bag up and sorted along the line of keys to find the one that fit the outer door.

'Hey,' The Crow said to the boy who looked to be about six years old. 'Who's your favourite football team, then?'

'Hearts,' the boy said proudly. 'Every other team is crap!'

'Lennox!' the woman scolded. 'Mind your language. God, I'm sorry, gets it from his daddy. Mild as you like until there's football on the telly, then you wouldn't know it was the same man.'

'Aye, well, if you can't swear a bit about football, when can you?'

She looked grateful not to have been judged and the boy accepted The Crow ruffling his hair with only the bare minimum of a grimace.

The Crow enjoyed playing the part. It proved what he already knew but hadn't had a chance to put into practice yet: that he was ready to become. He could change almost every aspect of himself to fit whatever role he needed to play. Nature was a clever beast. It allowed you to stalk your prey silently but gave you a roar that would deafen the herd. It provided you with the softest feathers, bones as light as air, but a beak that could gouge eyes and rip out a still-beating heart. He was stronger than ever because he'd learned to portray weakness.

Now the woman was talking about a toddler group. Did his imaginary wife want to join? And don't sign up with the doctor's surgery round the corner because you'll wait two weeks for an appointment. A longer journey and you could see a doctor the same day you phoned.

He smiled broadly as she talked, the grin becoming more and more genuine as they neared the door to the flats. It had been easier than he'd imagined. Integrate yourself into someone else's unit, look like you belonged, appear at home. If anyone was watching, they'd see a man walking comfortably with his partner and her children. What could possibly be suspect about that? And they were laughing, having a good time. Ruffling the boy's hair had been a genius touch. Helping with the pram for a minute, even better.

The woman pushed her key into the outer lock. He stepped back, holding the door as she pushed the pram in first. A siren wailed in the distance, coming closer. The girl – Pauline, who he'd so convincingly nearly fallen over – went next. The boy stopped in the doorway, staring up at him.

'You never told me who you support,' he said.

The sirens were getting louder now and The Crow stared up the road.

'Hearts, of course, same as you,' he smiled, wanting to get inside now.

'Doesnae make any sense,' the boy continued.

'What doesn't?' The Crow asked, wondering if it would spook the woman if he pushed past her son. He couldn't afford to arouse suspicion at such a crucial stage.

'You're from Fraserburgh, you said. Why would you support Hearts? My dad says you should stay true to your home-town.'

The sirens were nearer now, then there were lights, frantic flashed reflections in the windows at the end of the road.

'I was born in Edinburgh,' The Crow said quickly. 'I moved to Fraserburgh when I was a teenager. Your dad sounds like a very sensible man.'

'Would you come on?' the woman scolded the boy abruptly. 'Before the baby wakes up.'

'Sorry, Mam,' the boy said, stepping into the building and letting The Crow in, too, as the lights and sirens flashed past the end of the road and away up the hill.

He breathed out, enjoying the small victory, letting it mask his relief.

'I'll be off, then,' he said to the woman who was climbing into the lift. 'Good to have met you.'

'Be sure to tell your wife about the toddler group. It'd be nice to have someone to go with!' she called as the doors finally closed.

The Crow began climbing the stairs to the third floor.

Lance Proudfoot saw a child run around the slight bend in the road first, a boy, older than five but no more than eight. Now that his own son was grown-up, he found it harder to age young children accurately. He could see the heads of the adults accompanying him above the top of a row of parked cars, talking to one another, nodding occasionally, looking relaxed. Other people had come and gone, but none had looked out of place.

A young man had walked past having a loud row on his mobile about money, drawing attention to himself with his bad language. Not a tactic a potential killer would employ. Lance kept checking the vicinity for other people sat in their cars. He was sure the police would be around somewhere.

A car carrying two men had just taken off and he hadn't got a good view of them. He was mostly just surprised that no one had come to ask what he was up to, given how long he'd been sitting there.

Lastly, an elderly lady had shuffled along and into the building, struggling to get her key into the lock. Lance had fought with himself not to get out and offer to help, but that would have defeated the purpose of staying low, keeping the internal lights off, and avoiding using his mobile and streaming blue light onto his face.

The newcomers were fully visibly now, pram in front of the woman, and a girl, younger than the boy, struggling to keep up. As they walked slowly towards the outer door of the flats, the woman began searching in her handbag. Keys, Lance decided. His wife had never been able to find hers once she'd put them in her handbag, either. The man said something and the boy stepped forwards, trying to take hold of the pram. The man got there first, using his longer stride and height to take control. The look on the boy's face was thunder.

Lance sat up to get a better look at them. The woman pulled a set of keys from her bag with a relieved half-smile. By then the man was laughing and ruffling the boy's hair. The male was good-looking. Tall. And he was making an effort. A first-date kind of effort, Lance thought. Not a 'just bumped into your neighbour' kind of effort, or an 'aren't you a friend of. . .' kind of effort. The wide grin was way too much for people who knew each other well.

Then they were at the door. The woman opened up, pushing the pram through, the girl following, but the boy stood in the doorway, something approaching a scowl on his face. Sirens disrupted the quiet evening at a distance and the man looked away into the distance at their source, just as Lance did. He wondered what he was doing there, if he was missing the real story, sat in his own little world, having convinced himself yet again to follow his gut.

The sirens got closer and still the boy didn't cede the entranceway to the man. They were involved in quite a discussion and the boy's face was sombre, questioning. The man's smile held fast.

The siren grew closer and louder, but Lance told himself not to look away. He got the clear impression that the boy wasn't happy. Then it broke. The boy smiled again, the man was allowed to pass into the building and the reflections from the streetlights drew a reflected curtain over the action happening behind the glass.

Opening a packet of crisps, Lance contemplated his life. Since teaming up with Luc Callanach, things had become both more exciting and more painful – and teaming up was a vast over-statement of his own importance – but it felt good to be doing real work again. His younger days as an investigative journalist had got him in no end of scrapes and he'd loved them all. His now ex-wife hadn't shared his enthusiasm, nor been keen on the amount of time he'd spent travelling. So he'd compromised and settled down. Or maybe he'd just settled. Got lazy, to be brutally honest with himself. Now Callanach was out of the loop and Lance was stuck chasing hunches instead of cold, hard facts.

He hadn't liked the man who'd pushed the pram. The thought came to him, a non sequitur mixed into memories of other more successful points of his career. That was ridiculous, though. You couldn't dislike someone based on seeing them talk – not even hearing them – for three minutes as they walked along, or because their smile had seemed excessive in the circumstances.

Only he really hadn't liked him. He wasn't imagining it. It had been to do with the ruffling of the boy's hair. Lance closed his eyes and reconstructed the details in his mind. The man had been carrying a shopping bag, a full one, up in his arm. Entirely macho positioning, like he was too embarrassed to carry it swinging from his hand like a housewife. Balanced on the top of the shopping, prominently, had been a pack of nappies. A small pack. Usually when Lance saw them in the supermarket they were the huge bumper packs and the damned things were expensive. No point buying them unless you were buying in bulk. The man hadn't thought of that, apparently.

He saw the male ruffle the boy's hair in his mind once more. Just before that, the boy had positioned himself between the woman and the man, jostling for control of the pram. It wasn't just Lance. The boy hadn't liked the man, either. Hadn't wanted him next to his mother, or helping with the baby.

He'd ruffled the boy's hair. The image kept returning. No parent did that to someone else's child. You didn't do it to your own child because you knew children hated it. They *really* bloody hated it. Hair-ruffling was reserved for politicians who didn't have children of their own, or who – if they did – had a nanny and hadn't spent a single hour caring for the children without military-style backup.

Lance's next thought – and it came with a clarity that made his chest hurt – was that the man wasn't a parent at all. He knew it the same as he'd known when his wife had decided to leave him and when he'd known his son was experimenting with drugs. He just knew. But he'd been carrying nappies. Keeping them in full view, up in his arms. In the woman's face. Like a badge of domesticity. He might as well have been wearing a sign on his chest that read: I'm a dad.

Lance unlocked his car door and began to climb out, wondering if he'd finally lost the plot. Then there'd been the scene at the door. The boy had stood, scowling, demanding either an answer or an explanation, as if requesting the magic password. Open sesame. It had worked, only the man had been more interested in the sirens that had come and gone just as the boy had allowed him in. The smile, that big, broad smile, had seemed almost fixed in place. No, not almost. Utterly fixed, like someone auditioning for a game show. Look at me, the smile had said. Gosh, I'm a happy, friendly guy.

Lance took his mobile from his pocket and dialled Callanach's number. He was greeted by an invitation to leave a voicemail. He tried again. Still no answer. By now, he was at the door to the flats. He looked up the road. The area, of course, was deserted. No one was coming to open up who he could charm in his older-guy kind of way to let him in.

He should call Ava Turner instead, he thought. Only to say what? This guy walking towards Janet Vargas' flat had been carrying shopping that didn't match Lance's experience of parenting. And he had a creepy smile, too – mustn't forget that crucial bit of evidence. It was ridiculous and yet it felt as real as the bag of crisps he hadn't realised he was still clutching in his hands. He looked down into the sack of salt-and-vinegar flavoured saturated fat and knew he had to do something. Anything.

He phoned MIT, grateful the number was still in his phone from his previous work with Callanach.

'Hi, I need to speak with DCI Turner as a matter of urgency, please,' he said.

'Sorry, DCI Turner's out at the moment. We're expecting her back later tonight. Can I take a message?'

Lance racked his brains for other names.

'Um, wait, Max Tripp. Is he there?' he tried.

'No, also out. I'm afraid the department's a bit low on personnel right now. If it's an emergency, I can put you through to the switchboard to get police units to you?'

He thought about that. There was no emergency. Just a suspicion. And a block of flats with a possibly dodgy man inside, who could have a million different reasons for carrying a small pack of nappies and chocolate cereal. Perhaps his wife was pregnant and craving chocolate goodies, and they wanted the smallest pack of nappies possible for practising changing techniques. Lance felt like an idiot.

'No worries,' he said. 'If you could just leave a message for DCI Turner that I called. The name's Lance Proudfoot. She knows who I am.'

'Of course, sir,' the woman on the other end of the line said. 'I'll let her know.'

Lance almost hoped Ava wouldn't phone him back. The more minutes that went by, the less certain he was of what he'd seen, or at least of what he'd deduced from it.

The outer door to the flats opened as he stood, poised and

ready to return to his car, and to go home to a warm flat and a numbing hour of TV. The exiting teenagers didn't even look at him. He didn't exist to them. Not a threat, not a friend, not a girl. They left the door open, with Lance standing in range of it. His hands hung at his sides, but his foot was quicker, pushing out a toe to stop it from closing.

There was a stairway to the right, an elevator to the left and a passageway leading to ground-floor flats stretching ahead into the distance. Lance screwed up the nearly empty packet of crisps and shoved it deep in his pocket, putting his mobile away at the same time. He had nothing to lose except his evening and there were enough of those free in his diary not to be concerned about that. With one final look up the street, wondering where the sirens had been headed and if that was also where Ava Turner was right now, Lance Proudfoot stepped inside.

Chapter Thirty-Five

17 March

They raced through the city, using lights and sirens until they got near their destination. Other units joined them from all directions. Heading north-west, they took the Queensferry Road and made for Barnton Grove. Approaching RJ's flat on foot was a silent operation. Armed units were in place. They already had a view of the flat windows, although there was no sign that anyone was home.

Rufus Jacob Bott was the sole tenant of a one-bedroomed flat, unless he had a girlfriend they didn't know about. They'd accessed his Facebook account and there were no pictures of him looking coupled-up, so Ava was feeling confident about that. His Facebook page was all about him. Egotist central, Tripp had called it. Thousands of selfies. Rants. Links to videos, some of which were certainly illegal. Photos – many obviously real, some possibly Photoshopped – of dead bodies. RJ was a man obsessed, but the betting on suicides was clearly a new thing. An opportunistic element perhaps inspired by meeting Vicki.

The problem was that it seemed to have inspired something much darker than a simple desire to see people die at their own hand.

Ava briefed the squad.

'Keep it clean and quick. Don't make any unnecessary conversation with him. Take him down, caution him. I want his flat checked thoroughly and everything seized. All items of clothing. We don't know what might have a victim's DNA on it. Also, focus on electronics. We know his primary focus is on screening deaths and that he uploads footage regularly, so phones, computers, laptops, cameras. Keep the use of force to the absolute minimum – no one gets heavy-handed. I won't have his lawyers challenge us in court over procedure. No one talks to him in the van on the way to the station. The cuffs will be correctly applied and they mustn't leave marks. Questions?'

'The Jon Moffat killing suggests he's familiar with guns. What if he's armed, ma'am?'

'You're all wearing protective vests. If you suspect he's armed, stay back and let armed units deal with him. The priority then will be to establish that there's no one else in the flat. All other flats in the block must be secured before we go in.'

Tripp's phone rang and he walked away from the group.

'Right, moving in one minute,' Ava said. 'Keep in radio contact. Each team has been assigned a floor. Call it in once you have your area safe. No one uses a doorway after that until the safe signal has been given. Let's go.'

They started jogging towards the allocated building entrances.

'A couple of people have called the incident room for you, ma'am,' Tripp said as they got close to the building exterior. 'Lance Proudfoot, who I think is DI Callanach's friend.'

'Okay,' Ava said as they entered. Callanach was the last distraction she needed right now. 'And?'

'Someone from traffic. Not sure what that was about. They

left a number and asked you to call back. I've forwarded the details to your phone.'

'Follow me,' Ava said, taking the first staircase, nodding to other units along the way as they quietly knocked on one door after another, showing their ID badges before giving whispered explanations to each resident about their purpose and what was about to happen. Bolts could be heard slipping into place with each floor they left.

RJ lived on the fourth, and top, floor, at the end of the corridor.

'Limited neighbours who might hear or suspect something,' Ava said. 'Innocuous flat, within easy reach of the Queensferry Crossing. Makes sense that he managed to get to the Stephen Berry incident quickly.'

In front of her was a team of officers ready to use force, if necessary, to enter the apartment. She checked her body armour one last time and gave the go signal.

Initially, the door was knocked on quietly and without fuss. No response. They knocked again, listening through the closed door with a high-sensitivity microphone. The officer using it pulled away from the door, pointing to the other side of it, then giving a whirling signal with his forefinger. Someone was inside the apartment and choosing not to answer the door. Ava nodded her consent to move to the second phase of attempted entry.

'Police, move away from the door!' the officer at the front shouted loudly.

Ava covered her ears as an Enforcer was used to batter the lock section of the door. It gave way on the first ramming. The door flew open, slamming against the wall behind it, and a stream of bodies disappeared into the lounge area.

A new voice began shouting before Ava could even reach the front door, then there were yelled instructions and the heavy, dull thump of a body hitting carpet. A caution was given. The response was a stream of expletives followed by commands to stop struggling. Ava went in.

RJ Bott was face down on the floor thrashing his legs uselessly as officers restrained him. She looked around his flat, drinking in the chaos: three half-empty cereal bowls decorated the floor. There was nothing on the walls except a large TV screen. The furniture was mismatched and threadbare, and the only litera-ture to be seen was a tatty porn magazine that no one in their right mind was going to touch without heavy-duty gloves and a litter picker stick. The back windows looked out into a shared garden area surrounded by trees, but only through the cracks between the blackout curtains held up with gaffer tape.

'I'm guessing he doesn't use the place for romance much,' Tripp said, pointing to a pair of underwear left over the back of the armchair, obviously worn.

Ava looked away. Every crime scene, every house she'd raided, left a stain in her head. The man on the floor protesting some-thing about human rights and access to a lawyer may not have been expecting visitors, but that didn't excuse the foulness of his living space.

She walked into the bedroom – a mattress on the floor with bedding that was stained in a manner resembling bodily fluid tie-dyeing – and caught sight of a collage in the mirror in front of her. For a moment she didn't want to look. The last time she'd seen so many carefully displayed pictures of dead bodies was when she'd been studying a police course in forensic pathology.

Drawing breath, she swung round. Hangings, burnings, falls, gunshot wounds, knife wounds, apparent cult poisonings – it was all there. Some were old press photos, others newer and in colour, most taken from the Internet and printed off. More surprising was the love with which the images had been taped to the wall, each with a clear centimetre border, none overlapping. This was no desperate, disorganised fetishist. Whatever else was chaotic about RJ's life, this part of it was where he channelled all his concentration, his excellence. His love – if anything so macabre could ever be couched in such idealistic terms.

There was a sudden further eruption of noise from the lounge. Ava dashed for the door, to find Tripp yelling across everyone.

'Asthma inhaler. Locate it. Now!'

She fought through the crowd of bodies surrounding Bott and found the man gasping dramatically, if not convincingly.

'Need an ambulance,' Bott panted, leaning heavily on the officer at his side.

'Or a better drama teacher,' Ava muttered. Tripp gave what could only be thought of as an old-fashioned look. 'Fine, let's be cautious, call the paramedics in.'

'Ma'm, he's turning an odd colour,' an officer shouted.

Ava stepped closer to him.

'Mr Bott, you need to calm down and try to breathe in a more controlled manner.'

He rolled his eyes ceiling-wards and sank to the floor. Ava caught the slight smile at the corners of his mouth and fought the urge to knee him somewhere that would help to return him to full consciousness.

'Paramedics'll be here in one minute,' Tripp notified her.

'No rush. He's faking it,' she said, looking at her watch.

'Are you sure? Only he seems to have passed out, ma'am,' Tripp said, taking a knee at Bott's side and feeling for his pulse.

'Is his breath rasping now or has he relaxed?' she asked.

Tripp leaned over and listened at Bott's mouth.

'No, breathing seems normal, actually.'

'Neat trick,' Ava said. 'Rapid, excessive breathing. Made himself pass out. Buys time. Gives himself an opportunity to prepare for questioning.'

Standing aside as the medics entered, Ava forced herself to keep quiet and let uniformed officers answer questions.

'He'll need to be taken to the hospital and checked out,' was the conclusion. 'He'll have to be stretchered out.'

'Give me strength,' Ava said. 'Tripp, organise an escort and a guard at the hospital. Make sure he's not left unattended at any time. I want to speak with the doctor who assesses him as soon as they've reached a conclusion about Bott's stability.'

'Got it,' Tripp said. 'Any other specific instructions?'

'Only one. Get him into an interview room this evening at the latest. No lingering overnight in a hospital bed while he regains his strength. I want this bastard charged and in a cell before I go to bed tonight. Absolutely no mistakes.'

Chapter Thirty-Six

17 March

Lance took the stairs slowly, listening for signs of life behind each door he passed. Voices approached from the stairwell above, and he dragged an old receipt from his pocket and pretended to be reading it as a couple approached.

'So I told the doctor, there was no way I was going into hospital just for that . . .'

'Excuse me,' Lance said, an apologetic but winning smile, practised over many journalistic years to chivvy information from the unsuspecting, plastered on his face. 'I'm looking for Janet Vargas. I know this is the right block, but it seems I haven't got her flat number written down right.'

'Vargas?' the woman repeated. 'I don't know anyone by that name. You sure you're in the right place?'

'I thought I was . . . sorry, I don't want to keep you. She's about thirty, slim, roughly five foot five inches, dark hair, kind of Spanish-looking.'

'You mean Janet Monroe,' the man said. 'Pretty, brown eyes, dark hair . . .'

'Oh, really?' the woman chipped in. 'So she's pretty, is she?'

The man sighed and Lance felt a twinge of guilt at the amount of grovelling the man was going to spend his evening doing.

'That's her,' Lance said. 'Do you know her flat number?'

'Not sure exactly, but it's on the third floor, right-hand side near the end of the corridor,' the man offered, looking anxious to move on.

Lance didn't blame him. His partner had adopted a hands-on-hips stance that didn't bode well.

'Thanks,' Lance said. 'Appreciate the help.'

'Why do you want to know, anyway? She can't be expecting you if you didn't even have her name right,' the woman said.

However much of a hard time she was about to give her partner, Lance was pleased she was suspicious. Too many people gave out information thoughtlessly.

'I'm a journalist, actually,' he said, getting his semi-official credentials out of his pocket and handing them over for inspection. 'There was an incident in the city this afternoon that Janet was involved in. I'm just following up the story. Feel free to take a note of my name if it'll make you feel better about it.'

'What sort of incident?' the man asked.

'Why are you so interested?' the woman shot back.

As the argument got into full swing, Lance took the opportunity to raise a hand in both thanks and farewell, taking the stairs to the third floor two steps at a time.

The couple's raised voices began to fade as he moved down the corridor, pausing at each door on the right-hand side, having ignored the first few. There were lights on inside the final three, with televisions or radios playing in two of those. He fought the sense that something was wrong. Imagination was the most powerful tool in the world. It was the reason propaganda started wars and why horror movies were so popular. Hitchcock was directing a thriller inside his head and right then it wasn't looking good for the about-to-be victim.

He picked the middle of the three doors, beyond which he could hear a female with an Essex accent screeching at – in his head – a fake-tanned, plucked-eyebrows male, about how he'd cheated on her with her best friend. Reality TV was as easy to identify as the theme tune from *The Archers* had been when he was a boy. He knocked and waited.

The door was wrenched open by a teenager, chewing gum opened-mouth and staring at him.

'Hello, sorry to bother you, I was looking for Janet Monroe?'

'Mum!' the girl yelled, tongue piercing on full show, gum stretching from the stud to one of her back teeth. 'There's some old bloke here.'

'For fuck's sake . . .'

Sofa springs squealed in relief and heavy footsteps approached. The woman who came to the door clutching a giant 'sharing' bag of toffee popcorn didn't look any more impressed than her daughter had.

'What?' she demanded.

'I was looking for Janet Monroe,' Lance said. 'Do you—'

'Next door.' The woman poked a finger to the door at the very end of the corridor and slammed her own shut.

'Thank you,' Lance said out of habit, to the wood in front of his face, trying not to laugh.

Just like that, the spell was broken. It was just a block of flats with all the normal stuff going on behind closed doors. The reality TV watchers had plainly heard nothing to cause them any concern. There had been no gunshots, no screams, no thumps against the walls, or they'd have greeted his enquiry about the woman next door with more concern. Still, he'd come so far. It'd be ridiculous to waste all the effort he'd gone to. And maybe Janet Vargas – or Monroe, or whatever name she chose to go by – would appreciate a friendly face checking up on her. He knew what it was like to spend so much time alone in your own home that sometimes you forgot there was a world of friendly people outside your door who actually did care about you.

He knocked. No reply. She might be asleep, of course. Possibly sedated given the day she'd had. He knocked one more time. That time he heard a voice from within, asking who it was.

'Janet, I'm Lance Proudfoot. I appreciate you don't know me, but I was worried about you,' he said, feeling ridiculous, intrusive, like a kid caught peeping into a bedroom window. 'I just wanted to make sure you were okay. I saw a man come into the flats earlier and . . . you know what? Don't worry about it. I shouldn't have bothered you.'

The door opened halfway. Janet stood smiling at him. He felt relieved immediately. She was fine. It had all been in his head. The wave of relief was quickly flooded with a sense of terrible embarrassment. She was within her rights to consider him some sort of gruesome stalker. He'd be lucky if she didn't call the police as soon as he left. Only, she wasn't looking annoyed at all. She was grinning, which wasn't right at all. She didn't know him. In fact, her reasoning for opening the door at all suddenly felt . . . he struggled to find the word.

'I'm fine,' she said brightly, her eyes twitching towards the end of the corridor from which he'd come. Twice, three times. He wasn't imagining it. 'It was nice of you to check on me, but you should probably go.'

Wrong. That was the word. It was that simple. She didn't know him, should never have opened up. Only now she was trying to get rid of him, but she wasn't saying it.

'I didn't mean to disturb you . . .'

'I was just about to go to bed, so you should really go now,' she said, her throat as taut as a stringed instrument in spite of the radiance of her smile.

Lance took a half step to the side to get a better view inside her flat.

'Janet, if something's wrong I can call the police,' Lance said quietly.

The tip of a gun – just the tip, but Lance had seen enough of them to know what he was seeing – was aimed at him from behind Janet's shoulder. He couldn't see the face of the person holding it, but he already knew it was the man he'd seen worming his way inside the flats earlier. Janet's face fell. Her adorable attempt to save Lance from getting involved in whatever drama was unfolding inside her flat had failed.

'Inside, now,' the male ordered him.

'I don't think so,' Lance said. There were benefits to getting older and one of them was that fear, while in no way diminished, was often accompanied by a healthy dose of belligerence. 'I think you'll just have to shoot me in this corridor. I'm guessing the police would be here within a couple of minutes. The neighbours won't want their TV time ruined by gunshots.'

The gun moved fluidly to press into Janet's right temple.

'Okay,' the man said. 'Have it your way. Only it's not you I'm going to shoot.'

Janet closed her eyes.

'All right. Whatever you want,' Lance said. 'Just lower the gun, would you?'

'Don't come in here,' Janet blurted. 'I'll be . . .'

Lance stepped inside. 'The police are on their way,' he said.

'Really? I find that hard to believe, given you had no idea what the situation was inside this flat. I'm curious, though, as to what brought you here in the first place.'

'Who are you?' Lance asked.

'I'll answer if you will,' the man grinned. 'First things first, there's some rope in that bag there. Right down in the bottom. Throw out the nappies and the cereal. I won't be needing those any more.'

'I'm not handing you any rope,' Lance said. 'Why don't you let Janet go? You've got me now. I'll take her place.'

'Take her place?' he laughed. 'This isn't some random act. Nature has laws. There has to be an accounting when you take life for granted.'

He pulled the back of Janet's shirt down and she crashed hard onto the sofa.

'Survival of the fittest?' Lance asked.

'You wouldn't understand. I asked how you found me?'

'The boy you walked into these flats with didn't trust you,' Lance said, watching Janet slip her hand into the left pocket of her jeans and noting the outline of a mobile phone through the material.

'You're lying. The boy was fine with me. Why were you watching me in the first place?'

'I was watching the flats,' Lance said. 'I realised someone might come for Janet. That's why I called DCI Turner before I came in after you.'

'But you see, right now, DCI Turner's pursuing a suspect she has good reason to believe is a dangerous killer. She's going to be busy for a while. In fact, given how frantic she must be, I doubt you spoke to Ava at all.'

Lance liked to think he had a fair poker face, but it wasn't fast enough on that occasion. The man wasn't concerned in the least and that meant he was telling the truth. Lance's eyes returned involuntarily to where Janet was still furiously tapping buttons in her pocket. The man followed his gaze. Whipping the gun in front of her face and bringing it sharply upwards, he smashed the metal into the base of her nasal septum. There was a full second where no one moved or made a sound, then blood gushed down her T-shirt and she howled, leaning forwards and clutching her face.

'Give me the phone,' the man said.

Lance felt a sensation of self-loathing like he'd never experienced before. He'd thought he was being clever, distracting the man, keeping him talking, but it was him being played. Nothing like a well-educated psychopath holding a gun to ruin your day, he thought bitterly as Janet produced her mobile and handed it over.

'Good, now lie on your back on the floor,' the man instructed her.

Lance saw panic on her face and knew it reflected his own.

'You said an answer for an answer,' he said. 'I asked who you are.'

'I used to be someone,' the man said. 'Now I've become something more. I'm The Crow.'

Sod it, Lance thought, the last dregs of hope seeping into the carpet along with the blood from Janet's dripping nose. Not just intelligent but deeply deranged. That was just bloody great.

'No, I'm not,' The Crow said.

'Not what?' Lance asked.

'Not crazy,' he smiled. 'I know what you were thinking. You have a very expressive face. I doubt you've ever been able to hide anything from the people who know you best. Unlike Janet, here. Not a word since I arrived. Cautious, quiet, guarded. Not at all what I was expecting.'

Janet spat a mouthful of blood across the floor and took a deep breath.

'I called for help,' she said, gasping for breath.

The Crow laughed. 'Called for help? Who's coming? Who could you possibly have in your contacts book who's going to race in here and rescue you?' He picked up her mobile and tapped the screen. 'Max? He must be an impressive specimen if you think he's going to pick a fight with a man holding a gun. And what did you say to him?' He scrolled down the screen. '999. Very dramatic, except he might just think you've run out of petrol or lost your credit card. He's hardly going to be knocking your door down any time soon.'

'Max Tripp,' Janet said. 'You've met him.'

A shadow passed over The Crow's face. 'Tripp?' he repeated vaguely. 'Where do I . . .?'

'He's a detective from the Major Investigation Team,' Janet said. 'He works with DI Callanach.'

'Of course,' The Crow said.

He lurched forwards, grabbing the back of Janet's neck with his left hand and thrusting the gun under her chin, dragging her to the floor, shoving her onto her knees then kicking her hard in the hip and ribs.

'On your back,' he said. 'Right now. Enough talking.'

'Stop kicking her,' Lance shouted, flying forwards, sending a punch in The Crow's direction as Janet collapsed on the floor.

He stumbled and his fist struck air as The Crow brought an open hand towards the side of Lance's head and swiped towards the floor.

The Crow was simply planning on slapping him. That was Lance's most naive thought. A slap would have been a blessing compared to the crack of skull on skull as he ploughed into Janet. The Crow might be deluded, and Janet might have taken him by surprise, but the man/bird knew how to fight.

Lance heard groaning and realised Janet was badly hurt beneath him. He tried to move and realised he couldn't. His arms and legs felt like lead, and when he opened his eyes, the world had become a too-bright haze, accompanied by a high-pitch squealing.

345

Janet Monroe – of course . . . Lance joined the dots too late. They'd changed her name so no one realised she was a police officer. It had all been a set-up, her up on the roof. Trying to force the killer's hand. And it had. Only The Crow had been a step ahead of them all, deflecting their attention to someone else.

Lance stopped fighting the desire to close his eyes, letting his head drop onto Janet's shoulder, feeling roughness against his face and then a slithering. Rope, he thought, trying to recall if The Crow had explained what he'd planned to do with it. If only he'd got hold of Callanach earlier. Explained what he'd seen. If only . . . Now there was a phrase fit for a headstone. Concussion intervened.

Chapter Thirty-Seven

17 March

The coleslaw was vinegary and the bread was hard, but Ava was forcing the ham salad sandwich down anyway. She couldn't remember the last time she'd eaten and her stomach was a painful knot. Either she was hungry or she'd finally succumbed to the classic DCI peptic ulcer. RJ Bott was recovering from his Royal Shakespeare asthma performance, but he wasn't going to be putting in an appearance in an interview room until the following morning, which was the earliest the doctors would allow it. Meanwhile, they'd arrested the bookie Bott had gone into business with, offering odds on whether or not suicides would happen or be avoided, and Bott's detestable website and blog had been taken down by the tech team.

She knew she should go home. There was an opportunity for sleep that might not come around again for a couple of days, yet it felt wrong not to be at the station while so much remained unresolved. Work – as self-destructive as it was – could provide the only respite from her frustration.

DI Graham walked in carrying his laptop and a mug of coffee, which he put in front of her.

'You got him, then,' he commented.

'We've arrested him,' Ava corrected. 'We'll have got him when he's serving multiple life sentences. For now, he's lounging in a hospital bed, being brought easy-to-swallow, low-sodium meals and having his pulse taken every few hours.'

'I'm sure you'll be equally tender with him tomorrow,' Graham grinned. 'You wanted to see the footage from Bruce Jenson's care home again?'

He set the laptop down on Ava's desk and pressed play. She leaned in, still chewing rubbery ham, and stared at the screen.

'So when this is over, to the extent that any of it's ever really over, can I call in your raincheck on that drink, or were you deliberately avoiding the subject?'

'I was deliberately avoiding the subject,' she said, keeping her eyes focused on the body running through the grounds: slim, leggy, tossing her hair. 'You're junior to me. We work together. It's too complicated.'

'It's just a drink,' he said as she replayed the footage again.

'Nothing's ever just a drink, but I appreciate you asking. Did we get any footage of this person sneaking onto the care home grounds?'

'Nothing clear enough to be sure it's her. There was some shadowy movement through bushes, but it was three hours earlier and we couldn't define a body shape clearly enough. Whatever it was kept low to the ground. It could even have been a deer. I didn't add it to the briefing because there was a substantial possibility it might end up being a mislead.'

'Three hours earlier? So if that was the perpetrator entering the grounds, they'd have been there all the time Callanach was visiting Jenson. Depending on where they'd positioned them-selves in the garden, they might have been able to watch his visit through the patio doors,' Ava said, a sense of déjà vu making her wish she hadn't attempted the sour sandwich.

'You okay?' Graham asked.

'I think . . . I'm not sure,' she said, wondering if insomnia was pushing her imagination beyond its reasonable bounds or if she was finally seeing the bigger picture. 'That woman . . .'

'Ma'am!' Tripp raced in. 'The message left for you earlier by a traffic officer while we were at Bott's flat. I just chased it up.'

'Slow down, Sergeant. What is it?'

'The woman – the illegal worker – who was living with Jon Moffat, the farmer out at East Saltoun, has been found. She and several others were stopped trying to get on a truck bound for Amsterdam.'

'That's fantastic news.' Ava stood up. 'Get her here. Let's see if she can identify Bott in a line-up . . .'

'She won't,' Tripp interrupted. 'Mariam – that's her name – is still traumatised. She confirmed it was her who called the pub landlady to report Moffat as dead, so the information she gave is verifiable. Her description of Moffat's killer was limited. She got a brief glimpse in a mirror as she sneaked down the stairs to see what was going on. All she could confirm was that the perpetrator was male and that he was black.'

Ava froze. Pax Graham stood up slowly, reaching for his jacket.

'Oh, holy fuck! He was hiding in plain sight all the time, pretending to help us,' Ava said. 'It's Rune Maclure. He gave us Vicki who took us to Bott . . .'

'That's not all,' Tripp said. 'I've got units on their way to Janet Monroe's. We took surveillance off her place when we did the raid on Bott's, believing we had the murderer.'

Ava felt sick and it was nothing to do with off coleslaw. She didn't want to hear what Tripp was about to say.

'I got a text from her sent half an hour ago, but I only just got around to checking my phone. All it said was 999.'

Sprinting before she had time to register the command to her legs, Ava was shouting instructions as she took the corridor to the stairs.

'There's a car waiting for us,' Tripp yelled, only just keeping up.

'I'll drive,' Graham shouted, overtaking them both and leaping down the stairs in front of them. 'Tripp, you try to contact Janet. The chief can liaise with the other units.'

They concentrated their energy on making it to the car before Ava began a rushed radio briefing to squads providing backup, and an extended operation to attend at Maclure's home and place of work, covering all bases.

There was one last thing she'd been meaning to do just before Tripp had run into her office, but it would have to wait. It was only a suspicion, but there was a possibility the woman on the care home video was someone from Callanach's past. Someone with no direct grudge against either Bruce Jenson or Gilroy Western, but not without a motive. A woman who – once upon a time – would have done almost anything to get Callanach's attention, positive or negative. Someone disturbed enough to have lied to the police in the past, to have self-harmed for revenge, and with plenty of experience in stalking.

For now it would have to wait. Janet Monroe's life was in danger because Ava had followed the information given by the murderer himself. And that meant she was to blame for whatever happened next.

Chapter Thirty-Eight

17 March

The knocking came from a long way away. Then closer. Then Callanach woke. His clock flashed with the information that it was 11.42 p.m. He'd only been asleep half an hour, but that was enough to render him groggy and disoriented. By the time he was fully conscious, the knocking was more rapid and insistent.

'Ava,' Callanach said, the sure knowledge that it was her at the door both enervating and exciting.

He dragged on a pair of jeans and jogged to his apartment door, peeping through the spyhole for just a second before opening up, deferring to muscle memory rather than exercising caution. The mistake he'd made dawned on him only when the door was already fully open. He'd seen a woman's face in profile when he'd looked through the spyhole, a hoodie covering her hair, her features only semi-visible in the dim glow of the corridor's night lights.

'Hello,' she said, smiling wanly, looking more like a lost child than anything else.

'Astrid. What do you want?'

The question was only to buy him thinking time. He knew what she wanted. Him. Astrid Borde had disappeared from his life more than a year ago and in his naivety, he'd chosen to believe she was gone forever. Not so, and now it seemed utterly ridiculous that he'd let his guard down.

'We have to talk, Luc,' she said softly, her voice plaintive and silky in the silence.

'It's the middle of the night. If you give me your number or an address, we could meet up tomorrow. Now's not really a good time.'

He glanced towards his bedroom, keeping it subtle, hoping she'd believe there was someone else there. As much as he didn't want her in his apartment, aggressive rejection wasn't the right tactic for handling someone so unpredictable. Jenson and Western were dead, and suddenly the perpetrator of those crimes was no longer a mystery to him. If Astrid had been delusional and obsessed before, she'd progressed into full psychopathy.

'You're pretending there's someone here? Oh, darling, don't lie to me. It's beneath you. But I understand, this is a shock. You never did like being taken by surprise. Why don't you get us coffee and we'll make small talk while you get used to having me around again.'

Callanach glanced across to his neighbour's door. He could raise his voice, make a fuss, wake her up, but Astrid – this new Astrid – was an unknown quantity. Dragging anyone else into his mess was unacceptable. He had to handle it himself.

'It's not that I don't want to spend time with you. In fact, I've been wondering where you were and how you were doing. I'm glad we left the past behind us and moved on. You look great, by the way. Your hair's shorter.'

Astrid touched it then flicked it slightly, a smile flitting across her face.

'It's just that I have to be up early to go into work,' he added.

'Really? Only you haven't been into the station for a while. Why is that?'

'I've been off sick,' he lied. 'Stomach flu.'

'And yet you've managed several trips to the gym.'

Callanach decided against asking just how much time she'd spent watching him. What mattered now was her motive for revealing herself.

'If I'd known you were outside, I'd have invited you in before now. You should have let me know. There's no reason for us not to be friends any more.'

'I'm glad you think so. I felt that between us. It's why I came back. I always knew we'd get past that misunderstanding before. You're looking good yourself.' Astrid let her gaze meander down his torso and Callanach wished he'd taken the time to put a T-shirt on. 'Listen, Luc, I know it's late, but I really do need to come in. We have to figure out what we're going to do about this situation we've found ourselves in.'

'Situation?' Callanach asked.

'A certain pair of enemies of ours? The lovely Bruce and Gilroy. Probably best not to talk where anyone could overhear me saying their names,' she whispered with a conspiratorial smile.

Callanach thrust his hands into his pockets, keeping it casual, feeling his blood pressure rising. Enemies of ours. So that was it. It wouldn't have been a problem, only he'd lied in his statement to Pax Graham about his reason for visiting Jenson and at best he'd withheld information relating to Gilroy Western. The fact that Astrid had physically killed the two men was irrelevant if she planned on saying he'd asked her to do it on his behalf. That lie alone would be enough to end his career and might well be sufficient to put him at the centre of a double murder trial. He couldn't let her inside his flat. The presence of her DNA would only add to claims of a criminal conspiracy. If she wasn't going to leave the easy way, there was no option except the hard way.

'I'm sorry, Astrid, but we can't discuss that here. Whatever information you have, you should give to the police, anyone except me. I don't know anything about their deaths but I'm a potential witness, so I can't talk to you about their cases. You should probably go now.'

'At last!' she grinned. 'Some reality. Look, I didn't expect this to be plain sailing. We always have to get through a certain amount of bullshit with each other, don't we? At least this time we kept it brief. You have to let me in, Luc. There's really no choice.'

'There's always a choice, Astrid. Like I said, you can leave me your number, if you like, and we'll find another time to talk. I'm going to shut the door now. Goodbye.' He took a step back and began closing up.

Her foot intruded, which he'd been expecting. He was ready to use force to get rid of her if he had to. He had too much to lose to be gentle.

Astrid withdrew a hand from the generous pocket of her hoodie, her fist wrapped around something the size of an apple.

'No,' she said. 'I can't. I wish I could, but you did this to us, Luc. You called out to me. You gave me a cause. You knew I wouldn't be able to stop myself from helping you. Now, I need you to show your appreciation. We have to agree on our next steps. There are lots of options. I know people who'll give us alibis. Or we could simply disappear together. You're not happy here. I read your emails to your mother. She really shouldn't have used your name and year of birth as her password. The emails nearly broke my heart . . .'

'What's in your hand?' he asked, wondering why his heart was thumping so hard when his brain was still insisting that he was simply imagining the worst.

'You were an Interpol agent. You know what this is. How many arms dealers did you bring down? More than half a dozen, if memory serves me right.'

She opened her hand and pushed it forwards into the light. In her palm sat grey-green death, her thumb through the circle of the pin. While her thumb was there, any attempt by Callanach to grab it from her would have only one result. It would be the end for both of them without a shadow of a doubt and perhaps the start of a fire, which would also kill anyone else sleeping in the apartments.

'You'd better come in,' he said, stepping aside.

She pocketed the hand grenade once more, keeping her hand in there with it, and kissed him on the cheek as she walked past. Callanach shut the door behind them and wondered how long he had left.

Chapter Thirty-Nine

18 March

The Crow stared down at the two bodies on the floor. It was a mess, both literally and metaphorically. He knew who the male was now. Lance Proudfoot, journalist. Leech. Anyone who made a living out of reporting other people's misery deserved to die. Even if it had been outside the boundaries of his plan, he didn't need to feel guilty about ending the journalist's life. If Proudfoot walked free, he would go straight to the police and The Crow had no desire to be incarcerated. Some deaths were simply necessary. Janet, though, had taken him by surprise. He'd checked the entire flat. There was no evidence that she was a police officer, nor that the Max she'd texted was in fact Max Tripp, detective sergeant. But she'd known his name and that The Crow had met him previously.

He refused to believe he'd fallen for such a dramatic ploy. The woman had been on the roof for hours and The Crow had spoken to the attending counsellor about it at length. Charlie Packham had formed the opinion that the attempt was absolutely genuine and that without intervention, there would have been a life lost. If The Crow had made a mistake, it was relying on the skills and expertise of a colleague. Apparently, not everyone shared his ability to sniff out a lie when they were fed one. Yet here he was, in a flat with two unconscious people, either of whom could identify him if left alive. He'd had a plan. All he had to do was adapt it for two.

The punishment still had to fit the crime. Learning to appreciate the gift of life was the point of the deaths he inflicted. It was unthinkable that he could be so crass, so base, as to kill without purpose. He still had time, he told himself. He was a predator. Swift, decisive, almost supernaturally deft. He'd been given an opportunity to face adversity and come out stronger.

Reaching for his bag, he pulled out a knife, cutting the rope in half. It would serve his purpose to have it shorter now that he had to accommodate two rather than one. Lance Proudfoot was starting to groan and twitch his fingers. He wouldn't be unconscious much longer. He lay them both flat on their backs, the tops of their heads almost touching, feet at opposite diagonals of the lounge walls, as if he'd drawn a straight line with their bodies across the room. From his pocket he withdrew two cable ties, securing their wrists over their stomachs.

Now for the trickier part. The only heavy item of furniture in the room was an old sofa. That would do for one of them, but not both. He dealt with Lance first, wrapping a section of rope around his ankles then knotting it tightly multiple times around the distant legs of the sofa, lifting the old leather monstrosity to make sure there was no way the journalist was getting his legs free.

The window provided the other essential tether point. He knotted the rope to provide a large clump, which he could be sure wouldn't pull free, and wedged it through the top of the window – banal health and safety regulations meant it didn't open from the bottom upwards – before shutting it up tight. The other end he wrapped around Janet's ankles, congratulating himself for thinking to put her trainers on her to ensure she couldn't simply slip her feet free.

Both tied by the ankles, hands bound, they lay with their heads about two feet apart. He wished there'd been more space between them, but as improvisation went, it was impressive.

Lance woke, blinking wildly and shaking this head. A couple of strips of gaffer tape took care of any noise he was about to start making. Clumsy but necessary. From his bag, The Crow took the last item he needed. The length of bungee rope was professional grade – the sort used for thrill-seeking idiots to jump from bridges over rivers and pretend they could fly. Flight was reserved for the truly evolved. Such gifts could only be earned, not bought.

He measured the correct length of bungee cord and tied a hangman's noose at each end before casting a brief glance out of the window. No lights. Few vehicles. Crucially, no sirens. Vicki's friend, RJ, would be in custody by now. Ava Turner would be busy trying to trip him up in interview. He allowed himself a moment to enjoy the irony of it all.

'One for you,' he said as he slipped the first noose over Lance's head, ignoring the wild dance of his eyes as he began to struggle. 'If you do that, you're only going to kill poor Janet even faster. Best to lie still,' he cautioned. 'And one for you.' He put the second noose over Janet's head with an iron effort.

The bungee cord took all his strength to pull between their two necks, constricting as he let it go, pitting one against the other as the weight of their bodies strained against the rope on their legs. The industrial-grade elastic pulled their necks together and tightened both nooses at the same time. Janet's eyes flashed open, nostrils flaring as she tried – and failed – to draw a full breath. Both their hands went above their heads immediately, grabbing at the bungee cord and trying to pull it down to slacken the noose around their own neck.

'Now you want to live,' The Crow preached. 'Which of you is willing to kill the other to survive? Pull hard enough and your noose will slacken, but you'll speed up the other's death. Breathe slowly is my advice, try not to struggle. Thrashing your legs won't help.'

He looked at his watch. He'd already been longer than he'd intended. If the police were on their way, and he didn't think they really were, but if so, then now was the time to get out.

He picked up his bag, tempted to take a photo of his creation but knowing it was only vanity. Janet was blowing blood out of her nose again with every puffed breath. Lance's face was turning an unnatural colour. To their credit, they were doing a remarkable job of keeping their legs still while they tried to slacken the bungee that was cutting off their oxygen supply. It wouldn't last long. As they became more and more oxygen-starved, they'd each lose control. They'd kick, squirm, wriggle and finally thrash, each strangling the other. Then they'd know what a gift life was. They'd learn gratitude with regret.

Rune Maclure scattered a handful of feathers over the two of them, enjoying their glorious struggle, then slung his bag over his shoulder, gun in hand, as he reached for the flat door.

Chapter Forty

18 March

Tripp took the stairs up to Janet's flat at a fast jog next to Ava.

'We've had confirmation from Maclure's co-worker that Maclure would have had access to records for anyone helped by the Reach You charity, not just to those patients he personally counselled,' Tripp told her as he got off his mobile.

'So he just chose a victim, studied their files, or felt a particular connection to them and struck when he felt the time was right? That doesn't explain the sudden spate of deaths. Something must have happened to have triggered it.'

'Not necessarily. One of Maclure's co-worker's concerns was how far back this went. Dr Lambert noticed a fraction of a boot mark on Stephen Berry's finger, indicating that he might have been stamped on to release his grip up at Tantallon Castle, but that was maybe a lucky find. Who's to say Stephen Berry wasn't just one of many?'

They rounded the corridor, where a line of officers was waiting silently for Ava to arrive and the operation to start.

'How many years has he been a counsellor there?' Ava asked.

'Several,' Tripp confirmed. 'But he's also done counselling stints at local hospitals, hospices, even schools. His access to the clinically depressed, suicidal and suffering people of Scotland is probably not accurately quantifiable at this stage.'

'That explains opportunity but not motive,' Ava said as she nodded greetings to the officers waiting for her. 'Any theories on that?'

'Only that at one stage he was found to be self-medicating. He admitted it to a colleague, got help, took voluntary blood tests to show he was clean. It's quite common among therapists, apparently, to suffer depression at some stage. I guess when you spend your day listening to other people's problems, it's hard to go home feeling happy.'

'How long ago?' Ava asked.

'Six or seven months,' Tripp said, strapping on the protective vest he was handed.

'Did the co-worker say what drug he was taking?' Ava asked.

'Clozapine. I've not heard of it,' Tripp said.

'Ma'am, are we good to go?' the armed unit leader whispered to her.

'Sure,' she confirmed. 'Any noise from inside the flat?'

'Some movement, no voices. It's definitely occupied.'

'Right. Weapons lowered. If there's a situation in progress, he may well use Janet Monroe as a shield. I don't want any weapons going off unless there's a clean, clear shot. Otherwise, we're negotiating for as long as it takes. We don't need to announce our presence. Janet isn't going to complain that we didn't give her a warning to open up. Just get that door . . .'

It opened. For a split second, twenty police officers froze. Rune Maclure didn't. His eyes met Ava's fleetingly as he stepped backwards and slammed the door.

'Rune,' Ava shouted through the wood. 'You've seen the

force we have out here. Open the door – last opportunity – or we'll have to break it down.'

The response was a single gunshot that hit the door from inside the flat, hard enough for the impression to be seen from the corridor side, even if the bullet didn't quite make it through. Ava jumped clear of the door panel, one hand pressed to her stomach where the bullet would have entered had it got past the wood. Shaken, she mentally chalked off another one of her lives.

'You've made your point,' Ava said. 'Just let me in to make sure Janet's okay. If you can reassure me of that, you've bought yourself some time.'

An inhuman noise came from within the flat – a half-screeching, abrasive call. No words.

'Break it down,' Ava ordered. 'Right now.'

She stepped back as the door took a hammering, splintering before it slammed inwards to reveal not the one body they'd been expecting to see, but two.

Ava stepped through, backed up by half a dozen rifles pointed at the floor just behind her feet.

Rune Maclure had a gun and was aiming it at the top of Janet's head as she tried feebly to pull some slack into the rope around her neck.

'Put the gun down,' Ava instructed. 'This is the only way out. Whatever happens to Janet and . . .' She half recognised the other man's face, purple and swollen as it was, but couldn't place him immediately. '. . . this other man, you can't get out of here.'

'I wanted you,' Maclure said. 'I offered you the chance to know me. To truly know me. Perhaps if you'd taken it, this could have been avoided. No more silly traps and lies.'

'I'll give the instruction to shoot,' Ava said. 'Three seconds. Lower your weapon.'

'Shoot me and I'll shoot her. You know my muscles'll spasm. I won't be able to help it.'

'Then let me untie them,' Ava said, 'and we'll talk.'

'I can help you with that,' Maclure smiled.

Ava looked down at the two bodies, fighting the pressure around their necks less now, each barely breathing. The man's fingers had given up their purchase on the rope between them and were twitching on his chest.

'If I open the window, the rope will release. It may be too late, but it's worth a try. Tell your men to move away from the door.'

'I'm not negotiating at this point,' Ava said, taking a step further towards Maclure.

'Then they both die in front of you,' he smiled.

'Fuck,' Ava muttered. She didn't have the time or luxury of playing hardball when two lives were being lost right in front of her. 'Move back. Everyone up the corridor now. Guns down.'

'Thank you,' Maclure said, pulling the window down from the top to its lowest setting, leaving the upper half open to the elements.

The rope that had been wrapped around Janet Monroe's feet flew into the room and became a benign snake on the floor. Immediately, Janet was pulled towards the other man, neither of them moving, the nooses around their necks too tight for any quick relief.

'Let me help them,' Ava said. 'Lower your gun while I do that. Please.'

'Do whatever you want,' Maclure said. 'I don't need their deaths. I'm strong enough. I've already become. I was simply waiting for a sign. This is it.'

Ava glared at him. 'What's Clozapine?' she demanded, edging closer to Janet.

Maclure cocked his head to one side. 'A distraction,' he said. 'It was an attempt to deny my true self.'

Ava knelt down slowly and began releasing the knot that was preventing Janet from drawing breath.

'And who is the true you?' Ava asked, keeping the conversation going while her fingers worked too slowly.

Across the room, the other man's feet were drumming a death dance on the carpet, his body finally giving up the fight.

'Not who,' Maclure smiled. 'Like most humans, you lack vision. When I realised denying nature was wrong, when I gave in to it, it all happened so fast. It's blissful, Ava. I wish I could have shared it with you.'

Ava released the noose from Janet's throat, almost too scared to attempt to find her pulse. Instead, she moved across the room to help the man, turning her back on Maclure as she repositioned herself.

She heard his steps, heavy, purposeful, before turning to find him using an armchair to get himself into the window frame, thrusting his upper body out into the void. He lurched forwards, arms outstretched, face a vision of ecstasy as he tipped downwards.

Ava sprung across the space between them, screaming, grabbing at his right foot before it could slip out, wrenching her shoulder painfully. The weight of him dragged her body upwards. She used her legs to brace herself either side of the window, slamming her head painfully against the wall.

Rune Maclure smashed against the outside wall and window, cawing furiously, kicking Ava's face with his free left foot, dangling perilously head down and flapping his arms maniacally.

Then a second pair of hands reduced Ava's burden, and a third, a fourth. Bodies filled the room. There were cries for stretchers and medics. Someone told Ava to release her grip on

Maclure's leg and she did so gratefully, wondering why she couldn't use her right arm and why she was being slowly lowered to the floor.

The paramedics took over. Ava could see an oxygen mask being fitted over the top of Janet's face and someone else was performing CPR on the man on the floor. Lance Proudfoot, she realised – he'd phoned her earlier and she'd been too busy to return his call. Then several people were holding her and telling her to brace. The pain finally registered in her upper body, and a man's voice was counting to three and telling her it would all be all right in a moment. Her body was being pulled apart. The pain was blinding, almost surreal. Everything faded out of focus and she could hear a woman screech. In the few seconds before her world reassembled, she realised the screech had been her own.

'It's back in,' a man told her. 'It'll be sore but you're going to be fine now. You'll need to rest it and take anti-inflammatory painkillers.'

Ava sat up and allowed a sling to be fitted over her previously dislocated arm.

'Will they live?' she asked, looking across the room to Janet Monroe and Lance Proudfoot.

She had no idea what the journalist was doing there or how he'd been a step ahead of them, but at least someone had been there with Janet and for that she would always be grateful. Lance Proudfoot had a habit of being in the wrong place in the middle of the worst kind of police operation.

'Janet's in better shape than the man. They're en route to the hospital now. We have an air ambulance on its way,' Tripp said, appearing at her side and dismissing the other officers.

Rune Maclure had been lowered in through the window and was pinned on the floor, still making a bizarre, high-pitched animal noise deep in his throat.

'Help me stand up,' Ava told Tripp, keeping their backs against the wall as Maclure was handcuffed and removed from the flat.

'Are you okay? Your arm was badly dislocated. You'll be dizzy . . .'

Ava ignored his concerns.

'Call ahead to the hospital. There'll have to be a psychiatric evaluation asap,' she told Tripp.

'Is that how he's going to spin it? The procurator fiscal will get their own psych report. We'll have a chance to fight it.'

'Not this time,' Ava said, seeing Maclure's gun on the floor at the base of the window and taking an evidence bag from her pocket. 'The Rune Maclure I met before wasn't the man who was here today. And that noise he was making. He talked about becoming. When he threw himself out of that window, he genuinely thought he was going to fly away. No question about it.'

She bent down, using the bag to pick up the gun without adding her own fingerprints to it, making sure the safety catch was engaged before sliding it into her pocket. It would need to be added to the evidence log as soon as possible.

'Had Maclure taken drugs?' Tripp asked.

'I don't think so. More likely down to the lack of them. The man they're flying to the hospital is Lance Proudfoot. We should inform his family about what's happening.'

'Lance . . . I know that name.'

'Yes, you do, which brings me to our next stop of the evening. Could you drop me at DI Callanach's, please? Lance Proudfoot's a journalist and a close friend of Luc's. I need to go and break the news in person.'

Chapter Forty-One

18 March

Tripp dropped her off outside Callanach's flat and sped away to help oversee Rune Maclure's processing. Ava checked her watch. She could afford ten minutes, no more. Using her key, she let herself into the corridor and took the stairs quietly, keen not to wake any of his neighbours at such an antisocial hour. Police work had made her forget the relevance of time in so far as which part of the day or night it was. A clock was only for reminding you how urgently the next task needed to be handled.

She felt a stab of jealousy as she ran up the stairs for those people whose jobs started at 9 a.m. and stopped at 5.30 p.m., whose weekends were their own and who'd never had their holiday cancelled while they stood in line at the airport. How much easier for them to do classes, make social arrangements and have actual relationships. Ones that didn't crumble under the stress of their profession.

Ava knocked on the door. No answer. She knocked harder

then gave his mobile a call. When that, too, received no response, she tried his landline. That was engaged, which was strange in the small hours, given that she couldn't hear his voice inside. It was possible that someone from MIT was calling to update him, but then surely he'd have come to the door. She hadn't wanted to use her key on his flat door. It was one thing letting herself into the stairwell to the apartments, but going further was an invasion of his privacy. More than that, it assumed a connection between the two of them that was no longer active, if indeed it had even been real.

She caught movement from behind the door's eyehole. No more than the briefest darkening of the dim light beyond, a flicker, but the flat was definitely occupied.

'Luc,' she called quietly. 'It's me. I should have come before now, I realise that, but something's happened. Please, open the door.'

Waiting proved futile. Her watch showed she'd already wasted half the time she'd allocated. In five minutes, another police car would arrive to get her to the station. Perhaps Callanach was being stubborn, only that wasn't like him. What concerned her more was the prospect that his current suspensions – in all but name – had sent him into the same spiral of depression that had disabled him so badly at the end of his time at Interpol. If that were the case, there was only one thing to do.

'I'm coming in,' she said as she slipped her key into the lock and walked into the dark living room, clicking the door shut behind her.

There was a light on in the bedroom.

'Luc,' she called. 'It's just me. I apologise for letting myself in, but it's important. I hope you don't . . .'

Callanach was on the bed, bare-chested but wearing jeans, sitting with his legs stretched out but his arms folded. Perched on the window seat, one hand wrapped around something Ava couldn't quite see, was Astrid Borde.

'Hello,' Astrid said brightly. 'Luc was hoping you'd just go away, but I'm glad you've come in. Things were getting rather dull. You don't seem surprised to see me here.'

'I'm not,' Ava smiled. 'You appeared in some footage I was watching earlier today. You have quite an unmistakeable figure.'

'And you have a key to Luc's flat. Why is that?'

She addressed the question to Callanach, who simply shrugged.

'What, no attempt at excuses? No elaborate tales of working late together? Luc, are you not going to defend DCI Turner's honour?'

'DCI Turner can defend herself,' Callanach said. 'She has a key because we're friends. If you're looking for anything more than that, I'm going to have to leave it to your imagination.'

'Sweetheart, you sound almost bitter,' Astrid purred. 'Do you know, I actually believe that nothing's going on between you.'

'Ms Borde, did you smother Bruce Jenson with a cushion?' Ava asked.

'That's an oversimplification. I did many things. I helped Luc when he couldn't help himself; although I recognised from his email to his mother that he was asking for assistance. I also ensured that justice was done. Bruce Jenson and Gilroy Western raped Luc's mother. Did you know that?'

Astrid's cheeks were fevered, her eyes too bright. The obsession she'd had with Callanach was not at all diminished by the passage of time. Ava almost pitied her. Callanach, on the other hand, looked exhausted. Not scared, not even interested. Just done with it all.

'I did know, actually,' Ava said. 'Luc told me when Jenson was discovered dead. And Gilroy Western, that was your work, too?'

'Not just me. You keep saying that as if Luc and I weren't involved in it together.'

'We weren't,' Callanach responded dully. 'Because there is no we. I wasn't communicating with you, Astrid. The emails I sent my mother were private. You hacked into them, the same way you hacked into mine.'

'Hacking's a hysterical term. Your mother emailed me before when I was in contact with her. I just had to guess her password. You kept the same private email address from when you worked at Interpol and I had access to your personnel records, remember? Sloppy of you not to have changed it. I paid an online company based in Colombia to access your email account. It's not even a hidden Web service. Took them less than a day. But you knew I could do that, too. What I found in there was a clear call to arms and I responded exactly the way you wanted me to.'

'And the email to Western purporting to be from Jenson's solicitor?' Ava asked.

'The easiest part of it all. When people want to believe what they're reading, they get careless.'

Callanach looked Ava in the eyes briefly then looked away. She saw that he'd given up. Astrid had the sort of fixation that couldn't be reasoned with or persuaded. The sort of fixation, in fact, that made it possible for her to suffocate a terminally ill man and cut the brakes of another who had plenty of life left in him yet.

'You can't arrest me,' Astrid declared. 'I'll tell them Luc was in on the whole thing. He's suspended at the moment, isn't he?'

'No, he's not,' Ava replied, taking a step closer to the bed. 'Do you mind if I sit down?'

'Don't lie to me. He hasn't been into work for a while now. I've been watching. And yes, you can sit down, but don't touch Luc. I don't want either of you to touch each other.'

'He's on administrative leave, nothing more than that. He certainly isn't suspended.' She sat.

Touching Callanach was the very last thing she'd had in mind when she'd gone round there, but now Astrid was rattled for the first time and Ava could use that. The thought of her and the man she was obsessed with being intimate was what Astrid couldn't bear. Ava pushed herself far enough back on the bed to be next to Callanach's feet.

'What is it you think's going to happen now? Are you and Luc supposed to go sailing off into the sunset? Only if Luc disappears now, he'll make himself a suspect and I'm sure you'll agree he has a face that stands out in a crowd, so trying to stay out of sight might be tricky.'

'I know places we can go,' Astrid pouted. 'You forgot about me pretty quickly when I disappeared and I was right here in Edinburgh most of that time.'

'You weren't wanted on suspicion of murder,' Ava reminded her.

'And Luc won't be, either. You already told me it was a woman on the CCTV footage from the care home.'

'Do you think I'm just going to let you go?'

'Ava . . .' Callanach warned her quietly.

She laid a gentle hand on his ankle and rubbed it affectionately.

'Don't worry. Astrid and I can sort this out,' she said, giving him a warm smile.

Astrid got to her feet.

'I told you not to touch him,' she growled. 'Do you know what I'm holding? You really don't want to piss me . . .'

'Hand grenade.' Ava cut her off. 'I'm guessing you bought it in Sweden. They're easy to get hold of there and much cheaper than most people realise. You probably bought that for, what, no more than fifty euros?'

Astrid stared at her.

'You'd have taken multiple ferry journeys back. No way you'd have been able to fly with it. Hiding hand grenades in a car, however, is relatively low-risk. They're currently the favoured weapon of some Swedish gangs. It's becoming a problem.'

'You're so arrogant,' Astrid hissed. 'You think I don't have the guts to pull the pin?'

'And ruin Luc's face?' Ava laughed, reaching out to take hold of Luc's hand. 'Why would you do that?'

'Because if I can't have him, no one's going to.'

She stamped a foot, childlike, frowning, clutching her hand around the grenade. The end of her thumb was inserted into the ring and would require some manoeuvring.

Ava slipped her hands into her pocket, gesturing compliance and defeat.

'He's all yours,' Ava said. 'I'm seeing someone, anyway. To be honest, Luc's not really my type. All style and no substance, if you know what I mean.'

Astrid paused, looking from Callanach to Ava and back.

'You . . . you don't need to be rude about him. You shouldn't be. He works for you. You're supposed to respect him.'

'Respect him?' Ava laughed. 'After that sordid fling he had with the Spanish doctor? My God, she was all over him. It was embarrassing. She used to turn up at the station all the time – I actually had to ask her to leave once.'

'What Spanish doctor?' Astrid demanded. 'Who was she?'

Her attention turned to Callanach, who sighed deeply and rolled his eyes.

'No one. She was no one. It was a passing phase, nothing more. Don't get . . .'

'Are there photos of her on your phone?' Astrid demanded. 'Give it to me. I want to see.'

Callanach paused.

'Let her see,' Ava said. 'She killed the men who raped your mother, Luc. I think Astrid has a right to know what you've been doing while she was out there plotting and planning to assist you.'

'It's charging in the lounge,' he said. 'Help yourself. The unlock code is 9004.'

Astrid moved cautiously towards the doorway, peering into the lounge.

'You,' she motioned at Ava. 'Get it for me.'

'Fine,' Ava said, drawing her hands out of her pockets to push herself up from the bed, sliding Rune Maclure's gun, still in the evidence bag, under Callanach's ankle to shield it from Astrid's line of vision.

Walking slowly into the lounge, hands raised, she noted the part-open window and wondered how Maclure was doing. More importantly, how Lance Proudfoot was doing. Callanach would want to be at his bedside as soon as possible. She detached the phone from its charging cable and typed in the security code, swiping through until she found the photo gallery.

'Here.' She held out the phone for Astrid, who carefully swapped the grenade to her left hand, looping the new thumb through the pin.

Ava cast a look at Callanach, who'd taken the opportunity to reach down and take the gun in his hand, tucking it close in to his hip.

'This is her?' Astrid yelled, holding up a photo of Dr Selina Vega with her arms wrapped around Callanach, in some bar judging by the background. 'This skinny little bitch? Is this what you were doing while I was helping you to get justice for your mother?' She flicked through more photos, scrolling

– staring – scrolling, swearing to herself, beginning to pace. 'How could you do this to me?' she screeched, holding up a picture of Selina in a bikini that would have made the most secure of women turn green. 'I want to know where she lives. Is she in the city?'

Astrid took a step towards Callanach, leaving her back exposed and Ava behind her. It was the best chance Ava was going to get. She rushed forwards, grabbing Astrid. Pushing her thumb as hard as she could into the tendons in the back of Astrid's hand and forcing her to relax the fist partially, Ava wrapped her own hand over the newly exposed section of the grenade, wrestling Astrid for control of it. Callanach was up in a second, on his knees on the bed, gun levelled at Astrid's face.

'Astrid, let Ava take the grenade,' he ordered.

Astrid laughed, hurling the mobile into Callanach's face and freeing her second hand, then grabbing Ava's wrist to force her off the grenade.

'I will shoot,' Callanach shouted.

'I killed for you!' Astrid screamed back.

Ava elbowed her in the base of the throat and Astrid choked, her knees buckling, twisting towards the window seat. Getting a knee onto the window seat, giving her better purchase to pull the grenade from Astrid's hands, Ava yanked as hard as she could.

There was a moment of silence. The grenade floated into the air, a gracefully spinning ovoid. They watched as one, Ava's eyes the first to return to Astrid's hand, where the pin remained fixed around her thumb like a Christmas cracker trinket, ill-fitting and ridiculous without its counterpart. Then Astrid was jumping for it, with Ava reaching both hands out for the live bomb, as Callanach threw down the gun, scrambling to launch himself off the bed. Ava got to it first.

'Window!' Ava screamed at him.

Callanach shoved the slightly open frame, thrusting it completely upwards, leaving a big enough target for Ava not to miss. As she was aiming, Astrid thrust a knee into base of Ava's ribcage, folding her double. Astrid grabbed the grenade back again from Ava's hand, clutching it to her chest.

'At least I can die with you,' Astrid gushed, staring into Callanach's wide eyes.

Ava lurched forwards, grabbing Astrid from behind at the knees with her left arm and pushing her at the hips with her right – a carefully directed rugby tackle – which left Astrid falling head first across the window seat. Ava kept her own knees bent, using every bit of her weight to push Astrid up across the seat and out of the window, keeping her grip, following through.

'No . . .' Astrid's scream sliced the night air.

Callanach's own cry followed as he threw his body weight on top of Ava's on the window seat, reaching out to jam himself across the frame.

Ava tried to hold Astrid. She tried with every ounce of strength she had. But her grip was one-armed – the other was half tangled in its sling and weakened to the point of uselessness.

Astrid thrashed, grenade still firmly in her grasp. Ava's hand slipped down in excruciating slow motion until only the tips of her fingers were brushing Astrid's boots, then she was gone, falling the single storey to the ground, screeching furiously into the night.

The grenade unleashed its terminal force as Astrid hit the pavement. Ava covered her face with her good arm, where she hung from the open window. She heard nothing. There was a sensation of force, like being hit by an invisible wave. Then there was pain. Her ears filled with hot liquid. Her eyes were sandstorm raw. And the night was alive with light, with mirror-ball reflections on every surface. Glass flew. It was beautiful and terrible. The ground was awash with crimson. Ava wondered momentarily if she'd survived.

By the time Callanach lowered her body carefully to the floor of his bedroom, she was unresponsive.

Chapter Forty-Two

24 March

Machines beeped. The hospital bed was surrounded by wires. Screens flashed electronic messages to onlookers. At the bedside sat a white-coated man, staring at a clipboard, running his pen down the text on the attached sheets and frowning over his glasses. At the far end of the room was a mirror, and in the space beyond that another room allowed interested parties to watch and listen unseen. Not that the person in the bed didn't know what lay behind the mirror. There was nothing deficient about Rune Maclure's IQ. That wasn't an issue. The small group gathered in the observation room was interested in a much more specific function of his brain. A number of stickers covered Maclure's head, a lead trailing from each one.

'Right, Mr Maclure, if you're ready, I'll begin,' the white-coated man announced. 'I'm Dr Fox and I'm part of the psychiatric team. Your solicitor consented on your behalf to this procedure. Do you recall that?'

Maclure gave a single slow nod. The doctor lifted a page, checked something and looked up again.

'You've refused medication since you've been here. Is that right?'

'I don't need medication,' Maclure said, twisting his right wrist and loosening the covering blanket to reveal a handcuff attached to a low bedrail. 'What you call psychosis, I know to be evolution. I've moved beyond.'

Dr Fox made a note on his clipboard and cast a swift half-glance into the observation suite.

'What does he mean, "moved beyond", Professor?' a young woman in the group safely behind the glass asked.

An older female, around whom a semicircle had formed in obvious deference, smiled at her students.

'Beyond being human.' The professor switched on a monitor, upon which a variety of horizontal lines ran, some blipping neatly and regularly, others varying wildly. 'Keep listening, but watch this screen.'

'So what are you now?' Dr Fox asked Maclure.

'I'm The Crow,' Maclure said simply.

'Can you explain how you've become this creature and how it makes you feel?'

Maclure grinned. 'I feel free. Powerful. Invincible. I understand the world in a way no one else can. I see its patterns. The way it all fits together. How one creature is a resource for the next. We give life and take life. Nature is a pyramid, Doctor. Every one of us was built to consume the weaker among us.'

'And when did you first start feeling like this?'

'I always have. Always. I denied it for so long. Pumped my body full of chemicals to shove the animal inside me back down to the depths of my humanity and for a while I believed that was the right thing to do . . .' He tipped his head to one

378

side, then the other, his eyes flicking left and right. 'Do you hear that? Do you hear them talking about me?'

'Who?' Dr Fox asked.

'Them . . .' Maclure gave an upwards nod towards the mirror. 'The people in there, staring at me. They're fascinated. They feel how different I am to them.'

'We're all here to help you, Rune,' Dr Fox said. 'We just want to understand what's happening.'

Beyond the glass, as one, the medical students took a small step away from the glass.

'Can he really hear us?' one asked. 'I thought this was sound-proof.'

'He's bright,' the professor said. 'He knows he's being watched. The schizophrenia he was self-medicating for doesn't mean he's incapable of making rational deductions.'

'So is he making up this thing about becoming a crow to excuse killing? It seems too far-fetched. He's calm and controlled. The attacks seem to have been carefully planned and he chose to stop taking his antipsychotic medication,' another student continued.

'No.' The professor crossed her arms. 'He's not making it up. Mr Maclure is, in my opinion, suffering from clinical lycanthropy. It's rare – I've never seen a case myself – but well documented and is a form of delusional misidentification syndrome, where the brain ceases to be able to identify the self accurately.'

'So he genuinely believes he's no longer human?' someone else asked breathily.

The professor pointed her students' attention back into the hospital room.

'The people I killed had defied nature. They'd tried to take their own lives. They made themselves prey. What else could I do but consume their life force? I'm a predator and I was still forming my true self. I needed what they had to offer me . . .'

Inside the observation suite, two lines on the monitor began to pulse erratically.

'But what you did to them might be regarded as cruel. Perverse, even. There were elements to their deaths that went far beyond anything one could define as natural,' Dr Fox commented calmly.

'Nature's the beast, not the beasts themselves. You can't tame the wildness that comes from within. Tigers kill for sport. Coyotes make an art of it. Cats play with mice for hours before killing them.'

'Is that what you did with Stephen Berry?' Dr Fox asked.

'He was the easiest of them all. We went to Tantallon Castle as therapy. I told him he'd feel more alive if he took controlled risks, let himself feel wild. We climbed a fence, climbed a wall. He fell for it all so easily. Then he refused to let go. He clung on and cried and begged, just like I knew he would. He was weak like all of them. What part of natural justice do you not comprehend?'

'What about the farmer, Jon Moffat? How did you come to cross paths with him?' Dr Fox continued.

'He was the patient of a former colleague of mine for several years. I saw him coming and going, never improving, occasionally making an attempt at ending his miserable existence, but he couldn't even get that right. That one really was a mercy killing. In the wild, a creature that badly injured would be left to die. Why do human beings insist on patching people up, on prolonging life when it would be far better simply to let nature take its course? Moffat was burned beyond recognition. I saw the photos of him from before. You can't tell me it wouldn't have been a kindness for him not to have survived the fire.'

'But how do their deaths benefit you, specifically?' Dr Fox asked, making notes.

'How does eating a meal benefit you? Explain this. One of

the few natural threats to the crow is the fox. Is that why they sent you, Doctor? You're not at all what you seem in your white coat and your shiny stethoscope. Was that supposed to hypnotise me?'

'Because of my name?' Dr Fox asked. 'That's just a coincidence . . .'

'His stats are going wild,' one of the students interrupted. 'His brain function's not normal, at all.'

'Which has been documented before in clinical lycanthropy cases. These patients are so convinced that they've become another animal that their brain actually begins to function in new ways,' the professor said, changing position in the room to get a better view of Maclure.

'So what causes delusional misidentification syndrome?' another student asked.

'We believe it's right hemispheric lesions,' the professor replied, distracted. 'What's Maclure doing?'

'Do you know why I had to consume those people?' Maclure asked, eyes widening, panting. 'I knew I was about to have to fight for my life. I was expecting you to come for me. The fox stalks its prey only so long before it strikes. It may be silent and devious, but the crow is faster still. Every moment of the suffering I caused made me stronger, fiercer. I withstood all their complaints, their crying, their shame. I soaked it all up.' Maclure bared his teeth.

'Mr Maclure, please calm yourself. You're in hospital care now. I can assure you that no one here, least of all me, wishes anything but the best for you. My name is irrelevant. I'm human and I believe we'll be able to help you return to your former self.'

'Yeah?' Maclure whispered. 'Well then, you really are the enemy.'

He swivelled on the bed in a heartbeat, his right hand still cuffed, flinging his legs across to wrap them around Dr Fox's neck, creating a vice and squeezing, squeezing, squeezing.

Dr Fox's face was purple in seconds, his hands flapping uselessly at Maclure's knees. The students in the observation room were screaming. The professor shoved them aside, yelling for help as she burst into the corridor. By the time she was at Maclure's bedside, Dr Fox was on his knees.

Maclure was cawing victoriously, filling the room with a haunting, high-pitched screech. The professor grabbed a syringe and plunged it into the top of Maclure's arm. Still he didn't release his legs, his system defying the sedative. At last, two orderlies rushed in, taking a leg each and pulling them apart, leaving Dr Fox to collapse unconscious to the floor.

Maclure's eyes began to roll, the grin on his face undiminished by the coming darkness.

'I'm The Crow,' he muttered, his voice hoarse.

Chapter Forty-Three

25 March

'Lycanthropy? So he's a fucking werewolf, is what you're telling me?' Overbeck sat legs crossed, upper ankle bobbing up and down furiously, on the business side of Ava's desk.

'Lycanthropy's a generic term. I guess it originally referred to people who believed they turned into wolves, probably courtesy of folklore, but these days it applies to anyone who believes they turn into an animal. In Maclure's case, it was caused by his schizophrenia, which was why he appeared so normal and unaffected at times. He's convinced he's a crow. Every psychiatrist who's seen him agrees. He's not denying physically having committed the murders, but he will be running a mental disorder defence,' Ava replied, wondering just how long her detective superintendent was planning on making her visit and glad she had a briefing in a few minutes to use as an excuse to get away.

'What's the update on the doctor he attacked?'

'Badly damaged windpipe and I gather he's considering early retirement, but he'll recover.'

'And the other sick little fuck who distracted you? What was his name?'

Ava ignored the jibe. 'You mean RJ Bott, ma'am?'

'Yes, him, I want that bastard doing life for making us look like a bunch of incompetent dicks. Tell me he's been charged.'

'He has, in fact. There were a number of offences relating to the possession and distribution of snuff videos, and some unlawful gambling offences.'

'Is that all? Could you not have done any better than that?'

'Bott has a disturbed and frankly disgusting obsession with death and murder, but that's it. He was just a voyeur. There's no evidence he ever got involved in anything himself. He used the girl at Reach You for his own purposes. We believe Vicki Rosach was innocent in the whole thing. Stupid, but not culpable.

'Having spoken to the witnesses from the charity, they say it's not a terribly unusual thing. Suicide prevention groups attract people with an unhealthy fascination for death. When Vicki joined RJ's football club, it must have been an absolute gift for him. Not to mention a way to boost the number of his online followers.'

'Ban the whole fucking Internet, I say. Well, if that's really the best you could come up with . . .' Overbeck let the insult hang in the air for a few seconds. 'More importantly, are we going to be sued?' Overbeck asked, standing and straightening her jacket.

So that was the real reason she was there. MIT's liability. The potential exposure to criticism. The long-term damage to her career. Ava almost wished Janet Monroe *was* going to take legal action against the department.

'Janet Monroe will also make a full recovery,' Ava said. 'It was obviously a serious mistake that the units watching her flat were called away to the RJ Bott arrest scene, but everyone believed we'd found the perpetrator and that Janet was no longer in danger. It was extremely fortunate that Lance Proudfoot turned up. It looks as if he delayed Janet's attempted murder long enough for us to get there.'

'Fucking idiot, getting involved in police business. What the hell was he thinking?'

'Well, right now he's probably thinking he's glad to be alive. Technically speaking, he died. Paramedics revived him; although he'll be in hospital a while longer. They think he allowed Janet to pull all the slack from the bungee cord so she could live. The man's a hero.'

'But is he a litigious hero? That's what I want to know.' Overbeck walked to the door.

'No, he's not,' Ava replied, retaking her place behind her own desk. 'How are things between you and DS Lively? He's barely spoken all week.'

'None of your business,' Overbeck snapped before dropping her shoulders. 'Cut him some slack. I had to lower his expectations of our relationship recently.'

Ava took a breath. 'Will do,' she said, waiting until Overbeck had cleared the corridor before exiting herself.

Lowering the expectations of a relationship. That was a euphemism and a half. Lively would be crushed. In spite of the extreme differences between her sergeant and her superintendent, the former was very much in love with the latter. Policing really was a recipe for relationship disaster. She knew that better than most. It was her first full day back at work and she was about to pull her team apart.

'Good morning,' she said, glad everyone was in the briefing room and ready to start when she arrived. At least she'd managed to avoid making small talk.

The crowd was silent. She'd forgotten about her face. For most of them, it was the first time they were seeing her since the explosion. She was healing now, but her skin was still peppered with cuts from glass shrapnel. Both eardrums had been punctured. She had nosebleeds three or four times a day. Her eyes were sore and she was suffering some hair loss, likely from the shock as much as the impact, the doctors had told her. It would get better. She'd heal. More to the point, she'd deliberately thrown a woman out of a window. Ava had no idea how she was supposed to heal from that.

'Janet Monroe sends you all her regards. She's doing well and hopes to be back on duty in a week or so. No permanent damage. In true MIT form, she expects to have all of her drinks paid for over the next twelve months.' That at least got a small laugh. 'Lance Proudfoot, the journalist who intervened, was more badly injured, but he, too, should make a full recovery.'

'Are you all right, ma'am?' someone asked.

'Cut myself shaving,' she replied.

Bigger laugh that time.

Callanach wandered in, leaning against the wall, hands in pockets. She tried not to look at him, but it was as hard then as the first day he'd arrived. It was his looks that got most people's attention, but that hadn't been it for Ava. Luc Callanach was an enigma. He kept so much inside, so much gentle warmth that he covered with intense professionalism. He was funny, but he never tried to be. His instinct for police work was incredible. And when he looked in her eyes, it was as if no one else existed. As if no one else had ever existed, in fact. No one who mattered.

'The Maclure case is closed from our perspective. We now know that he was a regular visitor to Fenella Hawksmith's ward when she was an inpatient, although he never treated her. Same thing with Jon Moffat. It's a useful lesson in throwing the net wider for future investigations. Astrid Borde has been positively identified in connection with the murders of both Bruce Jenson and Gilroy Western. DI Graham will finalise his report shortly, but Miss Borde's obsession with DI Callanach seems to have been the motivating factor in both murders.'

That was all she needed to say. Astrid's DNA was a match for the blood spot on Gilroy Western's engine and the footage of her at Jenson's nursing home was all the conclusion needed to close the case. Thankfully, forensic testing hadn't shown any DNA link between Callanach and Bruce Jenson, avoiding both the need for an awkward explanation to Pax Graham, and breaking that particular bombshell to Callanach.

'What we actually need to talk about today is a new case,' Ava continued. 'Interpol has approached us with information that there appears to be a substantial flow of human traffic moving into Edinburgh through mainland Europe, highly organised. MIT are providing backup for Interpol's investigation; although it's very much an international effort. DI Graham'll be heading up day-to-day operations here.'

As one, every head turned to look at Callanach. The obvious question hung in the air.

'I've asked DI Callanach to handle matters as the Scottish police liaison to Interpol, based in Lyon. Given his experience with Interpol, that made the most sense. He'll be leaving for France later today, so if anyone has any matters to discuss with him, you have a couple of hours.'

'How long?' Lively asked gruffly.

Ava hadn't even noticed him in the corner.

'How long what?' Ava queried.

'How long will we be without one of our DIs?' Lively clarified, getting to his feet. He was red-faced and looked nothing like the habitual piss-taker they were all used to.

'For as long as the investigation's active.' Ava coughed slightly. 'It's a major international case, so we're making contingency plans for DI Callanach to be away from us for several months. In the meantime, you and DS Tripp'll be asked to step into his shoes.'

The room was horribly quiet. Ava tried desperately to think of a way to lighten the atmosphere and came up blank.

'The good news is, the French have better taste than you bastards, so I'll finally get some of the adulation I'm entitled to,' Callanach intervened to smiles all round.

Ava did her best to join in.

'I know you'll miss me, so I'll be signing photos in my office for the next hour.'

That earned him a few whoops.

Ava waited for calm.

'You've all worked a serious amount of overtime in the last month, so I'll be trying to get you time off in lieu.'

No response to that.

'Right, well, I'll be preparing a full briefing on the Interpol case. Expect a package on each desk tomorrow with details. Thanks, everyone.'

She left the room in silence, hearing chairs scrape as people stood, followed by murmuring and then the sort of backslapping that she knew were the team's goodbye to its most experienced detective inspector. The irony was overwhelming. Callanach's arrival had been met with an ill-disguised coldness, now it was as if she'd separated her team from their nearest and dearest. He'd won them all over. Even — perhaps especially — Lively.

'Who'd have thought it?' she murmured to herself as she wandered back into her office.

'Thought what?' Callanach asked, directly behind her.

'Holy mother of fuck!' Ava shouted. 'What the hell are you doing?'

'I thought you could hear me behind you,' he smiled. 'You must have been a million miles away.'

'Burst eardrums, remember?' Ava replied. 'Have you said your farewells?'

'Not all of them,' Callanach said quietly, clicking her office door shut behind him. 'Feels like you've been avoiding me since you phoned to say I was being seconded to France.'

'Just busy. Wrapping up two simultaneous cases is a paperwork nightmare.'

She leaned against her desk. Callanach walked over and stood right in front of her, close enough that the tips of their shoes were touching. Ava looked sideways across the room and out of the window.

He reached up and gently stroked her cheek.

'I'm so sorry you got hurt. This whole thing with Astrid, from start to finish, has damaged so many innocent people.'

Ava's face was aflame. She took hold of his fingertips and put them back down by his side.

'It's over now. You can get on with living your life. Really living it. Wherever you feel most at home. No more ghosts. Bruce Jenson wasn't your father. I know there's still a question about Gilroy Western . . .'

'I'm leaving that one alone, for now at least. When I got Jenson's DNA test back, it made me realise I'm better off keeping hold of the memories of the man I always believed was my father. No point making things any harder than they already are.'

'Sounds like you're starting to come to terms with it all,' she said.

'Is that why you're sending me back to France? To see if I settle there again? You didn't need to do that. I already know where I belong. Scotland isn't the place I ran away to any more. It's where my friends are, where my life is happening. It's where I want to be.'

'My decision was purely professional. You know Interpol like no one in the whole of Police Scotland, never mind MIT. If I'd sent anyone else, I'd be answering serious questions as to why I hadn't chosen you. I need to sit down, actually, could you just stake a step back, so I can pass . . .'

He shook his head, smiling briefly, reaching out a hand to put on her waist.

'Feeling faint?' he asked. 'You probably shouldn't even be back at work yet. What did your doctor say?'

'That's none of your business,' she said, the echo of Overbeck ringing in her ears. For a moment, self-loathing overwhelmed her. Tears came. 'I'm sorry. I didn't mean that. I'm tired. It's all the painkillers.'

'Let me drive you home,' he said. 'I've got time before my flight. I could even grab you a takeaway. I bet you haven't eaten for . . .'

'Luc, stop, please,' she whispered. 'I can't do this. Everything's broken. I killed Astrid. I failed to protect Janet and your friend, Lance, and I wonder if I haven't been so distracted by everything going on between us that I didn't miss evidence. Rune Maclure sat right here in my office, asked me out, for Christ's sake, and I never treated him like a suspect. Not once. I need to get my head straight and I can't do that with you here.'

'Ava, don't . . .'

'No. This is the end. I lied for you. I covered for you.'

'I hadn't done anything,' Callanach said quietly.

'That's not the point. I broke so many rules. The integrity of the whole investigation was compromised because of the way I felt about you.'

'How *did* you feel?' he asked, taking her face in his free hand.

'It's how I feel now that matters,' Ava replied stiffly. 'I don't want you here, Luc. Everything got too messy. I need to be able to get up in the morning knowing I can do my work, do it properly, make good decisions and that I'll be able to sleep when I get home.'

'I'm not stopping you from doing any of those things,' he said.

'Yes, you are. It's what you do. To Astrid, Selina, to me . . .'

'That's not fair. I didn't ask for any of this.'

'I know,' she smiled. 'You don't even see it coming, do you? There's just a trail of pathetic women left in your wake.'

'Ava,' he kissed her cheek. 'I'm sorry I took the prayer slate from your room. I'm even sorrier I never returned it. It was . . . weird and wrong on so many levels . . . even I can't explain it. But I think all this time I was waiting for something to happen between us, you were already waiting for it to go wrong. And no, I'm not blaming you. I take full responsibility for the disaster that happened at my flat, but still — I think there was something of a self-fulfilling prophesy to it for you.

'I'm going to France. I'm not here to persuade you differently. But I am coming back and when I do, you and I are going to sit down and work this out. Because I care about you far too much to give up on this — whatever it is — before it's even started.'

Callanach tightened his grip on her waist and pulled her body forwards to meet his, kissing her gently on the lips and holding her a second longer. Then he let her go.

Can't get enough
of the *Perfect* series?

Then read on for a sneak peek
of Helen Fields' next book,
Perfect Dark.

Chapter 1

At precisely the same time Bart was coming round from a distinctly chemically induced sleep, his mother was waking from a herbal insomnia remedy and wondering why the house was so quiet. It wasn't a Sunday. On Sundays, Bart neither had college nor work, and sometimes he slept in. Not all that often, but sometimes. Maggie rolled onto her side and rubbed bleary eyes, trying to focus on the small travel clock perched on her bedside table. 9 a.m. She'd overslept. Not that she had anywhere to be in a hurry, but mornings – it was a Wednesday, she realised – were marked with the clanging of crockery, the pouring of cereal, and the sound of the dishwasher being loaded before Bart exited the house. He was a good boy. The sort of boy her friends were rather jealous of. She was conscious of the fact, sometimes moaning about him a little to make it clear that he wasn't perfect, although secretly she knew he was. She might tell her neighbour that he'd played his music too loud, or pretend to her weekly library social group that he was forgetful about tidying his room. But Bart was neither loud nor untidy. In fact, he was independent, considerate and helpful. An exception among other twenty-year-old men. (Boys, Maggie thought. Twenty was no age at all. Certainly not mature enough to comprehend all the cruelties the world had to offer.) But then Bart had grown up quickly after his father had been killed serving in Afghanistan. Not in battle. That would have been devastating, of course. The truth had garnered more pity and less admiration from the community. Her husband had choked in the mess hall one night when a fellow officer had cracked a particularly hilarious joke. The meatball he'd been chewing was sucked up into his airways where it had stubbornly lodged and refused to move in spite of no end of back patting, then finally a desperate attempt at the Heimlich manoeuvre which had broken ribs but not allowed any oxygen to his lungs. How did you explain that to a fourteen-year-old boy? That his father, who had been a military man since before Bart was born, had been dispatched not by bomb or bullet, but by a ball of minced beef, egg yolk and breadcrumbs.

Perhaps Bart was ill, Maggie thought. Or maybe she'd taken too many sleeping tablets and not heard him leave the house. That had happened before. Distracted after a long shift at the call centre, she'd returned home and taken a SleepSaver, eaten dinner, then swallowed another pill without thinking. Such were the perils of tiredness. Living on a military widow's pension and her wages was too tight for comfort, even with Bart earning a few extra pounds waiting tables in the evenings.

'Bart, you all right love?' she called, pulling her tatty pink dressing gown over bare shoulders. Bart had bought her a new one for Christmas. It was exquisite. Cream, and so soft it was like one of the really posh cuddly toys you seemed always to find in bookshops, for some inexplicable reason. It was hanging on the back of her bedroom door, and she stroked it every time she entered or exited. But it was too nice to wear. She'd only spill coffee down it, or splash it with the remnants of the previous night's pasta sauce. The thought of spoiling something so luxurious and thoughtful was enough to keep her in her threadbare robes, at least for another six months or so. She'd start wearing it before Christmas came around, she told herself.

Bart hadn't replied by the time she'd reached his bedroom door, knocking politely, always mindful that her boy needed his privacy. He had never bought a girl back for the night, not that Maggie would have minded if they'd been discreet, but Bart conducted his relationships elsewhere. He obviously had girlfriends. He was a good-looking lad, and that wasn't just the blur of looking at him through mummy-goggles talking. At six foot he was big enough to stand out but not so tall that he attracted silly comments on the street. His father had been six foot four and once threatened to deck a man who had somehow imagined that no one had ever asked her husband what the weather was like up there. Maggie's husband – God rest his soul – had been a decent man, but not blessed with looks, all sharp features and eyes closer together than suited the average face. She was the exact opposite. Broad, flat face, wide eyes (wide hips too, and getting wider by the year, she reminded herself). Perhaps the differences between them was what had left Bart with that sort of symmetrical, well-balanced face that wasn't exactly attention-grabbing, but with which no one could find a single fault. Great skin, even teeth, good bone structure, and a fair brain. He was in his final year of a business studies college course that he was hoping would offer a potential career in London. Plenty of work in Edinburgh, Maggie always told him. Or Glasgow, if he wanted to leave home. Anywhere in Scotland. But London was the dream. Always had been.

In the absence of a reply to her knocking, Maggie opened the door slowly, calling his name softly as she put a foot inside.

The curtains were drawn and the bed was made. Nothing surprising there; his lectures started at 9 a.m. every day. He'd have left an hour ago to make sure he was in good time. Bart wasn't the sort of student who ever turned up late. But he hadn't woken her up. His normal routine was to wake, shower, have breakfast, clear up the kitchen, and to take her a cup of tea before leaving the house. She in turn would rise later, do the washing, shop and leave something tasty in the slow cooker before going off for her shift – telesales was thankless but they hadn't missed a mortgage payment yet – which started at lunchtime and went on until 8 p.m.

It wasn't the lack of a cup of tea that bothered Maggie. Her son was entitled to forget doing that for her. She counted her blessings on a daily basis for him, with or without his little kindnesses. What she couldn't understand was why his mobile was still sat on his bed, charging, exactly where he'd left it the night before when he'd dashed out to grab an extra shift at the restaurant. Another waiter had called in sick. Bart had been offered the hours, and the thought of boosting his savings account was too tempting to refuse. The pay wasn't great but the tips were, and he always attracted enough customer good-will to make a night's work worthwhile. His phone had been running on empty so he'd left it on his bed charging ready for the next morning. Maggie had watched him plug it in as she'd delivered a pile of freshly ironed clothes for him to put away. Those, too, sat waiting on the bed for his return.

She squashed the stupid maternal panic that made the stable bedroom floor feel suddenly more like quicksand. So her boy hadn't come home. Perhaps he'd met up with friends and gone for a drink, or had a better offer from a pretty girl. Only normally he'd have called her, however late. Let her know to put the chain on the door. Tell her not to worry. Bart was thoughtful like that. His father had taught him well. Maggie took the stairs carefully, and checked the answerphone on the landline. No message. She didn't have a mobile. It was just one more bill that she didn't need. Plastering an optimistic smile on her face, she popped her head through the door of the lounge, all ready to have a good laugh in case he'd had a few too many and slept on the couch. She was fooling no one with the false jollity, least of all herself. Bart wasn't an excessive drinker. He'd never reached a point where the couch looked like a better option that his own bed. Her mind began conjuring the ghosts of accidents before she could stop it. Somewhere in there, a misadventure with a meatball loomed large. Like father like son. Wouldn't that be the ultimate irony? Both of them gone, cause of death Italian cuisine.

'Stop it, you silly woman,' she scolded herself, wandering into the kitchen to make her own cup of breakfast tea. 'Your boy'll be back any minute.'

But the truth that Maggie had felt in that secret, vile part of the brain no parent ever wanted to hear pipe up, was that he wouldn't be back in a minute. Not by any stretch of the imagination. Because by then, Bartholomew McBride was 100 miles away.

It was the stench that woke him. Something acrid with a heavy undertone of sulphur had filled his sinuses and was threatening to make him gag.

'Mum?' His first thought was that she must be ill. That she'd gone down with food poisoning or a virus overnight and been too embarrassed or too thoughtful to have disturbed him. Only he couldn't remember getting home. And now that he registered the pain in his body, he realized he wasn't in his bed. Or any bed at all.

He sat bolt upright, head swimming, before collapsing back down to the floor. Everything was dark. Not the dark of Scottish nights away from the city camping by a loch. Not even the dark of the private rooms at the back of the night club he occasionally attended with his friends. True dark. Not one star. No bloom of pollution. No crack or spill from beneath a door or at the edge of a blind.

'Hello?' he shouted, braving movement again, sitting up more slowly. That was when he felt the tugging on his leg.

Bart froze. Something had hold of his left ankle. He breathed hard, twice, three times, tried to get to grips with his fear first and his imagination next, then he lost it.

'Get off me!' he yelled, wrenching his foot upwards, trying to scrabble away. He hit a wall with his head shortly before his foot locked solid and his hip popped from its socket. The scream he let out was loud enough to wake the entire terrace he lived on. He rolled right, instinct kicking in, and the displaced hip shifted again back into its socket, easing the dreadful pain and allowing him to lean forward to take hold of whatever had his foot.

He didn't want to extend his hand. There was something about reaching his fingers out into the black void that seemed to be inviting a bite. Like slipping your hand into a murky river in the sort of place where, when animals attacked, the general reaction to the news was – what the hell did the idiot tourist expect? What Bart found was both less and more terrifying. His ankle was bound by a leather strap. There was no bogeyman occupying the darkness with him. Not one that had hold of his leg, anyway. The strap was thick and sturdy, with a chunky metal link sewn through it. At the end of that, he realized miserably, was a chain. What was at the end of the chain, Bart wasn't sure he was ready to discover yet. So he did what all cautious people would do in a foul pitch-black room, finding themselves inexplicably chained up. He began calling out for help.

His cries echoed. He called for help. Stopped, listened. Called out again, this time louder. Stopped, listened. Bart could feel the rumbling below the floor more readily than he could hear the engine, but an engine it unmistakably was. He put his hand to the floor. The surface was rough but not cold. Neither wood nor metal. More like the sort of industrial liner that was used to insulate modern houses. He'd seen it being carried in huge sheets into Edinburgh's ever growing new housing estates. Perhaps he was in a factory then, in a room high above the machinery. That made sense. The low level growl of metal and the lack of sharp sounds from the outside world. He pressed himself closer to the wall and began yelling afresh.

'Hello! Anyone! Can anyone hear me? Help. I need help.' His cries got louder, his voice higher. He banged on the wall first then the floor between phrases, punctuating his cries for assistance. His cries became screams. Bart had never heard himself scream before. It was terrifying. Then he was hammering on the wall and stamping on the floor at the same time as he screamed. Just make noise, he thought. Someone would hear him. Someone would come.

But what if it was the wrong someone?

No, he told himself. Not that. Those thoughts were what would stop him being rescued. If all he had was a short window of time before whoever had chained him up was due to come back, he had to make all the noise he could right now. He took some steadying breaths. Think. The chain on his ankle allowed him limited movement. He walked along the wall as far as he could, tapping as he went, feeling for the edge of a doorway or handle, listening for a place where there might be an exit. Nothing. Then he walked the other way along the wall. Tapping all the time.

A crash at his feet made him leap backwards. He tripped and fell, scrabbling away from the metallic noise. The darkness made everything nearer and louder. He'd never considered what a threat the lack of light was before. Everything was alien. His sense of distance and direction had completely gone. As the noise faded, he reached out tentatively, groping on the floor for whatever it was he'd hit. The bucket was just a couple of feet away on its side, still rolling gently to and fro. He grabbed the handle and pulled it closer, exploring its edges, neither brave nor stupid enough to put his hand all the way inside. The smell coming from there was its own unique warning.

Human waste was remarkably distinctive. Neither cat, cow, dog nor pig excrement came close to replicating its odour. Bart contemplated what it meant. The bucket's handle was rough with what could only be rust. Its outside was dry and there was no liquid slopping anywhere. Not recently used then. Yet it was there for a reason.

'It's here for me,' he whispered, not liking the rawness in his throat from all the yelling. He'd lost track of the time he'd spent calling out to apparently absent listeners. He'd be lucky if he could speak at all within the hour.

Setting the bucket down, he took stock. There were two options left. Sit down, huddle, wait it out. If someone had brought him here – he had no idea how that had happened, but a dim recollection of being bought a drink by a very attractive woman after finishing his shift was blossoming – then it was for a purpose. They would be back. If he chose not to simply wait, he could assess the situation, explore his surroundings, try to figure out the state of play. It was a phrase he remembered his father using on his infrequent trips home from active duties. He summoned whatever genetic courage might inhabit his DNA. What he learned was that bravery was a myth.

In the end, fear was a far livelier motivator. If Bart waited, things could only get worse. He could think of no earthly reason why anyone would want him. Perhaps it was a case of mistaken identity by some chancer who thought he was from a wealthy family able to pay a ransom. Maybe it was some sort of bizarre terrorist event. And they were the better options. More likely – much more likely – it was some sick fuck who wanted to rape then kill him. He wasn't sitting on the floor and waiting patiently for that.

Forcing himself to get to his feet, he felt for the wall, arms stretched out so that only his fingertips were touching it, and tried to measure the space. Four walls, rectangular, maybe twelve feet by twenty. The chain was attached to a central metal loop in the floor and secured with a hefty padlock. No discernible door. Three other objects. A coarse blanket that reeked of damp and sweat. He bundled it up and kept it close to his chest, as much as a comforter as for warmth. A shoe, definitely belonging to a woman, with its high heel snapped and hanging half off, laying on its side in a corner. Finally something dangling from the wall, also chained, that he found as it squeaked back and forth when he knocked it. Reaching out, he identified its hexagonal shape, felt the chill of glass round its sides, then his fingers found the dial they'd been looking for. He turned the metal cog.

Light, enough to barely illuminate a metre radius, spilled from the lamp. Bart let out a soft coo. Amazing how such a simple thing could suddenly mean more than all the money in the world, given an appropriate degree of terror. The colours it shed were dappled. A sickly yellow nearer the top from the old bulb, graduating into a dull pink in the middle, then brown at the bottom. Bart stepped even closer, letting his eyes adjust. It wasn't that the glass panes were coloured, he realised. Nor that a special effect had been used on the bulb.

The outside of the glass had been spattered red. He reached out his fingers, wanting to know, not wanting to know. The lantern's panes were bloodied with delicate streaks, settling at the bottom. Different layers. Subtly varied shades. A mixture of very old, crackled blood, like a glaze on an antique vase, and newer congealed blood. A single blob came away on his finger. Congealed but not yet fully hardened.

Bart sank to the floor in the small circle of light, an actor mid-stage in a spotlight with no audience to appreciate the beautiful tragedy being played out. Then he pulled the blanket around himself, and wondered how long both the lamplight – and he – would last.

**Loved *Perfect Crime*?
Then why not get back to
where it all started with book
one of the DI Callanach series.**

On a remote Highland mountain, the body of Elaine Buxton
is burning. All that will be left to identify the respected
lawyer are her teeth and a fragment of clothing. Meanwhile,
in the concealed back room of a house in Edinburgh,
the real Elaine Buxton screams into the darkness . . .

Welcome to Edinburgh.
Murder capital of Europe.

A dark and twisted serial killer thriller that fans
of M. J. Arlidge and Karin Slaughter won't
be able to put down.

Available in all good bookshops now.

The worst dangers are the ones we can't see...

DI Callanach is back in the stunning third
novel from the bestselling Helen Fields.

When silence falls,
who will hear their cries?

Relentlessly dark and twisty crime that fans
of Karin Slaughter and M. J. Arlidge will love.

Available in all good bookshops now.